BLACK SWAN,
WHITE RAVEN

Other Fairy Tale Anthologies
Edited by
Ellen Datlow and Terri Windling

RUBY SLIPPERS, GOLDEN TEARS
BLACK THORN, WHITE ROSE
SNOW WHITE, BLOOD RED

BLACK SWAN, WHITE RAVEN

EDITED BY

ELLEN DATLOW
AND
TERRI WINDLING

AVON BOOKS  NEW YORK

AVON BOOKS
A division of
The Hearst Corporation
1350 Avenue of the Americas
New York, New York 10019

Copyright © 1997 by Ellen Datlow and Terri Windling
Interior design by Rhea Braunstein
Visit our web site at http://AvonBooks.com
ISBN: 0-380-97523-8

Library of Congress Cataloging in Publication Data:

Black swan, white raven / edited by Ellen Datlow and Terri Windling.
    p. cm.
   1. Fantastic fiction, American. 2. Fairy tales—Adaptations.
I. Datlow, Ellen. II. Windling, Terri.
PS648.F3B52   1997   96-33224
813'.08766054—dc20   CIP

First Avon Books Printing: June 1997

AVON TRADEMARK REG. U.S. PAT. OFF. AND IN OTHER COUNTRIES, MARCA REGISTRADA, HECHO EN U.S.A.

Printed in the U.S.A.

FIRST EDITION

RRD 10 9 8 7 6 5 4 3 2 1

For Alan Lee,
a connoisseur of fine fairy tales,
with gratitude for many years of friendship
and creative support.
—TERRI WINDLING

For Jack Heidenry,
who may not remember,
but got me started editing anthologies.
—ELLEN DATLOW

Contents

Contents

Contents

BLACK SWAN, WHITE RAVEN

Introduction
Terri Windling and Ellen Datlow

Many scholars over the last century have attempted to define why fairy tales and fantastical myths can be found in the oldest storytelling traditions of virtually every culture around the globe. Some scholars view magical tales as prescientific attempts to explain the workings of the universe; others see in them remnants of pagan religions or tribal initiation rites; still others dissect them for symbolic portrayals of feminist or class history. The most fascinating thing about fairy tales is that there is some truth in all these different views. There are many ways to interpret the old tales, whether as allegory or metaphor, as art or simple entertainment. No single deconstruction of a fairy tale is "correct," no single version of a tale is the "true" one. The old tales exist in myriad forms, changing and adapting from culture to culture, from generation to generation. Like the wizards who roam through enchanted woods, the tales

themselves are shape-shifters: elusive, mysterious, muta-
ble, capable of wearing many different forms. This fact is
at the core of their power, and is the source of their lon-
gevity. It is also what makes them such useful tools to the
modern writer of fantasy fiction.

"A true fairy tale is, to my mind, very like the sonata,"
said the nineteenth-century fantasy writer George Mc-
Donald. "If two or three men sat down to write each what
the sonata meant to him, what approximation to definite
idea would result? A fairy tale, a sonata, a gathering storm,
a limitless night, each seizes you and sweeps you away."
A century later, J. R. R. Tolkien compared fairy tales to the
bones from which a savory broth is extracted. Each storyteller dips his or her ladle into that bubbling cauldron of
soup, and then uses it as the base of a dish individually
spiced and flavored. The soup has been simmering for centuries—there are no cooks we can credit as the originators
of the first fairy tales; there is no single version of each tale
we can point to as "definitive." At best, we can point to
the authors of distinctive *variations* on old, common
themes: Charles Perrault's French "Cinderella" is the "ash
girl" tale we know best today; Hans Christian Andersen's
Danish "Little Mermaid" is the best known of the "un-
dine" legends; the Grimm Brothers' chaste German rendition of "The Sleeping Beauty" is the one found in
modern fairy-tale books (as opposed to much older versions in which the slumbering princess is impregnated by
a passing prince, and does not awaken until the birth of
her twins).

Each of these well-known fairy tales is based upon
themes that are universal. The earliest known versions of
"Cinderella," for instance, date back to ancient China; one
finds her in the Middle East, in Africa, and even here in
North America (in such stories as "The Rough-Faced Girl"
told by the Algonquin tribe). While the flavor of each tale

might change according to the culture, the times, and the teller, the core of the tale remains the same—because at their core, these are stories that speak of the most basic elements of the human condition: fear, courage, greed, generosity, cruelty, compassion, failure, and triumph. As a result, their themes are as relevant today as they were back in centuries past.

The old tales of the oral tradition have been entwined with written literature since at least the sixteenth century, when Straparola published his magical, bawdy *The Delectable Nights* in Venice. The literary fairy-tale form includes Basile's Italian *Story of Stories*, the *conte de fée* of the French court writers (D'Aulnoy, de Beaumont, Perrault et al.), works by Spenser and Shakespeare in England, and by the eighteenth-century German Romantics (Goethe, Hoffmann, Novalis). These were all works written and published for educated adult audiences—for it was not until Victorian times that fairy tales came to be considered stories specifically meant for children. Victorian editors, creating a new publishing market of books for younger readers, drew upon the magical tales of the past (a cheap source of story material) and changed them to suit their own ideas of what was proper for children's ears, turning feisty heroes and heroines into models of Victorian behavior. These are the versions of the tales that are best-known in our own century; as a result, most people now think of fairy tales as simple children's stories in which pretty, passive, feckless girls grow up to marry their rich Prince Charmings.

A look at the older fairy tales quickly disabuses us of this notion. Pre-Victorian tales were more ambiguous, more violent, more sensual or downright bawdy, and unflinching in their portrayal of the complexities of the human heart. "The Armless Maiden" is one such tale, of a girl brutally maimed by her own parents; "Donkeyskin" is another, with its frankly incestuous theme of a king determined to marry his own daughter despite her protestations and despair. Hansel and Gretel are abandoned in the woods; the son in "The Juniper Tree" is beheaded; Snow White's lovely mother orders her child's heart cut out, boiled, and served for dinner. In older versions of fairy tales, such acts were not foisted off on "wicked stepparents"; these were the acts of the parents themselves: of kings who are less than wise; and millers who are less than strong; of queens, housewives, and sisters slowly simmering with rage. In the universe of fairy tales, the Just often find a way to prevail, the Wicked generally receive their comeuppance. But a close look at the stories reveals much more than a simple formula of abuse and retribution. The trials our heroes encounter in their quests illustrate the *process* of transformation: from youth to adulthood, from victim to hero, from a maimed state into wholeness, from passivity to action. As centuries of artists have known, this gives fairy tales a particular power: not as a quaint escape from the harsh realities of modern life, but in their symbolic portrayal of all the dark and bright life has to offer.

In our century, fantasy writers (and modern poets) are the artists who speak this symbolic language best, using timeless themes and potent archetypes to comment on modern life. The late Angela Carter is a writer who has done this more thoroughly, more beautifully, than any other, particularly in the adult fairy-tale stories of her collection *The Bloody Chamber*. The poet Anne Sexton worked brilliantly with fairy-tale themes in her luminous collection *Transformations*. Margaret Atwood, A. S. Byatt, John Gardner, Marina Warner, and Sara Maitland are all writers who have used fairy-tale motifs for works published in the literary mainstream; while in the fantasy genre, Robin McKinley, Tanith Lee, Jonathan Carroll, Delia Sherman, Jane Yolen, and others have written works of adult fairy-tale literature as fine as any on the mainstream shelves.

Like the authors above, the writers in this volume have taken the themes of classic fairy tales and reworked them into stories of their own: stories that are both old and new, both bright as white ravens, dark as black swans. You'll find new takes on the fairy tales most familiar to Western readers: "The Sleeping Beauty," "Snow White," "Rapunzel," "Hansel and Gretel," and "Little Red Riding Hood"— as well as intriguing new reworkings of "Tom Thumb," "Thomas the Rhymer," "The Tin Soldier," "The Soldier and the Tinder Box," and other tales. Why do so many of us continue to be enspelled by fairy tales? Why do we continue to tell the same old tales, over and over again? Because we all have encountered wicked wolves, faced trial by fire, found fairy godmothers. We have all set off into unknown woods at one point in life or another. Such stories have been told, retold, passed on from mouth to mouth for thousands of years. The stories that follow are part of a tradition that is as old as storytelling itself.

> —Terri Windling
> Devon and Tucson, 1996
>
> —Ellen Datlow
> New York City, 1996

The Flounder's Kiss

MICHAEL CADNUM

Michael Cadnum lives in northern California and is a poet and novelist. He is the author of eleven novels including St. Peter's Wolf, Ghostwright, Calling Home, Skyscape, The Judas Glass, Zero at the Bone, *and an illustrated book based on Cinderella called* Ella and the Canary Prince *(Cobblestone Press). He has also published several collections of poetry, most recently* The Cities We Will Never See.

"The Flounder's Kiss" is based on the Grimm fairy tale "The Fisherman and His Wife." Cadnum's version follows the traditional tale of greed but transforms it into something more cheeky and simultaneously more sinister than the original.

The Flounder's Kiss

My beautiful bride said if you spend all your time fishing the river, you catch nothing but monkfish and bream. You get water wens all over your feet. If you want money, she said, you go sea fishing.

So there I was, a river man all my life, marrying after I had nine gray hairs, pricing fisher's small-craft at the weekly sale. Most of those belly-up clinker-builts belong to dead fishermen, their bodies feeding crabs, and everybody knows it. It keeps the prices down, but I decided to be a beach fisher, and I had some luck. You have to take the long view. You like whelks, you eat whelks. Shellfish don't bother me. When I don't catch anything, the tide all the way to the sunken merchantman in the mouth of Zeebruge harbor, I trudge back and start clamming. Eight, nine you have supper.

Yanni, my rose-cheeked wife, would say, "All day out

there, and you come home with what?" That lovely mouth of hers, working nonstop.

"I have six fine cockles," I would say. Or, if the tide had run well, two fine whiting. Or two soles, or John Dory, or a dozen pier mussels. Whatever it was, and they were always prime. I don't want to eat anything diseased or deformed or that looks peculiar. The fact is some days I can't bring myself to eat fish. It's not just that fish flop around with their mouths open. They have slits they breathe through and eyes that look up like pennies, and there's nothing you can do to tell a fish to lie still. You can use one of those mallets especially made for shutting fish up, head hammers, the dorymen around here call them in their usual jocular way, but about the only thing you can say to a fish is nothing.

Tourists love it. We put on these wooden mud-treaders, and you can hear them calling to their kids, "Look, how darling, wooden shoes." And I, for one, always wave and smile. I know they can't help it, so far from home and nothing to look at but a man going to work with about twenty ells of net on his back.

"You bother to catch one pilchard, Weebs, you might as well catch a hundred," my wife would say. Always sewing, needle winking up and down. Skirts, blouses, collars, gloves. "I might as well be a herring gull you come back with such tiny little fish."

"It takes a lot to maneuver the net with just two arms," I would answer. "You need a strong back and a feel for the current."

"You've got talent, Weebs," she would respond. "A rare genius. You ought to win a prize for being able to work for less money than anyone who ever scraped mud."

"You want me to catch flounder."

"Eels," Yanni would reply, squinting at her needle.

"Eels have two hearts," I would say. "They crawl over

land. They have conventions in the ocean, they have nests in the hills. An eel is too complicated to eat. I like pilchards. You can hold a fish like that in your hand."

"Men," my wife would say.

"There's something about a herring that says I'm made for eating, it's okay to eat me, I have an eye on each side of my head, and I am going to be eaten by something I never saw coming, it might as well be you."

"Catch something worth the effort," she would reply. Bored, having given up on me. But still talking about it, one of those people who can't shut up. She would walk into a room making announcements saying she was cold, I would be late for high tide, why was it so dark, where was her darning.

It was a glorious day for watching clouds. I had caught nothing. The sea was filthy, a gale out of the northwest. All the horsefishers were in their stables. The sailorfishers were sipping juniper spirits by their fires, and there was only I myself, on the broad flat beach. I didn't want to come home wet with rain and wet with brine, blue and nothing to show for it but a pocketful of limpets.

You cast your net and it looks pretty, black lace spreading out. When it drifts down over the water there is a splash where the netting settles, and the sound of it is what satisfies. Casting the net, you feel the waves calm under the span you mended, and sometimes I could do it well into the dark, regardless whether or not I caught a fingerling.

I was almost ready to quit for the night. One more cast, I told myself. Just one more. It's a serene sight, the net sweeping up, hanging over the waver, lifting with the wind. The net drifted onto the sea. And it happened. The net tugged, tightened. And there it was as I hauled in the net, the famous fish, the size of a Michaelmas tureen, fat and silver.

I have a great aversion to flounders. I can't stand to take them by the tail, much less slit one open. They have their eyes close together on one side of their head, and they swim around blind on one side, looking up at the sky with the other. I want something simple to eat, not a living curiosity.

I realized, however, that it was worth a guilder or two, a fish like this, an armload, and while I am not the most gifted fisherman alive, I am no fool. I pulled the one-sided creature out as it flopped in the net. I dragged it onto the beach and untangled the net, and then I heard something. I looked up, looked around, my head tilting this way and that. The wind was whistling, and I was not sure what I heard.

Maybe it was a tourist talking, one of the day-trip spinsters out of Southampton; they ferry across and flirt at a distance. They say things like "what a wonderful fish you have just caught," in German, as though I would ever speak a syllable of the language. The tourists are the equivalent of herring themselves, the poor dears. It would be just like one to be chattering in a rising wind in the dusk in the middle of nowhere. Not just talking, arguing, jabbering to make a point.

I stooped to gather in enough fish to buy a silver thimble and a bolt of silk when I realized that the muttering was close to my ear. I dropped the flounder. It smacked the sand and made that shrugging flopping I hate in fish—why can't they just fall asleep and die? The fish said clearly, but in a small voice, "Wish. Go ahead wish. Just wish. Any wish. Don't wait—wish."

I seized my gutting knife and just about used it, out of horror. But instead I asked it a question. My brother shovels waffles into the oven on a paddle and has a cellar of cheese. My sister married a brewer, and has beer and fat children. My father took tolls on a bridge with carved seraphim and saints, burghers and fair ladies and military men calling him by name, wishing him well.

And I was talking to a fish.

And the fish was talking back. "Any wish. Then let me go."

It was persistent, this idiot babble. So I made a wish. I asked for a bucket full of herring, pink-gilled, enough for tonight and a few left over for the market.

By candlelight Yanni picked a spinebone from her mouth and said, her eyebrows up, not wanting to admit it, "That was most delicious, Weebs. Most tasty little fish I have ever supped upon."

"There's a story behind that fish," I said.

She gave me one of her bedroom glances, dabbed her pretty lips.

"But never mind," I said.

"Tell me," she said.

I pushed my plate away, put my elbows on my table, and took a sip of beer, dark brew, tart, almost like vinegar. I smiled. I said, "You won't believe it."

Not a quarter of an hour later I was wading into the surf. "Fish!" I called. "Big fish! Flounder!"

It was raining hard. Despite what you might have heard, there was no poem, no song. There was a lump on my head, and one eye was swelling shut. I bellowed into the wind, now straight out of the north. "One more boon," I asked.

Waves broke over me, drowning the sound of my voice. There were no fish. The fish were vanished from the sea. I stood drenched, about to turn away, when the fish was there at my side, its eyes two peas side by side.

"One more!" I said. I was standing in a storm talking to

a fish, and before shame or common sense could silence me I repeated Yanni's desire.

I hurried back, running along the dike. Cows with their big, white foreheads stared at me from within their mangers, and when I half collapsed in my cottage she seized me by jerkin and turned me around. "Look!"

The kettle had unbent its hook, fallen into the fire, solid gold and impossible to drag out of the embers. "It's going to melt!" she cried.

"You wanted it turned to gold," I said.

"Go back and get this made into money."

I panted, dripping, catching my breath. "Money?"

"Coins! Sovereigns, ducats, dollars. We can't do anything with this."

"It's beautiful!"

"And then ask for brains, Weebs. For you. For inside your head."

"You should try to be more patient, dear Yanni," I said. I think it was the only time I had ever offered her such advice.

She put her hands on her hips. In her apron and her cap she told me what she thought of me. All this time I had thought her pensive, moody, emotional. But I thought she loved me.

I took my time. The wind was warm, out of the west now, and there were a few stars. When I was a boy I would want to stand outside in the wind and feel my sweater and my sleeves billow and flow, flying. Both feet on the ground, but flying in my heart.

"Fish! Magic flounder!"

It must have known. Once it began to trade in human desire it was finished. No net is worse. It nosed upward, out of the waves. Why it even listened I cannot guess. I thrust my hand into a gill, seized a fin, and hauled the creature with all my strength. I dragged it up where the sand was dry, black reeds, gulls stirring, croaking.

The fish was talking nonstop. I tugged my knife free of the belt and cut the flounder, gills to tail, and emptied him out on the sand.

There has been some question about my wife. Some say the fish renounced the boons, took it all back, and sent us into poverty. Some say my wife left me, taking the golden kettle with her, swinging it by one fist, strong as she was famous to be.

Proof against this is the kettle I still possess, heavy as an anvil, chipped at slowly over the years, shavings of pure gold to buy feather quilts and heifers. And this is not the only precious metal in my house. A golden pendant the shape of a woman's mouth dangles ever at my breast.

A parting gift? some ask.

Or a replacement for her, suggests the even-smarter guest with a chuckle, enjoying my roast goose.

Fish do not die quickly. They take their time. And even a magic fish is slow to understand. Give me silence, I wished, crouching over him, knife in hand. Silence, and the power to bring her back someday, should it please me, one kiss upon her golden lips.

The Black Fairy's Curse

KAREN JOY FOWLER

Karen Joy Fowler was born in Bloomington, Indiana, and currently lives in Davis, California, with her husband and two children. Her first book, Artificial Things, *was a collection of short stories. Her second, is the remarkable novel* Sarah Canary. *Her second novel,* The Sweetheart Season, *has recently been published. According to Fowler, it's packed with useful housekeeping tips and those alone will be worth the cover price.*

The story of Sleeping Beauty is one of the most popular fairy tales and it has inspired numerous variations. "The Black Fairy's Curse" is a brief, startling tale, the first of two new reinterpretations.

The
Black Fairy's Curse

She was being chased. She kicked off her shoes, which were slowing her down. At the same time her heavy skirts vanished and she found herself in her usual work clothes. Relieved of the weight and constriction, she was able to run faster. She looked back. She was much faster than he was. Her heart was strong. Her strides were long and easy. He was never going to catch her now.

She was riding the huntsman's horse and she couldn't remember why. It was an autumn red with a tangled mane. She was riding fast. A deer leapt in the meadow ahead of her. She saw the white blink of its tail.

She'd never ridden well, never had the insane fearlessness it took, but now she was able to enjoy the easiness of the horse's motion. She encouraged it to run faster.

It was night. The countryside was softened with patches

of moonlight. She could go anywhere she liked, ride to the end of the world and back again. What she would find there was a castle with a toothed tower. Around the castle was a girdle of trees, too narrow to be called a forest, and yet so thick they admitted no light at all. She knew this. Even farther away were the stars. She looked up and saw three of them fall, one right after the other. She made a wish to ride until she reached them.

She herself was in farmland. She crossed a field and jumped a low, stone fence. She avoided the cottages, homey though they seemed, with smoke rising from the roofs, and a glow the color of butter pats at the windows. The horse ran and did not seem to tire.

She wore a cloak which, when she wrapped it tightly around her, rode up and left her legs bare. Her feet were cold. She turned around to look. No one was coming after her.

She reached a river. Its edges were green with algae and furry with silt. Toward the middle she could see the darkness of deep water. The horse made its own decisions. It ran along the shallow edge, but didn't cross. Many yards later it ducked back away from the water and into a grove of trees. She lay along its neck and the silver-backed leaves of aspens brushed over her hair.

She climbed into one of the trees. She regretted every tree she had never climbed. The only hard part was the first branch. After that it was easy, or else she was stronger than she'd ever been. Stronger than she needed to be. This excess of strength gave her a moment of joy as pure as any she could remember. The climbing seemed quite as natural as stair steps, and she went as high as she could, standing finally on a limb so thin it dipped under her weight, like a boat. She retreated downward, sat with her back against the trunk and one leg dangling. No one would ever think to look for her here.

Her hair had come loose and she let it all down. It was warm on her shoulders. "Mother," she said, softly enough to blend with the wind in the leaves. "Help me."

She meant her real mother. Her real mother was not there, had not been there since she was a little girl. It didn't mean there would be no help.

Above her were the stars. Below her, looking up, was a man. He was no one to be afraid of. Her dangling foot was bare. She did not cover it. Maybe she didn't need help. That would be the biggest help of all.

"Did you want me?" he said. She might have known him from somewhere. They might have been children together. "Or did you want me to go away?"

"Go away. Find your own tree."

They went swimming together, and she swam better than he did. She watched his arms, his shoulders rising darkly from the green water. He turned and saw that she was watching. "Do you know my name?" he asked her.

"Yes," she said, although she couldn't remember it. She knew she was supposed to know it, although she could also see that he didn't expect her to. But she did feel that she knew who he was—his name was such a small part of that. "Does it start with a W?" she asked.

The sun was out. The surface of the water was a rough gold.

"What will you give me if I guess it?"

"What do you want?"

She looked past him. On the bank was a group of smiling women, her grandmother, her mother, and her stepmother, too, her sisters and stepsisters, all of them smiling at her. They waved. No one said, "Put your clothes on." No one said, "Don't go in too deep now, dear." She was a good swimmer, and there was no reason to be afraid. She couldn't think of a single thing she wanted. She flipped away, breaking the skin of the water with her legs.

She surfaced in a place where the lake held still to mirror the sky. When it settled, she looked down into it. She expected to see that she was beautiful, but she was not. A mirror only answers one question, and it can't lie. She had completely lost her looks. She wondered what she had gotten in return.

There was a mirror in the bedroom. It was dusty, so her reflection was vague. But she was not beautiful. She wasn't upset about this, and she noticed the fact, a little wonderingly. It didn't matter at all to her. Most people were taken in by appearances, but others weren't. She was healthy; she was strong. If she could manage to be kind and patient and witty and brave, then there would be men who loved her for it. There would be men who found it exciting.

He lay among the blankets, looking up at her. "Your eyes," he said. "Your incredible eyes."

His own face was in shadow, but there was no reason to be afraid. She removed her dress. It was red. She laid it over the back of a chair. "Move over."

She had never been in bed with this man before, but she wanted to be. It was late, and no one knew where she was. In fact, her mother had told her explicitly not to come here, but there was no reason to be afraid. "I'll tell you what to do," she said. "You must use your hand and your mouth. The other—it doesn't work for me. And I want to be first. You'll have to wait."

"I'll love waiting," he said. He covered her breast with his mouth, his hand moved between her legs. He knew how to touch her already. He kissed her other breast.

"Like that," she said. "Just like that." Her body began to tighten in anticipation.

He kissed her mouth. He kissed her mouth.

* * *

He kissed her mouth. It was not a hard kiss, but it opened her eyes. This was not the right face. She had never seen this man before, and the look he gave her—she wasn't sure she liked it. Why was he kissing her, when she was asleep and had never seen him before? What was he doing in her bedroom? She was so frightened, she stopped breathing for a moment. She closed her eyes and wished him away.

He was still there. And there was pain. Her finger dripped with blood, and when she tried to sit up, she was weak and encumbered by a heavy dress, a heavy coil of her own hair, a corset, tight and pointed shoes.

"Oh," she said. "Oh." She was about to cry, and she didn't know this man to cry before him. Her tone was accusing. She pushed him and his face showed the surprise of this. He allowed himself to be pushed. If he hadn't, she was not strong enough to force it.

He was probably a very nice man. He was giving her a concerned look. She could see that he was tired. His clothes were ripped; his own hands were scratched. He had just done something hard, maybe dangerous. So maybe that was why he hadn't stopped to think how it might frighten her to wake up with a stranger kissing her as she lay on her back. Maybe that was why he hadn't noticed how her finger was bleeding. Because he hadn't, no matter how much she came to love him, there would always be a part of her afraid of him.

"I was having the most lovely dream," she said. She was careful not to make her tone as angry as she felt.

Snow in Dirt

MICHAEL BLUMLEIN

In one life, Michael Blumlein is a practicing physician living in the San Francisco Bay area. In his other, he is the author of the novels The Movement of Mountains *and* XY *and the short works collected in* The Brains of Rats. *Many of his stories reflect his medical knowledge and use it to create some of the most fascinating, bizarre, and provocative science fiction/fantasy being produced in the short form today. His stories have appeared in* Interzone, Omni, The Magazine of Fantasy and Science Fiction *and in* The Year's Best Fantasy and Horror.

"Snow in Dirt," while lighter in tone than much of Blumlein's fiction, nonetheless has a typically keen edge. This second "Sleeping Beauty" tale is quite different from Fowler's in its time period (possibly futuristic) and in its tone.

Snow in Dirt

ONCE A LIFETIME

It can happen. Once a lifetime it should. I found the girl of my dreams in the garden. She was covered by dirt. I was digging a hole. Four feet down, three wide, a ditch for a foundation to prop up the falling shack at the back of the lot. Pine trees overhead. Bluest of skies. My oxlike shoulders, sweat running down my spine. She was hidden in soil, tucked between roots, still as a statue, beautiful. The shack, a ten-by-twenty-foot post-and-beam redwood cabin, had been built after the Great Earthquake, and in its time had been refugee shelter, wood shop, storage shed, chicken coop, teenage retreat, and hole-up for a drunk who beat his wife, then cried all night in remorse. It had been falling over ever since I took the time to notice, pushed down by the hill behind it, by clay, sand, and radiolarian

chert. After watching passively for years, I finally decided
to do something. I chased out the raccoons. I baited the
mice. Took two weeks off work, cleared the calendar,
jacked up the downhill side, cut a path through the fence
to the back. I was thinking of making a career move. I was
in between women. Hearing a mockingbird, catching my
breath, smelling the pine sap.

Very carefully, I dug her out.

THE WHEELBARROW

was newly painted, glossy and red as lipstick. I lifted her
over the front lip. She slid into the bed like satin. Her eyes
were closed. She wore a sort of bodysuit the color of dead
leaves. I picked a worm out of her hair. She had the face
of a young woman. My neighbor appeared on his back
porch, and I covered her with a tarpaulin.

"Gardening?" he asked.

"A little."

"Looking good." He meant me, not the garden. He was
drunk, and when he was drunk, he flirted.

"Thanks. Yours looks good too. I like your roses."

"Come on over. I'll give you one."

I begged off.

He leered at me. "Come on. I'll make sure to cut the
thorns."

It had been like this since his lover had died three years
before. He never talked about it, just drank and watched
sports on TV.

I beat it into the basement, parked the wheelbarrow, got
the girl out and onto a sofa inside. Her hair was long and
dark. Her skin was pale. I called my brother Frank.

"Yo," his machine said. "Talk to me."

I left a message, then washed up and hurried out. Mom

was waiting at the entrance of the nursing home when I arrived, freshly bathed and made-up. Her attendant was putting the finishing touches on her hair.

"Sorry I'm late," I said.

Mom smiled. "Hello, Frank."

"Martin," I corrected, pecking her on the cheek. "So what's your pleasure? You want to walk, drive, what?"

"The pie is very good," she said.

"You had pie?"

She smiled again but didn't answer. The attendant had tied a pink bow in her hair, something my mother would never have done. It made her look girlish and even more helpless than she was.

I took her arm. "I think we'll drive."

I took her to the beach, then backtracked through the park and up Twin Peaks, which was socked in by fog. We couldn't see a thing. My mother called it soup. She loved it.

Afterward, I drove her to my place. The woman was where I had left her. My mother frowned when she saw her, then glanced uncertainly at me.

"I found her in the garden," I said. "Just a few hours ago."

She strained to understand, looked at the girl, then back at me. Suddenly, her face broke into a smile.

"Marry?"

"No no no." I laughed. "We just met."

She smacked her lips. "Kissy kissy. Pussy pussy. Thing comes out."

"Thank you, Mother. I'll keep that in mind."

"Thing," she repeated, gesturing with her hands, struggling for the word. She became frustrated and started to pace, back and forth in forced little steps. This was always a bad sign.

"It's okay," I told her. "I get it. Thing. I understand." A

lie of course, and it didn't work. On the contrary. My mother halted in mid-stride, pointed an accusatory finger, erupted.

"Bad girl. Bad bad bad." She wheeled on me. "You."

I supplied my name. She frowned. Now she looked lost. Now she started to cry. I sighed, fighting back my own tears, and steered her out of the room. We had a cup of tea. I took the bow out of her hair and told her I loved her. Then I drove her home.

Frank came over around nine. He was all dressed up, and I asked where he'd been.

"With the Grizzly," he said, with a swagger. This was his newest flame, so named by him for her size and the ferocity of her embrace. "She has a friend, Marty. Someone you should meet."

He was always trying to set me up. For the thousandth time, I told him I was a one-woman man.

"Yeah?" He pretended to search the room. "There someone I don't know about?"

I took him downstairs. The girl was lying where I left her. Her eyelids were translucent and shaded ever so lightly blue. She had started to breathe.

"Well goddamn. My baby brother." He punched my arm. "What's that brown stuff she's got on?"

"I don't know. Some kind of protective coat or something."

"Looks like old newspaper." He sniffed at it. "Smells like dirt."

"No shit, Sherlock. I found her in dirt."

"What does that mean?"

I explained.

"Jesus," he said. "So what are you going to do with her?"

"I don't know. I'm taking suggestions."

He thought a minute. "We could ask Shirley."

Shirley was his other girl, his steady, ever tolerant (a requisite with Frank) and loaded with good sense.

"On the other hand," he said, "we could keep the lid on a few days. See what develops. Who knows? The lady wakes up, maybe she's as nice as she looks. Maybe the two of you get it on a little. Pardon me for saying, but you could use the action."

"Your suggestion being?"

"I'm just thinking of something a guy said to me today in the shop. We were making small talk, and I asked him how he was doing. He gave me a funny look and said, you know what the answer is to that, don't you? And I said, no, what's the answer? And he said, it's how many toys you got when you die. They can have wheels, buttons, skirts . . . it doesn't matter. Just how many you got on the day you croak."

"You liked that, did you?"

"The guy's an asshole, but yeah. I did. How many toys. I can think of worse ways to measure."

"You got toys, Frank?"

"You know I do." He winked at me, pulled out his wallet and handed me a foil-covered package nestled between two bills. "Safety first, Marty boy. You find her in the dirt, who knows? Maybe she's dirty."

So that was Frank's advice. After he left, I called my sister Carol to complete the family poll. She was on her way to bed, a ritual to be disturbed only on pain of death. She promised to stop by in the morning, which she did, arriving on the dot at seven, dressed for work in a snappy, tailored suit. She took one look at the girl and pulled a phone out of her purse, which she pushed at me.

"Call 911, you jerk."

To my credit, the thought had occurred to me, but the

truth was I didn't want to. No doubt this is why I'd called Frank first.

"She's breathing," I said defensively. "How bad can it be?"

"She's breathing. Terrific. Jesus, Marty."

I decided not to mention that she hadn't been breathing before.

"Does she have a pulse?"

"Sure she has a pulse," I said, thinking I don't even know if she has a heart. "She's sleeping."

"Have you tried to wake her up?"

"Carol. Please. I would never wake a sleeping lady. You yourself taught me that."

"Get off it, Martin." She took the girl's wrist and felt for a pulse, then slapped the back of her hand a few times. She spoke in a loud voice. She slapped her cheek.

"Get her to a doctor, Marty. If you aren't willing to call an ambulance, then take her yourself."

I suppose, at heart, this is what I wanted to hear. Sheepishly, I asked Carol to come with me.

"Can't. Got a meeting at eight." She checked her watch, pecked me on the cheek, and hurried out the basement door. A minute later she was back. Irritated but stalwart. My sister. Loyal to the core.

"Let's do it," she said.

"You're the best, Carol, but go on. I can handle it."

"You sure?"

I nodded. "I got the whole family behind me. Check it out: you say I should get help, Mom says I should marry her, Frank says I should fuck her. I can't lose. Anything I do is bound to be right."

THE PROBLEM OF CONCEALMENT

I solved with a blanket, wrapping her loosely, then sliding her in the back of my pickup and securing her with some bungee cords. At the hospital I swiped a gurney without being seen, hoisted her on top, unwrapped her, and wheeled her inside. Because she had no ID and no insurance, they didn't want to take her. I said I'd vouch for her: they looked at me with dried-up pity and shook their heads. I said she was homeless. They rolled their eyes. Was she a city resident? they asked. A native, I replied. Tenth generation (it was a wild guess). Deeply rooted in our illustrious past. They looked at me suspiciously. They looked at her. At length they sighed. Cash or credit? they asked.

We spent a total of six hours in the emergency room, complicated by the fact they couldn't get that brownish covering of hers off. Someone suggested it might be part of her skin, which prompted a call to the dermatologist, who came and discoursed at length on epidermal proliferation, psoriasis, ichthyosis, and generalized melasma, none of which, in his opinion, this was. Blood was taken from a vein in her foot, and all the tests came back normal. A chest x-ray and electrocardiogram showed nothing out of the ordinary. A scan of her brain showed brain. Because they could not find an opening in her bodysuit, they could not get urine, but some of her hair was sent to be screened for heavy metal poisoning. They tested everything they could, and then they called a neurologist.

His name was Dr. Aymen. He had salt-and-pepper hair parted on the side, a deeply tanned face, a prominent jaw. He wore a blue bow tie, and his knee-length lab coat was stiffly starched. His manner, by contrast, was smooth as butter. The other doctors treated him with deference, clumping around the gurney and observing in silence as he poked and prodded the patient. When he was done, he took a half-step back, slid his hands deep in the pockets of his lab coat, and struck a professorial pose.

"Thoughts?" he said.

There was a flurry of them. Encephalopathy, involutional melancholy, prolonged atonic epilepsy, drug overdose: I jotted down what I could, but I missed more than I got. All at once, Dr. Aymen seemed to notice me. He introduced himself, absorbed my name, then politely asked me to leave.

"I'll stay out of the way," I promised.

"Our suppositions are far-flung," he explained. "And strictly conjectural. They are easy to misinterpret. It would be a grave disservice to you if your hopes were falsely raised, or, worse, prematurely dashed. So please. Allow me a few moments alone with my colleagues."

He seemed a nice enough fellow, earnest if somewhat pompous, but I had no intention of leaving. Again, I promised not to interfere.

He regarded me sternly, then inclined his head. "As you wish."

Turning his back to me, he swept out of the room, followed immediately by his retinue of admirers. Twenty minutes later he returned.

"Speculation is inherent in medicine," he told me. "The possibilities of cause are, in every case, protean. This is both challenge and thrill for the diagnostician, but to others the process often makes us seem cold, if not downright callous. Please accept my apologies if such was the case. We are human beings like any other."

I thanked him. "So what does she have? Do you know?"

"Possibly." He glanced at her, then fixed his attention on me. "Are you sure you've left nothing out?"

The implication was clear, and simply by asking, he

made it a fact that I had. I thought back. The dirt? The worm in her hair? Family advice?

"No," I said. "Nothing."

He waited, giving me time to reconsider. I didn't need time.

"What's going on, Doctor?"

"THE THEORY,"

he said, "is hard to explain. Suffice it to say, there's definitely a literature on this. It seems that intact bodies are turning up all the time. There's actually a registry somewhere. I suggest we send a specimen of the patient's DNA for fingerprinting. Perhaps there's someone on file who's been lost. Or who's missing. Perhaps in this way we could identify her."

"Okay. Sure. But what does she have?"

He gave me a patronizing look. "What you really want to know is, what can be done."

"I want to know if you've ever seen anything like this."

"Certainly," he said.

"Someone buried in dirt?"

"Young man. In forty years I've seen diseases and afflictions beyond your wildest dreams. The range of human pathology, not to mention survivability, is nothing short of miraculous. Our ability to down-regulate vital functions, to enter at need into vegetative states, prolonged metaphases if you will . . ."

His soliloquy, which I barely understood, was interrupted by one of the other doctors, who handed him some papers held together by a clip.

"Yes," he said. "Good. Just as I recalled." He perused the papers, mumbling to himself, nodding. "You made copies for the others?"

"Yes," said the doctor.

"Excellent." Dr. Aymen addressed me. "This is an article . . ." He halted a moment, then resumed with an air of gravity and subtle condescension. "A scientific article comparing the efficacy of three regimens for the revival of found bodies. Cohort study, two-year follow-up, morbidity, mortality, proposed mechanisms . . . all of it. You see, young man, we are not living in the Dark Ages. We are not charlatans, nor do we operate by sleight of hand. No, no." He wagged a finger. "We adhere to science. The language we speak is strictly the language of reproducible results."

So saying, he pulled a pad from his pocket and scribbled out a prescription. "Two in the morning, two at bedtime. In a week increase it to three."

"What is it?"

He said a name so rapidly I didn't get it, handed me his business card with instructions to call for a follow-up appointment, and started out of the room. This put me in something of a panic.

"When's bedtime?" I asked. "She hasn't woken up yet."

He dismissed this with a flip of his hand. "Bedtime, nighttime, it doesn't matter. Just get it in her. The young lady should perk right up."

As it turned out, she didn't. On the other hand, she didn't get any worse. Carol was satisfied a doctor was involved. Frank suggested I try something more direct, more, as he put it, "physically stimulating." My mother, bless her heart, had forgotten everything.

THE KISS

was something I considered for days. It seemed the obvious thing to do, called for in some intuitive way, but in the end I decided against it, feeling at once virtuous, sexually repressed, and utterly confused. It was a vexing situation, so much so that this is what I began calling her. The closest I came to her lips was spreading them apart with my thumb and finger to pour the pills, which I dissolved in water, down her throat. I returned to the ditch, digging out and piling up dirt. When I got deep enough, I built the forms for the foundation, laid the rebar, and poured the concrete. By then it was three weeks since our visit to the hospital. Vexing slept on. I started on the framing. Her hair was black as coal. Foot plates, joists, studs. Eyelids like butterflies. Headers, rafters. Skin, clothed in parchment, like milk.

"OUR ARMAMENTARIUM

is vast," said Dr. Aymen, with the sweep of an arm that seemed to take in as potential allies not just the books and equipment that were in his own office but all information and knowledge that lay beyond as well. "If one pill doesn't work, we try another. It's what's called an empirical approach."

I heard only two words in that. Armamentarium, which brought to mind epic battles on dusty, medieval plains, and empirical, which made me think this guy doesn't have a clue. It was time to stand up for Vexing, who remained incapable of standing up for herself.

"What's this new drug?" I asked.

There was an edge to my voice, and he shot me a glance. Then he leaned back in his chair and bridged his fingers. He appeared to be thinking. Maybe he was. At length he mumbled something to himself and unclipped his pen. Barely looking down, he scribbled out a prescription.

"Start with two at night, go to three if no change in a

week, four if no change in two. After that it's up to you. You can split the dose, give two in the morning and three at night, or you can reverse that, give three in the AM and two in the PM, but under no circumstance must you increase more than twenty milligrams in any four-day period, unless you are prepared to watch assiduously for side effects, which of course you should do anyway. And call me."

"Call you?"

"If there's a problem."

I was reeling with his instructions. "What side effects?"

"The usual. Nausea, GI upset, headache, dizziness, twitchy muscles, sudden death." He let that sink in, then dismissed it with a bizarre smile. "Just kidding. But not really. I mention it only to assure you that it's very rare."

"What's the name of this drug?"

"Three, 5 dihydroxy, gamma-endoperoxide PGD. It goes by the trade name Resusinol."

"I've never heard of it."

"Are you a doctor, sir? A pharmacist, perhaps?"

"I work in a drugstore."

"Indeed."

I didn't tell him that the counter I worked was at the opposite end of the store from the pharmacy. I was angry.

"Do you have experience with it, Doctor? Have you used it before?"

"It's an excellent choice," he said. "I have no doubt it will be equal to the task."

"That's what you said about the first one."

He suffered me a look, then took a moment to compose himself.

"I realize your impatience, but understand. All things take time. This is Nature's decree, not ours. There are many conditions whose duration we can predict with great accuracy. Coma, unfortunately, is not one of them. An encephalopathic child may sleep for a day or a week. He may sleep for a year. Your young lady will awaken when she is ready. No sooner. No later." He paused, then added, "With or without drugs, I suspect."

"Then why give any?"

He smiled and stood up, indicating the end of the visit. "Because it's our nature to try. Because you, like us, like everyone, want to be able to fix what's hurt. Because sadly, we're too old for Band-Aids."

A week passed, then another. The cabin took shape, and the smell of fresh wood banished the smell of rot. I framed in a window facing east and one on the opposite side facing west. I had views of English ivy, pine trees, my neighbors' houses, my neighbors. From the roof I could see the bay. I roughed in the front door the third week of June. That Saturday, Midsummer's Day, Vexing woke up.

She stretched. She yawned. A moment later she sat up.

"I feel wonderful," she said. "I love naps."

Her voice was rough from disuse. The sound of it, and the sight of her awake, made me giddy.

"Naps? You've been asleep forever."

"Have I?" She took a few tentative steps. "Well, then I feel even better."

She spun around, arms outspread. Her hair fanned out. She laughed.

"And I suppose I owe it all to you."

I ducked my head. "Shucks. All I did was dig you out."

"You're a miner?"

"Not really." I stopped myself. "Sure. Why not. In this case, I guess I am."

Her chest swelled, and she let out a sigh. Her face seemed to catapult into some dream.

"God," she said. "I love miners."

She came to me. She smelled of dry leaves. She wrapped her arms around my waist.

"I guess that means I love you."

What can a man want in a woman? Good manners, good looks, good brains, good sex. Vexing had it all. To boot, she kept telling me how she'd never been so happy. When we made love, she said she forgot who she was.

For the first month or two we made the basement room our bedroom, because Vexing preferred the damper, cooler air. Her bodysuit, which had slid off intact the day she woke up, remained in a corner, retaining its shape but growing progressively paler and more translucent, except for what I took to be its supporting structure, thin threads that looked like the veins of leaves. These grew darker, and the more I looked, the more they seemed to represent something beyond mere structure. The way they intertwined and repeated themselves looked man-made, refined. A language? I mentioned this to Vexing, who denied knowledge of such a thing, but one evening after work I found her hunched over the suit, puzzling at it with great concentration. She acted as if I had caught her at something illicit, and the next day the suit was gone. When I asked her about it, she declined to discuss the matter further, begging my indulgence, which I gave freely. Shortly thereafter, we moved upstairs.

The heat in the upper story revved her up, frequently to the point that I couldn't keep pace. Not that I was old, but I was older than she was. Not that it bothered me. Not much.

After a particularly grueling and exquisite week of little food and less sleep, I suggested she find an additional outlet for her boundless energy. She was aghast.

"I don't want someone else."

"Not a person," I said with a choking little laugh. "God no. A hobby. A job."

"I've never had a job. I wouldn't know what to do." She scrunched up her forehead. "What do you do?"

"I'm a miner," I said. "I dig up riches."

She smiled.

"I also work in a drugstore. Talk to my mom every day, take her out twice a week. Be with you every other moment I can."

She seemed daunted. "Maybe I should start out working for you."

"What did you have in mind?"

"I don't know. What do you need?"

There were some chores. I listed a few.

"No problem," she said. "What else?"

"I can't think of anything."

"C'mon. You want to get your money's worth. Use your imagination. What do you want me to do?"

The vastness of her invitation made me tremble. "You can't make me tell."

"Please."

"You'll laugh at me. Either that, or you'll be offended."

"I won't," she promised.

"No?"

She shook her head. "Absolutely not."

As it turned out, I didn't need much encouragement after all, and I unburdened my heart of its puerile little fantasy. Her response?

She laughed.

"There," I said. "You've hurt me."

"No, no. I'm laughing only because you're so silly. Of course I will. And anything else. And as much as you like. I was born to this. I feel it in my bones."

"You're not vexing at all," I said.

She smiled. "You're kind. With any luck I never will be."

So she worked for me, and hard. Scrubbed the floors, the windows, swept every day, did the bathrooms. I had to help her with food, because very little in the supermarket was familiar to her. But she had a flair for cooking and learned how to operate all the kitchen gadgets in a day or two. She washed the clothes, changed the sheets, dusted, vacuumed, polished. It was a good life. Contentment reigned. For a while.

One night we were lying in bed, and she was obviously troubled. I asked if I'd done something wrong.

"I don't think so." She faced me, as innocent and fetching as the day I found her. "Are you happy?"

"Completely."

This seemed to baffle her. "Then why aren't I?"

I replied that I couldn't imagine. Which made her even more puzzled.

"I'm kidding," I said. "You can't depend on me for your happiness. You've got a mind of your own. A separate identity."

"It goes against the grain," she said.

"You need to get out. Meet people, do something besides housework. Part-time, volunteer, school, whatever. Something."

"I could cook," she said. "Be a housekeeper. A scrubber."

"You could do a lot more than that."

"Like what?"

She was beautiful beyond belief. It came to me without thinking.

"Be a model," I told her. "You've got the looks. The style. You're a natural. A knockout. Let the world see. Let them drool and dream."

THE LOOK

was all her own. Feminine, masculine, ingenue, queen. She liked to adorn herself with mirrors and other reflective objects, and this became something of a trademark. Sequins, foil, cut glass, polished stones; and mirrors themselves, appliquéd to her dresses or woven in the fabric itself, some large but most the size of dimes and quarters, reflecting light, faces, bits of the world around her. She loved it when people stared, for like all models she craved attention. To be the center about which all else revolved was her constant desire. For all the world, you might have thought she felt unloved.

On the advice of her agent she shortened her name to Vex, which rhymed so fluently with what she was selling. Initially, she did ads for Macy's and Target, and in a year graduated to the big time. *Vogue, Elle, Redbook*: you couldn't pass a checkout counter without seeing her face. She modeled for Dior, St. Laurent, Gaultier, Miyake; did the runways in Paris, Milan, New York. When *Playboy*, promising discretion, begged for a spread, her agent advised against it. But Vex went ahead, and a week after the issue hit the stands, she appeared on the cover of *Good Housekeeping. Working Women, Young & Modern, Cosmopolitan, Better Homes and Gardens*: Vexing had the moves. She had the talent. She had the ambition. By the time either of us got around to noticing what her career had done to us, she was famous, and we were both dedicated to her new life.

THE THING IS

she got more desirable with each passing year. She had a way of capturing your attention, pinning it, then extracting it as if it were some precious fluid. Sometimes the extract was envy, sometimes admiration. It didn't matter. She was greedy for praise and took what she got. She seemed to inhabit a different world from her public. A better one, loftier one by all appearance. It was funny, then, to hear her complain.

Her weight was a constant anxiety, but this was true of all models. Vexing also had a thing about height, not so much hers as that of the male models she sometimes worked with. Simply put, she hated short men. I was five-six (the same as her), no giant but no midget either, and it had never before been an issue. But one day after a long shoot with a "circus" motif, she came home in a rage, mouthing off against clowns and freaks and especially "stubbies," as she called them.

"What's wrong with short men?" I asked defensively, making sure I was standing as tall and erect as I could.

She had the broom in her hand, unconsciously prepared to sweep, although by then we had others doing the housework. "They're bossy and domineering. They're like old men. Or else they act like children. I've had it."

"Who are we talking about here?"

"Short men," she said sharply. "Don't you listen."

I cringed. "How short is short?"

She threw the broom down and held her hand dwarf-high. I breathed a sigh of relief.

"Hairy little buggers," she muttered. "I need a bath."

She had other anxieties, too, chiefly involving her looks. She was paid, I suppose, to be fastidious in this regard; in a sense, it was an occupational hazard. Like most of the models, she took stimulants, along with massive doses of vitamins. She did the exercise routine. She binged on ice cream. When she was high, she was magnanimous, charming, and full of fun. When she was strung out, she turned petty and vicious. At work she got away with this roller-coaster personality because she was, quite simply, the best. At home she got away with it because I, like the rest of the world, was in her thrall.

The tabloids dubbed her "The Queen," and if not omnipotent, she was certainly ubiquitous: TV, magazines, gossip columns, charity promos, web sites. At home I called her my queen and quit my job at the drugstore to be by her side. It was a switch for us: now I worked for her, fending off the sycophants and fools, doing my best to keep her from going insane. Typically, this involved making sure she had what she wanted when she wanted it, a short list of necessities that included food, speed, praise, solace, and sleep. To my knowledge, I was the only one ever to hear her confess to jealousy or self-doubt, the only one ever to see her cry. I was also the only one she ever truly loved, this from her own mouth. In the beginning of our relationship she said this often, but as the years passed, it was a sentiment she rarely expressed. This made the times she did all the more memorable.

There was one: it was early winter, and we were in a hut on a mountain above a lake somewhere in Switzerland, at the tail end of an exhausting day modeling swimwear in the snow. In the hut were a cot, a wood-burning stove and little else. Outside, the production crew was setting up for a final shot, and we had a few minutes alone.

Vexing was wearing a quilted cape over a lamé bikini. Her toes were blue from the cold, her face chafed by the wind. She was past the point of giving orders but bravely trying to keep up appearances. I helped her onto the cot, massaging her legs and putting her toes in my mouth to warm them with my breath. She made a sound and closed her eyes. Moments later she was asleep.

The hut was small and cozy. It reminded me of the cottage in our yard, which, since completion, I had barely set

foot in. The wind rattled the door, and Vexing opened her
eyes. Her hair at this time was short, her face rather gaunt
and undernourished. It was a look models aspired to, sug-
gestive of hunger, to be interpreted in so many ways. It
was nothing like the face of the woman I had dug up in
the garden. What was, however, was the way she seemed
to be asleep, even now, with her eyes open. They moved
without seeing, in jerky rhythms, as though she were following the flight of some insect, though it was far too cold
in the hut for insects. Suddenly, she fixated on something
invisible to me and uttered a sound. My father had suffered from epilepsy, but this was unlike any seizure I had
ever seen. I thought to yell for help, but then she started
to speak.

At first the words were too garbled to be clearly understood. Then it came to me that she was speaking a different
language, one I'd never heard, or, for that matter, could
imagine hearing, a combination of clicks, grunts, gurgles,
groans, and hisses. Except for her throat and lips, her body
was rigid. It was terrifying. At the same time it struck me
how little I really knew of this woman. True, I had dug
her up. I had given her her name and set her out on her
career. In a way she was my creation, or at least (to my
discredit), I thought of her as such. I shook her, gently at
first, then harder. The wind howled. I cried out to her,
stumbling over her name, feeling foolish for knowing no
other. I begged her to wake up.

Gradually, she did. Her sounds died away. Her body
relaxed. She opened her eyes, shivered, and sat up.

"Did I fall asleep?"

"Something like that."

She drew the cape across her chest. "I'm exhausted. I
need something to get me awake."

"What you need is sleep."

"Don't say that. Sleep is death. I'm done with sleep."

"You used to love naps."

"No more." She pushed herself to her feet. "Now I choose to be awake. As much as humanly possible. Alert and on the lookout. That's my new motto."

"I liked you better before."

"That hurts my feelings." Her tone was careless, rather mocking. Facing me, she let her cape fall open and struck an incredibly sexy pose.

"How about now?" she asked. "Is this better?"

I didn't answer. The point was made. She took my hand as if I were an errant child.

"I do love you, Martin. Even if it sometimes seems I've outgrown you. I haven't. You care for me. You put up with me. When I'm ugly, you always take me back."

"You're not ugly," I said.

"No?"

"Marry me, Vexing."

She laughed. "You'd take a woman like me?"

"And a child. Let's have a child too."

"Oh no." Her laughter rose in pitch, becoming a little out of control. "That would ruin me. A child would be my doom."

THE FERTILE MOON

smiles on some, but it didn't on us. Vexing stopped taking stimulants, and for five years we tried to conceive, without success. Although she denied it, I'm sure that Vexing was secretly relieved, as the prospect of pregnancy had from the outset filled her with dread. Models bearing children were, by and large, models on the way out. In the industry motherhood was tantamount to retirement. But beyond the threat to her career, I had the feeling that children were not much to her liking, as if in some other life she had had her fill. The role of mother and housewife certainly seemed familiar to her: she routinely graced the covers of *Family Living*, *Good Housekeeping*, and *Ladies' Home Journal* with that quintessential air of competence, good humor, and satisfaction. Sadly, this vision of motherhood rarely made its way home.

I wanted children. Always had. There was never a doubt in my mind. We went through all the tests, and the finger pointed at Vexing. Not infertile exactly, but "challenged." Her eggs seemed to kill any sperm that came within a yard. Not just mine, but anyone else's (this confirmed in test tubes), a quirk of nature for which she expressed regret, though once again I suspect that secretly she was glad. She didn't want a family, except for once or twice a year, when the idea would take hold of her and she would waver in her resolve. I took these rare opportunities to make my case for alternative solutions to our infertility problem. On one such occasion I broached the subject of artificial insemination.

"We've tried that," she said. "A million times."

"I was thinking of something different."

"Like what?"

I hesitated, which didn't help. "A surrogate mother."

It was a gaffe. I meant to say "egg," and I did, but it was too late.

"No way." She was hurt, and I sought to reassure her.

"You choose, Vexing. Any woman you want. We'll do it all in a test tube. I won't come near her."

"Forget it."

"Why?"

"Because it offends me."

"That's the furthest thing from my mind."

She regarded me with suspicion. "What if no woman agrees?"

"You're world-famous. You get hundreds of letters a week. Who wouldn't agree?"

"I wouldn't," she said.

"Think about it. Please."

"This makes me sad, Martin. Are you tired of me? Have I ceased fulfilling your precious needs? Are we drifting apart?"

I knew the tone. Foolishly, I told the truth.

"All of it. Yes. A little."

She looked at me with death in her eyes and threw a hairbrush. It missed my head and broke a mirror.

"Seven years bad luck," I said under my breath.

"I don't believe in luck," she replied coldly. "You know that. I believe in preparation and vigilance. And loyalty, Martin. If the thought of leaving me continues to enter your selfish little brain, I suggest you squelch it. Because while you might have a child with another woman . . . heavens, you might have a hundred . . . darling, you won't have me." She smiled patronizingly. "Such an old hag, I know. We'll just have to find a way to make you happy."

THE SEARCH FOR HAPPINESS

was not a great success. Our marriage had its moments, but for a match seemingly made in heaven, it felt an awful lot like hell. Frank was continually on me to take a mistress, while Carol brought me books on separation and divorce. Mother was the only one who was unaffected by our marital discord, chiefly because she forgot us from one visit to the next.

The years went by. Mom died, Carol took an advertising job in New York, Frank finally found it in his heart to marry Shirley and father a couple of kids. Vexing grew older, and her star fell. Not by any means completely, but to a person at the top, any movement is apt to be down. She became increasingly insecure in her looks and, as a result, increasingly vain. She got back in the habit of popping pills, which made her even more difficult than usual. She was, by turns, restless, aimless, grandiose, desperate and frightening. She had spasms of possessiveness, where she craved everything both within and beyond her reach, followed by crashing fits of despair. She lost weight and hair. Her face became pinched and drawn. Mirrors, which had always been allies, became enemies. She would stiffen at the sight of herself, eyes filled with condemnation and longing, lacking the strength to turn away. I, too, lacked the strength, to turn away from her. My dear and once beloved Vexing. As her star fell, so did mine.

I took to spending time in the cottage, which had become a refuge for me. The trees and birds and sunlight could still work their magic, and for short periods of time I was able to stave off hopelessness and resignation. I had never seen fit to decorate the inside, but now the bare walls, as if metaphors of our barren marriage, became oppressive. I had to do something, and one day in a fit of nostalgia it came to me what.

It took a week to cull through the magazines and another to cut and tack. When I was done, every surface, including the ceiling, was covered with her picture. Vexing the ingenue, the vixen, Vexing the girl next door, the starlet, the fresh-scrubbed housewife. Vexing the princess, radiant and happy, athletic, sultry and gay. She looked upon me wherever I turned. Vexing the pinup. The dreamboat. Vexing my lover, my queen, my wife.

I should have known better. More to the point, I should have been a better man. On the other hand, bombs exist to explode. After a terrible fight one morning I fled to the cottage. A few minutes later, there was a knock at the door. Vexing stood on the porch, in tears.

"I need help, Martin. I don't know what to do. I can't
stand it anymore."

I couldn't remember the last time I'd seen her cry, and
I took her inside and held her, feeling a closeness that had
been missing, a warmth, a hope. Gradually, she calmed
down, and by degrees became aware of her surroundings.
At first she was puzzled by what she saw. Then shocked.
Then furious.

"Jesus. Look at this. You're worse than I am."

I knew I'd done wrong and lamely tried to cover up.
"It's my scrapbook of you. My photo album. Aren't you
even a little flattered?"

"Flattered?" She was appalled. "Was that your intention? To flatter me?"

I pawed at the floor. "No. Not really."

"You're sick, Martin. I don't believe this."

"I'm sorry."

"Are you? Are you really?"

She walked the length of the room then back, stopping
at this or that photograph, shaking her head, muttering.

"So," she said at length. "This is what you want."

"What I want is for you to be happy again."

"Such happiness," she said. "You're a cruel man, Martin."

"I'm stupid," I said. "And careless. Some secrets are best
kept secret. Maybe I'd love you more if you loved yourself."

"If I loved myself, I wouldn't be who I am." She let that
sink in. "But if I wasn't who I am, you would never have
found me. Leaf and branch, sun and moon, cock and cunt;
we were made for each other, Martin. I do believe there's
life to this marriage yet."

The next six months were the most extraordinary of my
life. Vexing made an appointment with Dr. Aymen, whom
she had seen for various nervous conditions on and off for

years, to get a referral to a reliable plastic surgeon. She planned to do the whole works, starting at her legs and working up to her face, bottom to top, the natural direction, she said, of all regenerating things. She wanted a good technician but also someone with taste and style.

"I hear there is hardly anything they can't do these days," she told Dr. Aymen, who clearly had reservations.

"Certainly there are surgeons who do this work. Technicians, as you say. I suppose some consider themselves artisans. To me it seems a drastic approach."

"No lectures, Doctor. Please."

"You misunderstand me. There is an alternative. A new drug. I'm involved in the study. It's reached phase two trials." He opened a drawer of his desk and pulled out a folder. "QP 1500. It's a telomerase."

We had no idea what he was talking about, but then, before Hiroshima, few knew of the atomic bomb. For the next twenty minutes he regaled us with what, at the time, seemed pure science fiction. He used words like cellular senescence, apoptosis, feedback control, and defined homeostasis. Telomeric sequencing. Base pair deletion. Cellular immortality.

Cancer cells, it seemed, had a way of staying alive indefinitely, and it had to do with something called a telomere. They now had a drug that worked on this telomere. It kept cells from growing old, and miraculously, it didn't cause cancer.

"It's been tested in mice, sheep, and albino rabbits," the doctor declared. "We have animals that not only have halted the aging process but have literally reversed it, recovering eyesight, olfaction, mobility, and sexual function. These animals are shedding years from their lives before our eyes. In a very real sense, they are growing younger by the minute."

He shook his head at the wonder of it. "Do you understand? Do you see what this is? The Holy Grail. The Fountain of Youth. The end, perhaps, of illness as we know it. The beginning of a new, an ageless age."

The thought robbed him of words, and for an instant I saw him in a different light, as a younger man, a boy, starry-eyed and utterly self-absorbed, lost in a world of dreams, imagination and wonder. Slowly, he came back to his senses.

"We need volunteers. Humans. Would you be interested?"

"Are you kidding?" said Vexing.

Recalling the good doctor's propensity to exaggerate, I remained guarded. "Did you understand anything he said?"

"Does it matter? Did you?"

"Not much," I admitted. "How come we haven't heard of this drug?"

"You will soon," said Dr. Aymen. "Once you do, I can't promise supply will be able to keep up with demand." He let that register, then continued. "You certainly needn't participate in the study if you'd rather not. The choice is fully yours."

Vexing shot me a glance and proceeded to take control of the interview, questioning the doctor at length about the drug's effectiveness, its risks and expense. Nothing was certain and, therefore, nothing promised. The cost of the drug and any treatment necessitated by its use were covered by the study, which was funded jointly by Bristol-Myers, Microsoft, Revlon, and the Department of Defense. Weekly blood tests, as well as periodic measurements of bone density, skin turgor and resilience, arterial plaque, dental erosion, and the like, were required. There would be psychological tests, PET scans, electron microscopy, MRIs, cell cultures, and nuclear probes. PCR, RIA, Western blot, Eastern blot, ELISA, and GIR. Everything they could think of would be done. The Holy Grail was not a product to go begging.

"No problem," said Vexing.

"Sign here," said Aymen. "And here, and here, and here. You too," he told me. "Our witness."

"Beneficiary," said Vexing.

I told her that was cruel, and she patted my hand. "Now now, dear. That's only if I die."

She didn't, thank God. On the contrary. The pills actually worked. In a month she looked, felt and acted ten years younger. In two months, twenty. By three, she was, in every sense, the creature I had found in the garden, half girl, half woman, all sunshine and beauty and light. It was truly a miracle, and our happiness during this period was marred only by my anxiety that she wouldn't stop growing younger, that the process, once started, would somehow continue, with or without the pills, and I would be forced to watch in horror as my beloved went from woman to girl to infant to . . . what? Fetus? Ovum? Nothingness? Was this miracle drug to become nothing more than a new form of death?

It was a needless worry. She didn't keep getting younger, and she didn't die. What did happen was in some ways worse.

She fell asleep.

I should have foreseen it. If I'd had even an ounce of intelligence, I would have known. It happened quite suddenly: one moment she was animated and gay, the next in a deep swoon from which I couldn't wake her. I immediately stopped the medication. I called Dr. Aymen, who tried everything he could think of—drugs, shock, plasmapheresis, peri-cochlear stimulation, pulsed GHB infusions. Nothing worked. She didn't so much as stir. Nor age. Nor change at all. She simply lay wherever she was put, still, quiet, suspended.

I cared for her night and day, bathing her, dressing her,

doing her hair, rubbing lotion on her skin. Sometimes I read to her, sometimes told her stories, often simply sat. The years passed. I turned sixty, then seventy, birthdays I celebrated in solitude. I ceased thinking of Vexing as a lover or a wife; my feelings for her became more those of a father for his daughter. I began to worry what would happen to her after my death.

I looked into nursing homes, but we were poor now and couldn't afford them. The drug study, which by rights should have covered the expense, had long since been terminated because of an untoward number of "adverse outcomes." The lawsuits had been settled; because Vexing remained technically alive, we received nothing. I thought of setting up a foundation—there were certainly people who would sympathize with her plight and more who would pay to see the formerly famous model in state. But the idea of putting her on display, if only for the time it took to raise enough money to live on, was profane, as the idea of her having to alter herself at all should have been in the first place. I had been wrong, and in loneliness and guilt I was paying the price.

What I did do was move her from the house to the cottage, which was quieter and more detached from the world at large, as I myself had become. I tore down the photographs and in their place hung four of her favorite gowns, one on each of the four walls. On the day I turned seventy-five, Frank paid me a visit.

He was as spirited as ever: despite two hip operations, he still found a way to walk with a swagger. His face, like mine, was creased with age, and like me, he had hairs sticking out his nose and ears. Unlike me, he seemed to be enjoying life.

He clapped me on the back. "Happy birthday, old man. How're you doing?"

"Struggling along, Frank, thanks for asking. You?"

"Doing fine, Marty. Couldn't be better. And the little lady? How's she?"

"The same," I said. "I'm worried."

"You're always worried."

"Well excuse me, but now I happen to be more worried. I'm seventy-five. How many years do I have left? What's going to happen to her when I'm gone?"

"I'd say that's out of your hands, buddy."

"I can't just leave her. I don't want to."

Frank, bless his heart, seemed to understand. He squeezed my arm.

"Who does? But look, Marty. As long as you got breath, you got life. You got time. The point is, you got to make the most of what you got."

"I want her to wake up, Frank. Even if it's just for a day. An hour. Jesus, I'd take five minutes."

"Sometimes five minutes is all it takes." With a wink he suggested we pay a visit to the cottage. It had been quite a while since he'd seen the wife.

"So what have you tried?" he asked. We were standing on either side of her bed.

"Tried?"

"To wake her up, Marty. What?"

"Everything," I said. "I've tried everything."

"Lately," said Frank. "What have you tried lately?"

"I don't know. I talk to her. I move her so she doesn't get stiff. I read to her."

"Reading puts people to sleep, Marty. Maybe that's the problem right there. You need to get more involved. More active. Give the lady some stimulation."

"Like what?"

"Tell her you love her. Tell her she's wasting time. You got something for her, but you're not going to be around forever. Kiss her."

"I have kissed her," I said. "I do."

"Sure you have," said Frank. "Where? On the forehead? The cheek? Little get-well pecks. I love you, don't worry, everything'll be all right kisses. Like I used to do to the kids."

"This is embarrassing," I said.

"You've got to be bold, Marty. Nothing's going to work if you don't believe in yourself."

My big brother. Giving me a pep talk. I was touched.

"So what do you suggest?"

"I want you to kiss her. On the lips. Like you mean it. Like you care. Like it matters what happens next."

"She's asleep," I said.

"So?"

"It seems wrong."

He threw up his hands. "She's your wife, for chrissake. Kiss the woman, before I do it myself."

I did. I kissed her.

"Thataboy," said Frank. "Breathe some life into the old girl."

I tried. First tentatively, then with more passion. Life, heart, soul—whatever I had I tried to breathe into my Vexing.

Nothing happened.

Frank was undaunted. "Now kiss her tittie."

I looked at him.

"Her tittie," he repeated. "Trust me on this, Marty."

With trembling fingers I undid the first button of her nightgown. And the second. Then I stopped.

"I don't think so, Frank. Maybe later."

For a moment I thought he was going to ridicule me. But he didn't.

"Sure," he said. "In private. No problem."

I led him out of the cottage.

"You did good," he told me. "Keep it up. Every day.

Don't just tell her, show her you love her. Show her what she's worth. What she's missing. You do like that, no girl in her right mind is going to stay asleep."

So that was Frank. Carol was next. In honor of my birthday, she flew in from New York that weekend. She had put on weight, which was a relief. All her life she tended to run thin, due, I suspected, to the same chemistry that made her such an indefatigable go-getter, but thinness at fifty, or even sixty, is not the same as thinness at seventy, which was when I'd last seen her. At seventy thinness becomes frailty, or worse, the specter of some horrible wasting disease. But now her face was fleshed out, and her cheeks had the blush of health. Business was prospering, as was her marriage, her third. She asked after mine, and in reply I took her to the cottage. Upon entering, she had a quick look around, frowned briefly at the sight of the gowns on the walls, then approached the love of my life.

"So," she said, "she refuses to wake up. She insists on remaining asleep."

"It's been twenty years, Carol. This isn't news."

"I mean, since your renewed efforts. Your rededication toward raising her from wherever she is."

I felt the beginnings of embarrassment. "You talked to Frank."

She acknowledged this.

"And?"

"He thought you were acting a little strange. A little desperate maybe."

"What made him say that?"

"I'm not sure. Maybe because you took his advice."

This was meant as a joke, and being less than eager to hear exactly how much she knew, I let it die.

"I am desperate."

"Why, Martin? Why all of a sudden now?"

"I'm going to die soon," I told her. "I can feel it. I want to talk to her again. I want another chance to make it work."

"So talk to her," said Carol, ever the champion of free speech. "Maybe she hears everything you say. Maybe she gets it."

"I want her awake. I want her to move. To smile. To speak." My voice caught. "I want her to love me, Carol. I want to know that she cares."

"That's a lot of wants, Marty."

"Just one really. I want another chance. I want to show her I can be a better person."

She sighed and took my hand. "Don't we all."

Carol's was the rational approach. Practical, prudent and eminently reasonable. Her advice: get a lawyer. If I was going to die, I should definitely update my will.

This, of course, was the crux. My will.

We were sitting on the cottage porch the next morning over coffee. Carol was reading the business section of the paper. I was leisurely making my way through the obituaries.

"You want to know what I really think?" she said out of nowhere.

I was on McLamb, Yvette, beloved wife of Charles, devoted mother of Irene, Frederick, and Diane, adored grandmother of Adam, James, Portia, Kiki and Maurice, cherished great-grandmother of Laura, Gregory, Thomas . . .

I looked up. "Sure. What do you really think?"

"Put her away."

My mind didn't work that fast. "Who?"

"Your wife. The sooner the better. Especially if you're going to die. Which I doubt. And what makes you say so?"

"I'm seventy-five, Carol."

"Are you sick?"

"No."

"Are you thinking of killing yourself?"

"Not that I know of. On the other hand, I don't see the sense in needless prolongation. Life's been what? C+? B−? That's about an even shot that death is going to be better."

She didn't like that. "I thought you wanted another chance."

"Barring that."

"You know what, Martin? You're not desperate. You're depressed. You should see a doctor."

"No doubt." I folded the paper. "So, I should put her away. Tell me something, Carol. How does a person put away someone he loves?"

"We put away Mother."

"That was different. Mother was senile. She needed round-the-clock attention and care. She was like a baby that way."

"Exactly," said Carol, as if I'd finally seen the light. "A big baby."

She had never liked Vexing, had thought her spoiled and self-centered and generally unsuitable as a mate. The current situation did nothing to alter her opinion, and I felt pressed to my wife's defense.

"She's a victim, Carol."

"Victim schmictim. She's had everything a person could want."

"She lost what she had."

"What did she lose? Her looks? Her fame? What?"

"Both. Among other things. Or so she thought."

"Then give her to posterity, Martin. She'll be famous again."

"What does that mean, 'posterity'?"

"I don't know. A research foundation. A medical facility. Hell, give her to an art museum. They can put her on display, make her the center of attention, just like she always wanted. Design some new outfits for her, maybe work up a whole new line. She'd love it. You think she was famous before. How famous do you think she'll be when the world sees her like that?"

"It sounds awful."

"She'd be taken care of, Martin. That's what you want. Make the plans now, and you'll have that peace of mind. You'll have that security. And you know something else? I bet you'll be a happier man. She's a burden, Martin. When burdens are gone, life has a way of taking a turn for the better." She gave a self-deprecating little laugh. "I've been through two divorces. Trust me on this."

IN THE END

I took Carol's advice. In a way. And Frank's, too. I used the same shovel I had used to dig Vexing out, and I dug the hole to put her back. I did it at night, when no one was looking. During the daytime I covered the hole with a tarp. It took six nights. When I was done, I lined the hole with three of the four gowns from the cottage, mirrors and sequins and such facing inward, so that if she did wake up and could see in darkness, if her eyes could pierce dirt, she would catch a glimpse of herself. The fourth gown, white satin with a pale blue bodice encircled with moonstones, I wrapped around her. It was three in the morning when I finished. Fog hid the sky.

I hoisted her over my shoulder and carried her to the hole. The effort left me breathless. Her face was white as snow. I laid her in the ground. She was no longer Vexing to me, if ever she truly had been. She was the woman of my dreams, and I wished her well. Someday, I hoped, a new and better prince would come along.

I picked up the shovel. It was my finest hour. The night sang, as I covered her with dirt.

Riding the Red

NALO HOPKINSON

Nalo Hopkinson has lived in Ontario, Canada, for nineteen of her thirty-six years. She is a freelance writer and interviewer for Word: Toronto's Black Culture Magazine *and her short story, "Midnight Robber," tied for second place in the 1994 Short Prose Competition for Developing Writers, sponsored by the Writers' Union of Canada. She is the first of three contributors to have attended Clarion East 1995.*

"Little Red Riding Hood" is another fairy tale that has been interpreted by some of the finest contemporary fantasists, including Angela Carter, Tanith Lee, and Kathe Koja. It's one of the more suggestively sexual, even in its most innocent forms. Hopkinson says, "I was born in Jamaica, and spent most of my childhood in the Caribbean, where oral traditions of storytelling are vital. When I write, the rhythm and texture of the language are just as important to me as the meaning of the story. The words have to sing when I speak them aloud." And they do, in this, her second sale, adding a new voice to the canon.

Riding the Red

She never listens to me anymore. I've told her and I've told her: daughter, you have to teach that child the facts of life before it's too late, but no, I'm an old woman, and she'll raise her daughter as she sees fit, Ma, thank you very much.

So I tried to tell her little girl myself, listen, dearie, listen to Grandma. You're growing up, getting dreamy. Pretty soon now, you're going to be riding the red, and if you don't look smart, next stop is wolfie's house, and wolfie, doesn't he just love the smell of that blood, oh yes. Little girl was beginning to pay attention, too, but of course, her saintly mother bustled in right then, sent her off to do her embroidery, and lit into me for filling the child's head with ghastly old wives' tales. Told me girlie's too young yet, there's plenty of time. Daughter's forgotten how it was, she has. All growed up and responsible now, but there's more things to remember than when to do the milking, and did you sweep the dust from the corners. Just as well they went home early that time, her and the little one. Leave me be, here alone with my cottage in the forest and my memories. As it should be.

But it's the old wives who best tell those tales, oh yes. It's the old wives who remember. We've been there, and we lived to tell them. And don't I remember being young once, and toothsome, and drunk on the smell of my own young blood flowing through my veins? And didn't it make me feel all shivery and nice to see wolfie's nostrils flare as he scented it? I could make wolfie slaver, I could, and beg to come close, just to feel the heat from me. And oh, the game I made of it, the dance I led him!

He caught me, of course, some say he even tricked me into it, and it may be they're right, but that's not the way this old wife remembers it. Wolfie must have his turn, after all. That's only fair. My turn was the dance, the approach and retreat, the graceful sway of my body past his nostrils, scented with my flesh. The red hood was mine, to catch his eye, and it was my task to pluck all those flowers, to gather fragrant bouquets with a delicate hand, an agile turn of a slim wrist, the blood beating at its joint like the heart of a frail bird. There is much plucking to be done in the dance of riding the red.

But wolfie has his own measure to tread, too, he does. First slip past the old mother, so slick, and then, oh then, isn't wolfie a joy to see! His dance all hot breath and leaping flank, piercing eyes to see with and strong hands to hold. And the teeth, ah yes. The biting and the tearing and the slipping down into the hot and wet. That measure we dance together, wolfie and I.

And yes, I cried then, down in the dark, me and my Grandma, till the woodman came to save us, but it came all right again, didn't it? That's what my granddaughter has to know; it comes all right again. I grew up, met a nice man, reminded me a bit of that woodman, he did, and so we were married. And wasn't I the model goodwife then, just like my daughter is now? And didn't I bustle about and make everything just so, what with the cooking and the cleaning and the milking and the planting and the birthing, and I don't know what all. And in the few quiet times, the nights before the fire burned down too low to see, I would mend and mend. No time for all that fancy embroidery that my Mama taught me.

I forgot wolfie. I forgot that riding the red was more than a thing of soiled rags and squalling newborns and what little comfort you and your man can give each other, nights when sleep doesn't spirit you away soon as you reach your bed.

I meant to tell my little girl, the only one of all those babes who lived, and dearer to me than diamonds, but I taught her embroidery instead, not dancing, and then it was too late. I tried to tell her quick, before she set off on her own, so pretty with her little basket, but the young, they never listen, no. They're deaf from the sound of their own new blood rushing in their ears. But it came all right; we got her back safe. We always do, and that's the mercy.

It was the fright killed my dear Mam a few days later, that's what they say, she being so old and all, but mayhap it was just her time. Perhaps her work was done.

But now it's me that's done with all that, I am. My goodman's long gone, his back broken by toil, and I have time to just sit by the fire, and see it all as one thing, and know that it's right, that it must be so.

Ah, but wouldn't it be sweet to ride the red, just once more before I'm gone, just one time when I can look wolfie in the eye, and match him grin for grin, and show him that I know what he's good for. For my Mama was right about this at least: the trick is, you must always have a needle

by you, and a bit of thread. Those damn embroidery lessons come in handy, they do. What's torn can be sewn up
again, it can, and then we're off on the dance once more!
They say it's the woodman saves us, me and my daughter's little girl, but it's wolfie who gives us birth, oh yes.

And I haven't been feeling my best nowadays, haven't
been too spry, so I'm sure it's time now. My daughter's
hard, she is. Never quite forgot how it was, stuck in that
hot wet dark, not knowing rescue was coming, but she's a
thoughtful one, too. The little one's probably on her way
with that pretty basket, don't stop to dawdle, dear, don't
leave the path, but they never hear, and the flowers are so
pretty, just begging to be plucked.

Well, it's time for one last measure, yes, one last, sweet
dance.

Listen: is that a knock at the door?

No Bigger
Than My Thumb

ESTHER M. FRIESNER

*Esther Friesner taught Spanish at Yale for a number
of years before becoming a writer. She is best-known
in the sf/fantasy field for humorous fiction; it is only
in the last few years that she has attained recognition
for her darker works. She has published twenty-two
novels so far, including most recently,* The Psalms
of Herod, The Sword of Mary, *and* Child of the
Eagle. *Her short fiction and poetry have appeared in
many magazines and anthologies; she has also edited
the anthologies* Alien Pregnant by Elvis, Chicks in
Chainmail, *and* Blood Muse. *Friesner won the Romantic Times Award for Best New Fantasy Writer
in 1986, the Skylark Award in 1994, and the Nebula
Award in 1996. She lives in Connecticut with her
husband and two children.*

*There are numerous traditional fairy tales of
thumb-sized children. The Brothers Grimm's tale is
"Thumbling," the story of a boychild. The H. C. Andersen variation is called "Thumbykin" and is
about a girlchild. Many of us are familiar with
Thumbelina—particularly from the Hans Christian
Andersen movie with Danny Kaye. The one thing
that these tales have in common is that they are all
light and airy as a soufflé. Friesner's "No Bigger
Than My Thumb" is a far darker version from a dark
period for women in human history.*

No Bigger Than My Thumb

The old woman looked up from the fire, cocked her head to one side. "He is coming, Haldis," she said.

"Let him come, Idonna." Her companion never took her eyes from the fire. "Let him come."

The crone settled her bony rump on the splitwood bench and sighed as if at a leave-taking. "So you mean to see this through?" No answer. "He will not come alone, you know. He will have his men with him, and the law still stands, and—"

"I know the law." The younger woman was a statue for firelight to paint with blood and shadows. She sat on a chair with no back, her hands demurely tucked from sight beneath her clean white apron, as if she were the most common of matrons. "And I do not fear him or his men."

Idonna shook her head and fed a handful of dried herbs into the little black pot that bubbled and simmered on the hob. "I have lost one child already. I did not think to lose more this side the grave." She cast an imploring look at the other. "We may find we lack the power for this."

"In that case, he will call for all our deaths," Haldis replied evenly. Her mouth was the only part of her that seemed to live; the rest was stone. "If we die together, you will not miss me."

"Child, are you sure—?" A claw fell on the younger woman's knee, desperately clutched for the flesh beneath the layers of skirts and petticoats.

Haldis rose slowly, casting off the crone's grip like an afterthought. She crossed the room with the grace of carriage that had formerly drawn many eyes after her in the town, the grace that had once drawn one pair of eyes too many. . . .

"You are too much afraid, Idonna," she said, and she left the fireside for the sleeping room, closing the door after.

The old woman remained, her gaze drifting from the leaping fire to the singing pot above the flames to the door the other had closed behind her with such finality. Outside the chill breath of autumn's close whirled itself around the solitary cottage, seeking entrance at every crevice, like the talons of a cat. She sighed again, and the breath of it seemed to take a shape made of the sparks released from the crackling hearth fire.

"He will come," she told the flames. "And he is too cunning to come alone."

Let him come, said the pot.

Idonna's brows, gray and wiry, came together in a frown. "You too? I see you have as little sense as she. If we thwart him, you know our lot: The law still stands. He will have us for the burning."

Bubbles welled up from the center of the heaving brew, burst on the surface with a sound like chortling laughter.

Law or no law, he will have you, if that is his desire. You of all should know this.

Idonna's face drew itself into an even tighter knot of anger and perplexity. "It was you, wasn't it?" she demanded. "It was your counsel that turned her to this. It was different, better when she only heeded me!" She slammed a heavy iron lid down over the simmering vessel. "Curse the day she first summoned you!"

Steam sighed from between iron lips. *So old you are, and still so fearful-fond of life, and still without the wisdom to see. Old woman, she was never the one to summon me.*

"Then who? Not I! Not even if your coming gave us back what we lost that night. You were not meant to live. No spell's gone right since you've been one of our council."

The lid clanked and clattered against the rim of the pot, but the voice said no more.

Someone pounded at the cottage door.

The old woman shot upright in her seat, gnarled hands crossed over slack breasts like empty wineskins. Girlhood prayers long cast aside rose unbidden to her trembling lips. "Who—?" She felt cold sweat dew her papery skin. "Who's there?"

"Open!" A man's voice, harsh, loud. More blows battered the door. It was of good oak, thick, boasting iron hasps and hinges. Still it shook and groaned under the assault of heavy hands.

Idonna scuttled to the door and shot back the bar. She took her place a distance back, knowing what must come. Come it did: The door slammed open, sturdy wood hitting daub wall so that chips of whitewash went flying and dust sifted down from the cloth ceiling slung between the roof beams. Bootheels gouged small maiden-moons into the dirt floor as five men strode in, taking all the share of space they desired inside the little house.

Four were his men, the fifth was himself. He stood as tall and taller than the guards he'd picked to attend him here, and his hands in their gloves of supple leather were coarsened by the sword. The old woman sank to the ground in a ragged puddle of skirts, her fingers tangled in the fabric.

"She's here?" he demanded.

Idonna's answer did not come as readily as he'd like, or else was lost in a mumble of terror. He jerked his head toward the huddle of her bones and one of his men yanked the old one's head up by the iron gray plaits wound crisscross above her crown. The braids tore loose of their anchoring wooden pins but held one to the other; the man looked as if he'd picked up a cauldron by the handle, a pot with a woman's face.

"Lord—" Idonna licked her lips. "Lord, we had no thought that you might come—"

Another nod; this time the man served his master by slapping the old woman's face four times, with slow, careful attention to the blows. "Lie to fools, not to me. There's nothing happens for leagues around this hovel that you don't know. Not a mouse farts but you've word of it before the smell touches the creature's own nostrils."

Another darting touch of tongue to lips so wrinkled that they had folded in upon themselves. "Lord, she is here."

"In there, I suppose." He regarded the closed door. He did not even need to nod this time: A second of his men was on the spot, pounding on the planks, thundering for entry.

The door opened into dark. Haldis's face swam up into the flickering light, cool condescension spreading over her features like cream. "It was not locked," she said. "You did not need to prove to me that you're a brute beast." She turned her eyes to the man himself. "My lord . . ." (A smirk to take the deference off the curtsy she made him.)

His eyes and mouth were slits bitten out of his face with the blade of a battle-ax. "Leave us," he told his men. Their obedience was as natural as breathing. The last of the four to leave the cottage was the one who still dragged Idonna in his wake. A flash of skirt licked between him and the door.

"She will stay here with me," Haldis said, barring the guardsman's way.

He turned an ox's head towards his master, seeking instruction. "Do as she requests." His lordship made it sound like a great gift. The guardsman let the old woman drop and stepped back outside with his fellows.

His lordship claimed the splitwood bench, Haldis resumed her chair. The hag sat shivering on the floor where she had been let fall. Neither of the two took notice, and eventually she picked herself up and found a three-legged stool to drag into the shadow of the woodpile by the hearth.

"You know why I've come?" he asked.

"Will you tell me I'm lying, too, if I say no?" Her mouth was small and set, her lips pale.

He scowled. "No games, Haldis. I want no games; I'll have none."

"Not even for your own idle amusement?" Her voice scaled up unnaturally bright and giddy, though her face betrayed no change. "Not even to see how fast a lone woman can run before you catch her?" The tight mouth twitched. "But that was sixteen years past. We were both younger then."

He drew off the fine leather glove and leaned through the steam rising from the lidded pot. The glove struck her a solid blow across the cheek, sent her trim white headcloth flying. Dark hair streaked with gray tumbled out of its pins and down over her shoulders. In her corner, the old woman moaned in sympathy. "I said no games."

Haldis cradled her reddening cheek. "As you wish, my lord Galeran. No games. I knew you were coming—there has been talk of little else drifting down the mountain roads—but as for why . . ." She shrugged. "Rumors."

He clasped gloved hand and bare together between his knees. "Tell me," he said. "Tell me what they say, these rumors."

"That your third wife is dead. That your name is still yours alone. That three wives, young and fair and broad-hipped and sturdy, have gone one after the other into the grave without leaving behind any sign that you ever lay with them as a man lies with his bride. That not one had the courtesy to die in childbirth."

The hands unclasped, clenched into stones on either knee. "Three wives," he said through gritted teeth. "Three, and all barren bitches! What odds that?"

"What odds indeed?" She had the power to haunt her face with the ghost of a smile her lips never formed.

"You cursed me," he said, the firelight making his eyes burn red. "You cursed my marriage bed and me, didn't you? *Didn't you?*" His roar shook the rafters.

She never moved. "I am too wise to contradict your opinions, my lord. What good will it do me to deny what you already believe? And yet, those who know the workings of the Art will tell you that any casting—for blessing or for curse—would be impossible with only the two of us left, and I no longer a maiden, by your grace."

"I do not care to be lessoned in the dirt and dealings of witches." The firelight fled, leaving his face all darkness. "It is galling enough to know that you have black powers over decent folk. I praise the day I made it law that the fire should have any of you filth caught and convicted of sorcery."

She let the words pass over her, clouds across a summer

sky's serenity. "As my lord Galeran wills it," she said. "Then you have come to feed me to the fire for having placed that curse on you?"

"On *them*, damn it; on *them*! The only way you could touch me was through them. If the dead could speak, they'd tell you that it was their wombs your spells destroyed, not my manhood."

"Wombs are easily come by," she replied. "Especially for such a man as you. Why stop at three? I can tell you of fathers enough who are ready to sell you their daughters."

"And waste more years battering at a locked door? Don't take me for an idiot." He stood and measured out the length of the hearth, pacing back and forth over the baked and beaten earth before it. "Noble or common, lady or trull, no woman who knows my favor goes away full with my rooted seed. If I had stoked that fire with you and your granddam as well as your mother, you'd have had no time to cast the curse, but I spared you. There was talk that you carried my child. For that alone I spared you, and the old one to tend you when your time came. Maybe that was my error."

Her eyelids lowered. "My lord is as wise as he is kind."

He stopped in his tracks, back to the fire. "It was her death that made you cast the spell."

"Certainly nothing else," Haldis said softly, sweetly. "If you caught me in the forest, threw me down, had your joy of me, well—! It was your forest, my lord; you have the rights for hunting all fair game within its precincts. I hear some women say I should have felt honored."

Her words floated from her mouth, of no more substance to him than a water bubble.

"Damn you, will you not *see*?" He stamped his boot on the raised hearth. Caked red mud flaked down, staining the stones. "I had no choice! She left me none. She came and stood in the town square, a wild woman, baying accusations against me like a moon-mad dog. I did her a mercy by locking her away. It is no fault of mine if she was too stupid to accept it. She spewed curses against me from the cell, too, in my own castle, under my own roof. More than a score of my men were witness to her venom. They feared for their lives as well as mine, harboring a witch."

"And so you burned her." Haldis got the words out quickly, a mouthful of bitter roots. "You have not come to justify that to me after these sixteen years. What does my lord Galeran desire? I would be grateful to grant it as soon as I may."

"So that you can see the back of me, eh?" He managed a chuckle. His bare hand stroked the wealth of his beard, black badger-streaked with white and gray. "We're of one mind, then, Haldis. I can't shake the stink of this hut from my clothes fast enough. What a shame that you're a damned soul. We might have made a match of it, otherwise. I may wed where I like, you know, high or low. At this late date my vassals would be glad to see me wed to a wild pig of the forest, so long as I might get a child on it. But a witch—! They fear that worse than they dread the wars that must come if I die with no heir of my body."

"Wars?" Haldis echoed.

"Unlike me, they have never known a true war. They dwell safe under my rule, my lordlings, and grow fat. They would like to grow fatter. But if my holdings fall free at my death, each will turn on each; not from greed for land or thirst for conquest, but solely out of fear that if he does not strike his neighbor down first, his neighbor will strike him."

Haldis stood. She was a small woman; the top of her head did not come up to Lord Galeran's chin. "I do not

care for your lands or your wars or your rabbit-minded
lordlings. You have not come here to ask for my hand in
marriage—that much I know. If you have more to say, say
it."

"I have come for the child," he said.

In her corner, old Idonna gave a gasp that was half sob.

"Child?" Haldis's expression was guileless. "What
child?"

His gloved hand snapped around her wrist, a prisoner's
iron shackle. He tightened his grip until bone grated over
bone. "This can be your neck," he said.

She eyed him steadily, refusing the pain. Little white
lines twisted along the angles of her jaw, but she did not
cry out. At last he released her. She chafed the martyred
wrist and said, "You will forgive me; that was a light-
minded jest, and after I gave my word to speak frankly
with you. But you see, I did not have any idea that you
knew."

His eyes grew warm. "So the rumors spoke rightly.
There is a child; a girl?" Haldis nodded. "Well, even so,
she must do. I will wed her to the strongest man I can
find and for once I shall be able to sleep in bed of nights
without the belly-cold." He grinned, pleased with himself.

The grin paled as the silence crept back into its place
before the fire, like a cat hearthcome home. Haldis fed
upon it, drinking down the strength of quiet places, but
old Idonna whimpered, and the lord Galeran's teeth grated
out impatience, one against the other.

At last he could bear no more. "Where is she?" he
snapped. "Now that you know why I've come, what
keeps you from summoning her into my presence? God
witness me, the girl will be as glad to quit this place as
I. They claim you've kept her here secretly, letting no human eye see her from the day of her birth." A swift, sus-

picious frown touched his face. "She's not birth-marred, is she?"

"She is not birth-marred," Haldis said.

"Good! Fetch her, then, as you value your life."

"I will." And Haldis dropped his lordship another curtsy and went to the hook beside the fireplace to take the ladle down. She hummed a strange, half-hobbled tune as she wrapped her left hand well in her apron and took up the lid from the pot. The ladle dipped into the steaming brew, traced invisible whorled designs through the liquid. From her corner, old Idonna's voice quavered up in fearful harmony, both melodies twining into a braid with the wordless song of the bubbling pot.

Lord Galeran stared, at first too stunned at such outlandish doings to be angry. He had given a command, showed the power of his hand, and still the jade would not fly to obey! What was she about, this strange witch-woman he'd taken once for his pleasure? He was afraid, and he did not care for the feeling. He wanted to boot it far from him, like an importunate hound.

He lunged forward, bare fingers digging deep in Haldis's shoulder so that she gasped with the shock more than the pain. "Games? Games again? I want my child!"

"You want." The words slipped past him, little lizards of the breath. She hung the ladle back in its place. A measure of the liquid still sloshed in the small wooden bowl. Then, in a voice meant to be heard: "My lord, I am surprised at you. You know we are witches. Did you think we call our children home as common folk do?"

"You use a spell to call her?"

"Less than a spell. No casting can be made without three voices raised—maiden, mother, and crone. But when only two ring out, the third is drawn to answer. She will be with us soon. Will it please you to wait? I can offer no great refreshment for your grace, but I think we still have some peaches. I have heard they are your favorite."

Grudgingly, ungraciously he sat again and let her offer him the basket of bright summer fruit. When she volunteered to pour wine, he waved it away. "I have no wish to try the taste of your poisons, Haldis." He turned the peach around and around in his hand, examining the flawless, unbroken skin. "With these, at least, I could catch at your mischief. You cannot slip a black draught through a skin that shows the mark, even of a needle." She laughed and called him clever, then went outside to present a second basketful to his men.

He devoured two of the sweetly blushing fruits while she was gone, letting the juices trickle from the corners of his mouth, smacking his lips. She returned just as he was reaching for a third.

Her hand fell on his forearm, a gentle restraint. "You will give yourself loose bowels if you have too many," she said. "I tried to tell that to your men, but they were greedy swine; they guzzled down four and more apiece."

"Then let them pay for it later," he said, full of good humor.

"You were always kind, my lord." She palmed one of the peach pits and walked back to the hearthside where the ladle hung.

"What are you up to?" he demanded. "What's that you're mucking with?"

"Nothing."

He thought he heard a splash, but before he could question her further a faint tapping sound jerked his attention away. He could not for his life tell whence it had come. It was almost as if someone outside were drumming a finger against the iron fastenings of the door, but why would that be? His men would have raised a challenge. Besides, the wood of a door was for the knocking.

Haldis smiled, rubbing her hands together as if she

rolled a hot chestnut between them. "She's here," she said. She went to the door and opened it wide.

Galeran stared out into gray sky and black trees. If the moon rode full above leafless branches, he could not see it. Something white smeared the heavens, shining too bright to give honest men sight of the moon. He tried to rise from his place, to go to the door and have a better look, but his limbs were heavy and there was a seductive weariness lapped around him. He had ridden hard and far to come here; he deserved to have his desires brought to him.

"Where is she?" he blustered. "If you've got tricks in mind—"

Haldis knelt on the threshold, then rose and turned as if she were a silk-gowned lady weaving through the figures of a dance. Her hands she held joined together in the attitude of one who reads a holy book. "She is here," she repeated, coming forward to sparkle in Lord Galeran's sight.

For an instant he blinked his eyes, seeking to banish the dazzlement of pinpoint lights that dotted his vision like raindrops on a puddle. Then he saw *her*, and the faery lights were gone.

She stood with one tiny foot planted on either one of her mother's conjoined hands. Perfect in form, her breasts budding to the full, she was all smiles and curves and softness. Not a thread of clothing covered her, nothing kept her warm except the periodic gust of Galeran's astonished breath. From petal pink toes to dandelion-wisp hair the color of a raven's wing, she was only as tall as Haldis's thumb. Luminous dark eyes smiled up at him.

The breath of wonder could not hold against the sour fear now scaling its way out of Galeran's belly. "What sort of abomination is this?" he demanded. The words came out stumbling, flecked with spittle. "I want my child, not some—some faery-get, some freak of nature!"

The tiny creature in Haldis's hands shrank in on itself, a tender shoot of grass frostbitten. Head bowed into hands, back curved over, knees bent as the little one curled up on its side, shivering.

"Now see what you've done," Haldis murmured, raising her cupped hands closer to her face. "Poor thing; since I brought her into this world she's known only love—more than she knew while in my womb, I vow."

"Damn you!" he thundered. "This is the working of your witchcraft, worshiping barrenness, making cows run dry and women's wombs open before their time! It blights even your own belly. You've given me a monster for a child. You'll answer for it at the stake."

"My lord, complaint?" Haldis's hands closed slowly over the small pink curl of flesh within. "How would you have your daughter be?"

"How?" he echoed. "You must be mad to ask. Of a *woman's* size, rot your eyes! What spell has robbed her of human height?"

"I told you." Haldis spoke as if lessoning a child. "There could be no spells cast from this house since you burned my mother, flesh and bone; none woven until she came to us, the maiden to complete our triad. All we might do meanwhile, my granddam and I, was use the herbs whose properties do not rely on enchantment. And so I did."

Haldis's hands began to open like the waking of a flower, to move by wavering degrees toward Galeran's face. He tried to shift his weight and could not, tried to turn his head away and could not, tried to close his eyes and found that he had lost power over even that, although his lids felt heavy enough to drop and never open again. Dust and wood were under his tongue. All he could do was move his eyes in their sockets, for what comfort it gave him. To one side were shadows, to the other a table on which rested a basket in which hard, small, brown, and wrinkled things that stunk of mold had somehow banished the peaches.

So he knew, and with only his eyes to speak for him she could still understand his late-come knowledge.

"Peaches at this season?" she said. "Your desire for them would not let you make them a thing to be questioned, like the wine, even though offered to you under *my* roof. Greed outdoes you, my lord Galeran, more than a double dusting of all venomed powders that cling to surfaces, show no outward mark on a fruit's tender skin. What you want *must* be good by the simple fact that you want it. You see things as you would have them; we hardly needed cast our spell of seeming." She clicked her tongue over the once-were-peaches in the basket. "If I had let you eat more than two, it would be with you as it is for your men, poor souls. I hope that by your lights they did not die with too many sins on them, unconfessed, unshriven."

He tried to speak and found that the paralysis had cast its net over his tongue as well. His eyes maintained immunity. Their sight—now blurred, now dazzled—still owned flashes of awful clarity. Her cupped hands were half-open, coming ever nearer to his face. Soon it would not matter whether he darted desperate eyes to right or left: He had no choice but to see what she willed.

Haldis opened her hands.

It was curled in upon itself, small and soft, red with blood, free of glamour. Except for its outsize proportion to the delicate limbs—the miniscule, perfect fingers and toes—the head and face of it were human enough. Only the eyelids were fused shut, to trap the slumbering soul forever in the place of many dreamings. The torn end of the birth cord passed between the fingers of one hand, as if it told the beads of an elfin rosary.

"See how she sleeps," Haldis whispered over it. "See how she smiles!" She shifted her hands so that one was sufficient to cup the manikin. She held one finger of the other along the exquisite curve of the spine. "You see? No bigger than my thumb. So she was when we first brought her forth, the night my mother's pyre still smoldered in your castle's courtyard. So we kept her, once we saw the sign marking her sex. We kept her warm and safe." She nodded toward the small black pot still simmering over the fire. "We did not know, at first, whether her presence would be enough to make up the third that we had lost." The flash of her teeth blinded him. "It was."

She pulled her blouse from one shoulder, baring a breast, and brought her cupped hand up beneath it. An old, old lullaby purled from her lips as she gazed down with all a mother's doting love. Ice shrouded Galeran's bones as he saw a hand no bigger than a grain of wheat reach up to press itself into Haldis's breast. When at last Haldis lowered her hand, a single glistening drop of milk hung suspended from her nipple.

Without bothering to cover her breast again, she stood with both hands cradling her child. "You have come to me for a daughter, my lord; I have given you one. You complain she is not of a size to suit you? I will provide. You are in haste to have her? This, too, will be my care. I am a witch, after all. We would not thrive if we could not content those who come seeking our aid."

Her skirts whirled out as she ran to fetch the ladle. Standing it upright on the table, she slid the ungrown child into its flat-bottomed bowl. Hands stippled bloody, she began to tear open every fastening of Lord Galeran's garb, rolling him from his seat like a log to lie naked before the fire.

He felt the pressure on his chest as she straddled him, the ladle in her hand. Two fingers hooked his mouth open, wood clunked against his teeth as she tipped the ladle to his mouth. Something hot and wriggling slipped over his tongue, down the back of his throat. He tried to scream; he only gurgled.

"There," she said, dismounting, satisfied.

He fought to regain control of his body and found, with as much surprise as if it were a miracle, that his fingers would respond to the commands of his brain. He wiggled them, and his toes, and the tongue in his mouth that had lain so lately stiff and useless. A quivering life came back into his lips, crept up his legs and arms, until all the webs of animated flesh met and meshed above his heart.

She did not seem to notice. Once her gruesome task was done, she had stood up and turned her back to him. There she was—he could raise his head and see her plainly now. She stood against the fireplace stones, one hip outthrust, gloating into the dark. If he tilted his head a little he could see the old woman who rocked herself back and forth behind the woodpile, keening.

Trull! he thought fiercely. *To subject me to such affront, so disgusting a—* He could not bear to think of what he had suffered at her hands. He was afraid the memories would turn him mad with rage. His hands pressed hard against the earthen floor. He could see his castoff clothes lying in a spurned heap within arm's reach. Carefully, so as not to make the smallest sound, he stretched out his hand for the thick black leather belt and the dagger in its sheath.

It was in his hand. A twist of his hips and he was on one knee, the spring of sole to earth and he was on her. The dagger breached her chest above a breast still bared.

Haldis sank to the floor, breath whistling in her throat,

while Idonna shrieked and threw herself over her grand-daughter's body. He barked for the crone to move away and gave her a kick in the ribs when she would not. Bones snapped and blood flowed from Idonna's mouth. Teeth bared, he snatched up the fireside stool and brought it down on the old woman's head once, and again, and again.

"She was dead . . . with the first blow." Haldis's voice snapped his gaze away from old Idonna's shattered skull. "A true . . . victor . . . conquers no more than . . . enough."

His arm snaked down to parody a lover's embrace as it wound itself around Haldis's waist and hauled her up-right. She sagged against him, bleeding, but she still lived.

"*That* for your victory!" He spat in her face.

"Lord . . ." The word rasped from her chest. "Is this . . . thanks?"

"For what? For killing my men? For humiliating me? God's curse take you, and the devil, too, will you play games even now?"

"No game." Breath shuddered as the blood bubbled down. "I gave you . . . what you willed. Your daughter. Grown. Soon . . . soon grown." Another breath, shallow, wet. "Of a woman's size."

He had been to battle. He had heard the last breath leave many a man. Hers fled the flesh otherwise, as laughter. He growled a final curse and let the corpse drop.

He was just pulling on his tunic when he felt the first tentative movement in his belly. *Wind,* he thought, jerking on his trews. *Damn me if I don't have that* and *the griping gut from the bitch's demon-brew.*

He tried to pull the drawstring tight at the waist and found the ends would not meet over the swiftly swelling roundness. Smaller bulges poked out against the taut skin, subsided, moved to protrude in different places. He dropped to the bench, staring as his navel turned itself lazily inside out, then became a knot of flesh riding the humpback wave of his body.

When he read the purpose of the dead witch's spell in the small feet that kicked, the small hands that pummelled him mercilessly from within, he began to pray.

When he recalled her dying words, he began to scream.

In the Insomniac Night

Joyce Carol Oates

In addition to being a respected novelist and story writer, playwright, and essayist, Joyce Carol Oates is the Roger S. Berlind Distinguished Professor in the Humanities at Princeton University. She has won the National Book Award and the Bram Stoker Award for Life Achievement in Horror Fiction. Her novel Zombie *won The Boston Book Review Award for Fiction and the Bram Stoker Award. Her most recent books are* We Were the Mulvaneys *and* First Love: A Gothic Tale. *Her short stories have appeared in numerous genre and mainstream magazines and anthologies. She has three collections of dark fiction*: Night-Side, Haunted: Tales of the Grotesque, *and* Demon and Other Tales. *She recently edited the anthology,* American Gothic Tales.

Oates was inspired by the ballad version of "The Elfin-Knight," a story existing in different forms all over the world (including "Rumpelstiltskin"). Marina Warner, in From the Beast to the Blonde: On Fairy Tales and Their Tellers, *relates some of these variations. Generally, the pivotal character is a false suitor who kills the women he seduces. The heroine, often tested with impossible riddles, sometimes succeeds in tricking him, sometimes fails and dies (or loses her child). In the Netherlands, a medieval Dutch version has a bride disrobe to enter the sea, which is invoked as a bridal bed in which she will be drowned.*

In the
Insomniac Night

In the night, in the insomniac night, she lies in her bed whispering *Sleep, sleep!* But she isn't listening, listening instead to the sweet-mournful beat of the frothy briny greeny-bitter waves at the ocean's edge a half mile away in the night in the wind-buffeted liquidy moonlight spilling through partly closed venetian blinds onto the faded-wallpaper wall and a wedge of plaster ceiling shaped like an isosceles triangle floating. Moonlight calling to her, teasing. A man's face winking out of the moon. *Where are your children?* the voice asks pleasantly, and her reply is immediate and easy. *Both are here beneath this roof, asleep in their beds, safe in the night, miles from all harm.* For children are not inhabitants of the insomniac night. Children know nothing of the insomniac night. Sleeping deeply and innocently in ignorance. Holly who is eight, Mark who is five. Fatherless children. Yet happy children. Happy children because fatherless. *Both beneath this roof in their rooms close by my own and tomorrow Sunday: church.* In the old life of the city amid traffic, poison-exhaust, sirens rending the air like razor wire, there had been no church, not a thought of *church, faith, God, community, Jesus meek and Jesus mild.* And she herself nonbelieving, a skeptic. Yes and embarrassed. In the city in the old life. In the old life in the marriage. But the old life is past, is fled. Escaped. The old life is gone. Now the new life in the seaside town in the neat attractive stone-and-stucco slightly shabby bungalow on a street of similar bungalows inland from the ocean. Rented, leased in her name. In her name exclusively. Legally. Now the divorce is final, the custody suit settled. Mostly in her favor though of course the father, the ex-husband, has certain visitation rights. But now the children are in her care beneath a roof provided for them by her, by the mother. By this woman who is astonished with her unexpectedly fierce, possessive love for her children, like a lioness's for her cubs. She who had not seemed to herself as to others an inordinately maternal woman. But now this new life, this new adventure *Once upon a time, a very special time, there was a mommy and a little girl and a little boy who came to live in a town near the Atlantic Ocean where it was said nothing had happened in a hundred years that was not something happy, a happy surprise.* Except these nights, these autumn nights awake hearing the wind in the pines and the ragged clouds blown overhead scratching the pearly sky, hearing the *beat beat beat* of the waves against the pebbly shore that stir an old ache in her loins, an old weakness she would have wished to believe she'd overcome. Softly begging *Sleep! oh please,* for consciousness exhausts her, her weeks are strenuous bouts of commuting seventy miles to work, seventy miles back home, on weekends sleep is precious to her *Try to sleep! for God's sake! what is wrong with you, Judith!* even as her heart beats with a sullen stubbornness and her feet kick the bedclothes *I don't want to sleep, God damn I want to run to fly through the night. Where the night will take me.* Her long slenderly muscled runner's legs like the legs of a young horse primed to run, to run, to run. But she can't give in! Lying arms crossed still as the figure on the prow of a ship. Lying still, willing herself *Sleep!* for she is a single mother now, she must behave like an adult woman of thirty-two and not the irresponsible restless girl, the girl she is. Insomnia is a weakness to be overcome as she has overcome other weaknesses. Insomnia is not in her nature. In the old life in the city, in the failing miserable marriage to a man now a stranger to her were shameful sedative nights, sweaty oblivion nights of no dreams and by morning a mouth parched as if blistered and dazed headachy hours when for no reason her eyes leaked tears so Holly bit at her thumbnail *Mommy why are you crying?* and Mark pushed against her with his scared pouty whine *Mommy! Stop that!* But drugged sleep was not in her nature either. Nothing of weakness in her character is in fact her character. Except *I want to be outside, to run, to fly through the night where the night will take me.*

Finally, then, she gives in. Kicks off the bedcovers, rises and dresses swiftly, fastens her hair into a ponytail, puts on her running shoes. Her breath quickening like a child's on the verge of an adventure. *Only for a half hour* checking her watch which she wears night and day, rarely removes *back by 1:40 A.M.* This is the second time this week unless it's the third time she will slip away from the house too restless, too alert and yearning to sleep. How many times since moving to this quiet seaside town out of the old exhausting life of the city several months before. She ties the slightly frayed laces of the running shoes with mounting excitement, an anticipation of pleasure. Shoes that fit her long narrow feet so perfectly: like a caress. She smiles to think how ironic, how funny: these water-stained not-new

shoes feel to her more loving than any man cupping her
feet in his hands had ever been.

   She'd several times glimpsed him following her with his
eyes. Tracking her with his eyes. In town, once at the mini-
mart. This place new to her at the edge of the ocean:
Edgewater, New Jersey. A local handyman probably. Manual laborer judging by his walnut-dark skin. Carved-
looking face. Black hair that looked smudged as tar. He
was of less than average height for an adult man but com-
pactly, solidly built. Thick neck. Upper body development
like a boxer. Legs rather short, though by no means
stunted. A muggy September day he'd been wearing a T-
shirt that fitted his chest tightly and khaki shorts, unusu-
ally short shorts for a man. Hard sinewy-muscled thighs.
Legs and arms covered in dark hairs that appeared imbri-
cated, like an animal's pelt. His eyes easing upon her as
she kept in motion, not slowing to look around. *Never make
eye contact with a stranger especially a strange man* she'd gently cautioned both her children. Oh she couldn't be certain
the walnut-dark man had actually been watching her, each
of the several times was the sort of situation where you
can't be certain. So simply ignore. Forget. In the corner of
an eye. Watching? Can't know, so wisest not to imagine.
Not to alarm. She was not an excitable woman, not any
longer. Here in Edgewater, New Jersey, population 1,470.
The seaside town with the pebbly beaches unlike most of
the Jersey shore, not very popular with summer tourists.
A place where nothing has happened in a long time, the
real estate woman remarked, shaking her head. Median
age fifty-nine and rising. Great place to bring up children,
of course. The last time she'd seen the walnut-dark man,
the man with the carved face and swath of tar for hair,
she'd been hurrying to her car parked at the curb in front
of the post office. Holly and Mark were in the car, a Sat-

urday morning of errands in this new town at the edge of the Atlantic Ocean, where there was always a wind, always the briny smell of the estuary. And each errand pleasurable in itself. *This is our life now, our life, the three of us in Edgewater, New Jersey.* Where the children's father, when he came every third weekend to take them away, Friday morning to Sunday evening, was an outsider, a temporary visitor not at ease as in the city in the old life. After the post office was the dry cleaner's, then the video shop another time to rent *Pocahontas,* then Oleander Farm at the outskirts of town, where there was apple slush, cinnamon doughnuts, a mule and goats and a Shetland pony and many cats for the children to pet. So she hadn't given a second thought to the walnut-dark man on the sidewalk tracking her with his eyes.

Nor thinking at that time, of course, that there might be any connection between him and the lead-colored Chrysler van. That looked as if it might have been a workingman's van once, sides now crudely painted over. There was a crescent moon in silver on the driver's door, not very skillfully rendered. She'd seen this vehicle once or twice in town without taking any special notice of it except casually *Why is it parked there, motor running? for so many minutes?* while she'd been in the drugstore patiently waiting for the elderly pharmacist to fill a prescription. In the whitish glare of hot autumn the lead-colored van's windshield was blinding, she couldn't see who sat behind the wheel or whether in fact there was anyone behind the wheel, at all.

Quietly she checks the children in their bedrooms. The bungalow is a single story with an unfinished attic, her bedroom and theirs at the rear of the house. Next to her bedroom is Mark's, not much larger than a walk-in closet. But a cozy comfortable room whose walls she'd painted herself, cornflower blue. And the luminous Mother Goose plastic night-light on the floor, reassuring should the child wake with a start not knowing where he is. In the town house in the city *We don't want to coddle Mark, spoil him* the children's father had warned. *He will only see that darkness holds no terrors if he can experience darkness for himself.* But she is the mother; it is she who makes decisions now. So the luminous Mother Goose burns nightly in a corner of the five-year-old's room. Where is the harm? no harm certainly. And how hard Mark is sleeping! as he'd done as an infant in the crib. Sunk in sleep so he seems scarcely to be breathing, and his skin clammy-pale as if his body's heat has been sucked inside by the tension of his pumping heart and organs. In that region of dreams to which his mother, leaning above his bed, has no entrance, knows herself excluded. *Love I love you Mark-y, baby Mark-y.* She dares to bend closer, brushing her lips against his warm forehead, and dares to tug up the blanket beneath his chin. Mark doesn't wake, of course, he sleeps so soundly. Next is Holly in her bed in her room across the hall from Mommy's bedroom, asleep too, silky pale gold hair like her mother's at that age but resembling her father in the set of the eyes, set of the chin. Her daughter, her miraculous firstborn. Out of what starry dust, what maze of unnameable uncountable atoms. Out of what unknowable void. *What do babies dream?* the mother had asked as Holly, as an infant, fell asleep nursing, and twitched and flailed her tiny fattish arms, clearly enthralled by some sort of dream. And Holly's father had said *Obviously, babies don't dream, can't dream, lacking memory and language. No more than an animal can dream.* And the mother who was a new, young mother bold and giddy and flirtatious and in love at that time with the baby and with the baby's father and with herself such a success had laughed *How do you know, do you remember?* and he'd said with a smile but in finality *No of course I don't remember, haven't I said babies have no memory. Our daughter's brain is an emptiness ready to be filled.*

Holly is now eight years old, a third grader. Beautiful child if at times touch-me-not. High-strung. Quick to tears, quick to rages. But she loves her mother, hugs her mother tight a dozen times a day. *Mommy I love you Mommy when can I have a kitten?* At Oleander Farm there are kittens to be adopted, but not just now. Holly's room is a little-girl's room the two of them had decorated together, sunflower curtains, pumpkin-colored shag rug, white plastic glow-in-the-dark Kitty Clock on the bureau. Her mother doesn't dare lean over to kiss Holly, Holly is a notoriously light sleeper. A frown flickering over her face in profile on the pillow like ripples on the surface of water. Again thinking as she backs out of the room, shuts the door silently *What do children dream?* feeling a stab of jealousy for never will she know.

Of course the windows to the children's rooms are locked, and the blinds drawn neatly to the windowsills. Every night without fail. Double locks on both the front and rear doors of the house though there is virtually no crime here in Edgewater, New Jersey.

Where's the harm? no one will know. In sweater, slacks, running shoes slipping outside through the kitchen door and locking it, the key wrapped in a tissue in her pocket for safekeeping. She will not run far, or long. In the night in the wind-buffeted insomniac night her route has been a rectangle of which the approximate center is the stone-and-stucco bungalow on Spruce Street, the children sleeping in their beds.

Her heart quickens in rapture: running!

What freedom, what bliss: running!

Out through the carport, out the narrow asphalt drive-way and to the street and along the street of darkened houses in softened leaves lining the gutters and the fresh fragrance of the leaves stirred by her running feet, her heart beginning to beat strong and hard as a fist, confident in its rhythm, this speed matches her metabolism, this is the true rhythm of her being, this is where she belongs, not lying in bed beneath smothering covers trying to sleep, not helpless, not a passive cringing frightened woman: no longer. Running in the night in chill autumnal moonlight smelling of the estuary, of the ocean. *This is my life, no one can deny me my life, I am not a mother only, I am a woman before I am a mother, and I was a girl before I was a woman.* High overhead are wind-driven rags of clouds passing rapidly across the moon's winking face.

Why are you taking them so far away, it's a four-hour drive for me he'd complained bitterly. Her former husband yet not the children's former father. For he would always be their father, so long as he, and they, lived.

Only after the labor of birth, only after you've come home to your own private quarters bearing the precious gift of your baby, only then in the abrupt quiet and solitude of ceiling, walls, floor does the realization pierce you like a knife blade *I am responsible for keeping it alive.*

Alone she runs along darkened Spruce Street, past dim shapes of houses so similar to her own glimpsed in the corner of her eye they might be interchangeable, identical. It's October, it's night and gusty in chill liquidy moonlight, and her ponytail lifts and falls between her shoulder blades as she runs, swinging her slender-muscled arms, she runs, her fists lightly clenched, her feet flying lightly, touching the pavement and springing away, and on. And on. No one observing in the insomniac night she has claimed at last as her own. *How happy I am, how free I am, no one knows where I am, who I am no one knows.* Holly and

Mark are safe in their beds in their snug rooms she, the mother, has provided for them. The other nights she'd slipped away to run they'd slept undisturbed, not knowing she was gone, suspecting nothing. *Where's the harm?*—all the doors and windows of the house are locked, her car is parked as usual beneath the carport so it would appear she's home; no intruder would dare try to enter.

Here in Edgewater, New Jersey. Where nothing has happened for a hundred years. Where nothing will happen, to alarm. *The town that time forgot: Edgewater, New Jersey.* As the real estate agent said with a wink

Why can't I speak with my children without you monitoring our conversations on the phone he'd asked in a voice of aggrieved dignity, his scientist-voice by which as a young wife she'd been intimidated. But now empowered by distance she'd said quietly, just slightly provocatively, *Of course when you're with them, when they're in your custody no one is monitoring you, but when they're in my custody, beneath my roof, the telephone, too, is beneath my roof, it's my responsibility isn't it?* Unspoken between them were the bitter accusations she'd made and he'd denied, reiterated through their lawyers like echoes that reverberated without end. He said, making an effort to disguise his deep rage at her, *Judith please, it isn't necessary for us to hate each other just because we no longer love each other* and she'd laughed, stung, as if the man's words possessed still the capacity for hurt, she laughed *Why not?* and he said *Judith? What? I didn't hear* and she said *You heard me clearly enough, Gabriel* then rethought her position for of course she feared him, she feared him revenging himself upon her through the children, quickly relenting *Of course we don't hate each other, we're civilized adults aren't we?*

Still she continues to listen on the telephone extension when her ex-husband speaks with the children. Never can she imagine a time, her mind at ease, she will not be compelled to listen.

It isn't just their love, their allegiance he wants, but their souls. In all broken marriages it is the children's souls that are contested.

For though the man is her ex-husband and no longer shares her bed, he remains the children's father. DNA testing would confirm what she understands to be fact, fate. Out of what unfathomable void, what far-flung careening galaxies. Male seed, female egg. Brainless, eyeless. So simple! And the two children innocently linking them, so long as they both live.

Running in the night in the insomniac night she thinks of none of this. Truly.

In the night, in the wind-buffeted insomniac night, she runs. At the corner of Spruce and Highgate, passing the First Presbyterian Church of Edgewater; next morning at 10 A.M. she will take Holly and Mark to the Sunday school class in the basement, she'll eagerly attend services upstairs with the mostly retired, predominantly middle-aged and elderly congregation, only a scattering of women and fewer men her own age, she will make an effort to concentrate, to listen to the Reverend Heideman's drowsy sermon, she will hope to feel her heart expand with Christian compassion and elation as she sings from the hymnal glancing covertly right and left, hopefully *You see?—I am one of you, no different from any of you.* By night, however, the church that is a historic Edgewater landmark, built in 1841 of fieldstone and granite, appears scarcely recognizable. By wind-buffeted moonlight an awkwardly shaped mound of rubble, an untidy ruin beyond straggly trees, slovenly shrubs. What has happened to the church? Has she turned onto the wrong street, confused in the darkness? But no: she recognizes the minister's house adjoining the church, she has visited that house, but it too appears changed, squat and misshapen as if its foundation has partly collapsed. Running in the street in the dark she can't slow to look more closely; fear touches her heart and she keeps her gaze resolutely ahead, telling herself it's imagination merely, her fevered imagination, what had her smug pathologist husband predicted for her—*nervous collapse, dissolution of personality*—if she'd persisted in filing for divorce, demanding primary custody of Holly and Mark. But she'd defied him, proved him wrong. How wrong, he has fully to learn.

From Highgate she turns abruptly onto South Main Street, altering her route. She's shaken, confused. Running now past streetlamps that burn with a faint yellow-tinctured light. Past the Edgewater library, past the fire station, past the township office—all darkened. The pharmacy, the dry cleaner's, the barber shop—darkened. Yet there is Gino's Pizzeria, which usually closes by 9 P.M. weekdays, 11 P.M. weekends, still open; a few doors away, Edgewater Video is open, too, in fact glaring with light. Patrons in both places are mostly teenagers, she sees. High-school kids, here and there a familiar face—a girl named Sandy who'd baby-sat for her, a tall curly-haired boy named Todd, who's mowed her lawn. But most of the kids are strangers, hanging about on the sidewalk, idly smoking, drinking from cans, laughing raucously. She's surprised, disapproving—isn't Edgewater supposed to be a quiet village, not a gathering place for rowdy adolescents? She crosses the street, not wanting to pass too close to them, but sees nonetheless, to her discomfort, that several of the loutish long-haired boys are staring at her, grinning—as if they know her?—do they know *her*?—and on the steps of the video rental is a bevy of girls, startlingly young girls, in tank tops and jeans as if it's a summer night not a chill October night. The girls slyly cut their eyes at her, too, ducking and giggling, for they're passing what appears to be a joint among them, one of them a slender pale blond child so resembling Holly that Holly's mother blinks in astonishment, immediate denial *No: impossible* without hesitating for an instant in her running, head turned resolutely away and eyes fixed ahead, a sick trembling inside her *But no: impossible* and she does not glance back, she's eager to be gone from Main Street, which has been a mistake on a Saturday night and one she won't repeat.

Except: she'd jogged through downtown Edgewater last weekend, hadn't she, at midnight, it was deserted as a ghost town.

Except: the child wasn't Holly, at least eleven, twelve years old hardly an eight-year-old, *calm down you're imagining things, just calm down* the pathologist-husband's voice admonishes not unkindly. In fact Judith had scarcely glimpsed the girl's face, only the silky pale gold hair, so lovely, so like Holly's. Of the very hue her own had been, at that age.

The pathologist, the dissector. Amateur photographer. Fussy with his cameras, *Please don't touch my cameras.* Posing the children, developing his own prints, a perfectionist. How many portraits of her, the attractive smiling young wife so long as she was young. *Why did you ever love me if you can't love me now?* In such awe of him when first they'd met, she an undergraduate, nineteen years old, dismayed by organic chemistry, and he her section instructor, Gabriel, the very name Gabriel, great-winged angel bearer of celestial wisdom, *Gabriel.* Six years older than Judith but of another generation, in his presence she'd felt her personality so undefined, anxious, simply dissolve like vapor, felt her heart beat calmly as if with his magician's fingers

he'd reached into her rib cage to cup it. *But this isn't love,
this is a place you've walled me up inside, and the children,
please don't claim this is love.* The past several years he'd
taken up videotaping as a hobby, mostly of the children
of course, something fanatic in his zeal to record, record,
record. By then she'd ceased loving him but not fearing
him. Yet daring to object to the videotaping, Holly's seventh birthday and the child was overexcited, feverish with
Daddy's attention, exactitude, *Don't you believe anything is
real unless you've measured it and recorded it?* and he'd re-
torted as if she'd asked an idiotic question at the end of a
lecture *Every attribute of a thing increases its reality, every
truth we can discover about a thing defines it more precisely*
and she smiled angrily *Are our children things? Are we
things?* and he said *We share "thingness" with all matter,
animate or inanimate. Of what do you imagine we're composed,
Judith, except matter? The difference between us is that you seem
to be ashamed of such facts while I, a scientist, consider them
profound.* She laughed, stung. *Profound!*—the fury in the
man's face shut like a fist, steely eyes behind the lenses of
his glasses narrowed in contempt of her, a mere woman:
female body: unexpectedly resistant to his instruments of
dissection. She said stammering *It's dead matter you love!
Not living people, it's dead matter you love!* Lashing out at
him where he stood watching her the children hushed, in
the next room surely listening. How she hated losing control, a woman losing control to a man as if surrendering
her very body's heat to his as in his authority he sucked
it from her like that species of giant water spider sucking
life from frogs anesthetized by spider venom. *It's deadness
you love! Where nothing changes, everything is fixed!*—she
stammered, not knowing what she said as with a show of
patience Gabriel blew his nose, left nostril first, then the
right, fastidiously then refolding the handkerchief to return to his pocket. He said *There's where you're mistaken,*

Judith calmly, with professorial logic *"Dead matter" is not permanent, it changes as much as, or more than, "life matter." Its chemicals break down, it decomposes, as fascinating a process as "composing," I assure you—if you aren't blinded by convention, or your own narrow womanly perspective.*

Yet she'd won. In the end, the woman won. Taking the children from the man who'd been her husband for nearly ten years. Going into debt for thousands of dollars, borrowing to pay her lawyer, convinced she was right, would be vindicated. Gabriel had fought her, yet principled as he was, adamant in egoism, he had been forced to admit in court that his work schedule and his work addiction made it unlikely he'd be able to spend as many hours weekly with the children as she spent with them even with her commuting and her work. The judge, a black woman, had openly sympathized with the mother in this instance; there'd been a revolution in certain quarters regarding single mothers who worked. Judith had won, or nearly—she had not complete custody of the children, of course, the father had visitation rights, and had expressed satisfaction with the judgment. Not to the judge nor to the lawyers but in an undertone to Judith, smiling, shrugging *Well!—the children will be for my older years, then. I have plenty of time in which to win them.*

Beyond the estuary of the shallow Millstone River, smelling faintly of garbage rumored to be dumped by night, a harsher undercurrent of chemicals from factories many miles upstream, Judith is running now on the Shore Road, the third side of the rectangle. On previous nights this mile-long stretch beside the ocean has been the high point, the most pleasurable part of her run, despite the perpetual wind; tonight, already she's beginning to tire, her breath has lost its rhythm, there's a twinge of pain in her left knee. The Shore Road is gravel and sand and mud, she can't seem to find solid ground running in patches of darkness as, with a faint sound of jeering laughter, shreds of clouds race across the moon. Nonresidents of Edgewater, city people, own most of the property on this road, summer "cottages" large as houses, or mansions; all are shut for the season. Yet Judith sees, or thinks she sees, lights burning here and there, hears voices, outbursts of laughter. Drunken parties, at this time of year? She ignores such distractions, concentrates on her running, her breathing, her control.

In the night, in the insomniac night where sudden shadows loom gigantic and in the next instant vanish, much is exaggerated, Judith knows.

Thinking *Not Holly, don't be ridiculous. Not my daughter not now not ever.*

In the corner of her eye seeing, not seeing. What is it?—a vehicle parked in the dunes. Headlights off. On a beach trail amid tall rushes, whipped by the wind. She refuses to acknowledge it, will not be alarmed. The vehicle might be abandoned; if anyone is in it, probably they're teenagers, lovers aroused by moonlight; caught up in passion, sexual need, like water swirling deliriously down a drain; unaware of their surroundings, certainly of a lone woman jogging along the Shore Road. If the vehicle is a rusty lead-colored van, its sides painted over so the original words, like cuneiform, are indecipherable, she does not see. *Don't be ridiculous. Look straight ahead, mind your own business.* Yet forced to recall how early that morning the telephone had rung and she'd lifted the receiver to silence—a human, palpable silence. Whispering *Gabriel? Is that you?* Seeing her former husband's face: glinting eyeglasses, stubborn set of the jaw. *Gabriel? Please don't do this. I'm going to hang up now.* He wasn't to pick up the children until a week from Friday, he wouldn't violate that agreement—would he? A man of his professional stature and reputation would not risk any sort of embarrassing domestic scandal—would he? But that afternoon, a disturbing incident she'd since forgotten, odd she'd forgotten it for it had infuriated her at the time: she'd brought Mark to the Edgewater library for a children's reading hour, and afterward, crossing the street to her car, Mark's moist fingers securely in hers, she'd glanced up to see him—*him*: the walnut-dark man: and in that instant the realization came to her *Of course!—he's an emissary of Gabriel's.* A spy, a threat. A reminder. A warning. She wanted to shout *Leave us alone! You have no right, I'll call police! I know who you are.* But of course she said nothing, dared say nothing. Casting the gnomish creature a scathing look as he seemed almost to be preening himself, displaying himself, only a few yards from the rear of her car, one foot up on a sidewalk bench as he drank from a can—slowly, sensuously, even as his shiny eyes raked over her with a look of blatant sexual assessment. He wore teenage apparel as if in mockery of his age, which was not young, Judith's own age at least— bleached cutoff jeans ragged to his muscular thighs, one of those ugly mustard-yellow sweatshirts with WET- LANDS SUCK in black script. Judith flinched at his scrutiny, tugging at Mark, who stared at the man, unpredictable Mark lifting a hand to wave at him, at a malevolent stranger, in that way her younger child had of abrupt indiscriminate friendliness: *Hi!*

Judith plunged away with him, breathless into the car, fumbling to jam the key into the ignition, slapping at her protesting son, scolding *Bad! Bad! Haven't I told you never to—never to so much as look at strangers!*

The memory returns to her now, vivid and jarring. It isn't an exaggeration to worry that the walnut-dark man has driven the van out here to await her, knowing her itinerary—is it? *Don't think, don't think such things. He will have triumphed if you do.* She runs by, runs past. Bold, indifferent. Seeing how by moonlight the beach appears coarse and riddled as a lunar landscape, crevices and debris and sunken patches like quicksand and a lacy reeking mantel of long-tendriled glistening things that must be jellyfish, a terrible invasion of jellyfish along the Jersey coast, appalling, mysterious. Such mass deaths, desolation: the purposelessness of nature: a frenzy of reproduction, crazed life brought into being but fleetingly, much of it turned immediately back to pulp, protoplasm. *What is the point of it?* Judith had more than once inquired of her husband, bemused, yet disturbed, at similar anomalies in nature in the early days of her marriage to a man she'd believed to be a man of wisdom as well as merely of facts. And Gabriel had said, not unkindly, *Judith, questions about the "point" of things in nature suggest wishful thinking on the part of the questioner.* And Judith said, with a despairing little laugh, *But can't there be a point, a purpose, in nature, as well as just a "wish" in the questioner?* And Gabriel laughed, kissed her as he might have kissed a charmingly impertinent child.

Yes, those shapes are jellyfish, or their remains. Luminous by moonlight as if somehow still alive. And here and there amid tangled debris a glisten of dead fish, animal carcasses, bleached detached bones. Though Judith knows these things aren't human in any way human, merely creaturely remains cast up by the waves, she has to look quickly away. When first she'd brought her excited children to hike along the Edgewater shore the previous spring, at the time she'd signed the lease for the house, the state had just completed a massive cleanup after a devastating winter, and the shoreline had been beautiful in its modest way, hospitable for wading if not for swimming; by late summer, pollution and hurricane damage had altered it considerably. Erosion, inches each year, how many inches the entire Atlantic seacoast. Inexorable, inevitable. As life sucks at life, building up in one place even as another is depleted, exhausted. *I have plenty of time in which to win.*

The van's motor has started, the headlights have been switched on. Judith tries not to panic hearing the vehicle bounce over the dunes and down onto the road; headed in her direction; approaching her but not passing; keeping a distance of perhaps thirty feet; teasing? taunting? or out of courtesy not wanting to pass too close to her? She's running at the very edge of the road, refuses to run in the ditch. Refuses to break suddenly and run onto someone's property, into a marshy field, hide in underbrush like a hunted animal, try to escape her pursuer. Suddenly she's covered in sticky sweat, she can smell herself; her hair loose, slipped from the ponytail and whipping in the wind. *Why!* why had she come out to this lonely place, at such a time of night? Leaving her sleeping children behind, what could she have been thinking of? *Any punishment, you know you'll deserve.* The van's brash bright glaring headlights sweep onto her exposing her straining body as in an X-ray.

But Judith manages to run as before, or nearly. Trying not to limp so the driver of the van won't know there is anything wrong. As if she isn't frightened either. As if this—the loneliness, the late hour, the teasing pursuit—is nothing remarkable, nothing she can't handle. And finally at the intersection of the road with a narrower road leading inland the driver of the van speeds up to pass her and she swallows hard feeling a thrill of terror she'll be struck, killed instantly as the motor's roaring grows louder and louder and she can't stop herself stumbling into a ditch screaming as with a blare of its horn and derisive male laughter the van rushes past.

Leaving her sobbing in relief, cringing in pain at the side of the road, her ankle twisted.

Please don't make me hate you, hatred is exhausting.
A woman does not exult in hating: not like a man.
Wish only that he. Not death exactly, but.
Yes if he'd disappear! Simply—cease to exist.

Several times since moving to Edgewater she has had
the dream and it leaves her faint with shame, excitement.
In a foreign country, India perhaps, somewhere she has
never visited, he has died—attending one of his science
conferences, all expenses paid. But he has died, is dead. Is
vanished. It seems that the funeral (funeral pyre? crema-
tion?) has already been held, and the burial. No need for
her and the children to attend. The body has been cleanly
disposed of, the man himself erased. *Ashes, dust. Bones ris-*
ing from the earth as plumes of powdery smoke.
    Of course the children would grieve for their father, for
a while; and then forget. As children do. Healthy children.

Except. That incident of several weeks ago, alone and
possibly she'd been drinking (only wine, only a few
glasses) and she'd fallen asleep on the sofa anxious, headachy in sleep awaiting the children's safe return, Sunday
promptly by 8 P.M. he must return her children to the door
of the rented house like clockwork and he and she
exchange civil words like the civil, civilized adults they are
but afterward, at bedtime, she smelled—what?—ether?—
sweet sickish odor in their hair and on their clothes, no
mistaking it. Suddenly frantic questioning the little girl
Holly what did he do to you? Oh God, Holly—your father—
what did he do to you and Mark? tearing at their clothes to
examine them, their small quivering naked bodies, until
Holly began to cry pushing at her mother's hands and
Mark ran from her crying and she was left dull-eyed squatting on her heels her hair in her face realizing it must have
been a dream. Not the dream of his death but that other

so ugly she could only barely recall it by day. Confusing a dream with—whatever this is surrounding us.

Once upon a time, a very special time, there was a mommy and a little girl and a little boy who. Nothing not happy, a happy surprise. In the night in the insomniac night breathless and limping returning at last to the stone-and-stucco bungalow on a street whose name she has forgotten in a state of dread and guilt for it's very late—by her watch 2:20 A.M.— much later than she'd intended to stay out. And seeing with a shock of horror a light burning in a window at the rear of the house. One of the children's rooms: Mark's. She hurries panting to the window to peer inside, pushing away brambles, unable to see anything at first because the venetian blind is shut but she hears sounds, children's squeals, a man's deep teasing-cajoling voice, it's Gabriel? Gabriel with the children? taking advantage of her absence, her carelessness? Judith leans against the window managing to catch a glimpse through the blind's slats of pale naked squirming flesh, child-flesh, a man's straining back, video camera in his hands, she screams *No! Stop!* bringing her fist against the window pounding through the screen until the glass cracks, then she's at the back door *but the door is locked!* fumbling with her key the key in her fingers slippery with sweat but she manages to unlock the door, he'd forgotten to double-bolt it from inside, she's rushing through the darkened house as the floor tilts drunkenly beneath her as in an earthquake, she slams open the door to Mark's room crying *No! Stop! I'll kill you!* but to her amazement Mark is alone curled beneath the covers of his bed, only the Mother Goose lamp on the floor emits its gentle light and she switches on the overhead light furious and baffled seeing that the man is gone, the father has escaped, with a start the child wakes and opens his eyes blinking in a pretense of surprise and alarm as his mother shakes him *Where is he? what have you been doing together? I saw you! I saw you!* shaking the child's thin shoulders, hugging him tight against her, she's weeping angrily, sees his pajamas are back on, hurriedly Gabriel must have dressed their son and of course the child will protect the father as always, they are in league against her. She drags Mark into Holly's room again slams open the door, fumbles to switch on the overhead light seeing her daughter in a pretense of white-faced wide-eyed terror sitting up in bed, clutching the quilt to her chin *Mommy? Mommy what's wrong?* as Judith tears the quilt from her believing the little girl naked but in fact Holly, too, is wearing her pajamas, exactly as Judith had left her hours before, which upsets and infuriates Judith to know that the father and the children have plotted together so shrewdly! so capably! as if not for the first time. She has pushed Mark onto Holly's bed, she has seized both struggling children in her arms, she will protect them, she has driven their father away, always it will be within her power, the mother's power, to drive the father away weeping hot bitter tears *Thank God! Thank God! You're safe!*—knowing one day the hysterical children would realize what it was, their mother had saved them from.

The
Little Match Girl

STEVE RASNIC TEM

Steve Rasnic Tem lives in Colorado. His novel Excavations *was published in 1987, but he is better known for his fantasy and horror short stories and poetry. He won the British Fantasy Award in 1988 for his story "Leaks." He has recently edited an anthology of writing by Colorado writers, called* High Fantastic. *His poetry has been published in* Blood is Not Enough, Psychos, *and* The Year's Best Fantasy and Horror.

Tem's poem "The Little Match Girl" is based on the tragic Hans Christian Andersen story of the same title.

The Little Match Girl

"Fire—fill your eyes
with fire," the dead lady guides
and the granddaughter follows
with fingers seared
by Father's hard kiss.
"Fire!" the dying girl sings
to snowflakes bursting
with heart-felt flame. She's waltzing
through curtains of burning, each match
alive with good fathers, warm meals,
homes where she might sleep, and now
a mother unlike the cold one
whose sorrow melts with secrets
held so long her arms had
no more room for children. "Fire!"
she cries to rich houses blazing
from bitter firewood the poor
sold them for pennies and the girl
frozen in the pale light
promised by a dead match.

The Trial of
Hansel and Gretel

GARRY KILWORTH

Garry Kilworth lives in Essex, England. Since win-
*ning the Gollancz/*Sunday Times *short story com-*
petition in 1974 he has published sixteen novels, over
eighty short stories, six children's books, and some
poetry. His most recent novels are Archangel,
House of Tribes, *and* A Midsummer's Nightmare. *He and Robert Holdstock won the World*
Fantasy Award in 1992 for their novella, "The Rag-
thorn." Kilworth's most recent collection of stories is
In the Country of Tattooed Men.

Here Hansel and Gretel are realistically (perhaps
too much so for comfort) portrayed as German peas-
ant children who are either the perpetrators or victims
of sorcery and greed.

The Trial Of Hansel and Gretel

The oxcart rumbled over the cobbled streets of the town, heading toward the *Rathaus* on the east corner of the market square. In the back of the cart, dressed in prisoner's shifts, were two children. The large, dull-faced boy with the protruding bottom lip was aged thirteen. The lumpy girl with her squashed features was twelve.

Standing by these two was a bleary-eyed giant of a man in a stained and cracked leather jerkin. The man had bruises on his cheeks, and his nose was swollen. In his right hand he held a smooth truncheon with which he continually tapped his knees, as if itching for an excuse to use it. He was the town constable, and, having just dismissed his men, a band of drunkards and layabouts recruited at the inn the evening before, he was now delivering his prisoners to receive what passed for justice in the hands of the law.

"Don't worry, Gretel," said the boy, "I'm sure the *Bür-germeister* will believe us."

As he spoke, the boy stared stolidly not at his sister, but at the constable.

"I'm not worried, Hansel," said the girl, sniffing a runny nose. "Not if you're with me."

The constable looked up and sneered, his face moving in and out of the shadows of the houses that fell across the cart's path.

"You hear that, Dieter Schultz?" said the constable to the driver of the oxen. "They're innocent."

The driver, a small man with a squint, spat a stream of saliva down onto the slippery cobbles, covered in vegetable peelings.

"I heard. We believe them, don't we Johann Meyer."

Both men tittered coyly, as if they had participated in a joke of supreme excellence, which modesty forbade them to laugh at uproariously.

The cart pulled into the main square and halted, the driver allowing the oxen to drink from a water trough. The low sun was now creeping over the black spires of the *Rathaus*. Timber-framed houses, with wattle-and-daub walls, were struck by its rays. The *Rathaus* clock, a device made by a Swiss artisan, was winding itself up, ready to drop its clanging quarter tones upon the cobbles of the square.

In the north corner of the square was something horrible, which the children studiously avoided looking at.

The smell of animal droppings was everywhere. Horse and ox dung filled the cracks between the cobbles, formed the major part of wall daub, was splattered over windows and doors and up the stone legs of the statue of the king, which stood by the trough. It stained the town brown and attracted flies by the thousand.

In the summer heat the smell was so rank it turned the stomachs of strangers to mush.

"Did she sizzle?" asked the constable, quietly, as if wishing to be a confidant. "Did the old woman *crackle* when she went in the oven?"

"She screamed the place down," said Gretel. "Then she shriveled to crispy fat."

The constable's eyes opened wide, as if his fears had been confirmed.

"Lord save us," he murmured, turning away.

The driver fell asleep, stretched across the seat of his cart. The constable, too, dozed. The children, chained to the side of the cart, stared bleakly at the quiet town. The quartet remained thus for two hours, until finally people began to stir from their dwellings, throwing dirty water from upstairs windows, chucking swill into the streets, releasing their geese out of doors, sending fuzzy-headed children on errands.

When the *Rathaus* clock struck ten, a fussy-looking little man in blue leggings came out of the *Rathaus* carrying a small table, which he placed in the square. He went back inside and returned with a chair, then finally a quill, ink bottle, and a large book with a kid-leather cover and a brass clasp. He then sat at the desk and began to write the date on a blank page in the book with a neat, copperplate hand.

This was the *Bürgermeister's* clerk, ready to perform his duty as court recorder.

At ten minutes past ten o'clock, two servants staggered out of the same building, carrying a heavy, oaken throne. They placed this level with and at a short distance from the clerk's small table. Grubby peasants and grimy gentry began to gather now, in various modes of dress, forming a large circle around the triangle consisting of the cart, the small table, and the oaken seat. At last, on the first quarter stroke of the hour, the fat *Bürgermeister* himself, resplendent and sweating in his heavy scarlet robes, took his place upon the vacant throne. *Bürgermeister* was now *judge*, over life and death.

The constable suddenly became very erect, very alert, swatting the flies away from the sleep dust in the corners of his eyes, and clearing out the entrances to his nostrils with his fingers, prior to nodding respectfully to the judge.

The judge cleared his throat and began.

"These are the children, Hansel and Gretel, accused of murdering the blind old woman?"

"Yes, yer honor," replied the constable.

The judge glanced at the two young serfs, who seemed about as intelligent as a pair of retarded hogs. One of them was picking listlessly at a sore on her forearm. The other was staring vacantly into the middle distance, as if somewhere on the moon. They were dull, sluggish, and dense in appearance.

"Roasted her alive in an oven, so we understand?"

A shudder, like the ripple which goes through a deer herd when a wolf is scented, went through the crowd.

"Yes, yer honor. They don't deny that," said the constable, nervously licking his fingers. "They've admitted to doing that."

The judge leaned back in his throne and gave the constable a gesture of impatience. In these times, when children of nine were executed for stealing a loaf of bread, such pomp and circumstance was a waste of valuable time. The children had admitted guilt. What more was to be said? He wanted no elongated pleas for mercy, nor lengthy mitigating circumstances. He wanted the trial over and the sentence carried out quickly.

There were two reasons for his haste in this matter.

Firstly, he found local trials boring. He was a man who believed he had a quick, lively mind, and more often than not these affairs were dull beyond the extreme. He loved a good problem with which to wrestle, and most peasants involved in crimes had either killed their next-door neighbor, bedded his wife, or stolen his pig. These repeated scenarios presented no mysteries, only endlessly dull recriminations.

Secondly, and more importantly, if these children were found guilty and executed, the wealth they had taken from the old woman's cottage would become the property of the town, which in effect, meant it went into the pockets of the *Bürgermeister*, since he controlled the town's coffers.

"Constable, is there any reason why I shouldn't pronounce sentence immediately?"

"Please yer honor," grated the constable, "they said it was in self-defense. The girl . . ."

The judge sighed and shook his head slowly, while interrupting with, "Let the girl speak first."

"Your graciousness," began Gretel, "it was like this . . ." and the young girl told her story.

At first the judge only half listened. He had been up late the night before at a feast, quaffing beer by the jugful, and was in no mood for lugubrious and false protestations of innocence.

Nearby, the clerk scribbled away, trying to keep up with the girl's gabble, looking up once or twice as if to ascertain that he had correctly deduced a word or phrase, but never asking for confirmation. It was true that no one ever read the book, no one even looked in the book, except the clerk himself. He might have been writing in Arabic, or gibberish, for all anyone could care. Yet he did his duty with zeal, because it *was* his duty. One day someone might read these accounts, if only to extract tales such as the story being told now.

". . . then we woke up in the forest, covered in wet leaves, and didn't know the way home . . ."

However, as the girl's tale continued, both the judge and the clerk gradually began to take an interest. It was, after all, an extremely colorful story: worth retelling to visiting princes and prelates. They both knew that if she was a witch, the children were entitled to any money or valuables found since witches prey on travelers. But they were fascinated by the inventiveness of the tale.

". . . she had this big oven, like a small cave at the back of her kitchen," continued Gretel.

"Why so large an oven for so small a cottage?" asked the judge. "Was the woman a baker of bread in large quantities?"

"I never asked her," Gretel replied. "She didn't say. She only kept telling us we were too skinny and she liked fat children to eat. She was horrible and ugly—all warts and running sores, and a nose like a cobbler's awl."

"Unbecoming features do not make a witch," said the judge. "Otherwise, half the people in this square might be accused of participating in the black arts. What happened next?"

"She'd fired up the oven. I could feel the heat on my skin. When she opened the door, I gave her a push, and in she went! It was so hot inside, her body stuck to the wall of the oven. There was a kind of *hiss*, like all her breath had been sucked out of her body, then she let out a yell."

"What kind of a *yell*?"

Gretel suddenly opened her mouth and released a high-pitched, piercing scream that chilled the judge's blood. People in the crowd went white. Gretel's face seemed to twist into a demonic mask as she liberated the sound from her throat. It was a shriek which made eyes water with its shrillness. There was something of the actress in Gretel, who, unlike her brother, enjoyed the attention despite the circumstances.

"Thank you," said the judge, his eyes still closed when Gretel paused for breath. "That's enough."

"Then," said Gretel, turning to the crowd, "there was steam coming off her, and her skin blistered, the bubbles making popping noises when they burst. The stink was awful. After a few moments I slammed the door shut. She tried to curse me then, but there was a kind of *whumph* sound. I think she just went off bang."

By the end of the piece, the judge at least was puzzled and impressed. Surely two peasant children, offspring of an ignorant, unlettered woodcutter, could not have concocted such a strange and wonderful story between them?

"Where's your father now?" asked the judge. "Why isn't he here?"

"Father ran away," replied the boy named Hansel, slowly and carefully, "when he heard the constable's men coming to arrest us."

"Hmmm. And your stepmother? We haven't heard what happened to her."

"Father said she died," Gretel said, "before we got back from the witch's house."

"Convenient. And where is *her* body?"

"Father must have buried her somewhere in the forest—we don't know where," said Hansel.

"So, we can't inspect the corpse?"

"The what?" Hansel said.

"Never mind," sighed the judge. He began to pursue another line of inquiry. "Can either of you read or write? Is any member of your family able to do so?"

The children shook their heads, dumbly.

"There's only our father and us," said Gretel. "Our stepmother was a fish-gutter when Father met her."

"And your real mother?"

"Dead," replied Hansel. "Died having Gretel."

"No other brothers or sisters?"

"All dead," Gretel said, predictably. "Father said they died of want."

"Now, let me get this straight," he continued. "I can accept the trail of pebbles, the subsequent trail of crumbs—eaten by the birds—but then we come to a house made of sweetmeats."

"You could eat bits of it—it was made of icing and chocolate and toffee," said Hansel, swatting a fly away from his nose. "It was like a big cake with sweets on."

"And how do you account for this?"

Hansel shrugged. "The woman who lived there was a witch."

The clerk said, without looking up, "Your honor, it might be that some sugar was mixed with the mortar sand? There are sugar beet mills in the region . . ."

This made little sense to the judge, who could not imagine even a dolt like Hansel eating mortar.

"So, you ate pieces of this strange house?"

" 'Til the old witch came out and grabbed us," Gretel said.

"This frail, blind old lady managed to grip and hold two lusty young peasant children, one of whom is a sturdy youth who, on being told of his arrest, gave the constable a bloody nose and knocked that gentleman down twice before being subdued?"

The constable in question looked suitably aggrieved, staring into the crowd, obviously hoping for a show of sympathy. He was disappointed. He touched his bruises gingerly with his fingertips and sniffed loudly, before glaring at Hansel.

The two children looked at each other. The judge thought he recognized a kind of ratty sharpness in Gretel's eyes. For the first time he realized there might be more to the woodcutter's brood than first announced itself. It was Gretel who finally answered the question.

"She was quite strong, being a witch of course. She smelled me for a girl, then got me first, then Hansel had to come when she threatened to kill me. Her nails were like claws digging in my wrist, see . . ."

Gretel displayed some small, regular marks on her arm, which might have been caused by the smallpox, or a horseshoe with a protruding set of nails, or a hawk's talons—or anything.

"Let's get to the white bird," said the judge. "You say it led you to the cottage. What was this bird? A stork, an egret, a crane?"

"An enchanted bird," breathed Gretel.

"And it led you to the cottage."

"I think it was the witch's cat, changed into a bird," Gretel said, turning to the crowd. "It was leading us to her, you see, so she could cook and eat us."

Another shudder went through the rabble. This was a brilliant stroke on the girl's part. The peasants knew about witches' familiars. They hated and feared them. Pets and other animals were often strangled or shot out of hand in the belief they were familiars.

The judge continued. "So then your brother was locked in the stable?—Naturally this slight, blind old woman with a tiny cottage owned a horse . . ."

"It was an *old* stable," Hansel said quickly, his eyes narrowing with remembrance—or perhaps something else? "It wasn't hers I don't think. Probably belonged to someone else, but built near her house."

"Can we see this stable?" asked the judge, leaning forward in his throne.

"Burned down," Gretel said, regretfully, "when the oven caught fire."

"Quite," said the judge, leaning back again.

Then something occurred to the judge.

"You say you found precious stones and pearls, which

you considered yours by right since this, er, *witch* tried to kill you both. This treasure was *inside* the cottage. You were able to search the cottage while the fire raged and even reached the stable, some distance from the dwelling, without being so much as singed?"

A murmur went through the crowd, and there was much nodding of heads and exchanges of sage looks. This was all very entertaining. Worth the death of some old biddy living out in the back end of nowhere whom no one cared a button for in the first place. This was better than a puppet show.

Hansel stared directly at the judge in a very disconcerting manner.

"The blaze started when we'd left and walked away— we forgot to damp down the fire in the oven. It spread quickly . . ."

"Ever so quickly," interrupted Gretel.

". . . before we could get any water."

"But you managed to find the jewels before that happened?"

"There were chests full of them—we didn't have to look very hard," snapped Hansel.

The judge snarled, "Don't get sharp with me, young man, or I'll hang you for contempt if nothing else."

Hansel flinched and looked, for the first time, toward the north corner of the square. There stood the permanent gallows, with enough room to accommodate three tenants at any one dropping. Near to the gallows, hanging by a chain from a stone arch over one of the streets off the square, was the iron gibbet. The gibbet cage, only one as iron was more expensive than wood, still contained the rag-covered bones of a nine-year-old thief. The birds had not yet picked them clean of meat.

Gretel said, "He doesn't mean anything by it, your honor. He was beaten by the witch, after he tricked her with a knucklebone. He's angry at all grown-ups. That's why he hit the constable—not because of anything but being so angry—at grown-ups."

"Well, here's one adult who doesn't like being the target of a snotty youth's anger; understand, boy?"

"Yes, your honor," said Hansel, quietly, and with a studied lowering of his eyes.

"Good," said the judge, still feeling ruffled, but remaining keenly interested in the children's story.

There was no possibility of letting the children go—it was necessary that they hang, and, fortunately for the judge, the crowd expected it—but still the whole account, which might have been fabricated by a traveling storyteller, was so ingenious, it was worth plumbing to its very depths.

The clerk's quill scratched on, distracting the judge, who required a peaceful interlude in which to think. He held up his hand, and the clerk dutifully paused in his scrivenings, allowing the judge the quiet he needed. The crowd, used to the judge's idiosyncrasies, knew better than to breathe during such a time.

The judge considered the father of the children.

Clearly the father was a weak man, ruled by his second common-law wife, given to killing off his children when food in the hovel was in short supply. These two had implied as much. All very familiar, yet with an underlying intrigue the source of which still remained to be discovered.

The woodcutter's offspring themselves did not, by all accounts, command a great deal of learning. It was doubtful they received any kind of schooling from their fishwife stepmother, or their forest-worker father, or any neighbor. Yet, there was in their demeanor an intrinsic kind of cunning, the sort of craftiness and guile which might be found in certain peasants versed in the black arts.

"Now," said the judge, "we come to a part of your account on which you were a little vague."

The crowd leaned forward expectantly, some wearing the aprons of their trade—cobblers, butchers, carpenters, masons—others the hats by which they might be recognized—town crier, watchman, coachman—and still others by their general dress—landladies, goose girls, clog sellers. They all knew to what the judge was referring, and they were all eager to hear what kind of answer was to be had from either Hansel or Gretel.

"You say," said the judge, "that when you left the 'enchanted wood' you came to a great stretch of water, which you would not have been able to cross without the help of something—what was that *something*? Speak up now."

For the first time in the trial the children exchanged looks in which it appeared there was an element of panic. If left to his common sense, the judge might have decided there and then that the children had been rehearsed in their tale and that their memories were at fault: they had forgotten a vital piece of information at the end of the story. However, common sense had gone out of the window with the first telling of the narrative: the judge wanted to know the answer to his question.

"Well?" he boomed. "Answer, one of you. You, Gretel—you gave us the tale in the first place. What was it that took you over this lake or river—this 'wide stretch of water'?"

Gretel seemed to snatch something out of the air.

"A duck," she said, triumphantly.

The crowd gasped almost as a single body.

The clerk looked up from his book for the first time and frowned at the girl.

The judge leaned back on his throne and toyed with the edge of his scarlet robe.

"A duck?" he said.

"Yes," cried Gretel. "I—I used a rhyme to make it come to us."

"And this *duck* carried both of you—two great lumps of lard weighing I don't know how much—across the water on its back?"

Gretel shot another look at the frightened Hansel, then said, "Not—not both at once, your honor. One at a time."

"Oh," said the judge, his voice heavily laced with sarcasm, "only one at a time. Well, that makes all the difference doesn't it?" He leaned forward quickly. "What about the sacks of precious stones and pearls?"

"The—the duck carried those as well it was an enchanted duck."

"Another witch's familiar? But you'd killed the witch."

Gretel stammered, "I—I—I think . . ."

The judge interrupted sharply with, "I think that we can deduce from this statement that it is *you* who are the witch, not the little blind old lady? You're the one claiming to be able to command a duck and ride on its back over a lake. It might be a good idea to let the mob take you down to the pond now and put this theory of mine to the test . . ."

There was a spontaneous cheer from the crowd, and they moved toward the cart.

Gretel, faced with drowning, now screamed, "It wasn't me. I wasn't the witch. It was *her*—my stepmother. She changed herself into a duck, to get us across. She told us what to do. She told us what to say . . ."

At that moment someone with a loud, booming voice cried, "Wait!"

The judge stared out into the citizens of the town.

"Who said that?" he demanded. "Who interferes with the due process of the law?"

At that moment a huge, bearded man began to move forward. In his hands was an axe. The crowd parted, giving him space, those nearest keeping their eyes on the axe.

The bearded man spoke. "I don't mean to be disrespectful, your honor, but I'm the father of the two children. What my girl Gretel meant to say was 'a boat'—not a duck—a boat. She gets mixed up—it's since their terrible ordeal with the witch, you see. It makes her say things she don't mean."

All the while the father of the children was talking he was glancing nervously at the *Rathaus* clock.

The children, too, were staring at the face of the town's great timepiece.

The judge looked up at the time himself.

It was almost noon.

"A boat," said the judge. "Not a duck, but a boat?"

Gretel cried sharply, "Yes—I meant a *boat*."

"It—it was *shaped* like a duck," said the woodcutter. "That's probably why my little girl called it so."

"A boat shaped like a duck?" said the judge flatly, feeling the situation was now becoming ludicrous rather than entertaining. It was obvious to him now that the whole family was lying, fabricating this fascinating but clearly false story to cover up the murder of a rich and eccentric old woman. It was time to hang them all.

"I think we've heard enough . . ." he began, but was stopped by the clanging of the great clock. DONG, DONG, DONG, DONG . . . The chimes were too loud to pronounce sentence over, so the judge had to wait until the last note died away.

Just as that had occurred and the judge was about to open his mouth another person pushed her way through the crowd, having just alighted from a carriage that had entered the square while the clock had been chiming. The intruder was a thin, reedy-looking woman. She held a rolled parchment in her hand, which she held up for the judge to see. The royal seal, attached to the parchment, glittered in the noonday sun.

"Before you say any more, judge," said the woman, "I think you should offer congratulations to your new lord."

The judge was becoming irritated, but that parchment held his attention for the moment.

"My new . . . ?"

"My husband, the *former* woodcutter, has purchased the baronetcy of these lands, which includes this town. Purchased them from the king this very morning. I went there myself to collect the king's proclamation to this effect."

The woman handed the parchment to the town clerk, who broke the seal and read the document quickly. He then looked up at the judge and nodded. The judge stared at the woman. There was the feeling that he had been but a pawn in this fish-gutter's hands. It was well-known that he enjoyed a good puzzle, that he liked thinking through an enigma and finding the answer. It was one of the reasons he carried the office of judge, as well as *Bürgermeister*, because of his ability to see through tall tales and get at the truth. Given time, he could get to the bottom of any mystery. Given enough time.

"You are the fish-gutter?"

The woman lifted her head. "I worked in the fish market before I was married, yes—but my father was a peddler, but not in pots and pans—he sold riddles."

"Ah," nodded the judge, "that explains a lot. Riddles are very time-consuming puzzles, are they not?"

She said, "Once you hear one, it's difficult to let it go without solving it."

"Precisely. And you are not a *witch*, I take it? Your stepdaughter . . ."

"She gets confused, poor child, she's not very bright. No, the wife of a baronet, a witch? Why that would be coming to something, wouldn't it? Who would dare strip naked and search the body of the lady of the manor for marks? Who would bind and throw their lord's mistress into the pond? I wonder at such things, judge."

"I see what you mean."

She smiled thinly, and said to him, "The trial is over, I think?"

There was a clatter of hooves on the cobbles at the back of the square and the judge glanced in that direction to see a squadron of horse soldiers waiting by the carriage.

The judge cleared his throat.

"The trial—is over," he said. "The children are found—not guilty."

The crowd groaned in disappointment, but once they saw that no more excitement was to be had, they began to drift away.

The judge rose and took off his robes and became the *Bürgermeister* once more. The woodcutter lifted his children down from the cart, where the constable was engaged sheepishly, and wisely, in tying one of the straps of his own boots. The woman was looking triumphant, still staring at the *Bürgermeister*.

"So," said the man in question, ignoring the woman and speaking directly to the new baronet, "congratulations—my—er—lord. I take it the children were mistaken about your wife's death?"

"They must have misheard me."

"Yes, quite—and the money, for the baronetcy?"

"Came from a witch," said the wife, determined not to be ignored. "The witch who tried to kill our children."

The square was quiet now except for the sound of magpies rattling the gibbet.

"Ah," he said, "of course—*that* witch."

The expression on the *Bürgermeister's* face as he spoke registered his thoughts: he was not prepared to let a woodcutter and his slattern wife get away with a fortune which might be his. The baroness watched with narrowed eyes as he turned and began to cross the square, now empty except for her and her family.

By the time the *Bürgermeister* reached the water trough his appearance began to alter perceptibly.

His shoes became floppy on his feet, his hat was now too small for his head, and his clothes were tight in some places and hung loosely in others.

When he had passed the gibbet his ears had begun to grow coarse hair and developed points; something squirmed and pushed at the seat of his pants trying to get out; his skin had thickened and taken on a pinkish hue.

Not that he seemed aware of any of this, nor had he paused in his stride.

However, as he reached the steps of the *Rathaus*, he found them difficult to negotiate in an upright stance. He finally kicked the shoes off his hind trotters, went down onto all fours, gave a snort, and scampered up the stone stairs. During the climb he began to shed split clothing, until finally he was completely naked, his big belly hanging low, sweeping the flags, his snout twitching as he sniffed for the scent of food.

Rapunzel

ANNE BISHOP

Anne Bishop is a newcomer to the fantasy and horror fields, but already her stories have appeared in Ruby Slippers, Golden Tears, A Horror Story a Day: 365 Scary Stories, *and in small press magazines including* 2AM, Figment, *and* The Tome. *Bishop lives in western New York, where, in addition to writing, she is involved in a variety of arts and crafts, oral storytelling, and music, particularly Celtic folk music played on the hammered dulcimer.*

This tale, too, is a story of peasants and greed and sorcery. It is based on the classic tale of "Rapunzel."

Rapunzel

I've always craved what I couldn't have. At first, I craved
the blacksmith's son because, in our village, a good blacksmith was a respected man. Then I craved the miller's son
because he was handsome, and his father was prosperous.
Then I craved the merchant's son because he was educated, and his father was wealthy.

Instead I got Amery, because after the others had gotten
what they craved from me, they had continued to speak
flowery words of love but never spoke of marriage.

A simple, hardworking man, Amery knew—after the
wedding night, anyway—that he hadn't been my first
choice, but he did everything in his power to show me
how much he loved me.

When I craved the fancy lace and expensive silk some
of the ladies in the village wore, Amery worked extra
hours for weeks to buy them for me. He even paid the

village seamstress to make the dress so that I would have one fine garment to wear on special occasions, one fancy dress that wasn't put together with my indifferent stitches.

I wore it twice before I became ashamed of it.

When I craved a garden like the other women had, bright with flowers and bursting with fresh vegetables, Amery got up early for a full week and prepared the soil. When the ground remained empty, he paid good money for seedlings instead of buying seeds and planted the garden on his rest day while I was out visiting.

I was delighted to see my young garden appear like magic, but I lost interest in a week or two when the weeding and watering became a chore. After that, Amery cared for it whenever he had time.

There were so many things I craved, so many things that always seemed just out of reach, but what I craved most of all was a child. It shamed me to stand on the outside of the circle of women who would gather on market days and exchange stories and boasts and sorrows about their children. It shamed me that I had neither helpful hints to pass along nor reason to ask the older women's advice about childhood troubles. I was never in the center of that circle, being praised or soothed for no more reason than being a mother.

Amery failed me for years, but finally, miraculously, the day came when I knew I carried a child.

Overjoyed, Amery couldn't do enough for me. He worked harder than ever, more hours than ever to put aside a little money for whatever the child would need. On his rest days, he built a fine, sturdy cradle. He bought special brews and herb bags from the village granny to ease my sickness. If I felt too ill or weak to do my housework, he would do it when he got home. If I hadn't done any cooking or baking, he would heat the soup, set out the day-old bread, then encourage me to eat, waiting until I'd had my fill before easing his own hunger with whatever was left.

Best of all, I was now part of the inner circle when the women gathered on market day. I was the one being given soothing advice and gently ribald teasing. I was the one who received the sympathetic tongue-clucking when I hesitantly admitted to feeling so tired by the time I finished the housework.

For the first time in my life, I had everything I craved.

And then I went up into the cottage loft and saw Gothel's garden.

I don't remember why I was up in the loft. I never went up there because I didn't like the narrow stairs. Maybe I wanted to see if it would make a suitable room for the child. All I clearly remember is looking out the small window and realizing that, for the first time, I could see over the high stone wall that separated Gothel's land from our little piece of ground, could see the lush, vibrant garden that made every other garden in the village look pale and withered. Most of all, I could see the bed of fresh, green rapunzel lettuce.

I stood there in that hot, dusty little loft with my mouth watering because I could almost taste that lettuce and with tears streaming down my face because I knew I'd never get any. The village granny knew a bit about herbs and charms, but Gothel was a witch full and true, and that stone wall wasn't so high just to keep out the deer and rabbits.

Shaking, I managed to climb down the loft stairs. By then the craving was so intense it made me dizzy and weak, so I lay down on the bed. I was still there when Amery came home and found me.

It took him an hour of coaxing before, sighing and sniffling, I told him about the lettuce I so desperately craved.

His eyes blanked with shock. He rubbed my hands.

"But, Hedwig, dearest, that's Gothel's land. Besides, we have lettuce in our own garden. I'll pick some and then—"

"Not like that lettuce," I snapped, pulling my hands from his and hiding them under my apron. My lower lip quivered. "No one else has lettuce like that. *No one.*"

"Hedwig." His voice trembled with an unspoken plea.

Knowing better than to act sullen, I gave him a brave little smile and said, "You're right, Amery. Of course you're right. Lettuce is lettuce. Pick some from our garden, and I'll make a nice salad."

And I did, all the while apologizing for silly women's cravings.

Amery's relief faded during the meal as I nibbled the salad and kept saying how good it was so he'd know how hard I was trying to pretend these scrawny, wilted leaves tasted the same as the fresh, green ones I'd seen over the garden wall.

For a few days, I made sure there was a hot meal waiting for Amery when he got home, a hot meal I'd only pick at despite his coaxing. A couple of days after that, he came home one evening and handed me a square of cloth filled with large, fresh, beautiful green leaves.

"Amery," I said breathlessly, hugging the bundle. I knew exactly how they would taste, exactly how it would feel to chew and swallow those fresh, green leaves. "Amery, did you really . . . ?"

He wouldn't look at me. And I knew. Just as I knew I wouldn't be able to taste anything with so much bitterness filling my mouth.

"Mistress Olinda has the finest garden in the village," Amery mumbled. "I thought—"

"Not the finest." I opened my arms and let the bundle fall to the unswept kitchen floor. "Not *the* finest." I went behind the blanket that separated our bed from the rest of the room and lay down.

Amery apologized, coaxed, and pleaded for an hour, sounding as if his heart would break. Weary of him, I got up, fixed the salad, and tried to eat it to prove to him that I wasn't being stubborn.

As the days passed, I did less and less. Every morning I climbed the narrow stairs up to the loft and stared out the window at that bed of fresh, green rapunzel lettuce that I would never taste. When the dust and heat became too much, I'd go back to the kitchen and sit there, doing nothing, feeling nothing. I couldn't even rouse myself to meet the other women on market day.

Finally, one evening when Amery came home, I held out my hand to him and said quietly, "Amery, I'm not trying to be stubborn. Truly I'm not. But I want you to know . . . Amery, I will die if I don't taste the lettuce growing in Gothel's garden."

I saw the anguish in his eyes, and the fear. He stood still and silent for a moment before he sighed and left the cottage. A while later, he rushed back inside, breathing hard. He fumbled inside his shirt and pulled out a thick handful of green leaves.

Tears filled my eyes as I hugged him. I wasn't sure if I was laughing or crying the whole time I carefully washed each of those leaves. I quickly made a salad and ate every bit of it, sighing contentedly between each mouthful.

By the next day, however, the craving was three times worse because now I knew, *really* knew, how good that lettuce tasted. When Amery came home that evening and listened to my stumbling, tearful words, he just nodded and went out again.

He was gone much longer the second time. When he came back, he was shaking terribly and his skin was sickly gray.

"She caught me," he gasped, collapsing against the

kitchen table. "Gothel caught me as I was leaving."

I pressed my hand against my mouth, feeling sick with relief when I saw that he still had both of his big, callused hands. Weaving slightly, I fetched the bottle of spirits we kept for special occasions and poured a calming glass for both of us.

Minutes passed. Amery sipped his drink and stared at the kitchen table. I could see a little bit of green poking through his shirt ties. Finally my patience snapped. I wanted to know what happened. I wanted him to hand over the rapunzel so that I could make my salad. "So Gothel caught you. What did she say? What did *you* say?"

"What could I say, Hedwig?" Amery asked, sounding beaten. "Thief she called me and thief I am. I tried to explain about your need. I offered to do work for her to pay for what I'd taken. I even offered her the bit of money we'd saved up."

I choked back my resentment. I'd counted on that money to buy some things for the child so that when the other women offered clothes their children had outgrown they would understand I was accepting out of neighborly practicality rather than needing their charity.

"She took all of it?" I finally asked. "*All* of it?"

"No." Amery's voice shook. "She wouldn't accept money in exchange for what was taken." He tugged the leaves out of his shirt and laid them on the table between us. He tried to smile. "She said that, being a woman, she understood about these little cravings, and that you could have as much rapunzel as you desired."

"Well, then." Annoyed that he had frightened me by making such a fuss but willing to overlook it, I reached for the fresh, green leaves.

As Amery watched me gather the leaves, a terrible *something* filled his eyes. I thought about what he'd said. My hands wouldn't move.

"If she didn't accept the money . . ." Amery said nothing, forcing me to ask outright. "What does she want in exchange?"

Amery refilled his glass and took a big swallow before answering. "She wants the child."

"NO!" I flung the leaves at him and wrapped my arms over my belly. "I don't want it. Give it back to her. What were you thinking of to make such a bargain?"

"I had no say in this bargain, Hedwig. I had no say." He flicked a finger at the leaves scattered on the table. "And it makes no difference if I give these back. These, and all the other helpings to come, are a gift. The child is payment for what was already taken." He pushed away from the table but stayed long enough to rest a hand on my shoulder, as if that would comfort me. "I'm going to sit outside for a bit. Fix your salad, Hedwig. You don't want the cravings to make you ill again."

I couldn't stomach those fresh, green leaves, not that night or any night after. I never asked for rapunzel again, hoping Gothel might forget the bargain in the months remaining before the child was born. I never asked, but every morning there was a handful of fresh, green leaves tied with a bloodred ribbon waiting for me on the front step.

It rained the night I sweated and wept and screamed my daughter into the world. I remember because the sound soothed me and helped me rest whenever I could. I remember because the morning stayed dark long after the sun should have risen. I remember because I haven't seen a bright morning since then.

Amery stood beside the bed, crying silently, smiling bravely. When it was over, the midwife let him hold the babe while she fussed and soothed and tended me. Too soon, I was back in the freshened bed, washed and wearing a clean nightgown, and the midwife was gone.

I held out my arms. "Give her to me."

Just as Amery laid the babe in my arms, another voice said, "Give her to me."

Gothel stood beside the bed. Tall, thin Gothel with her witch-wild black hair and eyes so light they looked more silver than gray.

"Give her to me," Gothel said again, reaching for the child.

I couldn't speak. I couldn't move. I couldn't look away from those silver eyes.

And then she was gone, and my arms were empty.

Amery patted my shoulder. "Rest, Hedwig," he said in a broken voice, before he turned away from the bed. "Rest."

Alone, I lay listening to the sounds that came from behind the blanket that separated our bed from the rest of the room. I heard the scrape of a kitchen chair being pulled away from the table. I heard his heart-tearing, muffled sobs.

I listened and grew angry. What was I supposed to tell the other women when they came to see the babe? The midwife knew the child had been alive and well when she'd left. How could I say it died and not have a body to show? Even if I managed to keep them all away, how would I explain never bringing the child when I went out on market day? How would I explain that Gothel, the witch, had my child?

How would I explain?

Anger pushed me out of bed. I shuffled to the blanket, pulled it aside, and stared at Amery, his head pillowed on his arms as he sobbed.

"This is your fault." I leaned against the wall to steady myself.

Amery wiped his face with his sleeve and looked at me. "What was I to do, Hedwig? What was I to do?" He raised his big, callused hands. "If I'd lost my hands for thieving, how would we have lived? How would we have provided for the child?"

"Then you shouldn't have done it!"

"But you would have died."

He looked so bewildered I couldn't stand it. "Don't be such a fool," I said with all the contempt I felt for him at that moment. "Who ever heard of a woman dying from a little craving?"

He stared at me. Stared and stared. Then his face changed. It took a long time for me to realize that what I had seen was his love for me trickling away when he finally understood.

Saying nothing, Amery went to the chest at the foot of our bed and pulled out the cloth traveling bag he used whenever he had to work away from the village for a few days. He packed his other change of clothes, packed his shaving mug and razor, packed everything he could call his own.

It all fit in that one bag.

Still saying nothing, he brushed past me and picked up the wooden box that held the tools that had been handed down to him from his father and his grandfather.

Then he walked out the door.

The last thing I said to him, the last thing I screamed at him as he walked down the road and out of my life was, "You sold my daughter for *lettuce!*"

Men are thieves.

You put your heart and magic into something to make it beautiful, you build walls to keep it untainted by the world, you nurture it for the pleasure it will bring you, and they'll sniff it out, no matter how high the walls, and taint the pleasure, sully the beauty.

Like that thief spoiled my lovely garden.

Like that prince spoiled my Rapunzel.

I thought I'd kept her well hidden in the high tower in the heart of a forest. Not so. The princeling sniffed her out even there.

I remember the day her betrayal of my affection could no longer be hidden. I remember how she held her head up even though she trembled with fear. I'd given her everything she needed: good food and fine clothes, needlework and music to keep her occupied, my company when I visited the tower. And do you know what that ungrateful girl said when I discovered her deceit? "He loves me."

"Loves you?" I screamed. I grabbed her golden braid and began pulling it toward me, hand over hand. "Of course he loves you. Why wouldn't he love a beautiful girl so innocent and untouched by the world? But what kind of love does he feel for you, my sweet Rapunzel? Hmm? What kind of love? I'll tell you what kind. Passion's love. The body's love. The kind that fades with the dawn and returns with the twilight. You think not? Then why didn't he take you away?"

Her lips quivered, but she didn't cry. "He *is* going to take me away. I'm weaving a ladder from the skeins of silk he brings each evening. When it's finished, we'll go far away from here."

I laughed and drew more of the braid through my hands. "Skeins of silk? Weave a ladder? You're such a fool, Rapunzel. If he truly wanted to love you anywhere but the bed, why didn't he bring a rope? Better yet, why didn't he free you from *this* golden rope?"

She hesitated, didn't answer. I could see in her eyes that

she'd wondered the same thing, but, having no knowledge of the world and its thieves, she didn't understand.

"I'll tell you." Nothing but a few feet of taut braid between us. "Because this is a fine leash, sweet Rapunzel. A fine, golden leash. No other woman could cover his bed with such a curtain of gold. Out there, in the world, a woman would be chained by hair like this. But he didn't mention that, did he? Of course not. Do you want to know what would have really happened? Your prince would have continued to come each evening, bringing you silk so that you would spend your time weaving a useless ladder It's a high tower. How many rungs of this ladder do you get from a skein of silk? Long before the ladder was finished, you would become too big, too awkward for your prince to enjoy. The night would come when he'd have to sit and talk with you instead of showing you how much he *loves* you. He'd kiss you before he left, but he wouldn't come the next night. Or the night after that. He wouldn't return, Rapunzel, because you would no longer be the girl he craved, and you never would be again. But he would remember and love you forever—whenever he thought of you at all."

I jerked the braid. When she stumbled against me, I grabbed the hair at the back of her neck. "And I'm to care for his spoiled leavings while he goes away with sweet memories? I think not, Rapunzel. I think not."

I slapped her. Slapped her and slapped her. When she fell and tried to protect her face and belly, I pounded her with my fists. Pounded and pounded as if that would change anything.

It didn't. Nothing would change her back into what she'd been.

When I left the village all those years ago, I blighted the garden so that no one else would enjoy its bounty. Between one breath and the next, the flowers withered and the vegetables began to rot.

Nothing so quick for my sweet Rapunzel.

I dragged her across the floor until I reached her needlework basket. Then I snatched up the shears and cut off her braid.

She trembled when I put my arms around her.

She shuddered when I smiled at her.

Swifter than a fleeing shadow, I took her away from the tower and brought her to a desolate place. Oh, she could survive there, if she knew how to work, how to scratch a living from harsh land.

I took a sharp stone and drew a circle around her, a circle as large as the tower.

"Here's your new home, sweet Rapunzel," I spat at her. "Here's the bounty your deceit deserves."

She looked around, her eyes dulled by pain as she struggled to understand. Finally she looked at me and made an effort to stand straight and tall.

I wouldn't tolerate her pride, so I told her about her parents, about how she'd come to be in my possession. I told her *everything*. When I was done, she had no pride. She slumped to the ground, as beaten in spirit as she was in body. What was left of her hair hung limply around a face already swollen and discolored by bruises. Sitting there, she no longer looked like my Rapunzel.

And I was glad.

I returned to the tower before nightfall and prepared my magic. I didn't have to wait long before I heard him call out, "Rapunzel, Rapunzel, let down your hair." I secured the braid to the window and let it tumble down to meet him.

Such a fine, handsome boy, so eager for his love.

He wasn't eager to finish the climb when I leaned out the window, the shears in my hand, and smiled at him.

"A pleasant evening for love, wouldn't you say, princeling? But sweet Rapunzel has gone away. Far, far away. So far away, *your* desire will never find her. Nothing to say, princeling? Nothing to say? I thought not."

I swiped at him with the shears. He wasn't in reach, but he jumped back just the same, losing his grip on the golden braid.

As he fell, the thorns of my anger sprouted and grew. Grew and grew as he fell, screaming. They pierced his eyes, his ears, his heart. Then they melted away.

Shaken and bruised but otherwise unharmed, he looked up at me.

"Justice tempered with mercy, princeling. Another thief had asked that of me, many years ago. This is my justice. Your heart will never forget her. Whenever you look upon another woman, you will also see the innocent beauty no woman touched by the world can match. Whenever a woman speaks to you, you will also hear the voice no other can match in sweetness. She'll be with you always and never with you, and she'll become more lovely with each passing year because you will grow older but she will always be sweet Rapunzel."

I watched him stumble away, already grieving even though it would take some time for him to realize he'd just begun to grieve.

I pulled up the braid and coiled it in the center of the bed.

My sweet, deceitful Rapunzel. She'll spend the rest of her miserable life locked in a tower she'll never escape. When it comes to building walls, words can be stronger than stones.

Because the last thing I said to her, the last thing I

screamed at her before I left her in that desolate place was, "I bought you for a handful of *lettuce!*"

A stone wall surrounds my garden, high enough to keep the village dogs and other small animals out and low enough that neighbors can rest their arms on the top stones while they tell me the day's news. Everyone says I have the finest garden in the village. Ethelde says it's because there's magic in me, that the Lady of the Land, She of many names, claims me as a daughter, and any land I work with my own hands becomes fertile ground.

Who am I to argue with the wisewoman, the witch, my mentor?

I sometimes wonder if Gothel thought she was working magic when she left me in that desolate place. Did she think a circle scratched into the ground would hold me in the same way as a tower of stone? Or had affection warred with pride at the very end and was that circle the only way she knew how to set me free without admitting it?

For a long time I neither knew nor cared, but now that strands of silver weave themselves through my golden hair and my eldest daughter swiftly approaches the time when the women in the village will celebrate her first rite of passage between girl and woman, I find myself thinking about all of them: the parents I never knew, Gothel, my handsome young prince.

I don't remember much about the journey from that desolate place to this village. I remember I stayed within that circle the first night, too numb, too frightened to move. And then the sun rose, and some promise carried on the wind sang within me. With my feet planted firmly in the earth, I raised my arms to the sun and wind in an ancient, instinctive greeting.

I stood there for a long time. Then I said to She of many

names, "No more towers," and stepped out of the circle. After that, grief and fear clouded my mind and shadowed my thoughts so fiercely the world slipped away from me. Or I slipped away from it.

But I kept following the promise carried on the wind. Eventually it brought me to Ethelde.

For the first few days, I ate the broths and bread she set before me. I slept through the nights and most of the daylight hours as well. I walked in her garden, blind to the glory all around me. I saw the plants as strangers I didn't care to know, so I didn't ask their names, and Ethelde didn't offer to tell me.

But as the weeks passed and my belly swelled, as I watched Ethelde's garden grow and bloom, as my body learned what my mind was not yet ready to embrace, I began to change. I began following Ethelde around the cottage and garden as she went about her work. She welcomed my company but never explained her tasks. She sang while she worked, and the songs always fit the rhythm of the task.

After a while, I began to sing with her.

She just smiled at me and said nothing.

After a while, since my fingers had come to know the feel of every plant in the garden, I no longer saw them as strangers but as friends. So I asked their names. And she told me.

Gothel's words had been a vicious flood that had cut deep into the soul's landscape, leaving destruction in its wake. Ethelde's words were soft rain, quietly sinking in and nourishing parched land.

It wasn't until the day I went into the village with her and listened to the respectful way the men spoke to her and saw the way the women deferred to her that I fully understood that Ethelde was a witch as powerful as Gothel and that the choice I had made when I stepped out of the circle was to become one. I hadn't realized because Ethelde is everything Gothel was, and everything Gothel wasn't.

After the twins were born, the young men in the village began to come courting. The blacksmith's son, the miller's son, and the merchant's son brought little gifts when they invited me out for a walk. They came with charming manners and flowery words of love. But they always wanted to end the walks in one of the quiet hollows where the village girls offered their bodies for love and the young men took their bodies for pleasure. And after the flowery words, there was always the question, "Will you, Rapunzel? Will you?"

Since my answer never changed, they eventually stopped calling.

All except Imre, a simple, hardworking man who had no flowery words, who never invited me for a walk without inviting Ethelde to go with us, who never brought gilt trinkets, and who never failed to do some small chore around the cottage whenever he called. Imre, who, when he finally took me for a private walk and asked, "Will you, Rapunzel?" didn't bring me to one of the hollows but to a fine cottage he'd built with his own hands. It had a separate room for him and his wife and a divided loft that would easily hold two children or more. It had a workroom with its own small hearth. It had a small, private bathing area. It looked out on a large plot of empty, carefully turned land enclosed by a stone wall.

Imre said nothing while I explored each room. He said nothing when I stood in the workroom doorway that opened onto the garden.

Finally he said in his quiet, deep voice, "Will you, Rapunzel?"

Imre had no flowery words, but I felt his love in every stone.

So I said yes.

In all the years since, I've never regretted my answer.

That first spring, Ethelde helped me plant my garden. "Don't try to fill all the land all at once," she told me as we planted the herb, vegetable, and flower beds. "I'll harvest more than I can use and you're welcome to it. Leave yourself room to grow."

That first summer, Imre teased me when he saw the vegetable bed. "You've planted enough of your namesake to feed the village." When he saw the look in Ethelde's eyes and the way she nodded her head in understanding, he didn't tease me about it again. By the end of that summer, he, too, understood the truth of his words.

At first the men came to me directly, but as the years have passed and they've come to realize that, when Ethelde finally returns to the land, I will stand in her place, they've become a little shy with me. The women will come to me and ask, but if the men have to come, they'll wait until evening when Imre is home. They'll come up to him while he's leaning against the stone wall, smoking his pipe, and murmur their request. He'll bring me the net bag they gave him and say with a solemn voice and twinkling eyes, "Master so-and-so's wife has a bit of a craving." I'll fill the bag with fresh, green leaves from my rapunzel, and together we'll return to the stone wall and our anxious neighbor.

"A gift," I tell them every time because, sometimes, they aren't sure if they should offer something.

They would never understand what I get in return.

In the summer, after the children are asleep, Imre and I sit outside on the bench he built for me. I sit with my feet on the end of the bench and my knees up. He straddles the bench and sits behind me, his strong arms holding me close. Most of the time we talk about small things when we choose to talk at all. But sometimes Imre will press his face against my neck and say, "Are you content, Rapunzel?"

I always tell him, "I'm content. More than content."

Which is true.

He always goes in first to give me some quiet time alone to listen to the wind's music, to listen to the earth's wisdom. Some nights, when I finally come to bed, he just holds me, his big, callused hands stroking the silvered gold hair that I never allow to grow past my breasts. On other nights, we give each other another kind of pleasure.

I think about them sometimes, when I'm sitting alone: the parents I never knew, Gothel, my handsome young prince. I think about the twins who look like him and the son and daughter Imre and I made together. I think about Imre and the difference between the fire of a boy's passion and the strength of a man's love.

I chose well, and my life is rich because of it.

I think about them, and I'll tell you this. My daughters will never crave what belongs to another because they'll know they can have what they want most if they give it their hearts and their hands. And my sons will never be so blinded by passion that they cannot see the other textures of love because they'll know that love, too, has its seasons. They'll know these things because Imre and I will show them.

Sometimes my neighbors talk about misery or desolation, but they don't understand what they're really talking about. No one, not even Ethelde, understands misery and desolation as well as I.

Misery is a heart that can never be content with what it has and, by always craving something more, brings about its own destruction. And desolation is a heart so fearful of losing what it hoards that it never knows the richness that comes from being able to give.

In her anger, Gothel wished me a miserable, desolate life.

But having learned the lessons well, mine is the stronger magic.

Sparks

GREGORY FROST

Gregory Frost lives in the suburbs of Philadelphia and is the author of four novels. His first three— Lyrec, Tain, *and* Remscela—*are fantasies; the fourth,* A Pure Cold Light, *is a work of science fiction set in a dystopic alternate Philadelphia. His short stories have appeared in most of the major genre magazines and in various anthologies including* Intersections: The Sycamore Hill Workshop Anthology *and* Snow White, Blood Red. *He reviews for* The Washington Post *and* The Philadephia Inquirer *and has taught story writing at Temple University and the University of Pennsylvania. He is currently researching a nonfiction book about spiritualism, and a science program for the Learning Channel.*

Although it's got the usual cast of characters (an ugly witch, a brave soldier, a beautiful princess, and those wonderful huge-eyed dogs), Frost transforms "The Tinder Box" by Hans Christian Andersen into a contemporary treat.

Sparks

You never know what's going to sweep you up. You make plans, choose the direction, cover what you think is every detail. There will still be a million things you didn't predict. See, everything turns on what you *can't* prepare for. It can be as big as a war. As tiny as a flame.

Paney and I opened an office together after the big one, WWII. We didn't see much action together. Still, I think if we hadn't served two years side by side on the *Endymion*—hadn't been cooped up watertight inside and out—we wouldn't have been able to stand each other. War made us buddies. Nothing else. I couldn't even tell you whose idea the partnership was in the first place. We probably weren't sober at the time.

The routine we settled into kept each of us out of the other's hair. I did some security work—bodyguarding starlets who didn't need one. Chased down a missing wife, an errant son. Things like that. Eventually I started seeing a cigarette girl named Sally from the Belvedere Beach Club. Funny thing about her was she didn't smoke.

A few years later I went off to Korea with the Seventh Fleet, and Paney stayed homeside. They call that one the forgotten war, and I guess I'm proof of it: When I came back, Paney'd planted a new partner in my place and even managed to get Sally to say yes to him. I don't want to say he conned her. Maybe I didn't write enough letters.

Thirty years old, I came back to . . . well, I still had the license, and there was enough government pay to open a little hole-in-the-wall off Ladera Ave. I hoped to make enough to get along.

They invited me over to the house, you know, for old times' sake—"No hard feelings and come look at the kids" kinda thing. I always had something else to do.

Not work, though. I wasn't getting scratch. It was as if every boy who'd jumped ship after Korea set up an office while I was changing clothes. Even the negro kid, Elroy, who shined shoes in the lobby, was probably better set up than I was. He sure kept more of my money than I did. I started thinking pretty seriously about heading out to the East Coast. Maybe they needed shamuses out there.

The old woman showed up one afternoon while I was on the phone to Mapes at the bank about letting me slide a little on the loan for the Packard.

She was a knobby creature, I guessed Italian or Greek. Nose like a hawk and eyes as hard as pinballs; dressed in early Puritan. She carried a black leather handbag on her arm not much bigger than a steamer trunk. I gave her a smiling apology while Mapes droned on about finance charges. Finally he drew a breath, and I jumped in fast: "Gotta go, bud—duty calls." Even as I hooked the receiver, I could hear him shouting.

The old lady had time to scan the office while I was

stuck; she stared at the wall plaque with my medals like butterflies pinned under glass. I cleared my throat and waited. She finally tore herself away from the medals and hauled the only other chair, as big as she was, across the floor to the opposite side of the desk and sat down to point those pinballs at me. Could have been the Evil Eye for all I knew. I wondered if I would break out in a rash or maybe keel over the next time I crossed Pico and Sepulveda.

"What can I do for you, ma'am?" I asked.

"You work for hire." Her accent was thick enough I found myself leaning forward to get everything, and thinking of Peter Lorre in drag. But the accent was decidedly Spanish. I'd only been off by the width of the Atlantic Ocean.

"Yeah, I'm for hire. As long as I don't have to dig with a shovel or read consecutive Burma Shave signs all the way to Baker, I'm for hire."

"I hire you."

"All right, fine. What do you want me to do?"

"I lose something. I want you to find it. I pay you lots of money. Some now." And with that she hauled an envelope out of her bag, licked her thumb, and started flipping through a crisp salad of fifties. I got five of them. "Much more later. You'll get rich from this, young man."

"Really?" I slid the money under my palm and looked it over. It seemed the genuine article. "Rich from finding what?"

She gave me a big grin. Her teeth would have pleased a horse trader. "My lighter," she said.

I considered offering her a book of matches, but changed my mind because I liked the five fifties too much to be that stupid. I stuck the cash in the bottom drawer and stood up. "Okay. Let's go."

We walked to the door. I scooped up my hat on the way.

She pointed at the medals. "You a soldier, right? Deco-rated."

"Sure." I didn't mention that I'd probably been within a week of pawning them before she walked in the door. I thought about my pistol in its holster in the desk drawer, told myself I had to be kidding, and locked the door be-hind me. Unless she'd lost her lighter in the La Brea Tar Pits, I figured this was going to be the fastest money I'd ever made.

I had no idea.

The house was way up in the hills, far enough from the city to consider itself countryside. A thick grove of trees surrounded the place, mostly mountain pine and laurel. From the road you'd never have known it was there. You couldn't see it 'til you were halfway up the drive.

It was a gingerbread kind of place—a cabin-style design with lots of screened-in porch and those little semicircles in a horizontal line below the eaves, between some of the slats on the side, a Norwegian timberman's notion of dec-orative trim maybe.

There was a car parked beside the house. We got out of mine, and she led me across the lawn, which was patchy from the dense shade, and into the trees. I kept an eye out for somebody else: Cars generally don't drive themselves.

We threaded through the trees for what seemed like an hour. I didn't think there was this much gently rising ground between her place and the steeper slope, but I hadn't been paying much attention. Soon, I noticed that our feet crushing needles and leaves was the only sound. I'd heard the *kik-kik* of a woodpecker at first, but that had dried up. So had all the other bird cries. It was like we were walking in between the seconds.

Our destination was a strange, shadowy little clearing that would have been perfect for Druids on the solstice. In the center of it stood a single, blasted great black oak. Lightning had split the trunk almost to the ground. It must have continued to thrive awhile after, the result being a queasy, unnatural kind of flow, as though the tree had vulcanized as it laid its dead, snaking branches down.

She stepped over them and came to a stop beside the wide trunk. From the huge black bag she hauled out a large spooled rope. It must have taken up the whole bag. "Here," she proclaimed. "I lost it here."

I looked around on the ground. "What are we talking about? What kind of lighter?"

She made a buzzing noise like a sewing machine motor as she thought about it.

"Zippo," she replied finally.

"No kidding?" I could just imagine this old dame flicking back the top of a Zippo and lighting up a panatella. Sure. "Where, exactly, do you think it went?"

She pointed. "Down this tree."

I'd already figured out what came next. "You want me to climb in there."

"*Sí.*" She held up the rope. "You must tie this around your waist. I'll lower you in."

This tree was split to about four feet above the ground. If I jumped, I wouldn't disappear above the armpits, but she wanted to put a line on me. "Lady, you are too much." I looked closely at the dead tree, the splintered wood sharp as knives. The bole did appear to be hollow. "Why am I going to jump into the middle of a tree?"

"For ten thousand dollars." She said it as calmly as that, and the moment I heard it I wished I'd packed the gun. Whatever was lost in this tree, it wasn't a Zippo, not unless I'd come up here with Norma Desmond. Still, maybe that was exactly who I had here, and it was her money. I had too many debts not to be persuaded by the figure.

"You got a flashlight?"

She hauled a big one out of her handbag. The cash, the rope, the light—this was starting to look like a magic trick. I figured I could have asked for Krazy Kat and she would have dragged him out, brick-beaned and all.

I took off my coat and hung it on one of the dead branches. Adjusted my suspenders, rolled up my sleeves. Then I accepted the end of the rope and tied it into place. I put one foot in the notch of the tree and pulled myself up, looking down into the bole. It was plenty wide for a person. In that ungainly position I couldn't use the light, and I didn't see the ground. I glanced back at her. "Ten thousand dollars?"

"And fourteen cents," she added.

"Well, hell, in that case . . . Geronimo." I stepped into the tree.

Your body gets crazy when you're all set to land and your feet don't make contact with anything. It's instant panic. You scrabble for anything to break your fall. I was inside a shaft the size of a coal chute and smooth as the neck of a whiskey bottle. My palms squealed against it.

Then the rope snapped tight.

The air whipped out of me. I almost lost the light. I was hanging folded up around the lasso, staring into the darkness beneath me, listening to the creaking hemp. Nutsy ideas rattled around my head like BBs: This was a leftover bunker from WWII, when we thought the Japs were going to invade Hollywood. A mine shaft from the gold rush. A shortcut to Mongolia.

The old woman's voice called down, calm as a drill sergeant. "Turn on you light, soldier."

I responded to the order. It shone down the rest of the shaft to a dark surface not far below. The rope began to lower then. I thought of that frail little grandmother playing out the line with my weight on the end of it. How could she do that? There *had* to be someone else up there with her.

I touched down in the black dirt and shined the light all around. Now I knew I'd fallen asleep at my desk listening to Mapes, and this was just part of my dream.

Ahead of me were three big doors made of vertical slats of oak, each one set in the side of a solid rock wall.

I took a few steps 'til the rope stopped me. I untied it and let it drop. If the woman was worried about losing me, she never made a sound.

I went to the first door. There was a black iron key in the lock, its bow large enough that I could put all four fingers through it. I was annoyed that if this *was* my dream, I hadn't allowed myself to pack a pistol. I had nothing but the flashlight for a weapon. Cautiously, I turned the key. It flipped a tumbler, making a soft click. I opened the door, stepping back with it in case someone came charging out.

No one did. I leaned around the edge and shined the light inside. It was a room not much bigger than a flophouse bathroom. There were only two things in it: an old wooden chest like an ammunition box and, sitting on top of that, the biggest damn dog I'd ever seen. He was maybe the size of a pony. The light seemed to transfix him. "Hey, boy, nice fella," I said. The dog didn't move. I took a step inside. The dog didn't growl. I sidled close enough to touch him. His eyes bulged, big as tangerines that had been painted blue with tiny pupils. He didn't seem to see anything. I waved my hand around just outside the edge of the flashlight beam. He didn't react.

"Okay," I thought, and put a hand on the animal, ready to leap if anything happened. Nothing did. I was working with a fur-covered statue. I shoved the dog off the box. He settled onto the dirt as if he didn't weigh a thing.

The box wasn't locked. I lifted the lid on the biggest pile

of pennies I'd ever seen. They were polished and fresh like they'd just come from the San Francisco Mint.

I scooped up a handful, looked at the dates. Not that they would have meant anything to me. I don't collect coins, and I've never been good at those games where you try to guess the number of pennies in the fishbowl. If I'd hauled the chest out of there, I would have had maybe five hundred dollars? I don't know.

I stuffed some of them into my pocket, shut the lid, and put the dog back on top of it. Then I backed out and closed the door.

The second door was identical to the first. I opened it and peered inside, and was rewarded with much the same view—a larger room containing a larger version of the first dog with larger eyes. Eyes like inverted coffee cups. He stared at the flashlight beam the same as his smaller brother, and let himself be pushed off the chest. Inside this one were silver dollars. This time I was impressed.

I filled my pants pockets with them 'til I thought the seams might give. I put the bug-eyed dog back in place and went out.

The third door concerned me. After pennies and silver dollars, what could be left?

I unlocked the door and threw it open.

The dog inside was too big to get through the door. How had they gotten him in there? His eyes were bigger than coffee cups, too, more like dinner plates. Seated on another big box, he loomed over me. He didn't move, didn't even look down. Another statue, I thought.

I went around in back of him and tipped him off the box. I'd expected him to be heavier than the previous two, but my hands were shoving something as light as papier-mâché. The effect was dizzying, as if my balance were out of whack. In that disoriented state I opened the third box.

It was full of gold. Coins of every sort. Some I recognized: US Eagles, Frederic d'ors, British Sterling. There were others that I only learned the identities of later: crusados, moidores, napoleons, and pahlavis, and one called a *solidus*. I didn't spend much time thinking about them then. I just emptied as much of the silver as I could, refilled my pockets with the gold, and closed up the box. Picked up the monstrous dog, put it back, and hightailed it out of that room. Although nothing had happened, I still believed that at any moment the doors would crash open and those dogs, come to life, would charge out to tear me apart. I ran back to the rope and started to cinch myself.

The old lady's voice came drifting down to me. "Did you find it? Is it there?"

"Find it?" I was so crazy, I had to think about what she was asking. The lighter. The damned lighter.

I looked around me. Where the hell was I going to find that? There'd only been three rooms, and the lighter hadn't been in any of them. But she said she'd dropped it, right? So I shined the light at my feet, all around me, back toward the doors. There was nothing I could see and I wasn't about to let go of the rope. Finally, I thought to check where I was standing. I lifted my right shoe, and there, pressed into the heel of my footprint, lay a dented and scratched old steel Zippo. I'd seen a thousand of them; the military owned a concession in them. I brushed it off and stuck it into my breast pocket and fastened the button. "Got it!" I called.

I just barely got myself securely fastened when up went the rope. It was a long haul. All the time I rose I was of two minds. The first went skipping through all the things I could buy with this dough. The other speculated on what I'd find when I got out. Who was helping her pull me up? What waited for me outside the tree? Preoccupied with that, I didn't even try to sort through the subterranean fantasia. Leave the big-eyed dogs to Disney. Just let me live long enough to spend the cash.

At the top I clutched the split in the tree and dragged myself over it. Nobody helped me out. I had splinters in my hands, and a couple big ones in my shirt. I was expecting a shovel in the back of the head, and I dropped and rolled. Coins spilled out behind me. I came up on my knees, only to discover her by herself. This was almost worse than the weird weightlessness of the dogs. This little bird-eyed crone had pulled me up out of a mine using nothing but the strength in her arms. Hadn't even worked up a sweat.

"You give it to me," she said, as I brushed leaves off my shirt and pants. My gold was strewn all over the ground.

"Yeah, sure. Just let me get my breath, will you?" I pulled myself up along a large broken branch. Something jabbed me as I stood, and I drew a long sliver of wood out of my side, hissing from the pain. I reached over and grabbed my coat to get the handkerchief in the pocket.

"No, you give it *now*."

"Look, lady," I said as I dabbed at the spot of blood, "what the hell do you have down there? The river Styx?" I drew on my jacket, then picked up the big flashlight and turned to face her.

She'd pulled something new out of that bottomless bag: a nasty old Browning High Power. The gun made her hand seem about the size of a squirrel's paw.

"Where is it? You let me have it."

"Let's take it easy now," I said. "I don't want you to let *me* have it."

Her smile at my joke was anything but friendly.

I reached carefully under the jacket—thumb and forefinger only, so she could see I wasn't dangerous. I stared at all the gold lying there and figured I was dead in about two minutes, no matter what happened next. I couldn't understand why she hadn't shot me already.

I took out the lighter, held it straight in front of me as if to ward her off. Her smile became nearly beatific. "Now," she snapped.

I tossed it. I tossed it just hard enough to pass over her outstretched claw and past the gun. She turned automatically, clutching the air, and the instant she did I swung that flashlight as hard as I could. The gun discharged, blowing nine-millimeter hell right through the flap of my jacket, just missing my side. The branch behind me cracked. The flashlight smacked her beneath the ear, and it felt like I'd punched a saltine. She did a frog leap sideways and away, letting go the gun, spinning as she fell.

The sound of that gunshot dashed among the trees.

I checked her pulse and there wasn't one. I left her the gun, but I threw the flashlight down inside that tree. If the cops wanted it, they were welcome to rappel after it. I would've liked to hear their explanation for the doors and the dogs and the money.

I might even have gone back later to get the rest of it, but by the time I collected my earnings and found a way out of the trees and underbrush to the driveway, I was so lost I could never have hoped to find the way back inside.

The car was still parked by the house. It was unlocked. I opened it quietly and climbed in, then rifled through the glove box. Can't say what I was looking for. I think I just wanted something simple and tangible and sane to tie everything together. Like a pay stub indicating that she was the prop lady at Paramount. There wasn't much, but I came up with an envelope addressed to a "Madame Tzeil" at an address that could have been this one, and containing a handwritten note thanking her for all her help "mapping our daughter's future." There was a little hand-tinted photo inserted in the note, of a young woman with black hair and green eyes and the most perfect face I'd ever seen. On the back someone had scrawled "Janine."

I glanced at the signature on the note: H. W. Kildragon.

I closed up shop then. Left her car, got in mine, backed down that damn dirt drive, and drove like hell. Good riddance was what I was thinking.

But what I'd gotten into was like a stray dog. It followed me home. And there was no point in asking whether I should keep it.

The coins, when I'd finished cashing them in—selling them to dealers and collectors—and added in the advance fee she'd paid and the new pennies still in my pockets, came to exactly ten thousand dollars and fourteen cents. The old woman had been a little ahead of the game, it seemed to me. I couldn't quite square it. I didn't try very hard.

I paid off the Packard. Mapes wanted to have my children. I got myself a nice apartment downtown, bought a better wardrobe, and started making the club scene. No more cigarette girls, I decided. Why settle for anything less than everything? It was a great attitude for cutting a swath through the middle of L.A.'s nightlife. In retrospect most of the parties remain a blur. I can't remember what I was doing, only what I thought I was doing—showing Mr. and Mrs. Paney that I'd dusted them. And since they weren't actually around to get the message, I sent it to myself. With a vengeance. A blur did I say? Hell, I made Ray Milland look like a piker.

All through this period, while people I'd never met before showed up to help me spend my money, I would find some corner by myself and take out that photo and look at it. Before long I had Janine memorized. I'd even fashioned a torso to continue past the bottom of the frame. If I'd died any of those nights she would've been burned on my retinas. The last thing I saw—Kildragon's daughter.

I can't tell you how long this phase lasted exactly, since I missed a lot of it myself. I expected it to take considerably longer to go through that much money. One morning I just woke up and the party had moved on without me. I'd been beached, washed up with the debris. There was a *lot* of debris. Most of it in my head.

There was a little money left, about as much as I had sense to give up drinking while I still had something resembling a liver. I quit the expensively worn-down apartment and moved to a cheaper place more like where I'd started. Way up on the top floor, with a fire escape holding on by its last bolt and a broken elevator that wasn't going to be repaired in this decade. Not a flophouse, but not by much.

I'd paid the rent on my office for a year in advance, which turned out to be the second smartest thing I did with the cash after paying off the Packard. I went back to work. Elroy looked me over severely the morning I came back, while he buffed my Italian leather shoes. "You been hung out to dry while you's gone," he said critically. Caught red-handed, I could only nod. "Gotta git yourself some stability." I gave him two bucks for the sage advice, and for not rubbing it in.

It was like coming back from a new and different war, starting over a third time. In the dead hours of the day, after a couple hands of Canfield, I started looking into the mayor of Las Hadas.

Henry Wadsworth Kildragon, a Broderick Crawford of a politician. Meaty, loud, tough as a fifty-cent steak, and very connected. In his youth, he'd run illegal booze up and down the coast for rich clients. Rumor was, he'd eliminated the competition himself. That hadn't hurt his reputation, either. The society pages framed him regularly, him and his wife. She was the former Jenette Demarque, née

Pelata, star of no film you've ever seen unless you like
your film stars in black masks and socks, but still sharp
enough to have caught your eye from a chorus line. That's
where Kildragon spotted her. The dark hair and green eyes
of the daughter belonged to her. The nose maybe was H.
W.'s, but he had a pretty tiny nose for such a fist of a face.

The thing about the daughter was, I couldn't turn up
much on her. Oh, she'd been to good schools, mostly far
away. She'd been in the middle of some sort of graduate
studies, when something changed, something happened
that had caused her to move back into the family home.
End of story. Was she a spoiled little daddy's girl? No,
everybody who knew Janine thought she was a swell kid,
unconcerned with her own beauty and untainted by her
crummy, vain, and nasty parents. No one had any explanation for why she would have wanted to return to the
family nest. But from the moment she had, she'd vanished.
Nobody but me was seeing her now, and I was only dating
her on the inside of my eyelids.

You'll say this was none of my business and I should
have stayed out of the family closet. You're right. But
somewhere during my inebriate period that girl became an
obsession.

A few jobs floated my way while I was prospecting for
Janine Kildragon. One was for Señor Aranjuez, who
thought his wife was cheating on him—that's maybe half
of what a PI does, chase after one spouse or the other.
Usually it turns out the fears of the offended party are
wholly justified. In this instance, however, it wasn't what
he thought. His wife was taking a real estate course to
better herself and she didn't want him to know, 'cause she
wanted to surprise him . . . also she'd borrowed from their
savings to pay for it. Anyway, he was so relieved that he
gave me a box of decent Cuban cigars as a gift. A man of
his emotions, the Señor. In this case, joy.

It was early evening when I hauled myself up the stairs to my dingy apartment. I felt pretty good about clearing up somebody's affairs if not my own. Decided to give myself a reward. In the subterranean depths of my sock drawer I had a pint of Scotch. I took off my shoes and moseyed into the bedroom. Unwrapped the band from a cigar, slit the tip with my pocketknife, then went to light it.

I didn't have any matches. I hunted around the dresser but didn't find any there. Usually I have a book or two stashed somewhere.

Finally I went to the closet and started slapping through my suits, until I patted the old one I didn't wear anymore and felt the hard lump in it. By the touch alone I knew what I had.

The Zippo was back.

I couldn't remember having retrieved it; it ought to have been lying in the woods somewhere near that tree.

Maybe I should have thrown it out the window. Thing was, right at the moment I had a cigar in my hand.

I snapped back the top and thumbed the wheel. It sparked. Not your usual sparks, either, but colorful ones that spiraled out for a second like a miniature fireworks display. The wick didn't even try to catch.

Before I could thumb it a second time, the door to my bedroom opened as if of its own accord.

I must have looked like an expired mackerel standing in front of the closet with my mouth open and the cigar in my fingers. The dog probably didn't care.

He was as big as I remembered, about the size of a miniature Clydesdale. His bright blue eyes were larger than you'd find even on a stuffed panda doll.

What he wasn't was a statue.

The door closed behind him, and he parked in the center of the room, staring straight at me. I considered my options, debating how much damage I could do him with a fresh Cuban corona.

I never found out. The dog spoke. "What does my master bid?"

The cigar slipped between my fingers. I tried to laugh, but nothing came out.

"I—I . . . what?" I asked.

"What does my master bid?" repeated the dog. He could've waited all day for the answer.

Other people might not have a problem with this, but I never went to those Francis the Talking Mule pictures. I said, "Can I sit down?"

The dog went out and came back carrying one of my folding kitchen chairs in his teeth. Warily, I took it from him and opened it up and sat backward on it. That at least put the chair between me and him. I leaned off it and picked up the cigar.

"Okay, I think I'm getting this," I said. "I ask you for something, and you go and retrieve it. Whatever it is."

The dog nodded solemnly.

"Phenomenal idea. Let's see, I've used up my funds from the last time; how about you get me some money?"

The dog stood up and calmly went out. I listened but didn't hear him in the next room, but he couldn't have gone much farther in the time it took him to bring back the leather pouch. He placed it on the floor in front of me. I swung around the chair and retrieved it.

It was full of pennies.

Naturally. He'd guarded the pennies, and I hadn't specified the type of money. "Okay, tell me, how would I call your bigger brothers?" He said nothing but stared pointedly at the lighter. That was the key. That was how I'd called him. Now I did start laughing. No wonder the old woman had pulled a gun when I wasn't quick enough handing it over; and no wonder she hadn't shot me right away. She hadn't dared, for fear of nailing the lighter. And thinking about the old woman got me thinking about the mayor of Las Hadas and his interned daughter.

"Anything I want," I muttered, and the dog nodded again.

"I want you to bring me the daughter of H. W. Kildragon. Here, I've got a photo of her." I set down the bag and reached into my suit coat and took out my wallet. That was all the time he needed to disappear. I was holding her picture out to an empty room.

I got up and went to the dresser. The bottle was in with the socks where it belonged. I unscrewed the cap and took a good solid pull on it. The first swallow made my eyes water. I took a second pull before I replaced the cap. All I could think was, "Who's going to believe me?" Paney and Sally would've called the wagon after the first minute. Hell, so would I.

Out in the other room, there was no sign of the dog or his treasure. I thought about the bag of coins in the bedroom and decided to try an experiment. I flipped up the lighter and thumbed the wheel twice. More funny sparks.

The new dog came straight through the front door like the ghost of a train engine. He saw me and sat down and repeated what his little brother had said. Same question; very well trained. I asked him specifically for bills instead of coins and he went out the door and returned almost before his tail had gone. He carried a canvas bag by its drawstrings. I took it from him but didn't have to open it to know it was full of paper money. It looked like it had fallen off a Wells Fargo truck. I didn't ask.

I told the dog thanks. "Give yourself something *you* want," I said, and sent him away.

Once he'd vanished I took the bag back into the bedroom. The first dog was waiting for me there. He had a passenger.

She lay unconscious, sprawled along his back, her head resting between his massive shoulders and her black hair fanned across his neck. She was dressed in a satin night-gown the color of cinnamon that clung to every part of her. If the Scotch had brought tears to my eyes, the sight of the sleeping woman of my dreams and hallucinations robbed me of breath.

I walked around and around the dog but couldn't bring myself so much as to touch her for fear she would come awake screaming. I rubbed her hair between my fingers, though, and finally, unable to restrain myself, leaned over and kissed her as lightly as I could. Without waking she put her arms around my neck and kissed me back with more passion than I'd dreamt of. Then she let go, folded her arms across her breasts, and lay back. Her toenails were painted deep red.

I stumbled against the folding chair and collapsed on it. I ran my hand through my hair as I gaped at her. My apartment had become a broiler. I cleared my throat, and managed to say to the dog, "Take her back. Take her back right now."

Around the door he went. She wasn't out of my sight a minute before I sprang up and ran after her into the hall-way. I'd changed my mind. I didn't want to lose her. Ever.

I didn't sleep at all that night. Having had her in my arms—or, more truthfully, having been in hers—I couldn't be quit of her. I paced the floor, finally smoked that cigar, and steadily drained the pint of Scotch, which should have fogged my brain a lot more than it did. Bleary-eyed, I watched the sun come up; I didn't feel any smarter than I'd been the day before.

I took a shower, got some coffee and eggs at Albright's Diner, then went to my office. There, at least, I could pre-tend to work.

I reread everything I'd amassed on Kildragon, made a few more calls, but gained no further insights as to what was going on between him and the girl. The only significant blip on the radar was when my friendly police departmental contact (whom everybody called "Spanky" because of some long-forgotten joke) politely told me to stay as far away as possible from Kildragon and the Las Hadas cops he owned. "It's like another country there," Spanky said. "They get hold of you, no one here's gonna lead the charge across the border."

It was good advice. There was no reason for anyone to suspect me of anything to do with the mayor and his family, but that situation might change. So I got in my car and gave myself the nickel tour of the sights in Las Hadas. The police station was a two-story brick, about two blocks off the water. I drove inland from there, up past Kildragon's estate. He had walls that Schliemann might have excavated. There were a couple of doormen guarding the gate, too, the kind who had engine blocks in their family trees. I drove past a couple of times and parked on a side street, then loitered in the hedge across the road.

I finally caught a glimpse of the house when the laundry truck arrived. For a few minutes the gate opened on a long snaking drive up a low hill to a wide adobe-colored portico. Above that stood a house that looked like some clever child had fit together interlocking building blocks at crazy angles, leaving gaps between some, standing others on end. It was too clever a design for the Kildragon I'd read about; he must have bought it already assembled to show off to people.

Somewhere up there they had her, like a princess locked in a tower, but no one could have got in without a blueprint and maybe a squad of marines. Disheartened, I drove back to the office.

Elroy shook his head at me as I shuffled through the

lobby. I guess I looked like I'd fallen off the wagon again, and I didn't feel like explaining.

Late in the afternoon, out of sheer exhaustion, I put my head down on the desk blotter and slept. When I woke, it was dark, and I had a crick in my neck. Switching on the light, I checked my pocket watch. It was past eleven.

First I stepped into the little water closet adjoining the office and splashed cold water on my face. Looking in the mirror, I could see why Elroy had given me such a disapproving look. I toweled off, combed my hair, and decided I had to buy some new blades for my razor.

I took my hat and locked up, then walked along the avenue. It was a balmy night, not many people around. The walk cleared my head and by the time I got home, I was ready.

I took out the lighter and called my canine pal.

He came in like before, and asked the same question as if we hadn't done this last night. I sent him after her and he brought her back.

She looked the same, in the same spaghetti-strapped nightgown. My heart was racing again at the sight of her, but I wasn't giving in this time.

I picked her up and carried her over to the bed. She came to as I was setting her down. I don't know what I expected as much as what I hoped. She didn't fight, didn't kick and scream. She just looked up at me, green eyes searching, studying, confirming. I backed away and she sat up. She looked at the dog, then back at me.

"So it's real. Or are you a dream?" she asked.

"Funny, I've had the same question awhile now."

"How does he do it?" She meant the dog.

"You'd have to interrogate *him*. I just send him out."

She drew her knees up and wrapped her arms around them. "Is that how you pick up women? It's the most novel approach I've ever heard."

She was amazing. Unfazed by the circumstances, even laughing at me in a very pleasant way. I took her picture and the letter from her father out of my suit coat and handed them to her.

Her brow pinched as she read the letter, and her mouth curved into a scowl. "Bastard," she said.

"Sorry."

"No, not you. *Him.*"

"Your father."

She nodded. "How did you come by these?"

"That is the part that takes some explaining. May I?" She nodded again, and I sat on the bed beside her. Then I told her how I'd been hired by Madame Tzeil to retrieve the lighter and how I'd killed the lady in self-defense. I couldn't believe I was confessing it to her.

"And all you have to do to call the dogs is flick the lighter?" she asked, incredulously.

"Well, *you're* here, aren't you?"

She rubbed her arms. "So it appears. How come you didn't leave me asleep on the dog? You could pretty much have had your way if you did."

I didn't answer that. "Why's your old man got you locked up?"

"His reasons. They make about as much sense as your story. He inherited that old witch."

"Family heirloom?"

"She came with my mother. A *bruja*. You know the word? He used her to guard his little kingdom."

"He believes in that stuff? Witchcraft?"

She aimed a manicured finger at the saucer-eyed dog. "Don't you?"

"I hadn't put a name to it. Go on. He hired her to put the whammy on his enemies."

"Oh, much more than that. She told the future to warn him of trouble before it became trouble. That way he was always one jump ahead of everybody. She told him he would have a daughter. Told him what schools to send me to."

"Told him? What about your mother?"

She smiled crookedly. "She hates me. She's hated me since I was little. You know, fathers and daughters—sometimes they're close. He lavished a lot of money and attention on me. Not so much on her. Her career was over, her looks were going, and they were all she had. Too much sun made her a lizard on the outside, too."

"I'm glad you're not bitter."

She laughed. "Not much, no. She's the one who made him lock me up. The *bruja* claimed that I was going to fall in love with someone who would destroy his empire. I was away at school when this happened." She waved the note. "So all of a sudden my mother shows up and says my father isn't well and needs me back home. She enjoyed that performance, I'm sure—luring the competition into her web, which is exactly what she did. As soon as I was inside the walls of the house, I found out it was a prison. They'd prepared a room for me, a very nice room, but still one I couldn't leave. Servants, massages, pedicures, but no freedom. Over a year now. She comes to gloat every day. I've only seen him twice." She fought the urge to cry. I reached for my handkerchief, but she mastered herself, bowing her head. "He threw the *bruja* out, though, for making him do this to me. I know he despises my mother, too. But it didn't stop him from doing it. His power's more important to him than I am."

"So"—I cleared my throat—"the guy you were in love with, did they nab him, too?"

Her right hand slowly slid from her knee and down her leg to cover my hand. She raised her head, gazing with an incredible, wonderstruck look. "They told me he was a soldier. I hadn't met him yet."

I leaned closer, my hand on her arm, circling her, pulling her to me. The kiss lasted an hour. Maybe two.

I felt her breath warm on my ear. "I thought you were a dream."

"I *know* you are," I answered. "Nothing can be real and feel like this."

"Let me show you how real it is." She drew away gently and reached up to untie the straps of her gown.

The dog barked.

I was lost in a sexual fog and didn't want to emerge, especially for some prudish Hound of the Baskervilles. But I looked, in time to see him leap through the doorway. The hair prickled on the back of my neck. He wasn't barking at us.

"Janine, stay here." I got up, switching gears with the greatest of reluctance, but intuitively certain there was something wrong.

I charged through the front room, out into the hallway. I peered into the stairwell, but there was nothing. The hound had disappeared. I headed down the stairs, alert at each landing, expecting God knew what. I reached the street, opened the front door cautiously, and eased out onto the stoop.

The street was dead. Maybe, I tried to tell myself, maybe the dog had just needed to take a pee. I turned to go back inside, and saw the big blue "X" chalked on the door. I stepped down to the sidewalk to look at it, trying to make sense of it.

In that instant tires squealed up the block and headlights flashed against a building, turning the corner. I jumped back against the wall and ducked into the alley.

Three black cars came roaring up the street and drew up two buildings away. Half a dozen shapes climbed out. I heard someone say "This is it!" Then four of the shapes ran up and into the building. The other two stayed on the sidewalk beside the middle car. The goons were gone for maybe ten minutes. But by then one of the two beside the car had already spotted something else. "Hey, lookee there!" He was pointing at the building next to mine.

The door of the middle car opened. I'd expected Kildragon. Instead, it was a woman's silhouette that climbed agitatedly out and marched in my direction. She stopped at the next building, fists on hips, while the two bodyguards ran to catch up. Then she marched toward me again, and I drew back and crouched low behind a trash can.

"¡*Maldito sea*! It's on *this* door, too," I heard her say. I peered over the can at the furious harridan. "Go and fetch me Kevin this instant," she told one of the guards, and he ran off. She stuck a long cigarette in her cruel mouth. The remaining guard fumbled for a match and then, with hands as big as her head, lit her smoke. She glared at him in the light of the match. As Janine had intimated, she was thoroughly reptilian. She turned from him and started pacing. "I cannot believe this, can you, Stevie? The *idiota* manages to follow this damn dog all the way here, and then does he go in and plug the son of a bitch who's running it? No, he puts his mark on the door like—like El Zorro—and comes back to get the rest of us so we can see. He had him *trapped*."

The gang of thugs came marching up the sidewalk. The one named Kevin was easy to pick out. Despite his size, he looked terrified, and the others were keeping a respectful distance.

"¿*Quiubo*, Kevin? Did you find your mark?"

He glanced at the door of my building. "S-somebody's come along and marked all the doors same as me, *Señora*."

"A soldier, maybe? A soldier-boy who's right now having my Janine because someone else wanted to show off how clever he is?"

"I marked the door," Kevin pleaded.

"Which door is that, please?"

Kevin looked around at the buildings behind him, and the one past mine. "I'm not sure, *Señora.*"

Madame Kildragon drew a deep breath. "*De acuerdo.* Let's say you followed the puppy and somebody followed you."

"But the dog was in your house."

"*Sí,* I've heard this story two nights now. A dog is in our house, a dog we don't own, that's as big as you, Kevin. A ghost that walks through walls."

"That old lady—"

"Shut up!" She struck him in the mouth. "That old lady," she parroted. "Of course, that old lady! Who else could be doing this to us? But you left them alone, you idiot. You left them alone *together!*"

"I'm sorry, *Señora,*" Kevin whined. "You said—I thought the best thing was to get you. Please don't kill me."

She shook her head. "You listen to this?" she asked the others. She made a claw and gently raked her nails down Kevin's cheek, pausing to dab one finger in the blood on his lip. "I'm not intending to kill you, Kevin. I need for you to do something for me. If you do it, then maybe I never kill you. That's fair, isn't it?"

Kevin laughed shrilly, and started babbling thanks and promises that, whatever she wanted, he would do it. The others decided he was safe to be near again. They patted his shoulder. His buddies. They were happy they didn't have to shoot him. They went off together to get the cars. The *señora* and Stevie remained. She stared up at my building with those serpent's eyes, and for an awful moment I thought she could see Janine way up at the top. Then she said, "What I want to do, Stevie, is take care of that little *puta* once and for all, and her fat father, too. I want the whole world—*todo lo posible*—before I die. They slow me down.'' The guard said nothing, even as she slid her hand under his jacket and across the front of his trousers. "You and me, we take care of them. *Uno a uno.*"

The cars pulled up. The two of them got into the middle one, and they all drove off.

I exhaled and started to rise. My shoulder bumped into something, and I turned to find the face of that monster dog right beside me. I crashed backward into the trash can. The dog watched me stoically. It opened its mouth a little, and a large chunk of blue chalk dropped to the sidewalk.

The dog had saved my life. I hadn't told it to do that.

I led the way back upstairs. Janine was still on the bed, still sexually radioactive. I told her what had happened, what I'd overheard.

"I have to go back," she said.

"Are you crazy? They know you've been here."

"My father doesn't know about her. I have to warn him."

I sat beside her and took her by the arms. "Why would you think he'll believe you? This is the man you said had locked you away because his empire's more important to him than you are."

"And she means to steal it from him."

"She means to do a good deal more than that. Help me out here. Look at this reasonably. You're going to go back into the hornet's nest, and maybe I won't be able to get you out again. I won't let you—"

She put her fingers to my lips. "Shhh," she said, and kissed me. "You have that big dog and his brothers. They can find me anywhere, can't they?"

I glanced at the dog, and he nodded. I wanted to kick him.

"Please, let me go back for one more day," she insisted. "I'll try to warn him. If he won't listen, then at least I tried.

The way I feel about him now . . . there were years when . . ."

"He's your father. All right. One more day."

She wrapped herself around me and kissed me with her soul.

For her I could wait a lifetime. I only hoped I wouldn't have to.

The dog knew his part. He stood and came over beside us.

She said, "Pick me up, darling," and I obeyed, taking one final kiss before placing her upon his back. What else could I do?

Afterward, as the sun came up, I tried not to imagine what might be happening in the Kildragon house. I wanted to believe that she would warn her father, he would see the truth of her warning and lock his wife away instead, and Janine would be set free—wanted to believe but failed. I knew that to send the hound in broad daylight would prove disastrous. Even if they weren't waiting for him, he would be about as inconspicuous as a fire engine. Besides, I'd promised her the day. I might go crazy, but I wouldn't go back on my word.

I spent a couple hours cleaning my revolver, placing it on my hip, making sure I could get to it quickly. Then I set off for my office.

Once there, I hung out in the lobby, waiting my turn for Elroy's services. I sat in the chair with the cracked seat, with my feet on his homemade box and, while he buffed my shoes, I filled him in as best I could on the situation. He never batted an eye, as if magical hounds and bags of boodle were common events in his life.

When I'd finished, he asked, "What you expectin' if they come take you away?"

I shrugged. "I'm not sure. I just wanted somebody to know."

He nodded sagely. "You git carried away at night, I won't be here to help noways."

"They carry me off at night, I think you can have my office. I'm not likely to be coming back."

"Yeah. Las Hadas to L.A. what Diddy-Wah-Diddy be to hell."

I paid him a twenty for the shine. If I got through this, I figured I'd ask the dogs to give him his own shop.

Nobody showed up the rest of the day. No one called. I played at least three different kinds of solitaire, and lost every game. I went out and brought some Chinese food back to the office, bought an evening paper, too. The ribbon in my fortune cookie read: "You have a delightful personality and are liked by everyone." I laughed, wondering who'd gotten *my* fortune. I think I read the paper front to back, even the obits and the classifieds, and when I was done I couldn't tell you what had happened that day. The lighter in my pocket weighed more than the *USS Coral Sea*.

I didn't go home. The one thing I was counting on was that even if Kildragon stationed people on my street, by bringing Janine here we'd elude them.

I waited until eleven. I should have waited longer, but I couldn't.

The hound set off, and I started pacing the floor. He was swift but that journey took years off me. I must have stuck my head into the hallway a dozen times. Everybody was gone. The whole building was silent as a grave.

Finally, I heard his claws clicking in the hall. The door opened and he walked in. I thought for a second there'd been a mistake, but I saw those dark red toenails and I knew the only mistake was that I'd let her go back.

They'd shaved off all her hair. There were circular bruises at her temples and dried spittle on her chin. Her eyes were darkly ringed, almost sunken into her skull. She was encased in a heavy canvas straitjacket, the sleeves joined together into a single strap that ran up between her legs. That's all she wore.

I was afraid to touch her, afraid to lift her from the dog for fear she would wake up and not know me. How could they do that to their own daughter?

Finally, it became intolerable to stand staring and not do something. I touched her face, kissed her. I didn't have a couch to put her on, only a couple of chairs and the desk.

I bent down and lifted her, and something sprinkled to the floor. I looked down at a pile of dust like cornmeal. The straitjacket was leaking. Stupid with grief, I stood there following the trail of it leading across the office and under the door. I knew what it meant, but I couldn't think.

They kicked the door open as I turned to set her on the desktop. I had her in my arms in the first crucial seconds. I slid her away from me and went for my gun, but the two lead gorillas slammed into me before I could draw it. A fist drove straight into my eye. Something else punched my belly hard enough to wrap my liver around my spine. I dropped, still trying to stay up on my knees, and another blow rang like a buzz saw into the side of my head. I hit the floor chin first and lay there, barely aware of angry voices all around me, someone screaming, shots fired, and the clicking of dog's claws skittering away. I thought, *I should have just asked him to save us.*

Impressions remain of being tossed around, of a car and streetlights sparkling; like being driven home drunk. Eventually I would sober up and realize I'd fallen in love with a dream. Then Bing Crosby started singing between my ears: "Have you ever seen a dream walking?" and I started to laugh, it was so funny. Someone socked me unconscious. They might have hit me twenty or thirty other times that I can't recall.

Somebody threw ice water on me to get my attention. I was tied to a chair. My jacket was gone, as was my gun. My left eye wouldn't open past a squint. There seemed to be a boulder in front of it. It hurt to breathe, and I was pretty sure I had broken ribs and missing teeth. I focused on the figure of H. W. Kildragon. He had his sleeves rolled up, and his knuckles were bloody. I ran my tongue inside my mouth, tasting nothing. I knew I was in for it, and there was no point in pretending otherwise.

"I guess," I wheezed, "this means you're rejecting my marriage proposal."

He stepped up and slapped me. I played with the solar system awhile.

When I saw him again, he was smoking a cigarette, sitting in a chair, staring at my medals in their little frame. I wondered who had taken those from the wall in my office.

He looked as cool as you please. Janine had been wrong about the old man. There had never been any good old days, just days when she was too small to see the poison through the wrapper. Nobody sweet and kind would marry a Gila monster like the *señora*. Maybe she was feeding him a line about his daughter and me, maybe he knew perfectly well what was happening but couldn't bring himself to confront his wife and was taking it out on me; whatever, he'd passed the point where I was curious about his perspective on anything. All I wanted right then was a Bofors gun and enough time to pepper him into stew meat.

Someone behind me grabbed hold of my head and jerked it up.

Kildragon exhaled smoke and dropped the medals. "Soldier-boy," he said.

"Sailor."

He shrugged. "Where'd you get the dog, shamus? The old bitch give him to you? You on retainer?"

The questions seemed too crazy in the circumstances, I

couldn't answer. I said, "Did you know your wife and Stevie are planning to bump you?"

He jumped up. "What'd you say?" he exclaimed, and you could see he was somewhere on the far side of crazy.

"I said, what kind of pond scum are you, forcing electroshock on her?"

"Son of a bitch." He slapped me again. "Rapist bastard." Hit me again. There were more names, I'm almost sure, but after that every time he hit me they flew out of my head.

When I came to again, I was lying on the floor of a Las Hadas jail cell.

I lay there listening, making sure no one was nearby. If I let them know I was awake, they might just begin again.

My head cracked like lightning when I tried to move it—at the very least I had a concussion. They weren't done with me either. All the man had to do was place a call to the cops and they would take their exercise on me. Like Spanky had said.

I made myself roll over. It took maybe an hour. My left hand was swollen. I must have hit somebody; I hoped it had hurt. Amazing, I considered, how much you can take and still be functional enough to fight back. Someone besides the Nazis should look into it.

How long had they had me? I had no way of knowing, but I had to get out of it somehow. The problem was, I didn't have a weapon. My gun was gone but, more important, I'd lost the lighter. I knew Kildragon didn't have it or he wouldn't have asked me about the dogs.

Someone rattled keys and I heard the cell door open. Safe to say, I wasn't going to spring up and take anybody by surprise. They knew it. The guard set a tray on the floor beside my head and walked away without a word.

The smell of food worked on me. I was hungry and nauseous at the same time, and the latter finally won out.

That made me move. Stars circled my eyes and breathing was like inhaling a knife, but I didn't black out. After a while I felt better, and slid over to the tray, away from my mess. I drank the coffee and ate cold scrambled eggs, thinking this must be breakfast. I lay there, chewing every bite experimentally to find where I still had teeth.

Then I heard voices approaching. Someone was saying, "Jesus, I don't think you should."

"Don't matter what you think, they want him back up the house this morning," came the reply. "Still got lotsa questions."

"This is the worst it's ever been."

"You growing a conscience, McCandless? I wouldn't let it get out."

The keys rattled again and footsteps came up beside me. I was hoisted to my feet. Pain like a wire burned through my whole body. There was a goon on either side of me. The cop couldn't bear to see me straight on. I must have looked pretty awful.

The goons dragged me out of the station and toward a waiting car. There were fast footsteps behind us and a voice said, "You want a shine? You gentlemen need to get polished—ooh, *this* one polished already!"

"Beat it, ya little runt!" said the goon on my right. He jerked like he'd tried to throw a punch. I was tackled from behind, and then the footsteps pattered away. The goon let go of me altogether and took up the chase until his partner, not happy hoisting me alone, shouted for him to come back. When he did, he was muttering and cursing. "Little bastard tried to grab my wallet, you see that? Kick his ass to the moon."

They stuffed me none too gently in the car. I dazedly glanced at them both. They looked like any hundred other gorillas in the herd. As we drove to the estate, they chatted back and forth like I wasn't there. I sat with my head

down. We went up the drive to the portico and they
hauled me out again. I was dragged around the side of the
house and down steps to a cellar.

I recognized the room I'd been in the day before. Time
for round two. I didn't think I could make round three.

Today I was in the presence of the happy couple. They
looked like they could have feasted upon each other if I
hadn't been there. Stevie stood behind the *señora*, calm as
a billboard in spite of a cut lip. I hoped I'd given it to him.

When I was sitting in my chair, Kildragon said, "I want
you to repeat what you said yesterday about my wife."

I looked at those glittering eyes of hers and knew I
didn't have a prayer either way. "You wanted to know
about the dogs."

"Decided to talk?" he asked.

"While I still can."

He found that amusing. "So, talk. Where's the *bruja* hiding?"

"First, you tell me where your daughter is now." His
lip curled and he took a step to sock me. "Look, I want to
know she's all right. I want to know that you know the
shape she's in."

"I oughta beat you through the floor."

I lowered my head and made a point of wincing. "You
want information first. Just prove to me she's all right."

His look went squeamish when he glanced at the *señora*.
"Go get her."

"I don't take orders from his kind. What he did—"

"Shut up and go get her. Sooner you do it, the sooner
this is over with. And you *do* want this over with, don't
you, Jenette?"

She muttered something underneath her breath and sent
Stevie out. Now I knew he did know his daughter's condition, whether he liked it or not. He wasn't running the
show.

I gave it a minute, then said, "Can I have a cigarette?"

Kildragon glowered at me, then nudged one of the mouth-breathers. "Give the man his last request."

"I don't think you should," mused the *señora*.

"Shut up, I told you." Giving me a cigarette was a little act of defiance. I took one.

The door opened and Janine was wheeled in. Her gaze was absolutely vacant, no one home—until she focused on me. Then the blankness slipped a moment and I saw the horror underneath. Horror at what they'd done to both of us.

Everyone was watching her while I fished out the Zippo Elroy had slipped into my pocket. The hardest part was making my swollen hand operate it. I snapped back the top. The sound caught the *señora*'s attention. She said, "Who gave him a lighter?"

The heads all turned, as if in slow motion, as I dragged my thumb down the wheel once, then twice, then three times. The goon who'd offered me the smoke started to reach for my hand. I smiled up at him, said, "It's not working," and dropped my hand quickly. He didn't know whether to snatch the lighter or offer me his.

Janine's chair was propelled across the room as the first dog pushed in behind her. After him came the two others, cramming the hallway outside. For a second the *señora* and I traded glances. Understanding. Then I said, "Mop the deck with 'em," and the hounds leaped into action. The copper dog jumped on the nearest goons. The silver one bounded over him and bit through Stevie's throat. The idiot in front of me swung around to shoot. I managed to kick him in the back of the knee and he fired straight up. The third dog swelled into the room and, like the monster he was, reached over everyone and closed the goon's skull between his massive jaws. Threw back his head and slammed the body against the ceiling. The light fixture exploded and sparked.

Finished with the hired help, the dogs turned on their cornered prey—Mr. and Mrs. Kildragon. Even trapped, they wanted nothing to do with each other, and stood their ground separately. The pack closed on them, so massive that the couple vanished from sight. The screaming didn't last long. When the dogs parted again, there was nothing left. Not so much as a smear.

Janine rolled her chair to me, crying, "My God, my God," over and over. As best I could, I took her to me. Jagged fire shot through me.

The three hounds sat in a column, like those Russian dolls that fit one inside the other. In unison, they queried, "What does the master bid?"

"Heal us," I answered.

They came forward, circling us as they had the other two, then started to lick us. Tongues as big as bath towels, as big as bedsheets; as loud as surf.

Las Hadas is different now. I run it. So far as anyone remembers, I always have. Only Elroy knows otherwise, and he's too happy with his shoe shop to mention it. People attempting to maintain Kildragon's level of graft and corruption have mysteriously vanished in the night. The rumor is . . . well, you can probably guess.

The house is a lot nicer than you might think when you first see it, especially with all the mouth-breathers gone.

The dogs like it, too. Behind the high walls they can roam the grounds at their leisure. There are no better bodyguards.

Janine and I try to leave them pretty much to themselves.

The
Dog Rose

STEN WESTGARD

Sten Westgard's first story was published in Tomorrow Magazine *in 1994. Since then he has sold another story to* Tomorrow. *He attended the Clarion East Writers' Workshop in 1995 and "The Dog Rose" is the last story he wrote while there. His is the second fairy tale that came to us from that Clarion. Westgard works as a desktop publisher/video producer/programmer for the family software company. He lives in Madison, Wisconsin, and has recently married.*

It is the tradition of many fairy tales to have a prince *awaken or otherwise rescue a princess. "The Dog Rose" instead focuses on less royal folk who might have an interest in the outcome.*

The Dog Rose

In the middle of May, when irises grow their beards and bleeding hearts shed their first white drop, Edward battled the sun for the life of the garden. Father was too old to haul buckets, so Edward carried the rain of the absent clouds on his shoulder-yoke. But in spite of his dousing, the herbs and flowers sagged under the growing heat. Shepherd's knot leaves shriveled and turned brown, and Edward saw the fevers he would not cure. The petals of the peonies curled up and died, and Edward dreamed of the gout that would flourish in months to come.

"Every moment you waste costs us an herb, Edward," Father chided. He sat outside the stone-and-turf hut, watching Edward work. "Do you think we can trade dry twigs for food?"

Edward didn't answer. For every plant skeleton, he saw a man's bones. The ache in his shoulders grew worse with

179

each day, just as Father's words grew harsher with each withered plant. The patch of sweet peas, the stand of bellflowers, reduced to brown stalks and sapless twigs. His muscles felt as if they were ripping off his bones, as if he were being stripped as bare as the garden.

It was then that Edward heard the news of Thorn Castle. Dobelis the merchant told him when he came to trade with Father.

"Did you know the roses are about to bloom?" Dobelis asked, as he tethered his horse to the low stone wall surrounding the garden. Edward's limbs tingled, and his throat felt suddenly rough. He set down his buckets, sloshing water onto his boots and cuffs. He looked back at Father, and saw his tanned skin draw tight against his cheeks.

"We hear that rumor every year," Father said, looking up from the pile of primrose flowers before him. He set aside his bronze shears. "Nothing ever comes of it."

"Where did you hear this?" Edward asked. He extended his hand, feeling the callused grasp of Dobelis.

"I saw the buds myself," Dobelis said. His face and hair were dusted brown by the road. Dirt had gathered in the wrinkles of his face like gashes from a many-clawed beast. As he talked the dirt fell off him like a mist.

"How long ago?" Edward asked, helping Dobelis take his saddlebags off his horse. Thick scents emerged from the leather bags, a pungent odor that made Edward's nostrils sting.

"Four days' travel by slow-witted mare," Dobelis said, patting the flank of his horse. "I trade with an old hermit nearby. His garden is much like yours."

Edward's cheeks grew warm. "Was anyone else there?" he said quietly.

"No one," Dobelis said, smiling.

"What have you brought this time?" Father said, changing the subject.

"Squill bulbs and sicklewort, and some winter jasmine leaves," Dobelis said. Edward watched him survey the garden with his eyes, a practiced squint that took in the drooping lilies and the faded periwinkle, and a score of late-spring blooms struggling in the harsh sun.

"The drought has hit you hard," Dobelis said.

"The fields are worse—the King and court are traveling to survey the damage," Edward replied. "We'll lose everything if it doesn't rain."

Father's voice bristled. "We'll lose everything if you don't keep watering. Come, Dobelis, we'll go inside and leave Edward to his work."

Dobelis took his saddlebag back. "Perhaps later, Edward," he said. Edward watched the two walk inside the hut, Father muttering, Dobelis taking out his two-armed balance and a set of tally sticks.

Edward turned back to the garden, staring at the drying, dying plants. As he poured water around the base of the lilies, he found himself distracted by memories of Grandfather—hands like gnarled roots, a voice that ground like mortar and pestle.

Another memory stuck in Edward's thoughts, this one a blurry recollection of a dream that came to him with every summer. Edward was working in the garden, digging, kneeling on the ground and tending to the plants. Grandfather stood before him, but Edward could only see the cracked leather of his boots. He heard Grandfather speak, words falling from his lips like the first rains of April, like seeds falling from a tree. As he weeded, Edward only caught snatches of the story. The Sleep. The thorns. And Cleome. As the words hit the ground they sprouted, shoots that raced up along Grandfather's legs and chest, surrounding him, digging into his flesh until they ran in his veins. Belatedly, Edward abandoned his toil, attacking the prison of thorny vines and knife-edged leaves that held Grandfather. He shouted, but Grandfather did not hear, did not stop telling the story of Cleome. Not a princess but a peasant, he said, ivy trailing off his tongue, eyes growing hazel and face wrinkling like bark. Edward pounded his fists against the verdant harness, but the vines had taken Grandfather. At the end of the dream, his face burst open like a flower.

The empty buckets banged against his legs like drums as Edward headed out of the garden. Father would talk with Dobelis for some time, he figured. Setting the buckets against the castle well, he made for the smithy.

A blast of hot air greeted him. Glowing coals cast the room in orange and red. The smith pounded on the blade of a scythe, oblivious to everything but the glowing curve. On the other side of the furnace, out of view of the smith, Olaus pumped the huge bellows. Edward shouted the news over the roar of the fire, the clang of the hammer on hot iron, and the gasp of the yawning bellows. Olaus puffed out his cheeks and rolled his eyes. "You bet our chance on the word of Dobelis?"

"He's always been honest in his dealings with us."

"A merchant who doesn't lie?" Olaus scoffed. "I'm not about to stake my fate on a coin-biter's tale." He pulled the handle up. The bellows moaned like the gust of an approaching storm.

"Whose word *will* you trust? The next time we hear of the roses, it will be from the man who walked through them. We can't wait for someone else to get there first."

"I just want to be sure," Olaus said, leaning his shoulder into the bellows, pushing down, feeding air to the coals.

"You want to spend the rest of your life at this bellows, your arms hairless from getting too close to the fire? You want to grow deaf like the smith from pounding the anvil all day?"

Olaus paused. The muscles in his jaw pulsed. "And you really think your father will allow you to go? Leave him alone in the middle of this drought? You're going to have to desert him, and let his life crisp in the sun."

"He'll understand," Edward insisted. "If he doesn't, I'll go anyway."

Olaus stood still until the smith hollered to keep pumping.

"I know the road to Thorn Castle. The day I hear you left your father, I'll set out on it. Not one moment before." He turned his back on Edward to work the bellows.

When Edward returned from the well, Father was waiting, his arms folded tightly around him like climbing vines.

"You think because I'm trading with Dobelis I don't know how long it takes to draw water from the well?"

Edward began to speak, but Father interrupted.

"Don't bother. I'll lose everything down to the roots if I wait to hear the excuse. Just get back to work."

Father stalked into the hut, and Edward didn't see him until he went inside to cook the evening meal. Even then, Father didn't look up. He held his half of the tally sticks from Dobelis, recording the trade with similar notches on a special plank. Edward simmered barley and rye in a pot, adding goat's milk for flavor. The fire warmed the front of his legs and arms, but his face felt hotter.

Finally, Father broke the silence. "I should never have let your grandfather tell you that nonsense."

"Why would he lie to me? He gained nothing from the tale."

"By the time you were old enough to listen to his fancies, he was too old to remember anything clearly. He never visited Thorn Castle before the Sleep, and he certainly never met a woman there."

"If the roses are in bloom," Edward said, "they'll part for the right man."

Behind him, Father said, "Don't be ridiculous, Edward." Edward heard the scrape of pottery as Father got out the bowls for supper. "The court will return soon. When the King hears the news, he'll send the Prince. His seers have always said the boy was born to save Beauty—let him be the fool who tests Thorn Castle."

With shaking hands, Edward ladled the thick mixture into Father's bowl, then his own. "Why must you be a prince to face a rosebush? A gardener will do better, especially if he has a link to the people inside."

"We've got a garden to save and no time for folly. A prince can do what he wishes. A gardener must work."

Edward sat down at the small table, smelling the lingering scent of primrose. He looked across at Father. "I used to play with him in the courtyard, remember? When I wasn't bent down beside you, weeding and digging and hardening my hands. All the Prince has ever had are soft palms and servants. What makes him better than me? What does he know of thorns?"

Father slammed his hand down flat on the table.

"Not another word, Edward. Mention it again, and you'll be out in the fields, not under my roof."

They passed the rest of the meal in silence. Edward cleared the bowls and boiled the water for tea. As Father added new straw to the bed, Edward mixed a special brew. Wild hyssop rootstock, steeped in among the tea leaves, its flavor masked by still other cuttings.

Edward lay awake in the bed, waiting until he could hear the slow, even breaths of Father's hyssop-deepened sleep. When he was sure of Father's state, Edward crept out of bed and packed a leather satchel with barley and turnips. Grabbing the bronze shears, a hatchet, and gloves, he slipped out of the hut and over the garden wall.

As dawn began to heat the baked earth again, Edward found himself staring from his hiding place at the peasants carrying water into the fields, their feet kicking up clouds of dust. Leaning over to pour water onto the browning crops, they looked like stalks themselves, bending in a chaotic wind.

The sun had reached its peak before Edward spotted Olaus, his ruddy face framed by a dented helmet, a notched sword resting on his shoulder. As Olaus crossed the fields and joined the road, Edward saw that even the chain-mail vest he wore was rusty, with a wide gash running along the left side. Once Olaus had entered the forest, Edward stepped out from hiding.

"How can you stand the sun in that armor?" Edward asked.

"It may be hot to you, but it's cooler than the smithy," Olaus said, smiling. He stepped off the road into the trees.

"Thank you, Olaus," Edward said. For the first time since the drought came, he felt unburdened. "Thank you for coming."

"Well, I know you can't do it alone," Olaus said. "Who'll defend you from the bandits that lurk along these roads?"

"The only bandits will be rivals for Beauty. If we meet someone, it'll likely be the Prince catching up with us."

"You'll need my help then, too." Olaus paused. "What will you say to Cleome?"

"I'm not sure."

"She's more beautiful than Beauty herself, right, Edward?" Olaus asked. "Hair like the dawn, and eyes like the deep sea?"

"Grandfather said no such thing. Cleome wasn't a noble. She served in the hall."

Olaus smiled. "And Beauty?"

"Grandfather didn't know. He never saw her."

"She can look like a horse, for all I care. Just as long as I'm not at the bellows, so long as the smith can't hammer on me."

Curiosity overcame Edward. "Did you see my father?"

Olaus shook his head, a solemn look taking hold in his face. "I won't speak of it, Edward. From this point on, we can have nothing behind us—only the thorns before."

Edward agreed, and no more words of home passed their lips.

The days passed by in a slow, sweaty blur. Edward grew used to the soft crunch of dry grass beneath his feet. He watched his pants grow brown and stiff with dirt, the cuffs becoming worn, then stringy, then ragged. As they got closer to Thorn Castle, they ran out of food; the sun had dried up everything Edward could forage. Soon all he heard was the growl of his stomach and the pounding of his head with every listless step.

Finally, Edward spotted a village, wattle huts with fallen thatch. Trellises and vines covered the walls. Flowers filled doorways and stretched upward to form roofs. Every path was planted, flowers and herbs all green and healthy. Edward stepped between bright yellow rows of trumpeting daffodils, threading through the colorful labyrinth and looking for the most edible plant. He heard Olaus's footsteps follow behind him.

"Who's there?" an old, old voice said, cracking and hissing like a fire built with wet pine. Edward could not see its origin; it seemed to flow from the very plants themselves. He looked at Olaus, who shrugged his shoulders.

"Two traveling gardeners in search of food," Edward said.

"For a square of cloth, I'll give you what you need," the voice replied.

"That trade sounds fair to me," Olaus said, tightening his grip on his imperfect sword.

Edward shook his head. "Let us see you so we may seal this bargain."

The old man emerged from a gap between the pink sword lilies and a hibiscus shrub. His cloak was made of a patchwork of scraps, some faded, some bright, some covered by dirt. Edward had never seen so many colors. In the bits and rags, he recognized bright dahlia oranges, zinnia yellows, and iris blue-violets and still more exotic, foreign dyes.

Olaus gasped. "How did you get so wretched, old man?"

"Olaus," Edward warned. He had not noticed the old man's face, a pair of faded blue eyes and more wrinkles than there are veins in a leaf. His white hair hung down in long, dirty knots, obscuring a pair of cankered lips. Edward could not tell where the mud ended and the face began.

"Do not ask about my age. Pay me my price."

As Edward clipped off a square from the edge of his shirt, the old man produced handfuls of beans and pea pods from his cloak.

"Are you here for the thorns?" the old man asked.

"Yes, for Beauty and for another," Olaus answered, straightening his shoulders. "One of his relatives sleeps inside the castle."

"Oh, really?" The old man smiled.

"Not a relative," Edward explained, as he handed over his square of cloth. "My grandfather visited the castle before the Sleep, before the thorns, to trade bulbs with the gardener there. He met a woman in the feasting hall. While he was at home, getting the King's permission to marry her, the Sleep overtook the kingdom. The thorns grew up and he married another. Toward the end of his days, his thoughts turned back to her. He was very old when he told me this."

"That doesn't mean you'll cross through. Dirt-diggers won't penetrate the thorns."

"I know the ways of roses. I handle thorns without getting pricked. I weed nettles without getting stung."

"You're not the breed that will survive. The roses will not part for a common weed. Turn back and return to your garden."

"Who are you to command us?" Olaus shouted.

The old man grabbed hold of his cloak, running the back of his fingers over the multicolored patches. "For every square, there was once a man who came to prove his bravery. Peasants, soldiers, even knights, now only the cloth is left."

Edward looked at the patches, hundreds of irregular squares, wondering if the old man's story was true. He tried to picture a face, a man for every patch in the harlequin cape, an army of hundreds swallowed up and gone.

When he crested the hill, Edward got his first glimpse of the roses, a fierce red as if the sunset had nestled in a circle around the castle. As he neared, it grew larger and larger, swallowing up his view until there was nothing before him but roses, tall as a full-grown oak. He felt dwarfed by the wall of flowers, like an ant before an apple.

"It's like a barley field set on its side, with a rose for every seed," Edward whispered.

"No, it's like a fire," Olaus said. "A wall of fire like the summer burns that eat whole forests."

Edward nodded. Here was a fire of roses, its flames the waves and ripples created by the wind, flowers bobbing, swaying, dipping with each gust. The closer Edward and

Olaus got, the more the wall seemed to move. Edward thought he could watch it forever.

He brushed his hand against the leaves, a soft, gentle feeling like the touch of velvet. He closed his eyes and stepped forward, feeling the peculiar embrace of pliant flowers and stubborn thorns. Two steps in and he could go no farther. The wall resisted him, and he felt the prickles dig into his body like the tines of forks. He gasped and stepped back.

"It didn't part," Edward said, a coldness spreading through his limbs. He looked at Olaus, whose face had turned pale.

"Try again," Olaus said. "I'll try with you."

Edward walked into the red again, and again made no progress. The thorns stung like bee stings, and he withdrew faster this time. He looked to his left; Olaus had failed, too.

"It won't accept us," Edward said. A yawning pit grew inside him. All his plans suddenly destroyed. Grandfather had been so sure. He had been so sure.

"I don't recognize these roses, Olaus."

"They look like the ones you place on the King's table."

"No flowers of this sort have ever grown in a garden," Edward said. "Maybe we should turn back."

"I'm not leaving. I won't give up yet," Olaus said. Edward watched as he drew his sword and struck the wall. The blow chopped off the heads of a score of flowers in one sweep. The petals scattered on the grass, a spill of red on green.

"You see them fall," he shouted. "It's only a matter of how many blows."

"They were supposed to part." Edward looked at his arms and legs, watching his scratches swell with blood.

"They'll part—by sword or hatchet, they'll make way for us." Olaus kicked the cut flowers. "I won't go back."

Edward felt the beating of his heart, the panicked breathing of his lungs. The roses might still make way, he thought. Bending down on one knee, he peered through the hole, gingerly touching the sap on the exposed red-thorned canes. Where there weren't thorns, there were bristles, red and fine as hair, like spider legs dyed with blood. He could not see through to the other side.

"There's nothing to return to, Edward," Olaus said. He sounded nervous, his words quivering like the roses in the breeze. "The sun has turned your garden to desert by now. The King has made us outlaws by now. Neither the smith nor your father could take us back. We can't change that, but we can make the roses part."

Perhaps make way meant that they could be cut through, Edward thought. A barren garden and his life stood behind him, but only the thorns lay ahead.

"We'll not hack our way through, Olaus," Edward said, taking the leather gloves off his belt, "but you'll have to do some cutting."

Edward constructed a narrow tunnel through the thorns, pruning dead cane when possible, propping healthy cane to the side with branches when it wasn't. The air stank of roses.

"This is taking too long," Olaus said, setting down freshly cut saplings before him.

But Edward wasn't listening. "These must be wild roses. Dog roses. They grow along the hedgerows when the weather is fair. Never this color of red, but the shape of the petals is right."

Olaus answered with a bitter laugh. "Weeds among weeds, are we? No wonder I feel so much at home."

"So much deadwood," Edward whispered. "Black spot, canker, mildew—it's a wonder they've gotten so large."

"What did you say?"

"Nothing." He wiped his forehead with the back of his arm. "Keep the branches coming."

"The tunnel isn't even straight."

"Better crooked than cut, Olaus," Edward said, and turned back to his work.

As the hours passed, his arms ached with the effort of twisting the cane. Behind every obstruction lay another. The aches spread up his arm into his shoulder and back. The light waned, and the cane grew tougher, thicker than his wrist and more like trees than vines. Here the roses were choked with deadwood, a lifeless snarled knot in the heart of the thorns. Edward switched to his axe, squinting before each blow, trying to aim for a particular cane, but often surprised when he hit something closer than his target. As the sweat trickled down his face, Edward thought he tasted the roses.

"Let me take over," Olaus asked.

Edward handed him the axe. "Only trim the deadwood. Nothing alive. Make the cuts at an angle."

"Right," Olaus said.

Edward dragged the cuttings out to the clear space beyond the flowers. The thorns began to pierce through the gloves, and each armload felt like a mass of iron burrs. Each time he returned for a load, Olaus was panting worse, face flushed redder than his sunburn.

When they were forty feet in, and the pile outside was higher than Edward, he heard a ripping, cracking sound above him, like breaking sticks or the felling of a tree. The cane above them sagged and collapsed. Edward shouted as he saw the vines engulf Olaus, as if a great mouth were swallowing his friend whole. Olaus cried out, but the cry was cut short.

Edward ran forward. He heard a brittle snapping that became a roar. Before he made three steps, the cane crashed down on him, a crushing, bristling weight that embraced him like an iron maiden.

A wind blew through the bush, carrying the scent of rotting flesh and roses, sweet scent and sweet decay, brushing the rose hips against Edward's face. Their spiny hairs tickled his jaw, then his chin, then his lips, like a spider crawling across his skin. His stomach protested, but Edward turned away, feeling the thorns dig into his skull, clamping down on his head like a beast with misshapen fangs. He turned to the left, grinding his teeth against the piercing of his scalp, and the rose hips scuttled across his ear, pressing so close he heard them scratch against his skin. Edward twisted again with a groan, pushing back the cane behind, flexing his arms against his bonds. His head burned as his scabs reopened and new wounds were made. But he had made a tiny space, a bit of safety.

The wind picked up again, and Edward's nose filled with the stench of Olaus's corpse. He could see the body, a few feet away through the fog of leaves and red thorns, with its purpled skin and crusted, blackened blood, surrounded by cane that had grown quickly into his skull. Blossoms snaked in and out of the eyes and mouth, shifting in the breeze like flames consuming a log. The thorns made a scratching noise as they brushed against the chain shirt.

Olaus, what have we done? Why did we think we could outwit this place?

A half dozen roses hung just above his head, their wilting red petals covered with a film of dew. Edward's parched throat cried out for moisture, and he tilted forward, licking the drops off the sagging petals. Then he bit the flower off at the stem, trying to sate his hunger with the damp, chewy petals. His stomach protested even more. He surveyed the thorns around him to distract himself.

The edges looked even farther out of reach than yesterday, obscured by a tightening curtain of cane and thorn and blossom, swaying under the force of the wind. He caught a glimpse of the safe, open space beyond the blooms. Farther in, there was still darkness, although he could pick out bones and skulls, wedged in between the cane or pierced right through. Above, Edward saw tiny patches of blue and white. Clouds, he thought dully. Finally some clouds in the sky.

His belly twisted beneath his skin. He could take the ache in his stomach no longer. He closed his mouth over the rose hips, running his tongue over the slender, waxy surface of the bulbous tubes. Biting them off at the sepal, he savored the sharp tartness as he chewed the fibrous fruit. When he swallowed, the wind blew through the thorns like a sigh.

The hermit was right, Olaus. Weeds don't part for other weeds.

The aches in his body became less insistent. His eyelids felt heavy, and his head drooped forward from fatigue. He looked at the bloodred thorns poking into his chest and legs. Cane that gripped and twisted around him like jagged-edged ropes. Soft green shoots brushed at his fingertips, edged down the collar of his shirt. I could tear them off, he thought, or bite at the buds, but what would be the point? They would only grow back. The space around him felt snug, conforming to his body, comforting him, as if the cane was weaving him a womb of leaves and thorns.

As he drifted into sleep again, Edward thought he heard the sound of an army. A chorus of men, shouting and calling. The whinnying of horses and the thud of their hooves. The thwack of axes against wood and the singing of swords. And beyond that, even fainter, the brewing thunder of a storm.

*   *   *

He woke gradually, like a bulb awaking from winter, slowly sending out its first shoots. His skin damp and chilled, his limbs trembling, pressed down by a dripping mass. The smell of rain and wet leaves. A far-off sound of boots treading through mud.

Edward raised his hand, expecting resistance but finding none. The withered cane bent like limp straw. He pushed himself to his feet, wet thorns grating against him but giving way. The thornbush lay collapsed about him, a mass of broken cane, ripped leaves, and flame red petals, spread out like of pool of fire across the acres. A devastated space before the gray stone of the castle where the Prince's banner flew.

He looked at his arms and legs, dotted by red scabs as if he were stricken with pox. With slow, uneasy steps, he headed toward the spot where he thought Olaus lay. But his search yielded only sodden rose and blighted cane. Still he looked, ignoring the bite of the thorns, stumbling along on his weak legs. No body, no helmet, no sword. Even the bones were gone, consumed by whatever had consumed the thornbush. The wounds on his hands broke open and bled anew. He had ceased to care. He could hear the sounds of revelry within the castle, the cheers offered to the Prince. All Edward wanted was to find Olaus.

He didn't know how much time passed; he ignored the angle of the shadows and the heat on his back. After a while, he noticed a group of men-at-arms approaching from the castle, their shields displaying a familiar crest.

"By God, you're a lucky one," one of them said, his eyes roaming over Edward's ravaged limbs. "The only man to emerge from the thorns since they fell."

Edward stared at their unblemished helms, their perfect spears which sparkled in the sun. "Lucky," Edward nodded, "to travel from one dying garden to another."

The soldier seemed confused. "Come into the castle. A

barber will look to your wounds, and we've enough food to feast for a week."

Edward shook his head. "I'm not welcome inside those walls."

"You've nothing to fear. The Prince has declared an amnesty. All debts forgotten, all misdeeds forgiven—a new start for everyone in the kingdom."

"I belong here among the flowers. There's another here I must find." He walked away, wading back into the fallen thorns, eyes seeking out bones. He closed his ears to the sound of drums and trumpets, shut out the smells of roast pig and boar. If he could find Olaus, give him a proper burial, perhaps he could make sense of it. Perhaps Olaus was still alive and trapped like Edward.

With the twilight, another man came out to see him. In the growing darkness, he didn't recognize the face until he was very close.

"I was wrong about you, gardener," the hermit said. "You did know how to survive."

Edward gazed into the hermit's ruined face. "But Olaus did not. The roses have shrouded him."

"These thorns will never yield up their dead," the hermit said. "If they did, the bodies would choke the fields, and the Prince could not celebrate the rescue of Beauty."

"He came because I asked him."

"Finding his corpse won't cleanse you of fault."

The strength emptied from Edward's legs. He stumbled as the hurt and hunger overwhelmed him.

"Come in with me," the hermit said, helping him to his feet. Leaning on the hermit's shoulder, they walked into the castle, where the cries of joy echoed off wet stone. Pale, smiling peasant faces, whirling and dancing as if the maypole stood in their midst. Their feet were clumsy and their movements stiff, but they did not lack for bliss.

"The Prince arrived only three days behind you. With

him came woodsmen and sappers and the men-at-arms. As he set camp, the storm broke. While the wind and hail lashed through the cane, the Prince walked to the edge of the flowers. He pricked his thumb on the thorns, and the roses fell down before him like hounds before a master."

"How fitting. The King will be proud."

"He's the most willful of the lot, this one. Acted like he already owned the land, with no ear for word or warning. Didn't give me my square, either. No, he told his soldiers to strip the cape off my back instead."

Rushes and squill crunched beneath his feet as Edward followed the hermit into the feasting hall. At the far end, the Prince sat on the old throne, a goblet in his bandaged hand and the cape draped around his slender frame. On him, the cape seemed regal, brighter and more brilliant, as if all the colors of the world had gathered on his shoulders. The hall filled with the echoes of the laughter and boasts of his men.

The hermit guided Edward to the nearest table. As Edward stared at the worn, gray wood, the hermit looked around, clapping his hands to get a maid's attention. "Bring us ale, here.

"Not everything is lost, Edward. This castle, this Prince, will need a gardener."

"Always the gardener," Edward said, his words grating his throat. He felt hollow, empty of hope, empty of glory, a barren, lifeless seed. "As if there wasn't one here already."

The hermit grinned, his brown lips like worn roots. "There was no gardener here when the Sleep came. He was elsewhere, picking berries, doing his work."

Edward started to ask a question, but a maid interrupted, setting two pewter mugs on the table. She smiled as she poured them drinks from her pitcher, her eyes as blue as the sky above a mountain.

"Do you realize this is a hero you're serving?" the hermit said, lifting his mug as if to toast Edward. "The only commoner to enter the thorns and live."

The woman smiled as she handed Edward his mug. Her hair was as red as the sunset when it touches the horizon.

The Reverend's Wife

MIDORI SNYDER

Midori Snyder is the author of several fantasy novels, including a high-fantasy trilogy (New Moon, Sadar's Keep, and Beldan's Fire), and a western-Irish fantasy, The Flight of Michael McBride, *which combines the Celtic stories of the Sidhe with a Texas cattle ride. She has contributed to the punk fantasy series,* Bordertown, *and written "Barbara Allen" for artist Charles Vess's popular comic-book series,* Ballads and Sagas. *After living abroad in northern Italy, she has found herself entangled in two forthcoming fantasy novels set in sixteenth-century Italy among the actors of the commedia dell'arte.*

According to Midori Snyder, "The Reverend's Wife" was an oral tale collected from the Kordofan people of Sudan and was originally known as "The Muezzin's Wife." In that version it was the men, a muezzin and a caravan trader, who dupe each other's wives into having an affair. Snyder's version, set in rural America, is definitely not for children.

The Reverend's Wife

It was funny the way it turned out. Hard in fact to feel any shame about it at all. No matter the fire and brimstone pouring out of Preacher Thomas's sermons, God-afearing and God-avenging, hitting the Good Book hard enough to make sin jump up into your mouth and begin to testify. Me, I don't need to testify. God knows me. Instead I just stay quiet and get to thinking how God has a mighty good sense of humor and doesn't mind a little sinning now and again. That is, of course, if no one gets hurt and all parties wind up happy. I guess you could say Violet Thomas and I wound up pretty happy women. And our dear husbands, though they learned a thing or two about women, were never the wiser for it.

It started back about the time my husband Caleb and I returned from our honeymoon. The old buggy and mule had barely made it home, what with the mule getting cantankerous and refusing to move and the buggy losing bits and pieces of itself every time we took a bump. Caleb was furious, swearing at the mule and slapping the reins over its stubborn rump. But I was laughing my head off and could of cared less if the old buggy had fallen apart on the ground and left us stranded in the road. I was as happy as a lark. I was young, loose-limbed, and pretty. I'd just gotten married to the man I loved most and spent three days in a fancy hotel room with him, most of it on my back, my heels up in the air. My bones ached everywhere. I was bowlegged, rubbed raw, and my skin carried a strong musky odor. I got dizzy just bringing my fingers to my nose and inhaling.

"Hey now, Mr. Johnson," I said, when the buggy finally groaned to a stop in front of our hitching post. "Are you fixing to carry me over the threshold?"

Caleb looked at me with those sharp blue eyes and grinned, his boyish freckles darkening with a blush. Sore as I was, I got heated up quick just looking at him. He jumped down from the buggy and ran around in front of the mule over to my side. I'd already sprung loose from my seat, panting like a rabbit, and was waiting for him. Neighbors had gathered on the road and were calling out greetings. But we didn't pay them much mind.

Caleb scooped me up off my feet and after wrestling the door open, hoisted me into our little house. He kicked the door shut behind him and our neighbors' voices were suddenly drowned out by the sound of Caleb's heavy breathing. I can remember the smooth feel of the wood floor, and the fury with which we grappled right there in the front hall. My hands were too busy elsewhere, so I had to bite off his shirt buttons. My petticoats were all bunched up about my waist, my bloomers hanging off of one ankle. I yanked at Caleb's trousers and praised God that we'd left the hotel in such a state that my husband hadn't managed to put on his shorts beforehand.

Like a pair of cats on the stoop, we howled, rolled, and left stains on the wood floor with our joyous homecoming.

Well I guess that's what a honeymoon is all about. What I didn't figure on was that it could change so fast. A month after my wedding night I didn't see any blood come at the usual time for it. I waited a second month just to be sure before I told Caleb the news. He was out back fiddling with the buggy wheels, grease all over his hands, his face kind of distracted by the falling-down husk of that old conveyance. When he figured out what I was telling him, well, you would have thought I'd hit him with a brick. His eyes opened real big, and he shook his head in disbelief.

"You sure?" he asked.

" 'Course I'm sure," I answered, a little testy that he should doubt me. "It's something a woman knows, Caleb."

"Well, that's all right then," he said, smiling, his face finally opening up to the wonder of it all. "I'm going to be a father."

I was ready right then and there to go in and celebrate the moment with a good tumble in bed. But Caleb had other ideas.

"We've got to be more careful now, Rosalie. I don't want to hurt you and the baby none," he said. "Why don't you lie down a while and let me fix you a sandwich? You sure you feel all right?"

Well, I didn't want a sandwich, but I was touched by Caleb's sudden tenderness. So I figured there was no harm in letting him wait on me a bit. Later I'd straighten his thinking out and let him know that even though I was pregnant, I was still capable of doing almost anything.

I lay down on the velvet sofa with a book in my hands while Caleb spent the day waiting on me, asking after my condition every five minutes, his eyes staring at my stomach as though a baby was going to pop out right then and there. I loved it. Yes I did. Until evening that is, when he made me dinner and then disappeared out back again for a long time, leaving me very lonely and bored. I could hear him hammering on the buggy, and every now and again the old mule braying while Caleb cursed at it. It was late in the night when I heard him finally come in the back door. A moment later he joined me in bed, stinking of axle grease, straw, and manure.

It didn't matter though to me. I was waiting for him, feeling frisky and ready to start a night of play. After all I'd spent the day resting up. I had on my honeymoon nightdress, a band of lace just holding up a sheer drape of fabric over my newly developing curves. My breasts were rounder than a pair of peaches begging to be picked. But Caleb wouldn't have any of it. He just held me close and told me that we both needed to get some sleep, what with the baby coming on and both of us having a long road ahead of us. I didn't like the sound of that, but I let him have his way, seeing's how he'd been so nice to me that day. Tomorrow, I figured, I'd get my way again.

Next morning Caleb was up bright and early and woke me. He was shaved, his hair slicked down with a sweet-smelling hair oil. He had on his wedding suit, a tie, and a hat. In one hand he held a cardboard suitcase and in the other, my tattered carpetbag.

"Where are you off to?" I asked, still rubbing the sleep out of my eyes.

"To work, little mother. Got the buggy fixed up and I'm going back to the road. I'm a family man now, and the best damn traveling salesman in this county. I'm going out to earn us a living. Take good care of yourself and the baby, Rosalie, and don't worry none about me. I'll write you every chance I get."

"When are you fixing to come home?"

"Couple of months. Maybe longer if the money is good."

"Couple of months? What am I supposed to do on my own for a couple of months?" I complained.

"Well, don't you need to knit or something?"

"I don't know how to knit," I snapped.

"Well, there's no time like the present to learn."

And there it was. Just that simple. He leaned over and gave me a chaste kiss on the forehead and left, the mule braying, all the pots and pans tied on the side of the buggy clanking loud enough to wake the dead. But he was off to make our fortune. I sat on the bed feeling cheated out of a lover and cried my eyes out. As far as that man was concerned the honeymoon and all that sex was over and done for a while. We were now each in our respective places, him on the road to make money and me, stuck at home to get as big as a barn while I learned to knit booties. I wanted to throw up. In fact I did, though I can't be sure whether it was my anger or my pregnancy that caused it.

In the weeks that followed I did manage to find ways to occupy myself during the day. The church in our town has always been a holding pen for women with a lot on their minds and not too many ways to express it. They go every day, pray loudly, sing feverishly, and make more food for the church socials than a president's banquet. Every now and again I'd get an envelope from Caleb with a little money in it and a set of instructions on how much to save and how much to spend. I'd take my portion, buy a new hat and go to church, just to be surrounded by the company. And of course, to hear the preaching of the Reverend Joseph Thomas.

The Reverend Thomas was a man born with the fire of God coursing though his veins. He'd a long serious face that would grow pale as ice when the words come on him.

Flames of righteousness seem to shoot out from his raven black hair and black eyes. His lips were a livid red and his white hands beat a golden dust from the pages of his Bible during his preaching. We women filled the front three pews, sweating profoundly under our fine hats, eyes half-closed to the driving incantation of his voice. And when it was all too much to bear, we shouted, surrendering our sins to the scalding flames of Reverend Thomas's preaching. The man was like lightning let loose in the church, and we all held up our hands to receive a healing bolt from that electrified touch.

Church was all right for the day. But there was nothing to keep my mind off of myself and my loneliness at night. There I was, a healthy young woman with a growing appetite for life, burning alone in bed. My body was becoming lush, my limbs rounded and soft, my breasts standing up almost by themselves. Beneath the darkened brown nipples milk tingled like champagne bubbles. Even the surface of my skin had grown so sensitive that a breeze from the window might set me to moaning for something more. But there wasn't anything more. Just my left hand tucked up tight between my thighs.

One night I lay in bed and decided something had to be done. I loved Caleb, but I hated being without him. It wasn't enough just to possess his letters lying scattered over the bed beside me. True, he always told me how much he loved me and how much he missed me. But the last letter said he was staying on the road a while, maybe even until after the baby was born because the money was good. It made me miserable to think all I had of my marriage was a few dollars tucked away in an egg jar and a shelf full of pretty hats. I needed him. Wanted him. But if I couldn't have him, then I wanted someone to help me in my need until he returned.

It wasn't long before the image of Reverend Thomas

came to my mind. I figured as he was a married man and a pillar of the church, he'd be above reproach and gossip. His wife Violet Thomas was a beautiful woman, with dark auburn hair and deep green eyes. She sang like an angel in the choir, and many women in the church envied her being married to the Reverend Thomas. But I always thought there was a kind of sadness in her eyes. A hurt I couldn't figure. They'd been married five years and still no children. I wondered now if that was the cause of her sadness. I liked the woman and would have been more friendly to her if I hadn't come up with my plan. I didn't want to give her trouble. I was just hoping I could borrow her husband in a quiet sort of a way.

I counted on the Reverend Thomas knowing as little as Caleb about pregnancy when I went to him on that afternoon. He was at the church preparing his sermon in his office. He was looking very handsome to me at that moment, running his pale hand through his black hair, his head bowed to his writing. His stern features were full of intelligence and passion. He looked up at me and the breath quickened in my chest at the keen gaze of those dark eyes.

"Yes, Sister Rosalie? Can I help you?"

"I do hope so, Reverend Thomas," I answered nervously, and lowered my eyes to my trembling hands. "Forgive me for asking this, Reverend Thomas, but do you know much about having babies?"

I heard him shift in his chair. "A man must protect himself from knowing too much of the sin of Eve," he answered in a low voice.

I found his reply encouraging, figuring it to mean he knew little enough about it. I plucked up my courage, but kept my eyes on my folded hands.

"Well, Reverend, I'm newly pregnant. But the trouble is my husband, Caleb Johnson, he left to go traveling before we both knew about my condition. Well, that has left me in a terrible fix."

"And what fix is that?" the Reverend asked.

"Well, a baby gets put together so to speak throughout the nine months he is carried in his mother's womb. The husband does his job every night to see that all parts are well and truly made."

At that, I glanced up to see how the Reverend was digesting this new bit of biology. He didn't seem to find it strange. I went on.

"But my husband left before knowing that he had got me with child. And now I am afraid that without a man to help me every day, I will give birth to a deformed baby, without a body, without arms or toes."

"Sister Rosalie, this is a hard thing for you," he said, and I was delighted by the genuine concern in his face.

"I wonder, as you are a man of God, and the only one I can trust with this unburdening of my soul, if you would help me in my time of need. Help me to finish making my child, Reverend." There was a moment of silence, and I let the words hang between us. "Confidentially, of course," I added.

"You want me to help finish making your baby?" he asked slowly. I knew he understood me finally as a rosy blush started up from his collarbone and stained his pale throat.

"Yes, Reverend. There is no other man I could ask who would understand that this is truly a mission of mercy and not an occasion of sin. My husband and I need your help."

I waited quietly while the Reverend struggled with the idea of serving God while making love to me. I must say, I didn't make it easy for him. My blouse was tight, the buttons straining over my full breasts, and my skirt wrapped around the plump length of my thighs. Pregnancy had given my hair a soft gold luster, and my skin was polished fresh as an apple.

"When?" he said so softly I almost didn't hear him.

"I'll say I'm to have Bible lessons, and I'll come to you every day, here in the church office after the dinner hour."

"Here?" he asked, his eyebrows rising. The room was small and cozy. There were only two chairs and the huge old mahogany desk spread over with papers and books. The desk looked a hard enough surface for my backside, but I wasn't too particular at the time. There was more than enough room on it for two willing people.

"Well, I'd like it best here in the church, where I can keep my mind on the healing presence of God," I said, and lowered my eyes again to my folded hands resting in my lap.

"Come tomorrow then," the Reverend said, and I heard him swallow very hard.

"Thank you kindly, Reverend," I whispered, and, without looking up, left his office, my heart charging like a racehorse rounding the homeward stretch.

Well, I won't say too much against the Reverend Thomas. He was after all in his mind a man doing a desperate woman a serious favor. But when I began those Bible lessons I first learned that the Reverend was a man sorely lacking in the knowledge of pleasuring a woman. It made me understand at last the sadness in Violet Thomas's eyes. Caleb was a lusty soul, not afraid to use his body, not afraid to hold and rock me until I just had to howl. That's why I missed him so. Until I'd met the Reverend, though, it never occurred to me that another man might not be so generous of spirit as my Caleb.

But the Reverend Thomas had a fear about him, and a way of touching a woman that made her feel more like a serpent than a bedmate. I decided that as long as I was settled on the idea of getting the Reverend to help me out every afternoon, I might as well give him a few lessons.

Not that he knew they were lessons, mind you. He just thought I was explaining the right way to set about making up a child. "Please, Reverend, if you'd just kiss me here, it will be better for my baby. And here, too. Yes, I know it's my breast, but it will help make the baby's heart strong. And Reverend, move it in slower, that's right, no need to hurry just yet . . . oh yes, that's doing it nicely. Praise God, I think a little faster now if you please, Reverend. No sir, you're not hurting me. I swear it. We're making the legs today, and they've got to be strong. Give it to me strongly, Reverend."

Oh my. Those afternoons on that mahogany desk were some kind of education. The Reverend was a good student, and he got to know by the sounds of my sighs, the heaving of my chest, the curving of my spine that indeed, he was pushing the clay of my unborn baby around just right. The only thing I had to stop him from doing was singing hymns while we were going at it. I was afraid we'd attract too much attention. Most people already knew I was pregnant before I came to the Reverend, so it didn't raise too many eyebrows when I went every day for Bible lessons. They just figured that in my condition, I wasn't thinking too much about sex, but God.

Well, I did think a lot about God. And thanked Him often for the wondrous changes in my body and the strange joy I found in making love while being as big as a prizewinning pumpkin. I'd be up on all fours, my huge belly suspended like the full moon over that mahogany desk. My climaxes were slow and long, a contraction of pleasure that began at the very bottom of my belly and rose in a steady rippling wave of heat. My breath came in hard gasps as the baby, furious at having his small space squeezed even more tightly by my fun, kicked his tiny legs into my lungs. The Reverend, leaning over me and holding on to my heavy breasts, came away with palmfuls of milk.

One day, I got a letter from Caleb. He was finally coming home the following month, just around the baby's due date. I felt a kind of peace settle over me at last. I was so full and sated with my condition. The baby had turned and his head was like an orange wedged between my thighs, while the soles of his feet were tucked up under my heart. I went with heavy swaying steps to the Reverend's office and sat down in the chair. My knees creaked and I crossed my swollen ankles. I looked at that man and realized that over the last months I had grown rather fond of him. He was a good man in his own way. Gentle, and now, loving enough to please any woman.

"Well, Reverend, our work is done," I said with a sigh. "This baby is coming soon and thanks to you, I know my child will be born healthy and strong."

"It has been a privilege, Sister Rosalie, to help you in this endeavor. And may God shine his love on you and your new baby."

The Reverend looked disappointed when I left, but I was just glad that in all that time no one had ever found out about us. And I was confident no one ever would. I was pleased with myself that day and went home to await the birth of my baby and the homecoming of my beloved husband.

"You are one lucky woman, Sister Violet, to be married to the Reverend Thomas. How that man can speak. Why it must just sweep you off your feet!"

I looked at the older woman beaming at me, knowing her to be too kind to be envious, and smiled politely. "Why thank you, Sister Laurel. I am honored to be his wife."

It was true. I was honored to be Mrs. Violet Thomas, the wife of the very Reverend Joseph Thomas. But I wasn't particularly happy about it either. Being married to the

Reverend Thomas had its advantages and decided draw-backs. After all, he was well regarded in the community, and we lived in a comfortable style because of it. He was a man of passionate concern for his flock and for the teachings of God. But he didn't have the same passion when it came to me, his wife. It wasn't that he didn't love me after his own fashion. He just felt that as a man of God it was important to distance himself from the temptations of the flesh.

If I had only known that before I married. I wanted the fire of his words to be realized in the fire of his embrace. I wanted children, a son to look up to his father, a daughter to stand graceful as a lily by my side. But in five years of marriage, the sex had been so meager that it seemed impossible that I would ever know the pleasure of conceiving.

The Reverend Thomas came into my room on the night of the full moon once a month. And that was all. We would begin by praying on our knees. That done, I would lie on the bed, my eyes closed, my face turned to the wall as he had instructed. At first I used to pray to myself that maybe I could sway him in my arms to a more lingering embrace. But he kept his mind on God. And singing "Praise My Shepherd Walk With Me," he'd give me the solitary thrust of a man doing his righteous duty. No lover's kiss. No warm embrace. It was all to protect us from the stain of Eve's first sin.

There was nothing I thought I could do but endure the matter for the sake of my marriage and God. So I wasn't prepared when the Reverend told me the truth about Rosalie Johnson's baby boy. There had been a christening for the new baby and, of course, I was required to be there. Oh how the serpents of envy bit my heart looking at that beautiful child. He had red cheeks and strong limbs. He wailed, and both of his doting parents fussed over him.

My breasts ached, my own emptiness seemed to mock me even as I congratulated the young woman on her new child.

It was later, at our dinner, that my husband revealed to me his role in creating that perfect child. The longer he talked, the more I stared at him in mute amazement. It wasn't the sin of adultery that inflamed me. The man was innocent of knowledge and did only what he thought was right to help a member of his flock. But it was the sin of pride that I found intolerable. He was overproud of his handiwork. Proud that he had had some hand in sculpting the final form of that beautiful child. This man who would not give me my own child to hold, believed that he had been instrumental in allowing another woman to have hers. I was ill with hurt.

But I had my own pride to think of and my own dignity to uphold. I said nothing, other than a passing comment. I complained of a headache and went to my room to lie down. I took off my clothes and mother-naked lay down on the bed. All I could think of was the men that I had refused in the past. Those other men with warm hands and knees nudging me under my mother's dinner table. Men who seemed overeager to hustle me into their marriage beds. But I had been charmed when I met the Reverend, pleased at last to meet a man who spoke to me with a quiet voice and a restrained hand. Now, lying on the bed, the silk counterpane cool under my skin, I prayed to be visited by every one of those eager men. I didn't care about the extent of my sinful thoughts. I would have coupled with a hundred men if only one of them would have made me feel more like a woman and given to me a child. Bitter tears flowed out of my eyes.

The next day I packed my bags and, making an excuse, I took a coach and went to my mother's house. I stayed there three months, wondering what was to become of me.

Rage seared my soul, lashing out at the memory of that woman Rosalie leaning over her baby. Had I seen her wink at my husband at the christening? Had they really sprawled themselves like animals to copulate on the desk I gave him as a wedding present? Had he really been so undignified his trousers draped around his knees, while I sat at home, ignorant and barren? I thought of revenge, then dismissed it as too cold-blooded. What would I do? Steal her child, kill my husband, write a letter and then throw myself in the river? All of those ideas were worse than foolish.

But sometime later, when the heat of my anger had abated, I came to realize that there was a third road between angry-sorrow and angry-revenge. It was called the road to fair play. I would do unto another as was done to me, I decided. Not to hurt another, but to heal myself.

I sat down and wrote a letter to the Reverend. I wanted to come home. But as I was going to be carrying most of my mother's jewelry that she had recently bequeathed to me while still living, I needed an escort. I told my husband that I feared traveling alone with so much wealth on my person. I asked if that nice Brother Caleb Johnson who traveled far distances on his sales routes might not assist me by accompanying me home on his next journey out.

I sent the letter and two weeks later got a reply in my husband's firm clear handwriting. The Reverend had organized it all for me. Brother Caleb Johnson was arriving on such a date to bring me home again in his buggy. The Reverend figured it would take us about three weeks or so on the road as Brother Johnson had to stop at various stores where he had accounts. This suited me very well, and, for the first time in months, I smiled.

On the morning Caleb Johnson was to arrive, I took a good look at myself in the mirror. I was a still an attractive woman. I was older than Rosalie, but I had a full maturity that the younger woman had yet to acquire. She shone brightly like brass, but I was polished gold, gleaming with a rich elegance. I wore my long hair down, like an unmarried woman, and put a small dash of color on my lips. I was just finishing buttoning my cream-colored silk blouse when I heard the groan of the buggy wheels and the braying of Brother Caleb's mule.

I hurried down, kissed my mother good-bye, and walked to the buggy. I can't tell you how it pleased me when I saw Brother Caleb take one look and then another at me as I approached. He scrambled down from the buckboard with a quickness I could not have imagined and took my bags from me.

"Morning, Sister Violet," he said, lifting his hat with one hand while the other hoisted my bag into the buggy's hold.

"Thank you so much, Brother Caleb, for helping me in my time of need," I answered. I gathered up my skirts, raising the hem well above my ankles and calves as I prepared to climb up onto the buckboard. Brother Caleb took me by the waist to help me and I heard the sharp intake of his breath as he glanced down at my bared legs. I pulled down my skirt, and he let go of my waist finally with a shy grin. I smiled back and hoped that Brother Caleb knew as little about the workings of a woman's body as did my husband.

I didn't feel much like talking on the first day of our trip. I just watched the road curving away before us, feeling a new sort of strength well up in me. After five years of hiding what was sensual in me, I was well pleased to find it not gone after all. I could see out of the corners of my eyes that Brother Caleb was watching me. Too many nights alone on the road for you, I thought. Too many nights away from that wife of yours. I'd turn suddenly and catch his glance, pleased to watch him fumble the reins while his face bloomed brighter than a June rose.

That night we stopped in a small wood. The buggy carried everything we needed to set up a tidy and comfortable camp. Caleb unhitched the mule, made a fire, then set beans and bacon on to boil along with coffee and biscuits. He unrolled two sets of sleeping blankets, laying them a discreet distance apart. I made a point of tucking my jewel bag under my pillow. We ate, chatted a while and then said good night. Slipping under the blankets, I pulled off my skirt and blouse, just so he'd know I was sleeping in my shift. He pretended not to notice, but I saw him cast a lingering gaze on my lace-covered stays thrown out last on top of my skirt and blouse. I listened to him wrestle with sleep, twisting and turning as if the nearness of me agitated him some.

I stayed awake a long time, waiting until I was sure he was asleep. Then I got out of my blankets, and, going to the buggy, stuffed all of my mother's jewels into a second pouch hidden in my suitcase. I slipped back under the blankets and, staring up at the stars, wondered briefly if I had the courage. But when I looked over at Brother Caleb sleeping near me, I lost all doubts. He was partially uncovered and bare to the waist. He had a nice manly chest with a small patch of curly hair. One strong arm was flung out, and I started imagining what it might be like to be held tight by such an arm. So I pinched my cheeks until the tears come, then started crying out loudly.

"Oh, Brother Caleb, help me," I sobbed.

He sat up with a sleepy, confused face, his hair tousled.

"Wha-what is it?" he mumbled. "Are you all right, Sister Violet?" he asked.

"No, sir. I am not all right. Please help me. Oh God, help me."

"What's happening?" he said, now awake and alarmed at the sight of my tear-streaked face. "Are you in pain?"

"Yes, Brother Caleb, pain of the worst kind."

He scuttled out of his sleeping blankets and came next to me. His trousers, worn low, clung to the sides of his slim hips. I inhaled the strong scent of male sweat and damp earth, and it made my heart beat like a tambourine.

"Do you know what happens to a woman when she is alone without her husband for a long period of time?" I asked tearfully.

"No, ma'am," he said, with a light shake of his head, clearly puzzled by my question.

"Well, it happens that if a woman is not receiving enough fluids from her husband, then her body, craving that which it lacks, will begin to steal from the woman anything that is near it." I held up the empty jewel bag.

Caleb Johnson stared hard at the empty bag, his brow pulled into a frown.

"I don't quite understand you," he murmured.

"It's our bodies," I said patiently. "Women have sinful and greedy parts. We are saved from them by the labors of a man. It is his attentions that keep us from stealing from ourselves."

"Uh-uh," Caleb answered, but I could see I wasn't getting through to him. I drew a deep breath and decided to be blunt.

"In these last months that I have been away from my husband my body has turned against itself. It has stolen my jewels. Taken all them into itself. I can feel them cluttering up my womb. I need these jewels to pay for the new roof on the church."

Caleb's mouth dropped open. "Should I fetch a doctor?" he asked.

"No. I would be too embarrassed by my body's betrayal to seek help from a stranger. I wondered if I might impose on you to help me regain my jewels? If you could provide me with the same attention I receive from my husband, I know my jewels will be given up. It would be the Lord's work to save these jewels for the church, Brother Caleb."

"Can't it wait? You know, until you're home and with the Reverend again?"

"In another day, my blood will be poisoned by these very same jewels living in my body. Please, Brother Caleb, you've got to help me." I pressed my hands together in fervent prayer, aware that the neckline of my shift was gaping open. I saw the young man struggle to keep his eyes on my tearful face and not my heaving bosom.

It wasn't much of a battle, and after about two heartbeats, Caleb ran his hand through his tousled hair and gave me his shy smile.

"Well, I suppose I could help you out. For the church, of course. Do I need to do it in any special sort of a way? You know, so as not to make the pain worse?"

"Only be firm with me. It's the only way to teach that thieving part of me who's master," I said, nearly losing my breath in my excitement.

"Well, all right. I guess I can do that," he said, and unbuckled his trousers.

In gladness did I lie back on those blankets and allow Brother Caleb to teach my thieving parts a thing or two. Lord, the lessons they learned that first night. A few times over, in fact, before the dawn came. I had always believed it was meant to be like that—full of fire, pleasure, and sometimes just the edge of pain. I kept my eyes open that first time and saw everything that I had missed with the Reverend when my eyes were closed and my face turned toward the wall. I looked down the length of that man's naked body and saw how a man swelled with desire. I watched fascinated as it rose in a sturdy column, standing upright with a mind of its own. I even held it in my hand, astounded by its weight and the warm throb of blood. I watched the way every muscle in that man's thighs contracted as he pushed himself into me, the moonlight falling over the curve of his shoulders, the sweat slick on his chest. And then I looked up and watched his face as the surge come over him, making him grimace, growl like a wild animal, and then his features soften unexpectedly, like a child falling into sleep. How it all thrilled me.

The second time Caleb Johnson came to me that night, I didn't watch his face, nor his body. I wanted only to know how good it could feel in my body. I traveled through my limbs, opening my senses as a woman opens doors in a house too long closed and locked. I took that feeling of pleasure into my fingertips until they glowed, light and porous. I let it enter my mouth through his hot kisses and fill up my chest. Heat loosened the tightness of my throat, released the breath held beneath my heart, flattened my hunched shoulders into the hard ground, and arrowed down into my belly. Caleb then turned us over, pulling me on top of him. He put his fingertips into my armpits, the heels of his palms cupped around my breasts.

Never had sex been so frightening and so demanding. I was allowed to do something. I was asked to be alive and participate. Suddenly there were no walls imprisoning my desire. Out there in the open forest I experienced vertigo, as though I had been pitched high into the air. The wind was cool on my heated skin. I spread my arms wide to catch the dark shadows of the swaying trees in my hands. The man beneath me stirred, his hips locked against mine, and I remembered that I was staked to the ground after all. I leaned forward, my hands braced against his chest, and started to move. But no matter how high I rose on that white column of flesh, he found me and pulled me down hard over him again. The night echoed with the smack of our bare skin meeting and then parting over and over again.

And when early dawn brightened a corner of the sky, and Brother Caleb had fallen off into sleep after a hard night of helping out his church, I slipped back to the buggy and found my suitcase. I fished around in the hidden pouch and pulled up my mother's good diamond brooch. Getting back in between the blankets, I laid the brooch between my legs, like a shell washed up by the tide.

"Why look here, Brother Caleb, the first jewel has been returned," I said, shaking the slumbering man awake. "I'm starting to feel better already," I added.

Brother Caleb squinted at the brooch out of one eye and smiled. "Glad to oblige," he said. And then pulling the covers around us again and tucking me under his arm, he went back to sleep.

So it went for the three weeks of our journey home. Night after night, Caleb offered his heartfelt services, and every morning another jewel appeared on my thighs. If he ever had a contrary thought about what we were doing, he never mentioned it once. By the time we were in sight of our hometown my bag of jewels was filled up again. And I was ready enough to return to my husband, the Reverend. Perhaps that seems strange. But the truth was that while I more than enjoyed the nighttime company of Brother Caleb, I did miss the conversation and the passionate faith of my husband. Brother Caleb took things as they came, never seeking to find the hand of God in any of it. I sorely missed the better parts of my husband's learning and all the lively arguments we often had over issues of our church.

And there was something else, too. I knew that day when I stepped down from Brother Caleb's buggy in front of my own house again, that I was with child. I knew it in the way my palms broke into a sweat, the sudden flush that heated my cheeks, and the spark of pain that pricked the sides of my womb. I could feel it in the shift of my hipbones opening into a wide bowl to hold the full wonder of a new life. I think even God was happy for me because I arrived home on the night of the full moon, and my husband was only too happy to take me to bed. The child would come close enough to the remembered date that he might never know the truth. And maybe it was me, or maybe it was my long absence from home, or just maybe I have Rosalie and Caleb to thank, but for the first time since we had lain together as man and wife, my husband and I looked at each other without fear as he entered me. And for the very first time that I could remember, he didn't sing hymns but called out my name in the throes of his passion.

Well, as I said in the beginning, it was funny the way it all turned out. I might never have known that Violet Thomas got me back with my own husband if I hadn't gone and lost my jar of egg money. I'd hid it earlier in the day to keep the baby from swallowing the coins. But I was so fractious with work, that I clean forgot where I hid it. I told Caleb about it when he got back from one of his journeys, and, instead of helping me look, why he pulled me by the hand into the bedroom, laid me down, and made wild love to me all afternoon. And when he was done, he looked over at me with a smug grin and said: "There. That ought to fix it."

"Fix what?" I said, still confused by this unexpected turn of events.

"Your thieving woman part. It went and stole the egg money because I've been gone from home too much."

"Caleb Johnson, what are you talking about?" I asked, starting to get angry.

He told me then, and I almost wished he hadn't. Told me all about helping Violet Thomas and her thieving parts. How she was afraid for her life. And how they were putting on a new roof with that money because of him helping her out. I just stared at him, too shocked to utter even one word. I was thinking to myself, that bitch Violet Thomas, how could she? That stealer of husbands, that hussy, that wanton she-devil cloaked in the ministry of the church. Damn her to hell.

But it did me no good to swear up and down about Violet Thomas. After all, she was only returning the favor I'd taken off of her. And after I'd calmed down and thought longer about it, I figured I didn't really mind half so much. On account of Violet's little tale about a woman's thieving parts, my Caleb decided it was time he did his business in town, lest I go and steal all the egg money while he was out on the road. So now it's almost as much fun at night again as it was the day we were married.

And as for Violet Thomas, well I saw her in church the other day. I had Caleb sitting on one side of me, trying hard to listen, and the baby on the other side, fussing. Violet was sitting alone, leaning her back against the pew and her arms resting over the rising bulge of her growing belly. She had a glow of pure happiness about her. Though he was in rare form that day, the Reverend looked a little tired around the eyes to me. I got to thinking it was probably all that hard work every night of shaping the ears, the nose, the fingernails, and the rest of his coming child.

Violet glanced away from the Reverend and caught my eye. I looked at her and she looked back at me. And with the fire and brimstone of the Reverend's sermon hailing down around our ears, we just nodded at one another and smiled.

The Orphan
the Moth and
the Magic

HARVEY JACOBS

Harvey Jacobs began his career with the Village
Voice, *then published* East, *a weekly newspaper on
New York's lower east side. He joined ABC-TV,
where he became active in the early development of
the global satellite system as an executive with ABC's
Worldvision Network. Since 1973, he has lived as a
freelancer based in New York City, publishing the
novels* The Juror, Summer on a Mountain of
Spices, Beautiful Soup, *the forthcoming* American
Goliath, *and the short-story collection* The Egg of
the Glak. *His short stories have appeared in a wide
variety of magazines including* Omni *and* The Magazine of Fantasy and Science Fiction, *and in some
forty anthologies. He has also written widely for TV.*

 *Jacobs writes witty satirical fiction. His previous
story in our series had a thumb-sized female protagonist who looked a lot like Pia Zadora. "The Orphan
the Moth and the Magic" is based loosely on "The
Cottager and His Cat" from* The Crimson Fairy
Book *edited by Andrew Lang. Jacobs's "cat" is a
very lucky creature.*

The Orphan
the Moth and
the Magic

Once, in a time apart, a young man called Wilbur Winkle, burdened by terrible poverty—but otherwise gifted with a lithe and powerful frame, excellent good looks, glowing good health, and a warm and outgoing disposition—knelt at the bedside of his dying father.

While his mother lit candles and murmured prayers to a pantheon of gods and goddesses whose work she respected, Wilbur took his father's pale hand.

The old man had the habit of gesturing while he spoke, and used the little strength left him to move his arm up and down, up and down, in order to underline his last words. Wilbur had the feeling he was holding a pump handle which forced astonishing confessions from his progenitor's trembling mouth.

Wilbur's father had been a constant, if remote, presence in the boy's life, and Wilbur did not want to see him go, for reasons both emotional and economic. The family was very poor, living in the most dilapidated hut in a village of slums. There was hardly money for food or fuel enough to sustain their meager existence. His father's diligent labor kept the wolf from the door, but the sound of its snarling was never far away. Now Wilbur would be the sole support of his mother and himself, and he knew he had no talent for the business of business or anything else. He'd done a few odd jobs, but his income was hardly worth counting.

Which is why Wilbur was surprised to hear his father reveal that, far from being a penniless wretch, Mr. Winkle was, in fact, a seasoned miser who had amassed a considerable fortune.

"I have worked dawn to dusk my whole life long," the ancient said, "complaining only that the days were so short as to limit my profits. Each evening, before collapsing from exhaustion, I managed to secrete a coin or two in the wooden box that once held your mother's skimpy trousseau. Now that box is brimming with gold, and I am pleased to inform you that the treasure is there for you to manage for my loyal and devoted wife.

"I hope, Wilbur, that you will nurture the treasure wisely. Ideally, you will do as I did, which is to deprive yourself of all pleasure and luxury. Then you will have the joy of passing the hoard on, in due time, to your offspring. It makes the idea of death almost cozy.

"For a small indulgence, you might consider buying Mother a bolt of cloth with which to make herself a dress to mourn in, since the robe she wears is so frayed as to expose significant portions of her anatomy better kept covered. And as for yourself, I would not begrudge you some frivolous gift, considering your youth. Perhaps you might splurge on some delicacy like a fresh raisin, which you could chew slowly."

"I understand, sir," Wilbur said, trying to conceal his astonishment, which wavered between shock and delight. If his father was not hallucinating, he and his mother would be rich, and it would take more than a raisin to make up for the icy decades of wretched poverty. "Be certain, Father, that I will take your advice to heart. Rest well and without concern."

"And don't splurge on my funeral. Just wrap my corpse in old newspapers and bury me in the swampy section of the cemetery."

"I will follow your instructions to the letter."

Just then, Wilbur's mother came running through the sickroom chasing a fat white moth, shouting, "Your father will surely recover! I have asked for some sign and here it is. Hallelujah!" The moth, her omen, then dived into the only candle permitted to burn by her parsimonious husband. There was a sizzling sound and a sudden flare of light. The moth turned to smoke even as Wilbur felt life leave his father's honest hand.

"He is dead," Wilbur said, as gently as possible.

"Perhaps it was only a moth," his mother said.

"I mean father."

"So much for divine intervention," said the heartbroken woman. "Woe is me, abandoned by my protector and provider in this hovel where my garden is lucky to produce a gnarled turnip or bent asparagus in the best of times and burdened with an only child who is without prospects or ambition. Alas, the future looks as bleak as winter's bowels."

Wilbur decided to keep his mother from news of their fortune until he could at least confirm its existence. Besides, he sensed it wrong to speak crassly of money until his father's new ghost was a bit farther down the road to eternity. So he embraced the poor widow, and together they wept, lamenting death's dominion, until sleep came to soften her grief.

When he heard her sad snoring, Wilbur began a frantic search of their hut. After fruitless hours, just as he was about to yield to fatigue, he discovered a loose plank in the battered floor. When he lifted that splintery board, he found the box his father had described. He pried open its lid, and there he saw gold enough for ten lifetimes of leisure.

He replaced the lid carefully, and the floorboard, said a quick prayer for his father's repose, did a silent but joyful dance with his shadow, then went to bed.

Somewhere from night's mystery came a disturbing dream. The fat, white moth so recently broiled by the candle flame was newly animated. It flew onto Wilbur's nose, beating its wings in grotesque applause, and said, in a voice like a creaking hinge, "Wilbur, I hate to bring you so disturbing a message, but you must know that soon you will become sole heir to the contents of that brimming box. For your mother is herself living on borrowed time and soon will join her dead spouse. Her constant nagging has made the gods angry, and they will endure no more of it.

"As for the gold, brace yourself, lad, and be strong. For you must carry it to the nearest beach and hurl your inheritance to the tide. Keep not a single coin. That money is tainted and cursed. Your father, who seemed an honest laborer, became involved, through keeping bad company, in a series of outlandish pursuits including usury, kidnapping, theft, gambling, pimping, and dealing in controlled substances. He was an adulterer, a pornographer, he practiced medicine without a license and was not above plagiarism or the robbing of graves."

"Everyone has their little faults," Wilbur said. "And even if I believe those outrageous accusations, must the living atone for the sins of the dead?"

"Absolutely," the moth told him, hovering before his eyes, "for that is the way of things." Then the moth circled Wilbur's head and flew out an open window.

Wilbur woke in a sweat. It was already morning. His mother was up and cooking a breakfast of nettles and Spam. Brushing his nightmare aside, Wilbur leapt out of bed, and said, "Enough of that slop. I must show you something to help gladden this grey, miserable day."

While the puzzled woman watched, Wilbur exposed the hidden box and its astonishing bonanza. He explained how his father had slaved to accumulate so much, saying nothing of his dream or the dire pronouncements of the depressing insect. But instead of celebrating, his mother turned beet red with a rage she had never before demonstrated.

"All those months, days, hours, minutes, all those years when my arteries filled with the wet sand of despair, all that while I walked on a carpet of gold?" she screamed. Then she beat at her husband's cadaver and fell over in a heap.

Wilbur howled at his parents' grave site. His anguish was sincere, for he missed them both. Still, even as he cast final clods on their tombs, his mind flipped through catalogs and wandered through exotic cities.

Of course young Wilbur was eager to enjoy his new incarnation as a man of property.

But he soon realized he must do as the moth commanded. He was simply too good and moral a youth to prosper from treasure earned through evil deeds and questionable practices. So, like a sinner carrying a burden of guilt, he carried his box of gold to the lip of the land.

As a sullen fog wiped color from the world, Wilbur watched waves roll and listened to the heavy hiss of the surf. He breathed deeply of the salty air, shrugged, then hurled handfuls of shimmering coins into the bottomless void.

Orphaned, and destitute, Wilbur felt that he, too, might as well be a corpse. He fell onto the beach in a faint, hoping as he lost consciousness that the incoming tide would soon end his misery. And his bones would have been toys for a mermaid, but for a school of mindless sardines which ventured toward shore, attracted by the sparkles of gold that had rained on the water.

The dean of sardines informed his followers that the golden sparks must be caused by hundreds of fish-cherubs frolicking in the rollers. Thus, when the tide lifted Wilbur in its wet arms and carried him off toward the horizon, those misguided sardines formed a natural raft that supported his body and bore him to an alien part of the world.

While he traveled, Wilbur dreamed of the moth again. This time it was busy pulling itself free from the web of a smug and patient spider.

Considering that this moth had caused him to surrender all chance for happy affluence, Wilbur sided with the spider. It would be a cheerful thing to watch that winged conscience stung, then sucked dry of its preaching. But the resourceful moth managed to escape.

"You did the right thing," it said to Wilbur, gasping after its ordeal. "Your reward will be peace of mind. And remember, sometimes great sacrifice transforms to great gain." The frustrated spider snickered and broke wind, which Wilbur himself might have done had his responses been quicker.

"How could I have been such a fool as to take the word of a vaporized spirit from the realm of darkness? What must my father and mother think of me now?"

"Fair question," the moth said. "Frankly, I was taken aback by your gullibility. Most people give me short shrift or worse. I can only conclude that you are the product of excellent nurture, tranquil toilet training, and a mother who was close to a saint."

Wilbur woke, drenched and weak, on a foreign shore. He learned he was still alive when a scavenger crab bit his toe. While he howled in pain, he surveyed a landscape more barren and ominous than the one he had left.

Mounds of black ash and rock stretched to a forest where from a few stumpy trees dangled pinched, wrinkled fruit. Even the sparse population of birds looked exhausted and depressed. They wailed like mourning doves.

Wilbur took stock of his assets. His total currency was his youth and three wriggling sardines he found trapped in the pocket of his tunic.

At least he could have a snack before exploring this unknown kingdom. Wilbur laid the wrigglers on a flat stone and tucked a frayed handkerchief into his shirt to serve as a bib. But before he could enjoy even that modest morsel, it was stolen from him. The strangest beast he had ever seen came bounding out of nowhere, a black furry thing with a tail like a brush and a mouth full of menacing teeth. It moved quick as time, jumping and dodging every obstacle. In a blink, the creature gobbled up the doomed sardines and vanished.

Wilbur sighed, the experience confirming that this new country was no hospitable host. Still, he shook off his lethargy and trudged in the direction of the sunset.

After walking many miles over treacherous terrain, now with the moon at his back, Wilbur spotted a pinpoint of light. Falling into holes and stumbling on gnarled vines, he made the light his beacon, even as his nemesis moth would have done, driven by instinct, hypnotized beyond risk.

If that light was the fire destined to consume him, so be it. Wilbur was too weary, hungry, and thirsty to consider wiser choices.

Finally, Wilbur saw a nice enough house made more cheerful by a cluster of candles he could see through the window and the smells of hot food. He girded his loins, smoothed back his hair, tucked in his shirt, and ventured to tap at the door.

His tap got no answer so he rapped harder, then forgot the better rules of conduct and pushed at the barrier. The door swung open as if bolts and locks had not been invented.

Wilbur found himself in a well-furnished room. He heard sounds of creaky singing. He peered into a kitchen where a fire blazed in the hearth and quickly determined that the broken chords of song came from the oldest crone he had ever seen. As she chanted her buoyant, if fractured, melody, she leaned over a stove where delicious things fried, boiled, and simmered, making music of their own.

"Excuse me, grandmother," Wilbur said. "I am a famished stranger and mean no harm. I come in peace and ask only . . ." The woman paid him no heed. It did not take long for him to realize she was as deaf as indifference and blind as certainty.

While she carried a splendid assortment of vittles to her table, Wilbur reached out to touch her brittle shoulder. "Stop that, you ignorant cat," she snapped. "Where have you been? They came from the palace to fetch you and were very cross with me, I can tell you. Since the King's ambassadors will not return until tomorrow, have your dinner and sleep. I want you at your best, believe me, for you must justify your high price. Our beloved ruler is a fair and tolerant man, but a stickler for value."

"As was my father," Wilbur said, though he talked to a post. "I think you have confused me with someone or something you call *cat*, madam. Whatever *cat* may be, it isn't me."

Wilbur's own village was too poor to sustain pets of any

kind, or even support the notion of cats, dogs, or canaries. What scant edibles there were went to soothe growling human stomachs. The only animals he knew from experience were cows with strained udders, mules with visible skeletons, overworked chickens, and two anxious pigs who belonged to the tax collector. Past those, he had never even seen a mouse.

"Now, cat, let me fill your dish. Eat well. This is our last and final meal together," the woman said, while Wilbur, amazed, watched her spoon meat and vegetables into a plate on the floor. He could only conclude that this *cat* she addressed must be some kind of midget or infant with an insatiable appetite.

He knew he could correct her misconception simply by forcing her to run a hand over his amiable face. But the dish was tempting, the room was warm, and too much revelation might result in quick banishment.

"I must confess, cat, when you first entered my life I thought you intrusive. But I have grown to like you, and I certainly appreciate your talents. When the poor shipwrecked sailor who brought you to me gave up his ghost, I never dreamed what a treasure you would bring. But, being the only cat in this kingdom and something of a marvel, even a miracle, I have developed a feeling akin to affection for you. Though you are a self-centered, undependable wretch. I hope you will remember me fondly long after you shift allegiance to your new master."

Wilbur was already squatting to devour his feast. The crone bent over and patted the hair on his head. "What a mat," she said. "But I have combed you and bathed you once, and that is enough." Then she sat at the table and had her own supper.

Wilbur was so filled by the meal, so lulled by his comfortable surroundings, he dozed on the floor. His sensible plan was to rise at first light and depart with no harm done. The only possible problem might come from *cat* itself, who might return to resent the intruder. But he could explain himself easily enough, and if the thing called *cat* had an ounce of compassion, Wilbur could expect a reasonable chance for detente.

That night, Wilbur's sleep was untroubled. No moth flew through his mind spouting platitudes. But his awakening was abrupt. He felt a pull, then a yank. The woman had tied a leather thong around his neck, attached to a leash. Wilbur opened his eyes and found himself tethered, gazing at four grimly polished boots.

"That is the cat?" said a booming voice. Wilbur stared up at two soldiers in uniforms covered with acres of braid. The one who spoke held the end of the tether in a white-gloved hand.

"Of course that is the cat," the crone answered. "What did you expect?"

"I'm not sure," the soldier said. "Something different. But if that is the cat, then that is the cat and best we get moving. It is no short journey to the royal palace, and you have caused us to make the trip twice."

Wilbur remembered the woman's words about the only cat in the country and its unusual origin. He was about to speak up when he had second thoughts. These soldiers already complained of the inconvenience they had endured on their cat-fetching mission.

Now, if they learned that they had an impostor on their hands, he might well feel their wrath. And he knew of the wrath of soldiers. If they'd come for *cat*, he would be *cat* until he found a better time for explanations.

Wilbur rode to his new home in a coach shaped like a plum he had once been given for Christmas. The soldiers who escorted him rode magnificent horses decked out in plumes and jeweled bridles, a far cry from the spavined mules of Wilbur's acquaintance.

The regal procession reached a most satisfactory palace built on a high hill and guarded by a moat. Its drawbridge had already been lowered and lined with twenty trumpeters blowing rousing fanfares. King Axel himself stood at the palace gate, a round fellow wrapped in a cloud of ermine. Under a massive crown, his face was cherry red, jolly, and full of anticipation.

Wilbur jumped down from the coach, staying close to the ground since that seemed expected of him. The King could not restrain his curiosity. The monarch waddled to examine this cat he had heard so much about. Thus Wilbur was probed, sniffed, scratched, and even kissed on his forehead, no small greeting from one so supremely powerful.

"Something of a disappointment," the King said, "but nothing can match one's imagination. I wish that my Queen had lived to see this beast. At least the Princess will be delighted with our new courtier."

Wilbur followed King Axel into a fabulous throne room. When his majesty took his traditional seat on the grand chair Wilbur found a place at his slippered feet.

"Where is my daughter? Summon my darling Etoile this minute. For days she has speculated on what this cat of ours would look like and was nowhere close in her fantasies. Twelve dangling legs, five rolling eyes, a tongue as long as a hall rug. Ah, that child has a limitless capacity for fantasy. And someday she is destined to rule this land. Lord help the common folk."

Soon after, the Princess arrived with her ladies-in-waiting. Wilbur had prepared to announce his duplicity and throw himself on King Axel's mercy, but when he saw Etoile he could only let out a gush of astonishment. If he had never seen a cat, he certainly was unprepared for this Princess, in the full bloom of splendor.

Wilbur had heard tales of love and beauty but assumed

they were only the lies of minstrels paid to manufacture impossible trinkets in rhyme. Now he was struck by a barrage of honey-dipped arrows that pierced him in places that had never seen the sun. He heard himself issue another noise, a high-pitched squeal whose recipe called for equal measures of dazzle and delight.

"So that is our cat!" Etoile said. "And that is its voice! So much for rumors and secondhand descriptions. I envisioned it more like a truncated dragon."

"Yes," King Axel said, "you were way off the mark, my child. And who told you the real thing always falls short of its billing?"

"You did, my King," Etoile said in a twinkling tinkle. "I have learned yet another valuable lesson though; dragon or not, I think I am most pleased with this cat."

"Then take responsibility for its well-being," her father said, beaming. "Will you do so? That, too, should prove instructional for a future Queen. Life leaves messes, and each moment of joy demands compensation."

"Most willingly do I accept your mandate, Father. Until the chore challenges my attention. I am easily bored, as you know, Sire. I hope, though, that this cat does not defecate."

"The old crone who charged me a ransom has left a list of instructions and suggestions for its maintenance. It seems this animal is subject to fits of temperament and must be constantly cuddled and humored in order to perform its duties at maximum. As for its habits, we will be obliged to cope."

Then the King turned his large face to Wilbur, and said, "My daughter, the Princess Etoile, will be your keeper and protector until the time when your antics cause her to yawn. So, cat, do your best to provide her with a variety of amusements. But never forget your reason for being here. We all carry our weight in this palace, and some carry more weight than others, eh?"

The courtiers and ladies all chuckled and applauded the King's witticism. Wilbur kept silent and pretended not to understand a word. He did not yet know how a cat behaved, nor what were its virtues or limitations. But he did grin shyly and heard ooohs and ahhhs of approval at his enigmatic expression.

Then there was a scream from one of Etoile's attendants. She danced in place though no music inspired her. Wilbur saw a miserable object rush down her leg and skitter across the marble floor. It was the size of three large sausages, had a tail like a needle and eyes like the buttons on a devil's vest.

"Oh, good, good. A rat!" the King shouted. "A fat, obnoxious rat for the taking. Don't you see it, cat? Well, then? Pounce. Rip. Tear. Show us that what we have heard is the truth."

Wilbur made no move except to back away from the disgusting and arrogant invader. He was too frightened to breathe.

"What explains this reticence?" roared the King, with venom in his voice.

"Oh, Father," Etoile chimed. "Our cat has just arrived. It must be dizzy from so abrupt a displacement. Give it time to grow acclimated. Would you expect even your best warrior to draw his sword and slay an enemy before the traditional salute? Patience, as you have told me so many times, in all things."

"Patience. Yes. Let me be patient. It is only that I so despise those rebel rodents that I long to see their nemesis at work to free us from the plague of vermin."

"And so it shall be," Princess Etoile assured him. "Today, let this cat rest. Tomorrow, he will hunt."

Slowly, Wilbur realized the royal problem. The first rat

proved only an appetizer. Dozens of vile relatives emerged from hidden places behind curtains and under furniture. They rushed helter-skelter wherever they wanted without obedience to, or fear of, any higher authority.

When evening came, Wilbur watched them cavort on the King's table and suck up turtle soup from Princess Etoile's delicate bowl. It dawned on him that, as resident cat, his job was to end the invasion. That was the reason the crone had been persuaded, even commanded, to sell him.

Since he had not the slightest idea of how to accomplish such a task, he thought it prudent to flee for his life at the earliest possible moment. It was too late for honesty.

His decision to escape the palace created a treacherous undertow of emotion. The very thought of leaving Princess Etoile produced the most intense anguish. But continuing his dastardly charade would be terminal.

After the banquet ended, it was the Princess who led Wilbur to her chamber. It was already late. A bouquet of candles flickered around her downy bed. Etoile vanished into an anteroom, where her maids helped her dress for repose.

Wilbur curled on the floor, making note of possible exits. It would be out the window for him, then into the moat, a short swim and a long dash to safety. There was no other way.

He thought again of the duplicity of the moth who had caused him to divest his assets, then promised hope of some palpable gain. Now he faced obliteration or, even at best, the loss of the glorious Etoile and a pain he would carry forever.

"Vile moth," Wilbur said in a whisper as a hairy rat dashed for the Princess's nighttime snack of crackers and caviar. "Is it my fault that you are no butterfly? Why have you inflicted such punishment on a good person like me, who deserves only grace?"

Wilbur's self-pity abated when Etoile entered her boudoir. If she was radiant before, she was luminous now beyond suns and moons. A sound escaped him so primitive that even the rat dropped a bead of Beluga and sprinted for cover.

"Sad cat on a cold floor," Etoile hummed. "Come share my bed. In the manual your last owner provided, she explained how you liked nothing more than to cuddle and snuggle.

"And so you shall. But first let me throw off this burdensome gown. It is our little secret, cat, that Princess Etoile greets her sleep wearing only the fabric of darkness."

On that day so filled with variety, Wilbur now found himself gazing at the landscape of Paradise. The mountains and valleys, the cliffs and the clefts, the endless plains, the forests of silken hair left him beyond all dimension of gratitude.

He turned crimson as Etoile extinguished the last small candle flame with her perfumed breath. It was very wrong to take such advantage, but Wilbur jumped onto her bed as he was commanded and there did his best to be more than the cat she wished him to be.

"Come out of your garments," Etoile coaxed him. "Be naked. I have never enjoyed seeing God's lesser creatures forced to wear costumes that only mask their true nature. There is pomp enough in my species, sweet cat, and no need for you to hide the beauty of your natural body."

Wilbur allowed himself to be undressed by hands as gentle as spring zephyrs. Following the list of instructions drawn by the crone, the Princess proceeded to snuggle and cuddle her curious cat, making sonorous noises for a lullaby. This was past all endurance for Wilbur, who felt his sap rise until he feared bursting.

"There is something you must know. I am a man, not a cat," he said. While he said it he could feel the executioner's cold blade. He would be split like a melon and thrown to the crows.

"As you wish," Etoile said, "and it is a charming conceit. You are the man and I am the cat and let it be so. Who thought of this game? I did, I am sure, since I could swear I heard you speak, which is, of course, quite impossible. But tomorrow it is you and not me who will chase away the nasty rats, and that is your purpose. My purpose tonight is to make you feel at home and entirely pleasured."

In the hours that followed, Wilbur blessed the moth many times over, apologizing for past lamentations. But when Etoile dozed, an angel at peace, he remembered it was the hour for urgent departure. The last night birds were already seeking their nests. Wilbur dressed with stealth, left the marvelous cocoon of Etoile's bed, and climbed to the window ledge. If he survived the dive to the moat without excessive breakage, and if the guards were distracted by dreams of their own, there was a last chance at freedom.

But Wilbur stepped down from the window and returned to kiss his Princess one last time. She drew him to her and wrapped around him and he knew he was lost and accepted destruction.

"Oh, cat," Etoile said, "if you are only half so ardent in your work and a fraction so expert, I do not envy your enemies."

In the morning, when Wilbur roused from his best-ever sleep, Etoile was already dressed and ready for breakfast.

"I hope you are as hungry as I," she said. "Rejoice, little cat, for your diet of rodents awaits you. Hurry downstairs, for the King's expectations must be promptly met, lest you feel his displeasure. My father is kindly, but he can be a vengeful old son of a bitch if riled."

Wilbur followed his beloved downstairs, quaking at the

tortures that awaited him. He crawled to King Axel, who was engaged in a tug-of-war with a huge rodent over a slab of crisp bacon. On the verge of confessing his terrible history, Wilbur heard a chorus of unearthly shrieking as if all the imps in Hell joined in choir.

Every rat in the place ran for the door, which was left open to let in some air. Whole battalions, in panic, hurled themselves into the fatal waters of the brimming moat. Their ghosts rose in bubbles that burst like boils.

Wilbur saw that the cause of this carnage was the very same beast who had snatched away his trio of sardines when he first came ashore in King Axel's domain. It had somehow accessed the palace through a breach in the wall and was now ripping and tearing and snarling and feasting in an orgy of feline virtuosity.

"What is that thing," screamed Princess Etoile, "that is gobbling cat's breakfast?"

Undoubtedly inspired by love, Wilbur jumped over a chair and pounced on the voracious lump of fur which, he quickly realized, must surely be the cat he'd reluctantly replaced. He wrestled it to submission, then proclaimed, "At last I am liberated! My soul is my own!"

The King and his Council requested an immediate explanation.

"There is your cat," Wilbur said. "There, with the blood on its jaw and eyes like time. That remorseless demon found me helpless on your beach and, in its greed, made off with my very essence. The brute attempted to live as a man but this morning old appetites betrayed it. And thank God for that, since it came here to pay court to the Princess Etoile."

"Who are you, then?" asked the King.

"I am without disguise, Your Highness. Only a loyal subject in love with your perfect daughter and ready to serve her all the days of my life."

"Well which of you has the power over rats?" the King questioned. "For it is that one who has my full appreciation."

"The cat has that power," Wilbur said. "But it is now in my debt, and will follow only my commands."

Princess Etoile wept at that disclosure. But she quickly regained her composure and asked friskily, "And which did I minister to last night, the cat or the man? And which shall I snuggle and cuddle tonight?"

Wilbur blushed. He fervently hoped Etoile's choice would come clear as the day wore on. Had not the moth made implicit commitments? But, then again, were the utterances of so ambiguous a moth to be trusted?

Wilbur glowered at the cat, who first arched in tribute to King Axel, then came to curl at Etoile's dainty feet.

The good youth now knew that there are some for whom no blessings come easily, nor can they ever be certain of privilege, however deserved. For those, fate and effort are indelibly linked, yet they must trust to their luck in the long run.

Three Dwarves and 2000 Maniacs

Don Webb

Don Webb lives in Austin with his wife Rosemary. His recent books are A Spell for the Fulfillment of Desire, Stealing My Rules, *and* The Seven Faces of Darkness.

This is one of the strangest versions of "Snow White and the Seven Dwarves" we've read. Manic and moving and slightly twisted, it's the perfect introduction to Don Webb's oddly unclassifiable fiction.

Three Dwarves
and 2000 Maniacs

For Bill

I've heard it said that many people study psychiatry on
the "physician, heal thyself" plan. Well, it was certainly
true for me. I was neurotic in high school, psychotic in
college, and saw my first padded cell during a Jung sem-
inar in graduate school. During my postgrad research—
when they let me around sharp objects again—I discovered Spencerzine, which as any well-informed reader
knows, cures even the most violent forms of aberration.
My wonder drug is emptying most of the mental hospitals
on this planet *and* filling up my pockets rather well. My
name is Alfred Byron Spencer, and I am known as the
Prince of Psychotherapy.

When *People* named me the most eligible bachelor in
America, something new came into my life—women.
Now, I've always liked women. A lot. I liked women in
high school, although I was too shy to talk to them. I liked

women in college, although I believed them to be controlled by a hive-mind on Uranus. I liked women in graduate school, although I had a hard time distinguishing them from Brussels sprouts. But I did not like the women who were in love with my newfound millions. I did not like the women who were merely grateful that I had freed their minds from a thousand and one horrors. I did not like the women who were in love with the flashing cameras that followed us during our dates.

I was a very lonely guy.

So I began calling up old friends. It was a real rush trying to track them down. Oh, I know there are services that will find anyone in America for $50, but I had more fun doing it myself.

Here's a sample conversation:

"Hello."

"Hello. Is this Ed Graham?"

"Yeah. Who's this?"

"Remember on the first day of the first grade when we discovered we had more Elmer's Glue than anybody—so we decided we had better stick together?"

There's a *long* pause, and I'm afraid I've found the wrong guy or Ed thinks I'm a nut.

"Al? Al Spencer?"

Whew.

We talk for a long while. How he is. How I am. Eventually Susan Pelham's name comes up. We'd both had a crush on her in high school. She was a year behind us.

"You remember Susan's mom died," said Ed. "And, you remember Bertha Jackdawe?"

"Only in my nightmares," I said.

Bertha was not what could be called a looker. She made up for physical ugliness by being twice as ugly spiritually. She had once set a math teacher on fire.

"Well, when Bertha's mother buried her fourth husband, she sent a note to Susan's father saying 'Let's get married—on one condition—Bertha becomes your heir, and Susan becomes our maid.' "

"You're kidding."

"So Susan's dad says he can't decide. He tells Susan to hang up an old boot with a hole in it on the wall of the garage. She's to fill it with water. If the boot holds water, he'd marry Bertha's mom. Well, the water made the leather shrink, and the hole closed up, and the boot held water. So he married Bertha's mom."

Now I hear a lot of things like that because I deal with crazy people every day. There are a lot stranger things in the suburbs than are dreamt of in your philosophy, Horatio.

"So," I asked, "what happened?"

"Well, they all move in together. It was a pretty bad trip—some kind of scene where Susan was their slave in everything. Susan starts wearing this French maid's outfit and looking wonderful. I used to see her at the 7-Eleven picking up things for them. Bertha's around town in a fur coat. About then I moved away. I guess if it's still going on, Susan's dead of starvation or abuse by now."

We talked a little longer, and after the phone call I decided to seek after Susan. What's the use of riches or power if you can't free the occasional poor soul?

I have a couple of busy days at the Institute. A very small percentage of the world's crazies don't respond to the standard Spencerzine therapy. They need careful balancing of the secretions of ductless glands, electrolyte balance, and, above all, movie therapy. Gore films work well. The violence excites the patients, and after a while it causes the Spencerzine to kick in. So I live in the Institute, which stands like a Rhine castle atop Mt. Gainsborough here high above the town of Pleasant Valley. Myself, my small staff, and my 2000 maniacs.

*   *   *

After a month of trying to track down Susan on my own, I went to professionals. I was afraid I'd get hold of Bertha or her mother. I had never met Bertha's mom, but I imagined her to be as evilly formed in body and soul as her repulsive daughter.

My spies did discover that Mr. Pelham had died, Bertha had inherited the household, and that very recently Susan had been seen fleeing the house late at night.

There were rumors that something hideous had happened in the house. All the windows had been painted over—and strange smells polluted misty mornings.

There were also rumors of saints and angels in the city, of strange monetary bequests, and of monsters and toad armies . . .

Clearly my old hometown needed vast amounts of Spencerzine. So I left my castle with a small entourage, a truck full of the drug, and instructions to call me if there was any emergency.

The mayor and the chief of police were overjoyed to see me. The mayor was a gracious woman, dark and tall; her name was Beth Tillman. The chief was a short, fat, and nervous man named Louis Chang.

"You can't imagine how bad it is, sir," said Chang. "Last night a small cache of antique Spanish gold was found in a Goodwill drop-off bin, and four teenagers claimed to have seen a creature with the body of a bear and the face of a squid foraging the trash cans at Memorial Park. There's a wide-scale attack of madness, here. Can you just dump your drug in the water—like LSD in reverse?"

I told him that might be feasible; I'd need to talk with the waterworks, run some blood work on a significant cross section of the population, and check to see if madness really was stalking the town.

"But," I said, "I don't get the gold. I mean, we're talking real gold here, right?"

"The gold's real," the mayor said. "We've had it assayed, tested, numismatically typed. Gold doubloons. A popular theory is that the squid-monster has brought them up from some sunken Spanish galleon. This notion appeals to fans of a horror writer called H. P. Lovecraft and has also spawned—if you'll excuse the pun—a local industry: selling I ♥ Squidman bumper stickers."

"Well if the gold's real, why do you think people are crazy?"

"Look," the mayor said, "we've got a cargo cult worshiping a squid god in mid-America. That's crazy."

They set me up at the best hotel in town, where two days later I met the most beautiful woman in the world.

The moon silvered the swimming pool, and the hum of the air conditioners had almost lulled me to sleep when she appeared. She walked to the pool—her black hair starkly beautiful against her naked body. She plunged into the pool with a graceful arc. It was Susan Pelham.

So beautiful was she as she swam through the hotel's pool that I was afraid to move—even to breathe loudly lest the vision prove to be a dream and my actions end it. Perhaps my drug was wearing off. If so, then a madness that could bring such beauty was not a madness to be feared.

For three nights she came and swam at three in the morning, and on the third night I was waiting by the pool when she emerged wearing only the glistening second skin of chlorine-scented water.

"Susan?"

So fearful was the look she gave me that I thought she would dart away, like a frightened doe.

"Susan, it's me, Al Spencer. I've come to rescue you."

"Al? The geek?" she said sweetly, and when she opened her mouth to speak a gold coin fell onto the concrete.

Minutes later, wearing my bathrobe, she sat in my room telling her story. When she would open her mouth to begin a new sentence, another coin would fall.

"At first," she said, "I didn't mind being the maid. In fact, I kind of liked it—the whole Cinderella bit—dressing up, humiliation. I was always sort of bent that way. Dad didn't seem to mind 'cause it turned on my stepmom so much that she and Dad were always at it. I didn't really think they had cut me out of the will in favor of Bertha. I thought it was all a game.

"Then Dad died. And they chained me up and wouldn't let me go to the funeral, but they let me go to the reading of the will. Sure enough, Bertha got *everything*. I should have bolted from the lawyer's office right then, but I was too stunned.

"When I got home I told my stepmom that I was leaving, and she laughed cruelly and said, 'Go ahead.' I realized that all I had were two shabby French maid outfits, no diploma, no driver's license. Other than a possible career of talk-show appearances, I had nothing. So I continued to play.

"My stepmom got a lot rougher after that, bruising me black-and-blue pretty often. The games got more complicated, and I think they were giving me drugs because I remember some mighty strange doings on my stepmom's part.

"One day in bleak December she gave me this little paper dress to put on, and a crust of bread to eat, and told me to go pick some strawberries. I know she wanted me to freeze to death in the snow. I decided I would go to the police, and at worst I'd wind up in some kind of institution.

"But somehow I wasn't in our neighborhood. My step-mother had done one of those weird things she could do—like when she made that boot hold water so dad had had to marry her. I was wandering through a cold and blustery forest where the snow was at least a foot deep. Eventually I saw this little house shaped like a gray toadstool.

"I knocked on the tiny door and three filthy little men popped out. They asked what I wanted, and I said as po-litely as I could that I was looking for strawberries. They told me to come in, and I thanked them profusely. Inside everything was dark and dirty and cold.

"The three little men asked what I had brought them to eat. I gave them the crust of bread that my stepmother had given me. Then they told me to take this ratty old broom they had and sweep their porch.

"I began sweeping away the snow and I found big, fresh, juicy strawberries there. I put as many as I could in the pockets of my paper dress.

"Then the three little men came outside. They inspected my work, and told me how glad they were to meet some-one as hardworking and polite as I. Then they had a con-ference in their own language.

"They said they wished to reward me.

"The first one said, 'Every time she speaks, a gold coin will fall out of her mouth.'

"The second one said, 'Every day she will grow prettier and prettier.'

"The third one said, 'She will marry a prince.'

"I started to tell them that the biggest reward they could give me was to let me stay with them. But when I opened my mouth to speak, a gold coin dropped out. That scared me so much I started to run. I ran and ran through the snow, and, before I knew it, I was back at my stepmother's home. So I went in, said 'Here's your strawberries,' and fainted.

"When I came to, they had one of the coins, and they had me tied up. I told them about my experiences. They made me talk and talk so they would have more coins.

"Finally Bertha said that if a simpleton like me could get such benisons, a real pro like her could rake it in. She asked me how to get to the three dwarves' cottage.

"Her mother told her not to go, but you remember how Bertha is—remember how she got into that all-boys club in high school?—anyway she talked her mom into Opening the Way to the dwarves' world. She put on her big fur coat and her mom made her some cakes and cookies to eat and she set out.

"I don't know what happened to her, but I got the feeling it wasn't pleasant. My stepmother put Bertha up in her bedroom and began caring for her night and day. She was so wrapped up in Bertha's welfare that I was able to escape.

"Thanks to the gold coins I could afford a room here, but I don't know what to do next."

Susan went back to her room and slept. In the afternoon we talked some more. I told her the story of my life since high school. It seemed kind of uneventful, after her tale. Finally I asked what I had come to ask her. Would she come back with me and be my wife?

Yes, she said, yes, yes, I will, yes.

They were showing *Blood Feast* when I got back to the Institute. Everything seemed normal and happy. The only changes had been cosmetic ones, like getting a new head day nurse. It used to depress me to find that the Institute ran as well without me as with me, but now I was in love, and my life revolved around Susan.

We celebrated our marriage by showing a double bill of

Scum of the Earth and *Color Me Blood Red* and giving the patients a double dose of Spencerzine.

We loved each other, and every day Susan grew more fair (and those gold doubloons really began to pile up, too).

I didn't attend well to business, I was—for the first time—truly alive. Love is a kind of madness that tears away as much as it builds up, and Venus in her diaphanous green robes is a strange and harsh mistress. I noted only the occasional film title as the days passed into weeks and the weeks into months: *Moonshine Mountain, Monster a-Go-Go, Something Weird, A Taste for Blood, The Gruesome Twosome.*

Some of our patients were cured, others took their places.

Susan told me she was with child.

I had never thought of kids before, just as I had never thought that anyone would find me lovable. The second knowledge had so transformed me that I found the first to be the most magical news in the world.

I hired the best doctors and had a wing built onto the Institute with a large garden and a small lake.

I would give my child all the love I could as well as the treasures of the world—which were still accumulating at a good rate.

My son arrived. I ordered banners flown at the Institute ramparts, and I endowed a college in his name.

But my year of love had had its costs. I had neglected my patients. Some—even with massive doses of Spencerzine and all the gore movies they would watch—were not improving at all. Business questions had piled up as well. Where should I invest my money? The counting room wanted to know what to do with the pile of gold doubloons—and there was the continuing annoyance of the

American Psychiatric Association's lawsuits against me for loss of livelihood.

So I turned my attention to business—putting in long and hard hours. Eventually I heard the message every husband dreads most, that my beautiful wife was ill.

I rushed to our bedroom, but the Institute's very efficient medical staff had whisked her away.

She was photosensitive, they told me, she was in quarantine.

I stood outside her darkened room—wanting more than anything to run to her to crush her to me to know that she was well to let her know how much I loved her.

I decided to enter the room, but the head day nurse almost tackled me.

"You can't go in," she said. "We think it's contagious."

My wife moaned. Something fell out of the bed. Something small, brown, and slimy. It hopped toward the door. A toad.

"As you can see," the nurse said, "it's very serious."

She turned to the toad and brought her white nurse's shoe down on the disgusting creature. An overpowering smell of corruption rose up, and I had to duck down the corridor to avoid vomiting.

Every day I would come and talk for a few minutes to the nurse. I gave her messages for Susan. I sent flowers. I prayed. I cried.

I even canceled the patients' movies. In my shameful state I wanted everyone to suffer.

Dead leaden days passed.

The staff told me that they were having trouble with one patient—a woman who continued to hallucinate despite high doses of Spencerzine. I decided to see her. Maybe I could reawaken my love of mankind by seeing the state she was in.

She had strawberry blonde hair which could have been pretty if washed and combed. Her light brown eyes could have sparkled if she knew happiness. Her thin pale pink lips could have been beautiful if they found the way to smile. I looked at her and knew that I would continue my quest against madness even if the forces of disease took my Susan from me.

"What's your story?" I asked.

"Oh, Dr. Spencer, I thought I was getting better. But the other night I sneaked into your wife's private garden. Oh, I know it's not for us patients, but it was a beautiful night and I was so happy, so very happy, at the return of my mind to me. Then I found out that I was still crazy."

"How did you find out?"

"A duck swam across the pond to me and then it talked," she said, her voice cracking on the final verb.

"What did it say?"

"It asked me in your wife's voice if I thought everyone was asleep. I said yes and then it said it wanted to look in on its baby, and it flew up to a window and looked in. I just sat and cried because I knew I had lost my mind forever."

"Is that all?"

"No. It flew back down and told me not to be sad, that I wasn't crazy. Then it said you should get a sword and swing it over the duck three times."

I did something I had never done before. I hugged my patient and told her she wasn't crazy. At least I didn't think she was crazy. We would visit the pond together that night.

I drove into town and bought a sword. It cost a pretty penny—it had belonged to an obscure Confederate general.

When the moon silvered the lake, I went out followed by my patient.

One duck swam over to us.

I swung my sword three times over its head.

And its white feathers became *her* white flesh, and the black of the night coalesced into *her* hair, and my wife stood beside me.

I called my most senior and trusted staff.

"Today is a very special day. You have all been faithful to me and we have accomplished great things. We have nearly ended madness on this planet, and we have all become wealthier than any of us have ever hoped. I love and respect each of you, and I will ask of you my friends to do some very unusual things for me. Firstly, I want you to isolate the head day nurse and give her this personality test. Mainly, I want to keep her busy, but I am very interested in her answer to the last question. Secondly, I want my sick wife to get a healthy injection of sodium pentothal. You needn't worry, her condition isn't contagious. Thirdly, I want an outdoor picnic prepared for the truly hard-core patients—those we've never been able to stimulate enough with the gore films. Fourthly, I want to introduce my new chief of operations, Ms. Rebecca Wayne. Many of you remember Ms. Wayne as a patient from just days ago. Rebecca has one patient to care for now, but she will be chief of operations beginning tomorrow."

Rebecca Wayne smiled, her strawberry blonde hair shining and beautiful, and her eyes burning with a mixture of intelligence and joy that told me she would go far. Beside her in a cowled white robe sat the mystery patient.

My staff began their jobs.

I waited for the drug to take effect, then I went to confront my "wife."

The thing on the bed had at one time been human. The fibrous tumors, warts, and scales that had replaced the skin were not as noticeable as the clear elongation of certain bone structures. No wonder she had scared the kids on lovers' lane.

"Bertha," I asked, "what did the dwarves do to you?"

Its voice was liquid and slurred. With each new opening of the thick blubbery lips of its fetid mouth, a brown toad fell out.

"I went to their house and the three little men came out. They asked what I wanted, and I said platinum since they'd given gold to Susan. They invited me inside and I told them how filthy and cold it was. They asked me what I had brought to feed them and I told them I only had enough for me. Then they told me to sweep their porch, and I told them I was not a slave. Then they said that I would get uglier each day, that each time I spoke a toad would fall from my mouth—and I would have a horrible death."

"Bertha," I asked, "how did you come to be here?"

"Mom said that if she could keep me close to you long enough, the dwarves' doom would be broken. Your concern directed toward me would do it."

"Bertha," I asked, "why didn't you kill Susan?"

"It is better for her to suffer. All of our power comes from her suffering."

"Ms. Wayne," I said, "you have read the test and consulted with the carpenters?"

"Of course, Dr. Spencer."

The dying sun had turned the clouds all lemons and oranges, and a sweet breeze swept up from Pleasant Valley. Birdsong and lunatic laughter filled the twilight. The patients kept looking at the high outdoor movie screen and the four coffin-length objects draped in white sheets before it.

There was potato salad, barbecued chicken, pickles and relishes, cheeses of a dozen nations. In fact it was a picnic that only the richest man in the town could afford to put on.

Toward the end of the picnic I went up to the podium and addressed my beloved maniacs.

"My friends, tonight we are here to honor the head day nurse. Now many of you know her as Sharon Stone, but her real name is Rachel Jackdawe."

Nurse Jackdawe jumped up, but three orderlies grabbed her. She struggled manfully during the rest of my speech. I shan't reproduce her foul language because I am a gentleman.

"Rachel Jackdawe took the standardized Spencer Appreciation Test—the same SAT you all remember taking. And she had the most extreme scores for cruelty of anybody, anytime. But there was a trick question on the test—involving this woman."

Two orderlies pulled the sheet away from a box my wife lay in. They helped her to her feet, and the crowd gasped and screamed at the most beautiful woman in the world.

"The question was, 'What should be done to someone who throws an innocent woman out of bed and into cold, cold water just to see her suffer?' Now Rachel threw my wife"—I pointed at the incomparable Susan—"into our little pond—" Boos and hisses.

"—with the help of this creature."

The orderlies pulled the sheets away and forced Bertha Jackdawe to stand.

The maniacs screamed and laughed at the ugliest woman in the world.

"Do you want to hear Rachel's answer?"

Two thousand screams of "Yes!"

" 'They should be taken and put in a barrel lined with sharp nails—and the barrel rolled down a hill.' "

The orderlies pulled away the last two sheets—showing long barrels filled with glisteningly sharp nails. The orderlies thrust the struggling Jackdawes into the barrels—the nails already beginning to cut and redden them. Then they carefully carried the barrels to the edge of the hill.

Then they kicked them down the hill.

As the barrels spun ever faster, rains of blood struck the hillside. The screams of the madmen and madwomen drowned out the tortured cries of the Jackdawes.

I knew that this was enough excitement for the last group of the mad in the world to be cured.

When the barrels had rolled to a stop on the base of the hill, I took the hand of the Most Beautiful Woman in the World, and we watched the last movie ever to be shown at the Institute.

Wizard of Gore.

The world is a beautiful place.

True Thomas

BRUCE GLASSCO

Bruce Glassco, like several others in this anthology, is a graduate of Clarion East 1995. Before that he took shelter as a student at the University of Virginia during the twelve years of Republican administrations, ending up to his surprise with a Ph.D. in Romantic literature. He currently teaches at a small college in Wisconsin, land of cheese.

According to the author, "True Thomas" was inspired partly by the famous ballad, and partly by an article by Carl Sagan which describes a thirteenth-century girl's description of how she was taken by fairies into "a city up in the clouds." Sagan uses the story as an example of why a certain type of experience is a fundamental part of human psychology, and thus not necessarily founded in reality. What Sagan conveniently ignores, though, is that the tale could just as easily be used as evidence for the opposite viewpoint: namely, that we aren't alone, and, furthermore, we never have been. Incidentally, Thomas of Erceldoune was a real person who lived in Scotland in the late thirteenth century, a time of tremendous upheaval. He wrote a number of famous prophecies, and a long version of the love story "Tristram and Isolde." No one knows who wrote the ballad that tells the story of his abduction.

True Thomas

True Thomas lay on Huntlie Bank;
A ferlie he spied wi' his e'e;
And there he saw a lady bright
Come riding down by the Eildon Tree.

Four laborers are drinking to pegs, sitting as far away from me as the cramped alehouse will allow. The pegs are fixed in a row down the inside of the tankard, and each man must uncover a new marker before passing the ale on around. "Wassail," they cry in the Saxon manner as they watch one another's Adam's apples bob and swallow. "Drink hail." Ninescore years ago, when I was young, the Archbishop Anselm spoke out against peg drinking, and I paid him as little heed then as these men would to their bishops of today.

Today no man or woman would dare to share my cup,

but still the men have spilled enough ale for me to taste its scent in the air, warm and sour and flat. Nowadays I take my communion wherever I can find it.

My fingertips taste the red-faced alewife's scent on the goblet of mead she has handed me. Her sound name, Kate, is nothing but a short harsh bark; it is over as soon as it is begun and leaves no aftertaste in the ear. The Word that is her sweat on the blue-fired clay, though, sings whole ballads to me of her loneliness and desire. Since her husband was put below ground her skin has ached for the touch of a man's hand. I smell an egg within her as well, ready to begin its long journey to the womb. If she is ploughed tonight, she will crop.

I smell her heat rise as she stops to jest at a table—ah. The priest, then. Father Owens. I am tempted to pass his table and sniff whether he returns her heart's longing, but I remain where I am. Father Owens does not approve of my Language, or the Queen who taught it to me.

Beneath the proud belches of the workers and the exaltations of Kate's sweat and the tart disapproval of Father Owens's thin spittle, a single sour bass note lurks: the acrid taste of fear. They fear me, one and all, as I drink my solitary mead. They rarely speak to me, for fear I will answer them. Even Father Owens, who damns me regularly from the pulpit of his kirk, would hesitate to speak against me to my face. Even men of God fear the Truth.

A blast of bitter cold air comes through the narrow window, and with it the sounds of men and horses. They have evidently seen the green branch tied outside that shows this place to be what passes for Erceldoune's tavern; they are dismounting. Soon a slender, smooth-shaven man strides through the door. Using no senses but my eyes, I can tell that he comes from the court; he dresses in the French fashion, with pointed shoes and long dagged sleeves that show he is far too important to work with his hands. The flower of a purple heartsease is pinned to his tunic.

The stranger has no difficulty in singling me out as I sit alone, and I stand as he strides forward to shake my hand. It is a new custom, brought with the Crusaders from the East, and it is a great help to me in my trade. What the handshake does not tell me, my knowledge of the court fills in.

"You are Alexander Macdougall of Argyll," I say. "Yesterday morning you left Roxburgh while the dew was still on the grass, accompanied by a single servant. You rode through most of the night, stopping only to water your horse. Your highland manservant admires you greatly, but your mistreated horse fears your touch. Now tell me, what is it that you wish of True Thomas the Rhymer?"

My juggler's trick has the desired effect, and the Macdougall loses some of his cockiness. There is an awkward pause. "If you know all this," says the laird, "then you must know why I have come."

I have already told him everything I know, but Kate comes to my rescue. "Our Thomas has never claimed the power to answer every question," she tells the visitor. "All we know is, whenever he speaks, he speaks the truth." She does not look at me as she speaks. She has truths she would rather not hear spoken—which of her bairns are not of her late husband's get, to begin with.

The laird looks annoyed. "Have I ridden all this way for nothing, then?"

"We shall see," I say. "Ask your question." I seat myself, and he looks around the room carefully before taking a seat across from me. Kate brings the laird a bottle of Gascon wine—too dear for our local custom, but Macdougall is not the first nobleman who has come to me with questions. He pours off a tankard and drinks it without hesitation.

To me she brings more mead, and I lean back and take a few drops on my tongue. It is metheglyn, spiced and potent, brought by sea from distant Wales. Overland would have been easier, but these days the Border is too dangerous for traders. I taste that there was not enough rain in the spring for the flowers that fed the bees. The spices were not adequately dried, and there was mold in the hivestraw.

"Hmm." Macdougall clears his throat nervously. "Yes, well then. In a fortnight I will be married to Isabelle Stewart, granddaughter of Alexander Stewart and connected to the throne. My question is, when she comes to be delivered of a child, will it be a boy, or a girl?"

"What is this to you?" I ask him, annoyed. Put five of them in a sinking ship, and they would squabble over the cargo instead of the boats. If I could speak to them using my Language, I would tell them how thin their words are, empty sounds holding empty meanings that flicker and die in empty ears. Sometimes I marvel how it is they have ever managed to communicate anything resembling thoughts.

The laird is taken aback by my question, but still treats me with respect. He begins to talk of the death of the Princess Margaret on the sea, and the chaos in the court that her death has created.

They have reached the end of their golden age, these nobles. All of their pretty royal family gone in a few short years, and nothing ahead now but a hundred years of strife and misery. They can sense it dimly, even this young man, who seems already enmeshed in some plot to ally himself through the engagement of his unborn child to one of the rivals claiming the throne.

I can smell the gold in his purse, and I ask for my fee. Five kings ago when I was a lad, there were no coins in Scotland, but King David had them struck while I was away. They are fine things to have, for an old harper.

Metheglyn is dear this far north, and will grow dearer in the coming wars.

While the noble is distracted with his purse, I reach out and brush my fingertips against the purple heartsease he wears, for it has all the look of being pinned to his jerkin by a lady. What I find there surprises me mightily. The lady was his betrothed, that is sure enough. I recognize the bloodline of the Stewarts. But her fingers, when she pinned the flower to her lord, had the taste of true heart's longing. I have known few noble couples, very few, who have felt truelove for one another in their marriages of state. Yet there it blooms in Isabelle's heart, simple and strong, like a rose in the heather. I cannot tell whether or not he returns her love, though.

There is a darker scent beneath. A weakness of her heart, and blood leaking into her lungs—I have tasted it before.

"Was your betrothed feverish as a child?" I ask. "Do her joints sometimes swell, as with dropsy? Does she tire easily?"

"Isabelle is as healthy as any woman in Scotland!" cries Macdougall, and the sharp scent of his fear strikes me like a knife. "What are you saying, Rhymer?"

The truth forms like honey beneath my tongue, but I hesitate. Whenever I have smelled this leak of the heart's blood in a woman's body, she has not outlived her first childbed. What will he do if I tell him this? Will he leave her at the altar, blaming the abandonment on me? Or will he marry and get her with child regardless, either not believing me, or not caring as long as the midwife has a chance to save the child, and he can enjoy his wife's sweet body for a few short years? Or will he marry her and take care that no child will come, sacrificing his noble line for her own true sake, so that together they can sit before their fire in old age?

Will love endure? The question has haunted me like a

knife beside the heart. I cannot stop myself from watching young lovers in the springtime, though their endearments can make my eyes smart like soured wine. Sometimes I imagine I will find my Queen in their muddled Language, like a slice of sweet apple hidden in a pot of porridge.

Will love endure? It is a question I ask myself when the rain beats on the thatch of my tower and this world seems like a prison to me. The down from the birds beneath the eaves carries in it Words speaking of family and hope. The clammy Words of the mold on the windowsill tell me that nothing lasts, that all will be eaten by the earth.

The truth is often easier to find than it is to tell. I could keep my silence. But if I do not, if I try to tell him what I know in his language, how should I go about it? What would my Queen in the stars say of this?

I ask Macdougall to wait for a moment, and open my purse. Inside is a tiny bottle, filled with the drink I prize above all others. I untie the cap and pour a single, golden drop onto my fingertips, letting it soak into my skin, breathing a scent as rich and deep as a king's treasure-house. Much of its depth has faded over the years, but when I put the drop on my tongue there is still enough to bring back the Queen's memories, like a book spread before me, written in gold.

> "Light down, light down, now, true Thomas,
>   And lean your head upon my knee;
> Abide and rest a little space,
>   And I will show you ferlies three.
>
> O see ye not yon narrow road,
>   So thick beset with thorns and briers?
> That is the path of righteousness,
>   Though after it but few enquires.

And see ye not that braid braid road,
That lies across that lily levin?
That is the path of wickedness,
Though some call it the road to heaven.

And see ye not that bonny road,
That winds about the fernie brae?
That is the road to fair Elfland,
Where thou and I this night maun gae."

It began with the fairy caught in the tree.

I had never seen a fairy before, so I examined it closely. The spindle-shaped body was covered with thick green fur, topped by feathery antennae and six eyes laid out in a pair of triangles. Its thin waist had snagged in a cleft branch of the Eildon tree, and four wings the size and color of the Eildon's leaves beat frantically to pull it free. A dozen stick-thin legs trailed from its torso; half of them clutched struggling beetles.

I gently bent the branch and freed it, and it buzzed off in the direction of the high meadow as the twilight deepened. I followed at a distance, burning with the curiosity of the young. Three days before my lady love had jilted me, and I felt as sad and as free as air. My father had decided that my destiny lay as a good-for-nothing scoundrel, and had told me to begin looking for other lodgings. Hunting was my excuse for wandering the hills, but I had brought my harp as well, for a new ballad would be worth more to me than a deer. I knew forty-seven ballads, nine of them of my own making, and when I was in my cups I would sing them to the applause of my friends, proudly off-key. I was a fortnight shy of my seventeenth year on earth.

In the meadow was a hill where no hill had stood before, towering high as Stirling Castle rock. The fairies had scorched a circle around it, and scores of them, large and small, were going and coming through the holes set into the hill's side, all of them dancing to the deep bass fiddle-sounds of their humming wings. I saw spirals and patterns more intricate than the most lordly roundel, leaps and starts more graceful than an estampie. The entire pattern seemed chaos, but wherever my eye rested, there was or-der.

I heard a noise behind me and turned. Three fairies, wingless, large as cattle and with crab claws the size of baskets, were almost upon me. Even as they attacked, my excitement outweighed my fear, for I knew that if I ever returned to Erceldoune, I could write a ballad to end all ballads. I had my father's knife with me, but I did not draw it, for they were beautiful, and I did not wish to harm them. My harp fell and broke against a stone. They spat webs of sticky rope around me and carried me into the hill.

> *"I have a laef here in my lap,*
> *Likewise a bottle of clarry wine;*
> *And now, ere we go farther on,*
> *We'll rest a while, and ye may dine."*

The room where they took me must have been near the surface, for I could see the sun through the ceiling dimly, as through a sheet of wax. I knew the ballads of Faerie, and knew that above all else I must not eat the food or drink the wine. But I had little choice, for a sweet cloudy liquid was poured in my mouth as I lay bound, until I choked and swallowed. My tongue went numb, and my eyes filled with mists.

Then I felt as if I were floating above my body, watching it from a distance as one would watch a child playing with a doll. I felt nothing as they swarmed in, dozens of them, probing the doll with pincers and nippers and long thin tongues, dissolving the bonds with more of their spit. I felt nothing when a swordlike foreleg sliced a hole beneath my tongue, and another slipped a waxy yellow coin inside. I felt nothing when they slid pink ribbons into my nostrils, or red beads into holes they drilled in my skull, or when they peeled the skin off my hands as I once saw a bishop remove his gloves, and did something to the skin and slid it back on again.

Then they forced more honey between my lips, and as two of the largest ones picked me up and carried me into the heart of the hill, I could feel my senses slowly returning. There was no pain, but I smelt my blood behind me on the floor.

> *"Harp and carp, Thomas," she said;*
> *"Harp and carp along wi' me;*
> *And if ye dare to kiss my lips,*
> *Sure of your body I will be."*

The chamber they took me to was larger than St. Giles kirk. It was lit by hand-sized fairies glowing brighter than fireflies, perched on ledges or flitting about. As high as one could see, the walls were pocketed with chambers tiny and large. Many were filled with large leathery bags, or grub-like creatures that pulsed behind waxy walls. But other cells held things even stranger: a frozen fountain made of silver, a mushroom twelve hands tall, a unicorn's skull, a blob that smelt like calf's-foot jelly but pulsed and moved. I wondered how it was that I could smell the thing from across the room, and then I realized that the air was full of scents I had never known before, and that each one could speak to me and tell me exactly what it meant, if I cared to read its message.

Then I saw the Queen. Her height was slightly less than

mine, and she rode across the floor to me on the backs of three guards. They set her down before me tenderly.

The fur that covered her body was as green as the sun appears when you swim deep underwater and look upward on a clear day. Twelve wispy arms grew from her slender torso, and a set of furled wings behind. Her waist was even narrower, and hairless: a band of wrinkled brown skin that seemed appallingly naked amidst the downy hair. Her lower body was heavy and pendulous, but compact, like a ripe fruit. Her feathery antennae stroked the air above her like the Eildon's branches. She smelled of honey and roses, and as her scent reached me I seemed to hear Words, and the Words said ★ Do not be afraid. ★

A small flat fairy flew up to her, and she grasped it with her upper arms. She held it up to her mouth, and at first I thought she might devour it. Then her flat mouth opened, but it held no teeth: only a soft, fleshy tube that stretched out until it almost touched the smaller fairy's back. The tube pulsed and narrowed and spread, and out of it fell a single, golden drop that landed on the small fairy's back. The fairy flew and landed before me, and the Word that was the smell of the drop said ★ Eat of my sweetness.★ And I knew that I had gone through too many doors to turn back now, so I scooped up the drop with my finger and ate.

How can I describe the Words of the Queen? Imagine that you are feasting on the finest banquet ever served to a king or pope. It has been prepared by the finest cooks from Ireland to Inde, and they have studied your body until they know your favorite foods better than you know them yourself. Now imagine that, with every bite, you taste every course of the meal at once, but preserve the flavors separately as well, the way five strings of a harp struck together sound sweeter than one string plucked alone.

Now imagine that, with every bite of this banquet, you are also reading a book, whole and entire. And this book is as sacred as the Mass, and as merry as a bawdy jest, and as sad as the saddest ballad, and yet you know that every word in the book is as true as the Word spoken by God when he made the heavens and the earth. And this book is not written by some stranger, but by a person who knows you and understands you and loves you for your own true worth.

The Word opened up rooms in every direction that I could have explored for days, but at its heart there was a question: ★ By what name shalt thou be called, man of the island? ★

I wondered how to answer her, and as I wondered I tasted sweet Language forming beneath my tongue. The Language took form to fit my thoughts, and I spit it onto the back of the fairy before me. My Word was flat-tasting and crudely formed, like a child's first burblings, but it said something like ★ Hail great Queen.★ Then I thought on my name. Thomas had no translation, so I picked a meaningless symbol that felt like Thomas in my mind. But I am also called Rhymer, so I formed a Word that said, ★ I am He-who-joins-similar-things-together.★ When it had both of my Words the fairy flew back to her.

As we spoke back and forth I grew more fluent with her Language, and she asked more and more questions about the world. Many of them were about the ways of men and women, but she seemed equally interested in what I knew of the other creatures of the earth. She seemed fascinated by our breeding of animals, and the way our ships traveled from one land to another. She showed a great curiosity about beetles, a subject about which I could tell her little. I asked her questions about Faerie as well, and what was to become of me, but her only reply was the Word that said ★ Do not fear. ★

We talked for what must have been hours. Then, ★ Thank you, Thomas-Joiner,★ she said at last. ★ Thou hast performed great service for Life this day, though thy world may not know of it for dozens of dozens of thy years. Now we shall give thee another drink, that shall make all that has passed beneath this hill seem like a dream dimly remembered at waking. But before thou dost return to thy world thou mayst claim one gift of me, and if it be in my power, I shall grant it. I can tell thee where gold is buried, within a day's journey of thy town. Or if any of thy family is ill, I can give thee medicine that shall make a deep cure. Or I can give thee a wallet of honey that will keep thy family and friends fed for a mortal life-time. Choose, Thomas-Joiner. ★

★Lady,★ I said in return, the Words dripping golden from my tongue, ★ In a fortnight I shall be seventeen years upon this earth. My lady love has left me for another, and my family cares but little whether I live or die. And in all the wide world I have traveled, from Berwick to fair Dundee, I have seen nothing as lovely as the room in which we stand, or tasted any food as sweet as your Words. The gift I ask is that you give me no drink of forgetfulness, but that you allow me to stay here in Faerie, and eat of your Words, and learn of your ways. ★

★Well said,★ the Queen's scent told me, and her laughter rang out like a field of wildflowers. ★ For when there are none to speak to but my own children, it seems betimes as if I am talking to myself. If thou dost truly wish to travel with us, then give thy knife to my chamberlain. We will begin our journey soon, and the forces that will take us on the first step would rip thy knife from thy side and send it tearing through flesh and floor and fairy. ★

I drew my father's knife and handed it to the fairy who

appeared at my elbow, and he flew upward. ★ Journey?★
I said as he disappeared through one of the holes in the
ceiling. ★ I will not change my resolve, but what journey
do we undertake? Are we not already in Faerie? ★

★You have much to learn, Thomas-Joiner,★ she said,
and this time her laughter smelled like strong wine.

> O they rode on, and farther on;
>   The steed ga'ed swifter than the wind;
> Until they reached a desert wide,
>   And living land was left behind.

The Queen's Word for the hill we were in was the same
as her word for Home. She put me in a soft couch, and
then I felt as if a giant's thumb was pushing me deep into
it.

Then, suddenly, I found myself flying without wings. I
tried desperately to grab onto the couch or anything stable,
but only succeeded in making myself turn slowly in the
air, smelling laughter as the Queen flew by me with her
wings outspread. Then a sheep-sized fairy with strong
wings flew up to me, with one of the Queen's Words on
its back.

★Hold on and follow,★ said the Word, and so I
clutched the fairy and followed the trail of her Language
through the air to another room. One wall, or ceiling, or
floor was filled with stars and the moon and a great round
thing that was green and blue and white.

My questions began flowing beneath my tongue, but she
had already made answers that floated in the chamber air.
★ The great sphere you see is your world,★ she said.

★In St. Giles in Edinburgh I have seen a map of the
world,★ I told her. ★ Scotland and England and France
and Burgundy and Norway, and as far away as Egypt and

sacred Jerusalem. I do not know what you mean when you say this is my world. ★

★The island of thy birth is there,★ she said, ★ slipping beneath that cloud.★ And my eyes went wide, for I knew then that I resembled an ant who has never left the nest, and who believes that the nest is the world.

But soon the blue-green sphere had vanished from the sky, and the sun was nothing but one spark among more stars than I could count.

> O they rade on, and farther on,
>   And they waded through rivers aboon the knee,
> And they saw neither sun nor moon,
>   But they heard the roaring of the sea.

I learned many things during my years in Home.

I had thought that I knew the shape of the universe, and I guessed that the Queen was taking me toward the sphere of stars. I thought that perhaps Heaven was her ultimate destination, or Hell. But she taught me the truth that our sun swims in a sea of stars, like a single stitch in a great tapestry. And I learned the task that the Queen's people have set themselves.

Suppose that there was one person on Earth for every star in our sea of stars.

Now suppose every person on Earth who lived outside of Scotland stood for a star without worlds. The Language of these stars is a thin, high-pitched scream that goes on forever until they have burnt themselves to a cinder or exploded. These stars have no life—imagine that everyone outside Scotland has died. Now take the people from our kingdom and spread them out through all the empty lands.

Now take away everyone but the inhabitants of Berwickshire. This time the vanished ones stand for all the stars whose worlds are nothing but empty rocks, speaking the dry Language of rocks.

Now remove all those of Berwickshire but not of Erceldoune: these are worlds with life, but no more life than the green scum growing in an unused well. Each world has its own Language, true, but with few Words. And if the residents of Erceldoune are worlds with life, perhaps only your own family would stand for worlds with life that can become aware of the Language from which it is made. A handful of people, spread out over the vast lonely Earth; a handful of worlds in the vaster desert of stars. And in between them flies the Queen's race, preserving Language in its cells before the night can snuff it out.

The place called Home was very old, older than some stars, and it carried Language from a dozen dozen worlds back and forth through the desert. Some Language, like that of the silver fountain, was carried inside the creature it belonged to, and some had been translated by past Queens into pure drops stored in the deep vaults. I explored the twisting tunnels of Home as far as I could until they grew too narrow, but still it seemed as if every chamber I entered held a new surprise. I have held trophies that brought the destruction of continents who fought over them, and I have read the poetry of races that were wise while our world was still without form and void, and I have touched the sloping skull of one of my ancestors who lived before the great flood.

Between stars, the Queen and I spent months eating one another's Words. She told me that she had been lonely, and that few other races were brave enough to quit their homes for Home. I sang her my ballads, which she dimly sensed through her feathery antennae, and tried to translate them to her Language. She showed me how she mated and grew her children, and how she fed them the Language that would teach them their tasks when they were fully grown. I showed her one or two ways that a human woman can please a man. Her lips were hard, but her hollow tongue was soft and warm. She said that human seed kicked harder and stronger than the seed of her males, with a taste like life on fire. She taught me how to laugh in her Language, and all of Home smelt like honey and like roses.

> It was mirk mirk night, and there was nae light,
>   And they waded through red blude to the knee;
> For a' the blude that's shed on earth
>   Rins through the springs o' that countrie.

My eyes could see nothing on the world where we stood but gray mud tinged with yellow flecks, lying under dark clouds. The air was so foul that the Queen had made us special fairies to blow fresh air into our mouths through a tube. Still, to me the place was beautiful. It smelt like twenty-three flavors of life, and I was there with my Queen.

Her wings were too weak to lift her from the surface of a world. She had dismissed her guards and allowed me to carry her myself. My hands stroked her fur and the wrinkled brown skin of her waist, and her wings quivered against my naked chest.

Life clung to the planet's surface like a climber on the side of a cliff in the midst of a storm. Tiny creatures clustered around pits where hot mud bubbled to the surface, and when the mud cooled they died.

We were giving them new Language. It came from a world whose star had exploded many Queens ago; here it would live again, and teach the creatures to grow new chambers inside themselves that would store food during a drought. The next time the Queen visited there might be a thousand life voices, instead of only twenty-three.

Then I saw what looked like a falling star punch through the clouds, and my world fell apart.

It was another faerie hill, and six males came to us as emissaries from its Queen. My Queen spoke to them for some time, and then she told me to take her back to Home, and they followed us. When we were back in the place between stars she retired to her central chamber with them, and told me to wait elsewhere. I could not be jealous of her own kind, but I made Words and chewed them in silence.

Finally, she sent for me. The chamber smelt of new things planted and growing.

★Thomas-Joiner,★ she said, ★ the time has come for you to return to your own country.★ But I had been speaking her Language for seven of my years now, and I could read more of the volumes that were contained in each of her Words. I knew that she was going to die, and my tongue went dry.

★Do not fear,★ said her scent like a reassuring field of grass. I tasted her Words over and over in my mind, and at last I understood. She was old for her people; I had never realized that before. The males had performed a mating flight, so that she could exchange Language with another of her kind. Pulsing somewhere in the deep vaults, tended by its own workers, was the egg of a new Queen.

★When she crawls into this chamber she will eat me,★ said the Queen, ★ eat me and many of my children, and the ones she does not eat will die. Then she will form a cocoon and sleep for a dozen of your years. When she awakens, she will have my memories, my Language. ★

★No!★ said the smell of my fear. I grabbed the dead body of a crystal creature from its cell and used it to cut my arm, and my blood mingled with my Words and added a Language of its own. ★ I will not let her do this . . . I will fight . . . I . . . ★

★You will go now,★ said the Queen's sharp scent. But then she took pity on me, and gave me a last lingering Word as a good-bye, rich as a thousand feasts, deep as a thousand songs. ★ Thou wouldst die here while the new Queen slept,★ she said, ★ and when she awakens in the place between stars, time will have bent and there will be nothing left of thee but dust in the earth. But she will remember thee, Thomas-Joiner. For of all the Language I have found in the stars, thine was the sweetest.★ That was the Word that I carried from Home with me, when Home launched itself back into the stars, and I turned my back because I could not watch; that is the Word I carry in a bottle around my neck, though time has caused its depth to fade. Contained inside its rooms are all the worlds we saw, the Words we spoke, and the memory of her body on mine.

After the hill had gone back into the sky, I found the rusty hilt of an ancient knife in the grass, and the tuning pegs of a harp. It was winter, and the side of the hill was cold.

> Syne they came to a garden green,
> And she pu'd an apple frae a tree—
> "Take this for thy wages, true Thomas:
> It will give thee the tongue that can never lee."

The Queen told me that time bends when one travels between stars, and I told her that I knew the stories of Faerie. Seven years had passed for me, and over a hundred and fifty in the kingdom of Scotland: No one I had known remained alive. St. Giles kirk in Edinburgh had been torn down and built up again, with slender pillars this time, and pointed arches instead of round ones.

But most things in Erceldoune were the same. I went back to telling my ballads. I translated the old tale of Tristram and Isolde, who drank a love potion and fell in love and destroyed their young lives. I used my Language to read the hearts of men and women, and I spoke the truth. There is no way to lie in the Queen's Language, and I found I had forgotten the trick of it.

Some people are grateful for my words and pay me to speak them, and some fear them and pay me to keep silent, and I survive. I have built myself a tower; I have begun studying beetles. I have grown old. Every night I watch the stars.

The Macdougall is asking his question again. "Well?" he says gruffly. "I traveled two days for this! Will my wife be delivered of a boy, or a girl?"

There are truths one needs to hear, as well as the truths one wants to hear. "Life," I say, "is the most precious, the most costly, the rarest thing in all the wide desert of stars. That flower you wear on your jerkin could buy worlds; your battered horse in the stable is worth a thousand thousand empty stars. Life that can know love is rarer than a diamond washed into your hand from the sea. How can you judge the value of lives, man of Earth?"

But this is not the truth he came to hear, and his muscles are stiffening with anger. I sigh and set my goblet on the table, for I fear it may spill when he strikes me. "I do not know whether your child will be boy or girl," I say, "but it will be your wife's last. If she is brought to childbed, she will die there."

The next instant I am almost drowned in the wave of his feelings: terror, despair, fury at God, fury at me. I dimly hear his shouted curses as his fist smashes into my chin. Then Father and the peg-drinkers pull him away from me and carry him toward the door, still screaming. "Liar," he cries. "You lie, Thomas of Erceldoune!" Then the door slams behind him, and the only thing of his that remains is the salty smell of his tears.

In spite of his words, he believes me. And now at last I can smell his love for her, strong the way the smell of a fruit is strong after you have stabbed it with a knife. Whatever choice he makes, it will be from love.

To me his tears smell like hope, like love that may endure, waiting for me somewhere under the hill, between the stars.

While Father Owens brings me a rag to clean my bloodied lip, I let a drop of blood trickle onto my tongue. It tells me that the organs the Queen put in me are working perfectly, that I am free of disease, that barring accidents or murder I will live for many decades more on this good green world. I reach for my mead and sip it, and I taste the memories of distant bees, a very long way from Home.

The
True Story

PAT MURPHY

Pat Murphy has published four novels, The Shadow
Hunter, The Falling Woman, *and* The City, Not
Long After, *and most recently, an historical feminist
werewolf novel, titled* Nadya: The Wolf Chroni-
cles. *A portion of this novel (*"An American Childhood," *published by* Asimov's Science Fiction
Magazine *as a novelette) was a finalist on the Hugo
ballot. She has also published numerous stories, some
of which have been collected in* Points of Departure.
Her second novel, The Falling Woman, *won the
Nebula for best novel published in 1987 and the same
year, her novelette* "Rachel in Love" *won a Nebula,
the* Asimov's Readers' Poll, *and the Theodore Stur-
geon Memorial Award. More recently,* Points of Departure *won the 1990 Philip K. Dick Award for best
paperback original and her novella* "Bones" *won the
1991 World Fantasy Award.*

*"The True Story" departs from its inspiration in
almost every respect but will be easily identifiable
nonetheless.*

The
True Story

When storytellers talk about weddings at the palace, they speak of love and enchantment and living happily ever after. The storytellers are liars: these things have little to do with royal nuptials. Desire plays an important role in a king's marriage plans, but it is generally not desire for his intended. More likely, it is the desire for power.

I was seventeen years old when I married the king. He asked for my hand in marriage because my father's kingdom lay just to the south of his own, because he wanted access to the fine harbor in my father's land, because my father had a powerful army that could oppose the king in his war with the weaker kingdom to the west.

My father agreed to the betrothal because he desired certain trade concessions, because the king was a powerful ally—and rumor had it that my father's cousin was amassing an army and planning an attempt to usurp the throne.

The king had been married before, but his queen had died in childbirth the previous year. I met him only twice before our marriage—once when he asked for my hand and once when my father formally accepted the offer. The king was polite to me, but little more. He was twice my age, a brusque soldier not given to courtly ways. But my ladies-in-waiting told me that I would win his affection with my beauty. I was innocent and foolish enough to believe them. After all, I was the fairest in the land.

The organ played stately music as I walked up the aisle toward the altar. The cathedral was crowded with members of the court in all their finery. The air was thick with the scent of incense. The king stood beside the bishop at the altar. He watched me walk up the aisle, watched me and the sweet little girl who scattered flower petals on the carpet before me. I saw a glitter of excitement in his eyes, the excitement of a man who lusts after a woman. In that moment, I thought that he wanted me.

When the bishop pronounced us man and wife, the king kissed me with passion, pressing me against his jewel-encrusted robe. But when I looked up, I saw that he was not looking at me. Though his lips were pressed to mine, he was looking past me, staring at the little flower girl who stood at my side.

Perhaps I should have known then. But I was young, and I was innocent. There were many things I did not know.

At the wedding banquet, noblemen and courtiers offered toasts—to our health, to my beauty, to the king's valor in war, to the glory of the kingdom, and so on. So many toasts. I drank too much wine.

My memories of our wedding night blur and shift, like reflections in a pool where wind has rippled the water. I remember the king led me to my bedchamber. My ladies-in-waiting had gone away, leaving us in privacy. He laid me on the white featherbed and unlaced my gown, his thick fingers fumbling with the delicate fastenings, catching in the lace. Dizzy with drink, I did not resist him; nor did I help him. I lay still and let him undress me as one would undress a child.

I remember lying naked on the white featherbed. I looked up at the king, waiting to see the lust that I had seen on his face when I walked up the aisle toward him. But there was no lust in his eyes. With one rough hand, he casually pinched my nipple.

"I'm not much of a one for lovemaking," he said, his voice low. "But it's our wedding night, and certain things must happen on our wedding night."

I remember the weight of his body on mine, I remember his hands fumbling between my legs, I remember his cock pounding against me, forcing its way into me. I remember crying out in sudden pain. But I was drunk, and the pain seemed far away. When the king rolled off me, I slept, drunk on wine.

And so I became the queen and mother to the king's daughter. I had the tiny princess brought to my chambers the day after the wedding. She was less than a year old.

The peasant woman who was the child's wet nurse let me hold the baby and rock her in my arms. "She's a sweet bairn," the peasant said, her low country accent so thick I could scarcely understand her. "Skin as white as new-fallen snow. Hair as black as coal. The most beautiful baby in all the land. Her mother, the good queen, wished it so."

The woman let me hold the baby, but she stayed close by my side. She did not trust me, I thought. Now that I am older, I understand that good woman better. If I could barely understand her accent, she must have had trouble with mine. The good queen, the mother of the child she held in her arms, was dead, and I was a foreigner, come to take her place. I was the child's stepmother, and in the storytellers' tales, stepmothers are often wicked.

When I gave the baby back, she smiled in relief and rocked the child, cooing nonsense words to make her smile.

The king did not come to my chambers that night. He was planning a new campaign in his war on the kingdom to the west. Just a few days after our wedding, he went off to battle. For my ladies-in-waiting, I made a show of being concerned. I climbed to the high tower to watch his army ride away. But in my heart, I was relieved that he would not be visiting my chambers for a time.

For the next few years, the king was frequently away. He was in the west, conferring with his generals. He was in the south, negotiating trade agreements with my father. He was in the north, subduing the barbarian hordes that left their mountain strongholds in the winter to raid towns in the river valleys.

When the king did return to the court, I did my best to please him. At the advice of my ladies-in-waiting, I powdered my face with talc to make my skin white; I dabbed sweet-smelling oils behind my ears and between my breasts and on the soft skin of my thighs; I wore low-cut gowns and braided my hair in the latest style. But I could have dressed in rags for all it mattered. He came to my chambers occasionally, but only when he was drunk. Then he simply fell asleep, taking up most of the bed and snoring loudly.

I did not have the king's attention, but I had everything else a queen could want: pretty jewels, ladies to wait on me, sweet foods to eat, and a beautiful baby to play with. The child was my pet, my plaything, my darling.

Skin as white as snow, hair as black as coal, and a temperament as warm as a summer day. I doted on her. At my knee, she learned her alphabet. I taught her to play the lute and sing as a princess should. I taught her to embroider. I told her stories, and she listened gravely.

Even then, young as I was, I did not care for the tales that the storytellers told. Even then, I thought their stories were half-truths at best. In their tales, the only thing that mattered about a princess was her beauty—she did not have to be clever or bold or strong. In their tales, a princess who married a prince always lived happily ever after—she was never lonely for her own people, her family and friends.

I did not like the storytellers' tales. So I made up my own stories to tell to the child. I told her of a princess who outsmarted the dragon that carried her off—and rode home in triumph with the dragon's gold. I told her of a peasant girl who planted a magic bean and grew a magic beanstalk. I told her of a little girl in a red hood who fooled a wolf and chopped off his head. In my stories, there were no wicked stepmothers, no helpless but beautiful princesses. In my stories, each princess was clever and kind and bold and strong—as well as beautiful.

The child was seven years old when the king finally won his prolonged war with the kingdom to the west. At the victory dinner, she sat between us. I fed her sweets from my plate, and the king did the same, smiling down at the child.

The next day, the king came to my chambers looking for his daughter. I did not think it strange that he loved the child. How could anyone fail to love her? He bounced her on his knee like any fond father.

Just a few days later, I noticed that something was wrong. Always a fair-skinned child, the princess had grown even paler. She had lost her appetite. She would not eat her dinner. She did not want the treats that I offered her. When I asked her what was wrong, she shook her head, bright tears in her eyes, and did not speak.

I called for the king's doctor, a gruff man more accustomed to performing amputations on the battlefield than to coaxing children to talk of their pains. He thumped her back and peered in her mouth and said there was nothing wrong with the child, she was as healthy as her father. But I knew that something was troubling her.

That night, I woke from a deep sleep, suddenly worried about the child. I don't know why I rose from my bed and threw on my robe. I was cold and frightened and I had to see her.

Wrapped in my robe, I went to the outer chamber where my ladies-in-waiting slept. If one of them had been awake, I might have spoken of my worries and been comforted, but they slept soundly.

I went to the chamber where the child slept, but her bed was empty. The peasant woman who had been nurse to the princess since she was a babe sat in a chair by the bed, her hands busy with her knitting.

"The king's man came for her," she said, before I could ask. Her needles clicked in a furious rhythm and her accent grew broader in her agitation. "He made me get the poor poppet up from bed, so that the king could see her." When she looked up from her knitting, I could see tears glittering in her eyes. "I had to let her go," she said. "I had no choice. I have no power here."

I hurried through the cold, stone corridors. I was near the king's chambers when I heard the sound of a little girl weeping. I paused in the hall, frozen by the sound.

The corridor turned ahead of me. A large mirror hung on the wall. In the mirror, I could see that the curtain that closed off the king's chambers had been carelessly left open. I stood still, staring into the looking glass.

The king sat on his fine bed. In his nightshirt, without his crown and finery, he looked like any other man. The princess sat on his lap, her head bowed. She was weeping softly.

"There now," the king was saying, his voice a low rumble. "Don't cry, little one." As I watched, his rough hand lifted the hem of her nightgown and began stroking her thigh. "Your father's here." I watched, unable to move, as his hand crept higher, exposing more of the child's soft skin. Just seven years old, she was.

Watching her now, I thought of the flower girl who attended me at our wedding. I thought of the look of lust on my husband's face when he saw her walking down the aisle.

"What are you doing here?" I heard a voice behind me. I turned to face one of the king's guard, a young man who had served in the army.

I straightened my back and faced him. "Is that how you speak to your queen?" I asked in a proud voice.

He stepped back, startled for a moment.

"I have come for my daughter," I said loudly. "It is past time for her to be abed."

Not waiting for a response, I swept around the corner. The king had heard my voice. He had pulled the child's nightgown back into place, and he was bouncing her on his knee. I snatched her up and hurried away.

I was twenty-three years old, and I did not know who to talk to. I knew that the bishop would only tell me to pray for release from the devils that whispered such evil thoughts in my ear. I knew that my ladies-in-waiting would turn away and murmur among themselves that I had gone mad. In the end, I spoke to the peasant woman who was nursemaid to the princess, and she helped me send the child to safety.

Over the passing years, the storytellers have made up lies about me. They said that I was jealous of the princess, envious of her beauty. She was the fairest in the land, and I could not bear that. And so, the story goes, I asked a huntsman to take the little girl into the woods and kill her. I asked the huntsman to bring me her heart, so that I might eat it and know she was dead. Over the years, the story-tellers have claimed that I was a monster, that I was wicked, that I was jealous.

It makes no sense. But the world listened to these lies. After all, I was a woman and I was a queen, a powerful position. Everyone knows that women can't handle power. I was a beautiful woman and I was growing old, and everyone knows that drives women mad.

Let me tell you the truth of it. The peasant woman took me to a nunnery that was on the edge of town. And I spoke to the sisters there of my troubles. The nuns told me of a group of women who lived in a cottage in the forest, where they meditated and prayed. I kissed the princess good-bye and sent her away with the nuns, to hide in the forest and be safe.

The storytellers say that the princess stayed in a cottage in the forest with seven little men, seven dwarfs. In the stories, old women rarely play an important role—unless, of course, they are evil. Old women make evil potions, old women work black magic, old women envy the young and the beautiful, poisoning them, killing them, turning them into frogs. That's what the storytellers say.

In truth, seven old women in the forest cared for the little princess, keeping her safe. They taught her how to brew herb teas for the sick, how to tend a garden, how to knit and sew. The princess made friends with the animals in the forest—the birds sang to her, the squirrels and the field mice frolicked at her feet. She learned to be clever and kind and bold and strong, as well as beautiful.

The king searched for her, of course. I told him that she had been spirited away by magic. He did not believe me, but he could do nothing to prove me wrong.

He called me a cold woman, an evil woman. He shouted

and blustered. But though he longed to strike me, to lock me up, to torture me, he could do none of that. He was preparing for war with the kingdom to the east, and he needed my father's goodwill.

Sometimes, I would slip away to visit the princess, to assure myself that she was safe and happy. I went in disguise, wearing a cloak like a peasant woman, so that the king's men would not follow me. And she remained hidden in the woods and safe.

While she was hidden, I kept myself busy. Before I had been content to amuse myself with stories and embroidery, but now I had a new interest in politics and power. Whenever the king was off fighting his battles, I engaged in court intrigues, determining which of the king's councillors were weary of war, which were interested in ruling well, rather than conquering more lands. I aided these men wherever I could, providing them with status in the court, with money, with information gained from contacts at my father's court.

It took time to erode the king's power, longer still to find an officer in the king's army who could be bribed to do my bidding. But at last, when the princess was eighteen, I received word from the north. The king was dead. Killed in the heat of battle, when arrows were flying and barbarians had crashed through the king's guard. Who was to say which man's hand had killed the king—a barbarian prince or a soldier whose loyalty was no longer with the king?

I knew that the people of the kingdom would not trust me—a foreigner about whom strange stories were told. It was then that a knight, wandering in the forest (and carefully following instructions I had given him), discovered the princess in her hidden cottage. He brought her back to the palace in triumph. There, with the aid of the noblemen I had cultivated over the years, she took the throne.

The storytellers say that a prince found the princess and took her as his bride. That's not quite so. The princess became a queen—not by marrying a prince, but by taking her father's throne.

The storytellers say that the wicked queen went to the princess's wedding, where she was forced to dance in red-hot iron shoes until she was dead.

The storytellers have a great deal of imagination—but only in certain areas. They cannot imagine a king lusting after his daughter—but they can imagine a wicked queen killing a child for jealousy. I don't understand why the people believe these foolish stories. Don't they ever wonder, in all the times they hear about the evil queen, what the king was doing while the queen was sending the princess away and working her terrible spells? If the king was so good and the queen was so evil, why wasn't the king protecting his daughter?

After the princess returned to the palace, I remained for a time to make certain that there were no threats to her sovereignty. But the people loved her, and I had chosen her advisors well. She had learned wisdom in her years in the woods, and she knew how to rule fairly.

Having had enough of court intrigues, I retired to the cottage in the woods where the little princess had stayed so happily. That's where I live now, with the seven old women who saved the princess.

The men in the nearby village fear us, thinking we are witches. Women who live without men—especially old women who grow herbs, heal the sick, and befriend wild animals—are always suspect. The men fear us, but the village women know better. They stop by the cottage when they are out gathering firewood in the forest. They sit by the fire and drink tea, while they listen to my stories.

Sometimes, I tell them of Snow White, the true story rather than the storytellers' lies. I think the true story should be known.

Lost and Abandoned

JOHN CROWLEY

John Crowley lives in western Massachusetts. He is a master of the literary fantasy form, for which he has twice won the World Fantasy Award. He is the author of several novels, including Engine Summer, Little Big, Aegypt, *and* Love and Sleep, *as well as two excellent collections of short fiction,* Novelty *and* Antiquities. *Crowley rarely writes short fiction nowadays, and "Lost and Abandoned" is the result of three years of, shall we say, "encouragement?"—by the editors.*

The protagonist of "Lost and Abandoned" has a dilemma that is utterly contemporary in this rendering of a traditional tale that will soon become apparent.

Lost and
Abandoned

1. LOST

The logic was perfect and complete; there was a beginning, a middle, and an end. The beginning was love, then
came marriage, then two children even before I got out of
graduate school and got a real job. There was even a baby
carriage, a real one, the blue-black kind with great rubber
wheels, chrome brightwork, and a brougham top with a
silver scroll on the side to raise and lower it. I wonder
where it is now.

The next story element, therefore, was divorce. She with
the kids, I with the job (it wasn't logical but as a story
element it has verisimilitude, meaning that it was always
done that way then). I taught. I taught American poetry to
children, to college students, and over time began to forget
why. I thought about it a lot; I did little else but reason

out why I did what I did, and whether it was useless or not, why they should be interested, why I should try to capture their attention.

None of this intellection helped my chances for tenure. The word was that I wasn't a team player; I wasn't. I was an Atom. I had no reason beyond physics for anything that I did.

Then she showed up again. With the kids, she and he. She had a lot of plans. She was moving, she told me, to Hawaii. She'd already shipped over her cycle, and the rest of the guys were waiting for her over there. The kids were going to love it, she said. Water and fishing and cycles.

And when would I see them?

Whenever you can come out.

Money?

Somebody had told her somebody was opening a speed shop in Maui and she might work there.

It's odd how quickly two people who have seemed to be practically one person since before they were wholly out of childhood can diverge as soon as they part. I was awake most of that night, lying beside her (old times' sake), and by dawn I'd made a decision. I wanted the kids. She couldn't take them. She said she sure as hell was taking them. I said that I would take her to court and get custody before any judge: I worked, I was a college teacher, I had a suit and tie, she was a biker, or could be made to seem one. It might not have been true, that it would have been so easy; but I made her believe it. She wept; she talked it out; she hugged them a lot; she left them with me.

And when I went back to classes in September I had, instantly, a reason to teach American poetry to adolescents, and do it well, too. Love costs money; so love makes money, or is willing to try. What I could not find a reason for doing in itself became quite easy to do when I did it for them. I went and talked all day about Emily Dickinson and Walt Whitman to put bowls of oatmeal before them, bicycles in the garage for them. And oddest of all (maybe not so odd, how would I know, I've only done all this once) I think I was a better teacher, too.

Unfortunately I had stumbled into all this—ordinary life, I guess, the thing that had kept all of my colleagues at their work and playing for the team—just that little bit too late. Despite my new need and my new willingness, I got turned down for tenure. And that in academe being equivalent to dismissal, I now looked into a kind of abyss, one I had heard about, read about, been touched by in stories, and had not thought was possible for me to encounter, though a moment's thought would have told me that countless men and women live facing it all the time.

Did I think of shipping them to Hawaii? No, never. Some doors cannot be gone back through.

So the next scene is the dark of the woods.

I used all my contacts to get a job that almost no one, it would seem, would want to have, thereby entering into another level of this thing, where the hewer of wood, the drawer of water, grows desperate not for release but for more water to draw, wood to hew, so his kids and he won't have to beg.

An inner-city enrichment program for no-longer-quite-youthful offenders, which had tenuous state funding and a three-story house downtown that had been seized for taxes. They were given courses in basic English and other work toward a high-school equivalency diploma, and seminars in ethics and self-expression. They got time off their probation for attending faithfully. Do you have better ideas?

The group I taught English to was about the same age as my old students, a group who had appeared ordinary enough then but now in hindsight and from here appeared as young godlings awash in ease and possibility. Days we worked on acquiring the sort of English language in which newspapers and books and government documents are written, a language different from the one most of them spoke, though using many similar words. We diagrammed sentences, a thing I am the last teacher of English on the continent to remember how to do; they liked that. In the evenings we met again. We were going to write stories.

They have stories, certainly. They tend to spill them rather than tell them. It seemed grotesque to try to chasten them, and make them shapely, make them resemble good stories; but that's what I was hired to do, and simply to listen is too hard. "A beginning, a middle, and an end," I say. " 'The king died and then the queen died' is a story. 'The king died and then the queen died of grief' is a plot. Who, what, when, where, how." And they listen, looking at me from out of their own stories, inside which they live, as street people live within their ragged shelters. Not one grew up with a father: not one. I know what crimes some of them committed, what they have done.

Late at night then I bus over to the adjacent neighborhood, one small step up in the social ladder, and climb the stairs to my apartment; let myself in, awake the sitter, asleep before the glowing television, and send her home.

They grow so fast. In the city even faster. Most of my salary goes to their private school, called fatuously the Little Big Schoolhouse, but really a good place; they love it, or did. They're getting restive, weirdly angry sometimes in ways they never were before, which leaves me hurt and baffled and desperately afraid. They don't want sitters anymore. I am going to come home and find them gone; or find one of them gone and the other silent, looking at me in reproach, can't have her, couldn't keep her.

*   *   *

"Let's retell a story," I told my students. "Just to get our chops. We'll all write the same story. Not long. Three pages max. A story you all know. All you have to do is tell it, from beginning to end, not leaving anything important out."

But it was not a story they all knew, and so I had to tell it to them. They listened with both eyes and ears, as my children had once. My boy, at the point in the story when the two lost children understood that the new protector they had found intended them not good but mortal harm, had cried out *It's their mother!* Which seemed to me to be an act of literary criticism of the highest order; and for the first time I noticed that indeed the mother, like the other, is dead at the story's end.

A girl named Cyntra wanted to know: Was I going to do this, too?

I said yes I would. I would do it in three pages. I hadn't thought of doing it but yes I would.

I know this story. I know it now, though I didn't before. I will write mine for me, as they will write theirs for themselves; we will trade them and try to read them with eyes and ears.

Three pieces of mail in the box on this night when I got home. A postcard from Hawaii. An official letter telling me that the enrichment program is being zeroed out, and my services will not be required. An answer to my personal ad in the *Free Press*, written in a clear strong hand. A picture, too.

My children still there, asleep but not undressed, unwashed and sprawled over the couch and the floor: they would not permit a baby-sitter, said they could take care of themselves. They are at least still here.

I will write my story with a beginning, a middle, and no end. No bread crumbs, no candy, no woods, no oven, no treasure. No who, what, where, when. And it will all be there.

Where will they go, those kids?

2. ABANDONED

Poverty is not a crime. Infatuation is not a crime either; and when a man who has loved his wife dearly, and had two children with her, boy and girl, children he loves deeply and in whose eyes he sees her every single day—when that man falls helplessly in love again, those children might find it in their hearts, if not then perhaps later on, after a period of transition, to forgive him. And to love this new woman, too, as he loves her, without ever forgetting—as he himself cannot—the other and earlier woman.

Children, though, spring from but one mother; and they, even if they cannot remember her, can't forget her either. The fact that he can see in their eyes the reflection of the woman who bore them can come to seem a reproach. Perhaps it is a reproach. That's certainly the way the woman who comes to replace her in their home might see it: a constant reproach, a claim never able to be made good and yet never withdrawn. And it's possible that—she being as infatuated as he, filled up with that domineering love that allows no rival (no crime; it happens), might scheme somehow to remove them, shut their eyes, shut their mouths for good. Especially if there weren't enough for all of them.

Was it a crime that he listened, that he chose between her and them? That was a crime, and he knew it when he abandoned them. Abandoned: went away from them when he thought they could not return, though at the same time he brought them back with him, of course, he would have to, have to bring them with him back home where they would trouble his sleep thereafter.

But we are always abandoned. We abandon our parents as we grow, and yet it seems to us that they abandon us; that's the story we tell. And often—usually, not always—we discover that abandonment is flight, too: our flight away. We leave a trail to guide us back, but it can disappear behind us as we go on.

Harder than it seems, abandonment; they who are to be abandoned are often more resourceful than we who abandon expect them to be or than the act or the name of the act (abandonment) allows them to be. Often enough they will not suffer being abandoned, must be shed or forced out or tricked into remaining behind when we go. Often they must be abandoned not once but more than once, each act of abandoning hardening our hearts further, until in the end the logistics of the deed are all we can think of, the awful logic, just get it over with.

Abandonment implies redemption, the finding of the lost, not always but sometimes: safety discovered in the midst of danger, altering the new equation of loss and abandonment again, and posing a question usually, a judgment to make though we aren't wise enough to make it; we make it anyway because we have no choice. Look how wonderful, all sweet, all good, and we so hungry and needy.

Finding out then that we have made a wrong decision, the worst possible decision, one we can't help having made and that we know as soon as we have made it was the wrong one, and that it can't be taken back. Finding out that this is what abandonment means: death at the hands of those we have relied on. They taught us to rely on them, on the two of them, their love, and then abandoned us: but still we only know how to rely on others, and have done so, and we were wrong, and now we will die. We didn't know this about life.

Only perhaps it isn't death, perhaps there is an exit from the cage, the death; perhaps we know better than we thought. Perhaps we have ourselves got reserves of cleverness, and will, and cruelty. Yes we have. We, too, can fool. We can do as we have been done by. And it is abandonment that taught us.

So this is life not death after all. It's even profit. We didn't know this about life either, what can be won from it by need and the willingness to be cunning, and cruel.

It was a long time ago. You find that even if you have lost the way home there is a path that reaches out to you from there, a path that you are bound to discover like it or not: and then, when you return there with what you have won, it isn't the place you left. You can forgive them, if they are still there to forgive: or you can refuse to. What you did and learned from abandonment—yours of them, theirs of you—has made home different. Now you can go or stay.

The Breadcrumb Trail

NINA KIRIKI HOFFMAN

*Nina Kiriki Hoffman lives in Oregon, with four cats. She is the author of two solo novels—*The Thread That Binds the Bones, *which won the Horror Writers Association's Bram Stoker Award for Best Achievement in First Novel in 1994 and* The Silent Strength of Stones, *published in 1995. She also collaborated with Tad Williams on* Child of an Ancient City, *a novella.* Common Threads *contains the text of* The Thread That Binds the Bones *plus fourteen other stories about the characters in the novel. Her more than 150 short stories have appeared in numerous magazines and anthologies. This is her first professional poetry sale.*

Nina Kiriki Hoffman says "I owe my life to fairy tales. My mother had a radio program called Stories Children Love, *in which she read fairy tales aloud, and needed a recording engineer; my father had a recording studio. That's how they met. As a child I grew up listening to records of my mother reading fairy tales aloud. Sometimes she read them to us in person."*

The Breadcrumb Trail

Only breadcrumbs mark the trail—
Breadcrumbs, which the waiting birds
Like as much as anything.
When stones led the way home, stones lay
    undisturbed.
White stones are valued only by themselves and
    children.
Breadcrumbs invite all the world to eat.

When all we have in our pockets is bread,
And we are led into the woods to die,
Our only hope of salvation is to follow our own trail
    home.
All we have is breadcrumbs to mark our trail
And night is coming.

We enter this dark forest of the mind
Led by the only person that we trust
Who leaves us
Leaves us here with shadows
And witches
And dangerous sweets.
We have spent our last bits of home
To mark our trail.
Spent, and brought birds who fly away.

Nothing is safe here.
Every shadow hides a tooth.
The sky is dark. The ground is damp.
The trees are too tall to climb.
We scuff up leaves
And hide beneath them
Hoping for warmth from this place of fear.

In the morning our crumbs are gone.

The tale would lead us deeper into the forest
To the house of the witch
Who waits for unwary orphans
Who offers us food in order to feed
Who offers us shelter in order to cage
Who teaches us to fear the forest
And everything in it.

But we have slept deep and we have dreamed earth.
Last night we left a trail of bread,
Brought birds who flew away
And left behind
Little star-shaped footprints
Little four-toed presses
Into earth.

Earth can tell us where we walked yesterday
For we have left footprints too
Where our prints and the birds' lie
There is the path we need
If we are careful and watchful.
There is the path we can follow,
Though it no longer leads to home and safety
For at its other end are the ones who left us here.
Still, the trail takes us back to where we started
So we can pick our own path next time.

On Lickerish Hill

SUSANNA CLARKE

Susanna Clarke lives in Cambridge, England, where
she spends most of her time editing cookbooks and
watching people take photographs of food. For her stories she likes to blend history with magic. She is currently working on a novel set in a nineteenth-century
Britain where magic is a respectable profession, more
or less. Her other stories appear in the anthologies
Starlight *and* Neil Gaiman's Sandman: Book of
Dreams.

*According to Susanna Clarke "On Lickerish Hill"
is set in East Anglia in the seventeenth century,
when the distinctions between superstition and scientific investigation were not as clear-cut as they are
today. The* Brief Lives *and* Miscellanies *of Miranda's "deare Friend," John Aubrey, are full of accounts of fairies and spirit-possession that he got from
"eye witnesses." Confusion between the fairies they
heard about from their neighbors and the Pharisees
in the Bible was commonplace among country people.*

On Lickerish Hill

When I waz a child I lived at Dr Quince's on the other side of Lickerish Hill. Sometimes in a winters-twilight I have look't out of Dr Quince's windowe and seen Lickerish Hill like a long brown shippe upon a gray sea and I have seen far-awaie lights like silver starres among the dark trees. The Pharisees live there but I never once sawe one.

My mother was mayde and cook to Dr Quince, an ancient and learned gentleman (face, very uglie like the picture of a horse not well done; dry, scantie beard; moist, pale eyes). This good old man quickly perceived what waz hid from my mother: that my naturall Genius inclin'd not to sweeping dairies or baking cakes or spinning or anie of the hundred things she wish'd me to know, but to Latin, Greeke and the study of Antiquities, and these he taught me. He alwaies meant that I should learne Hebrew, Geometrie, the

Mathematiques, and he would have taught me this yeare but Time putt a trick on him and he died last summer.

The day after the pore old doctor died my mother baked five pies. Now malicious persons will open their mouths and lies will flie out and buzz about the World, but the truth is that those pies (which my mother baked) were curiously small and, for certaine pressing and private reasons of my owne (a Great and Sudden Hunger) I ate them all, which was the cause of a quarrel betweene my mother and me. Angrilie shee foretold that terrible Catastrophes would befall me (povertie, marriage to beggars and gypsies, etc., etc.). But, as Mr Aubrey sayz, such Beautie as mine could not long remain undiscover'd, and so it waz that I married Sir John Sowreston and came to Pipers Hall. Pipers Hall is the loveliest old house—alwaies very smiling in the sunshine. It waz built long ago (I thinke in the time of King Solomon). About the house are many lawns where stand ancient trees that overtop the roofs like Gracious and Gigantique Ladies and Gentlemen from more Heroique Times, all robed in dresses of golden sunlight. Its shadie alleys are carpeted with water-mint and thyme and other sweet-smelling Plantes so that in a summerstwilight when Dafney and I walke there and crush them with our feet 'tis as if an Angell caress't you with his Breath.

Sir John Sowreston is two-and-thirty yeares of age; size, middling; eyes, black; legges, handsome. He smiles but rarely and watches other men to see when they laugh and then does the same. Since a boy he haz been afflicted with a Great Sadnesse and Fitts of Black Anger which cause his neighbours, friends and servants to feare him. It is as if some Divinitie, jealous of the Gifts Heav'n haz bestowed on him (Youth, Beautie, Riches, etc., etc.) haz putt an eville

Spell on him. There waz a little dogge borne upon our Wedding-daye. At three or four weeks old it would always goe a little sideways when it walked and would climb upon Sir John's shoulder when he sat after dinner and sleep there, as if it loved him extreamlie. But, being frighted by a horse looking in at the windowe, it fouled a coat belonging to Sir John with its excrements and Sir John putte it in a sack and drowned it in the horse-pond. We called it Puzzle because (Dafney sayd) whatsoever happen'd puzzled it sorely. (I thinke it was puzzled why it died.) Now Sir John haz gott three great blacke dogges.

Two months after Sir John and I were married we travelled to Cambridge to seek a cure for Sir John's melancholie from Doctor Richard Blackswann, a very famose Physitian. We took with us a little cristall flask that had some of Sir John's water in it. Dr Blackswann went into a little closet behind a curtain of blacke velvet and prayed upon his knees. The Angell Raphael then appearing in the closet (as commonly happens whenever this doctor prays) peer'd into Sir John's urine. Dr Blackswann told us that the Angell Raphael knew straightway from the colour of it (reddish as if there waz bloude in it) that the cause of Sir John's extreame Want of Spirits was a lack of Learned Conversation. The Angell Raphael said that Sir John muste gather Scholars to his howse to exercise their Braines with Philosophie, Geometrie, Rhetorique, Mechanicks etc., etc., and that hearing of their schemes would divert Sir John and make his thoughts to runne in pleasanter courses.

Sir John waz very much pleased with this Scheme and all the way home we sang Ballads together and were so merry that Sir John's three great black dogges raised their voices with us in praise of learned Dr Blackswann and the Angell Raphael.

The evening we came home I waz walking in the garden by myselfe among the Heroique Trees when I met Mrs Sloper, my mother. Mrs Abigail Sloper, widow; person thin and stringy; face the shape of a spoon and the colour of green cheese; cook and nurse to the late Dr Hieronymous Quince; made nervous by Dr Quince's talking Hebrew on purpose to discompose her (she mistook it for incantations)—a cruel Satire on her Ignorance, but I could not gett him to leave off; talkes to herselfe when in a fright; haz two old English Catts (that are white with some blewnesse upon them)—Solomon Grundy (four yeares old) and Blewskin (ten yeares old) and a Cowe called Polly Diddle (one yeare old); in 1675 she buried a little blew pot of shillings at the bottom of Dr Quince's garden, under some redd-currant bushes, but he dying shortly after and the house being sold very suddenly, she was cast into a Great Perplexitie how to recover her monies which she haz not yet resolved.

"Good Evening, mother, my deare," sayz I. "Come into the howse and have some vittles and drinke."

But she would not answer me and cast her Glances all over the garden, a-twisting and a-twisting of her apron. "Oh!" sayz she (with her eyes fix't upon a Beech-tree, so that she seemes to address it). "My daughter'll be so vex't."

"No, I won't," sayz I. "Why are you in such a pickle? Take time, my deare, and tell me what you're afeard of."

But instead of a Replie she rambled about the Garden, complain'd to a Briar-rose that I am Ungrateful to her, told two little Oringe-trees that I doe not love her.

"Oh, mother!" sayz I. "I doe not wish to be angrie, but you will make me so if you doe not tell me what the matter is."

At this she hid her head in her apron; wept very piteously; then suddenly reviv'd.

"Well!" sayz she (apparently to a monument of Kinge Jupiter that look't downe on her with much contempt). "You remember the day after the pore old doctor died I baked five pies and my daughter ate 'em all, first and last!"

"Oh! Mother!" sayz I. "Why doe you perpetuate these old quarrels between us? Those old pies waz such tiddly little thinges!"

"No, they warn't" sayz she to Jupiter (as if he contradicted her). "Howsomediver," sayz she, "I were so vex't an' I muddled about an' I told little old Solomon Grundy and old Blewskin . . ." [she meanes her Catts] ". . . I sayz to 'em, My daughter haz ate five pies today! Five pies! And I lookes up and I sees Sir John Sowreston a-sitting on his hobby-horse—as bewtiful as butter. And he sayz to me, 'What are you a-saying of, Mrs Sloper?' Well! I knowed Sir John Sowreston waz extreamlie in Love with my daughter an' I knowed he'd come to looke at her through the holes in the old Elderhedge an' I didn't like to say as how my daughter had ate five pies. So I sayz, right sly like, I sayz my daughter haz spun five skeins o' flax today . . ."

"Mother!" sayz I. "You never! You never told Sir John such a lie!"

"Well then," sayz she, "I did. An' there ain't nothing but good come to my daughter a'cos of it. Sir John Sowreston lookes at me with his bewtiful Eyes like two dishes o' Chocolate a-poppin' out of his Head and he sayz to me Stars o' mine! I never heerd o' anyone as could do that! Mrs Sloper, I'll marry your daughter on Sunday.—Fair enough, sayz I, an' shall she have all the vittles she likes to eat and all the gowns she likes to get and all the company she likes to have? Oh yes! sayz he. All o' that. But come the last month o' the first year she must spinne five skeins o' flax every day. Or else . . .''

"Or else what, mother?" sayz I in a Fright.

"Owww!" she cries. "I sayd as how she'd be vex't! I knew she would! I have made her a Grand Ladye with such a bewtiful Husband and all the vittles she likes to eat and all the gowns she likes to get and all the company she likes to have—and her never a bitt grateful. But," she sayz a-tapping herselfe upon the nose and lookinge sly, "no harm will come to my daughter. Sir John Sowreston is still ex-treamlie in Love an' he haz forgott those old skeins of flax completely . . .''

Then, having vindicated her-selfe in the Opinions of all the rose-bushes and Beech-trees and monuments in the garden, my mother went away againe.

Now Sir John Sowreston does not forget anie thinge and I knew very well that, sure as there are Pharisees on Lick-erish Hill, come the first daie of the last month of the first yeare of our marriage, he would aske me for those skeins. I waz very much tempted to sit down and weep oceans of bitter tears but then I thought of the noble and virtuous Roman matrons that Dr Quince told me of, who never wept no matter how great their sufferings; and I thought how I had a very ingeniose head and alwaies a thousand notions flitting about inside it and how I waz besides as beautiful as an Angell. I dare say, sayz I, there is some verie cunning way to overcome this Fate. And I determined to discouver what it waz very suddenlie.

Sir John went to London to seek out Ingeniose Gentlemen to cure his Melancholie. In this he waz shortly successful for nothing is so agreeable to a Scholar than to goe and stay in a rich man's howse and live at his expense. Mr Aubrey and Sir John Sowreston gott acquainted, and Sir John waz very pressing with Mr Aubrey to come to Pipers Hall and Mr Aubrey who waz pressed another way (Great Debts he could not Pay and Danger of Arrests!), waz glad to come immediately.

Mr Aubrey is writing downe all that he can remember of the customes of former times. He smells of brandy and chalke and is finely spotted all over with Inke. He haz pieces of paper in all his pockets on which he is writing his Histories. He is a Member of the Royal Society. He is my deare Friend. He is putting down all the lives of Great and Ingeniose men so that their Genius may not be forgot. Mr Aubrey sayz that he is like a man plucking out spars and relicks from the Shipwreck of Time and tossing them upon the sand. But, sayz Mr Aubrey, the Waters of Oblivion have the best of it.

For severall years Mr Aubrey haz wish'd to come into this Countie which is stuff't with Ancient Persons who, as Mr Aubrey sayz, may suddenly die and cheat Posterity of their Remembrances, if some Publick-spirited and Ingeniose man does not come and sett them downe; and Mr Aubrey wish'd very much to carry out this Design but was prevented, having no money and no friends residing in this part of the Countrey whom he could suddenly delight by arriving for a good long visit. Mr Aubrey waz once a very rich man with lands; estates; pleasant farmes; cowes; sheepe, etc., etc., and (I thinke) great boxes of silver and gold. But he haz lost it all through Law-suites, Misfortunes and the Unkindnesse of his Relations. Mr Aubrey sayz that nothing so distracts a Scholar or drawes so many teares from a Scholar's head as Law-suites. But, sayz Mr Aubrey, I am now very merry, Miranda, my Troubles are at an end. And he asked me to lend him three pounds.

The other noble Scholars arrived shortly afterwards. They are all very memorablie famose. Mr Meldreth, a sweet, shy gentleman the colour of dust, is for Insects and haz 237 dead ones in a box. Mr Shepreth haz discovered the date upon which the Citie of London waz first built. This, being like to its *Birthe-daye*, haz enabled him to caste its horoscope: he knowes all its Future. Dr Foxton haz shewne by Irrefutable Arguments that Cornishmen are a kind of Fishe. His beard curles naturallie—a certaine sign of witt.

All winter the Learned Conversation of the Scholars delighted Sir John extreamlie. But it is part of Sir John's Affliction that whatever pleases him best at first, he most detests at last. In spring he began privately to calle them Raskall-Jacks, Rumble-Guts, Drunke, Ungrateful; complain'd that they ate too much, despis'd their Learning and frowned very blacke upon them at dinner until the poore Scholars had scarcelie anie Appetite to eate so much as a bit of Breade and all satt with a kinde of Lownesse on their Spirits. Summer came againe and it waz almost a yeare since Sir John and I were married. I tried very hard to conjure a cunning Scheme out of my Head but could think of nothing until the verie last daie.

Upon that daie the Scholars and I were sitting together beneathe the great Beeche-tree which stands before the dore of Pipers Hall.

Mr Meldreth sighed. "Gentlemen," he sayz, "We are very poor physick. Poor Sir John is as unhappy as ever he waz."

"True," sayz Mr Shepreth, "but we have made Lady Sowreston . . ." [he meant me] ". . . very merry. She loves to heare our Learned Conversation."

"There is no merit in that," sayz Mr Aubrey. "Miranda is alwaies merry."

"Mr Aubrey," sayz I.

"Yes, Miranda?" sayz he.

" 'Tis a very curious thinge, Mr Aubrey," sayz I. "I have lived all my life neare Lickerish Hill, but I never once sawe a Pharisee."

"A Pharisee?" sayz Mr Aubrey. "What doe you meane, child?"

"They live on Lickerish Hill," sayz I. "Or under it. I doe not know which. They pinche dairymaides blacke and blewe. Other times they sweepe the floor, drinke the creame and leave silver pennies in shoes. They putte on white cappes, crie Horse and Hattock, flie through the aire on Bitts of Strawe—generally to the Kinge of France's wine-cellar where they drinke the wine out of silver cups and then off to see a wicked man hanged—which person they may save if they have a minde to it."

"Oh!" sayz Dr Foxton, " 'tis *Fairies* she meanes."

"Yes," sayz I. "That is what I sayd. Pharisees. I have never seen one. Dr Quince haz told me that they are not so common as once they were. Dr Quince haz told me that the Pharisees are leaving and will never more be seen in England. For my-selfe I never sawe one. But many Ancient Persons worthy of Belief have seen them on Lickerish Hill, trooping out of the World on Ragged Ponies, their heads bowed downe with Sadnesse, descending into dark hollows and blewe shadowes betwixt the trees. My Opinion is," sayz I, "that there can be no better taske for an Antiquarie than to discouver all he can of the Pharisees and I thinke there can be no better place in all the World to look for Pharisees than Pipers Hall under Lickerish Hill, for that is where they live. Mr Aubrey," sayz I, "Doe you know anie Spells to conjure Pharisees?"

"Oh, severall!" sayz Mr Aubrey "Mr Ashmole (who is a noble Antiquary and haz made the Collection at Oxford) haz putt them downe in his Papers."

"Mr Aubrey," sayz I.

"Yes, Miranda?" sayz he.

"Will you shew me the Spells, Mr Aubrey?"

But before he could answer me Mr Meldreth ask'd with a Frowne if they worked?

"I doe not knowe," sayz Mr Aubrey.

"Who shall we conjure first?" askes Dr Foxton.

"Titania," sayz Mr Shepreth.

"A common Pharisee," sayz I.

"Why, Miranda?" askes Mr Shepreth.

"Oh!" sayz I. "They can doe a hundred clever thinges. Bake cakes, gather in flockes of sheepe, churne butter, spinne flaxe . . ."

All the Scholars laugh't very much at this.

"So can your mayde, Miranda," sayz Mr Shepreth. "No, 'tis fairie politics we chiefly wish to learn. And for this purpose the Queen is best. Besides," sayz Mr Shepreth, "she may give us presents."

"Tut," sayz Mr Meldreth. " 'Tis onlie young men with handsome faces that she woos with presents."

"We are handsome enough," sayz Mr Shepreth.

Dr Foxton sayd that it waz one of the many inconveniences of discoursing with Fairies, that they may at anie moment disappear and so the gentlemen agreed to draw up a list of questions—so that when they discouvered a Fairie willing to speak to them all pertinent questions should be convenient to hand.

Quaere: if the Faeries have anie Religion among them?

Oh! sayd Dr Foxton. There waz a Fairie-woman in Cornwall who heard a Reverend gentleman saying his prayers. She asked him if there were salvation and eternal life for such as shee? No sayd the Reverend gentleman. With a cry of despair she instantly threw herself over a cliff and into the foaming sea. This, sayd Dr Foxton, he gott from a very Pious person who all his life abhorred Lying. Dr Foxton sayd he would not believe it else and Mr Meldreth, who is of a sweet and gentle nature, wept a little to think on't.

Quaere: if they have anie marrying among them?

Mr Shepreth sayd he believed they did *not* live together like Christians and turtle-doves, but had all their ladyes in common. Tut! sayz Mr Meldreth. Ha! cried Mr Aubrey and wrote it down very fast.

Quaere: if it is true (as some people say) that they are a much-decayed people and not so strong as they used to be?

Quaere: their system of Gouvernment: if a Monarchie or a Com-monwealthe?

Quaere: if a Monarchie then whether it is true (as we have heerd tell) that the Queen and King of the Pharisees have quarrelled?

Quaere: if it is true that the Queen cannot in one thinge gou-verne herselfe?

This went on until the Scholars all fell a-quarrelling, having now gott fortie-two questions to ask the poor Phar-isee when they found it and Mr Foxton sayd a Christian could not bear to be so putt upon let alone a Fairie. Mr Aubrey sighed and sayd he would trie to reduce the num-ber.

"Here is Sir John Sowreston!" whispers Dr Foxton.

"Mr Aubrey!" sayz I.

"Yes, Miranda?" sayz he.

But I had no time to aske him what I muste because Sir John hurried me into the howse.

"Oh, my deare," sayz I to Sir John. "What is the matter? Do not let the noble Scholars see you looke so Melancholie! They still hope to chear you."

"Where are we going, Sir John?" sayz I. "I never sawe this little staircase before. Is it some secret place that you dis-couvered when you played here as a boye? Is that what you wishe to shew me?"

"I never saw this room before," sayz I. "And here are your three goode dogges, fighting with each other for some bones. Sir John, doe such great big dogges like to be shutt up in such a little room? And what is this little spinning wheele for?"

"Miranda," sayz Sir John, "you are very younge and for that reason I have often gouverned my-selfe when I should be angrie. Your lookes are often insolent. Your speech is full of Conceit and not womanly."

"Oh no, my deare!" sayz I. "You mistake. Those are lov-inge lookes I give you."

"Perhaps," sayz he. "I doe not know. Sometimes, Miranda, I half believe . . . But then againe, all men lye—and all women too. They drinke in Lyes with their mother's milke. As little children they delight to bear false witness one against the other. The Lyes and deceits that are practised

on me every day by the common sort of people . . ." (He
meant our Servants, Neighbours, Lawyers, Relations, etc.,
etc.) ". . . pricke my flesh like the stinges of bees and mos-
quitos. I scarcelie regard them. But a Lye from you, Miranda, will be a long, sharp sworde that slippes between
my bones and cuttes my Heart. You swore when you married me that you could spinne five skeins of flax every
daye for a month."

(This is not true—it waz my mother that sayd it.) But all
I say, is, "Spinne five skeins of flax in a daye . . . Oh, Sir
John! I never heard of anie one that could doe that!"

"I hope, Miranda, that you have not lyed. A wife, Miranda,
haz her Husband's conscience in her keeping and muste
so order her actions that they tempt not her Husband to
sinne. It is a wicked thinge to tempt others to sinne. To
kille someone in anger is a sinne."

He wept a little to thinke on't, but it waz not for me he
wept but for his owne Unhappy Spirit, thinking that when
he murdered me 'twould be all his owne Misfortune and
none of mine.

"Oh!" sayz I chearfully. "Doe not be afraid, my deare. I
shall spinne you thread so soft and fine. And Dafney and
I shall make you shirts of the thread I spinne and at every
touch of those shirts you will thinke I kisse you."

But he shutt the doore upon me and lock't it and went
awaie.

From the windowe I sawe the Scholars sitting beneath the
Beeche-tree. They were all very merry now that Sir John
waz gone. As the twilight deepen'd they dranke each oth-

ers healthes and sang a ballad of their youth about a shep-
herdesse that some gentlemen liked. Then all joined armes
and sang againe and off to bed together.

The kitchen door opened and let out a little firelight upon
the lavender bushes. Dafney look't out. (Dafney Babraham:
mayde to Lady Miranda Sowreston that is my-selfe; yellow
haire; smelles of rosemary and other good thinges; haz two
gownes, a blew and a redd.) She called faintly, "Madam,
Madam." She came along the path; cast her lookes this
way and that; seemed quite distracted from not knowing
where to finde me. She feared Sir John had alreadie
drowned me in the horse-pond.

"Oh!" she cries, spying me. "What are you a-doing up
there? Where did that little windowe come from? I'll come
to you directly, my deare!"

"No," sayz I. "Go to bed. I shall sleepe in this little room
tonight. 'Tis my fancy."

"I heare terrible fierce noyses," she sayz.

" 'Tis onlie some good dogges that keepe me safe," sayz
I. "Good night my deare. God blesse you. I am not a bitt
afraid."

But all through the night the three dogges growled and
twitched as if in their sleepe they hunted me on Lickerish
Hill.

In the morning Sir John brought me flax and vittles. Then
he went awaie againe. Outside my windowe a silvery mist
like a Cloude cover'd Pipers Hall. Everything in the world

(*scilicet* Trees, Hedges, Fountains, Monuments, Dwellings of Men, Cattle, Hens, Bees, Horses etc., etc.) waz grey and faint in the silver Aire. There waz a golden glory all around Lickerish Hill but the Sunne did not yet peepe above the brow of the hill. All the birds sang and all the grey roses hung downe their heads with heavie dew.

Four grey figures in long robes approached the Beech-tree that stood before the doore. One grey figure sneezed and complained of the freshnesse and sharpnesse of the Aire that, he sayd, waz not wholesome for Men. Another grey figure regretted eating too much cheese and pickled herring the night before. And a third waz fearful that the Pharisees might steale him awaie.

Dr Foxton had gott a magickal hatt that (he thought) once belonged to the old, wicked magician, Simon Forman. He putt it on. The Sunne peep'd over Lickerish Hill. Mr Aubrey beganne to read the Spelle in a clear voice. It waz stuff't as full of magic words as a puddinge is of plumms.

"I, John Aubrey, call thee, Queen Titania, in the name of . . ."

And I listened very carefully and repeated the words after him—but where he sayd 'Queen Titania' I sayd 'Pharisee Vulgaris.'

". . . conjure and straightly charge and command thee by Tetragrammaton, Alpha and Omega and by all other high and reverent . . ."

The miste that cover'd Pipers Hall turned to rose and blew and silver. I heard a noyse in the orchard. But it waz onlie three birds that rose into the Aire.

". . . meekely and mildely to my true and perfect sight and truly without fraud, Dissymulation or deceite, resolve and satisfye me in and of all manner of such questions and commands and demandes as I shall either aske, require . . ."

The miste that cover'd Pipers Hall turned to golde. I heard a noyse by the hen-houses. But it waz onlie a foxe that ranne home to the woods.

". . . quickly, quickly, quickly, quickly, come, come, come. Fiat, Fiat, Fiat. Amen, Amen, Amen . . ." Mr Aubrey paused. "Et cetera," he sayz with a Flourishe.

The miste that cover'd Pipers Hall turned to little droppes of water. I heard a noyse beneathe the windowe but I could not tell what it waz.

There waz a long silence.

Then Dr Foxton sighed. " 'Tis well-known that the Queen of the Fairies is not to be trusted. Shee is capricious," he sayz.

"Perhaps," sayz Mr Shepreth (meaning to be Satirical), "shee did not like your hatt."

Suddenly the three dogges beganne to howle and runne and leape in a manner very strange to see as if they had fallen into a kinde of Extascie. It waz so violent and continued for so longe that I hid my-selfe in a corner.

"Woman," sayz a Voice. "What are you a-crying for?"

"Oh!" sayz I. "Are you the Pharisee?"

A small black thinge. Hairie. Legges like jug-handles. Face—not a bitt handsome. It had a long blacke taile—at which I waz much surprised. Irishmen have tailes neare a quarter of a yard longe (as I thinke is commonly known) but I never hearde before that Pharisees have them.

"Are you a good Pharisee or a bad?" sayz I.

The Pharisee, a-twirling and a-twirling of his long, black taile, seemed to consider my inquiry. "Never you minde," it sayz at last. It cock't its head in the direction of the win-dowe. "There be four peevish old men a-standin' in your meadow, wi' queer old hatts on their heads, all jammerin' together."

"Oh!" sayz I. "They are disappointed in their Spelle which haz had No Success. Whereas mine haz summoned you promptlie to the proper place."

"I don't take no notice o' frimmickin' old Spelles an' such like," sayz the little black thinge, picking his teeth with a bit of old rabbit-bone. "But I waz extreamlie kewrious to know what you waz a-crying for."

So I told him my historie, beginning with the pies (which were so curiouslie small) and ending with the five skeines of flax. "For the truth is, Pharisee," sayz I, "that my na-turall Genius inclines not at all to brewing or baking cakes or spinning or anie of those thinges, but to Latin, Greeke and the study of Antiquities and I can no more spinne than flie."

The Pharisee consider'd my Dilemma. "This is what I'll doe," it sayz at last. "I'll come to your windowe ev'ry morning an' take the flax an' bring it back spun at night."

"Oh, a hundred thousand thankes!" sayz I. " 'Tis a very generous turne you doe me. But then, you know, I have alwaies heard that Pharisees doe wonderful kind thinges and never ask for pay of anie sorte or anie thinge in returne."

"You heerd that, did you?" sayz the little black thinge, a-scritch-scritch-scratching of his armpit. "Well, woman, you heerd wrong."

"Oh!" sayz I.

The Pharisee look't at me out of the corners of its little blacke eyes and sayz, "I'll give you three guesses ev'ry night to guess my name, an' if you ain't guessed it afore the month's up, Woman, you shall be mine!"

"Well then," sayz I, "I thinke I shall discover it in a month."

"You thinke so, doe you?" sayz the Pharisee and laugh't and twirl'd its taile. "What be the names o' they old dogges?"

"Oh!" sayz I. "That I doe know. Those dogges are called Plato, Socrates and Euclid. Sir John told me."

"Noo, they ain't," sayz the Pharisee. "One on 'em's called Wicked. The other un's Worse an' the third's Worst-of-all. They told me theerselves."

"Oh!" sayz I.

"Happen," sayz the Pharisee with great satisfaction, "you don't know yer own name."

" 'Tis Miranda Sloper," sayz I. ". . . I meane Sowreston."

"Woman," sayz the Pharisee laughing, "you shall be mine."

And he took the flax and flew awaie.

All daie longe there waz a kind of twilight in the little room made by the shadowes of leaves that fell over its white walls. When the twilight in the room waz match't by a twilight in the World outside the Pharisee return'd.

"Good evening, Pharisee," sayz I. "How doe you fare?"

The little blacke thinge sighed. "Kind o' middlin' like. My old ears is queer an' I have a doddy little ache in my foot."

"Tut," sayz I.

"I have brung the skeins," it sayz. "Now, woman, what's my name?"

"Is it Richard?" sayz I.

"Noo, it ain't," sayz the little blacke thinge and it twirl'd its taile.

"Well, is it George?" sayz I.

"Noo, it ain't," sayz the little blacke thinge and it twirl'd its taile.

"Is it Nicodemus?" sayz I.

"Noo, it ain't," sayz the little blacke thinge and flew awaie.

Strange to say I did not heare Sir John enter. I did not know he waz there until I spied his long shadowe among the shifting shadowes on the wall. He waz entirelie astonished to see the five skeins of thread.

Every morning he brought me flax and vittles, and whenever he appear'd the blacke dogges seemed full of joy to see him there, but that waz nothing to their Frenzie when the Pharisee came. Then they leap't in great delight and smelled him extreamlie as if he were the sweetest rose. I satt thinking of all the names I ever heard, but never did I chuse the right one. Every night the Pharisee brought the spun flax and every night it came closer and closer and twirl'd its taile faster in its Delight. "Woman," it sayz, "You shall be mine." And every night Sir John came and fetched the thread and every night he waz greatly puzzled, for he knew that the three fierce dogges that guarded me obeyed no man but him-selfe.

One daye, towards the end of the month I look't out of my windowe and waz entirelie astonished to see a great many people with sorrowful faces trudging out of Pipers Hall and Dafney's yellow head among them, bent in Teares. Beneathe the great Beeche-tree the four Scholars were equally amazed.

"Sir John, Sir John!" cries Mr Aubrey, "Where are all the servants going? Who will take care of Lady Sowreston?" (Sir John had told them I waz sicke.)

Sir John bent low and sayz something to them which I did not heare, and which seem'd to them a great Surprize.

"No, indeed!" sayz Mr Shepreth.

Mr Aubrey shook his head.

Dr Foxton sayz gravely, "We are Scholars and Gentlemen, Sir John, we doe not Spinne."

"Truly," sayz Mr Meldreth, "I cannot spinne, but I can make a pie. I read it in a booke. I believe I could doe it. You take flour, cleane Water, some raisins, whatsoever meate you like best and, I thinke, some Egges and then . . ."

Dr Foxton (who waz once a teacher in a grammar-schoole) hit Mr Meldreth on the head to make him quiet.

After Sir John had gone the Scholars told each other that Pipers Hall had gott very dismal and queer. Perhaps, sayz Mr Shepreth, it is time to goe and take their chances in the wider World againe. But all agreed to wait until Lady Sowreston waz well and all spoke very sweetly of my kindnesse to them. Then Mr Meldreth look't up. "Why!" he sayz. "There is Lady Sowreston at that little window among the leaves!"

"Miranda!" crie the Scholars.

Dr Foxton waved his hatt. Mr Shepreth kiss't his hand to me twenty times, Mr Meldreth putte his hands upon his Heart to shew his devotion and Mr Aubrey smiled chearfully to see my face.

"Good morning, deare Scholars!" I crie. "Have you dis-couvered the Queen of the Pharisees yet?"

"No," sayz Dr Foxton. "But we have got eightie-four more questions to aske her when she does appeare."

"Are you better, Miranda?" askes Mr Aubrey.

"My Opinion is," sayz I, "that I shall be cured by the end of the month. Meanwhile, deare Scholars, I have had a strange dream which I muste tell you. I dreamt that if a Scholar onlie knew a Pharisee's true name then he could conjure it quite easily."

"Well, Miranda," sayz Mr Aubrey, "many fairies have se-cret names."

"Yes but doe you know anie of them?" sayz I.

The Scholars putte their Heads together for Grave Debate. Then they all nodded together.

"No," sayz Mr Aubrey. "We doe not."

Today is the last daie. Earlie in the morning I look't out of the windowe and sawe a shower of cool rain upon Lick-erish Hill that stirr'd all the leaves of the trees. When Sir John brought me flax and vittles I told him what I have seen.

"There are Deer upon Lickerish Hill," sayz Sir John thoughtfully.

"Yes," sayz I, "and many other thinges besides. When you and I were first married, my deere, you used to say that you had no greater pleasure in the world than to goe hunt some wild creature on Lickerish Hill and kille it and then come home and kisse your owne Miranda. And my Opinion is that you should take these goode dogges and let them know againe how grasse smelles. Take your learned guests, Sir John, and goe hunting on Lickerish Hill."

Then Sir John frown'd, thinking that the dogges should still remaine in this little room, for the month waz not yet over. But the breeze that came in through the windowe carried with it the sweet scent of the woods on Lickerish Hill.

In the shelter of the Beech-tree I heard Mr Shepreth tell Mr Aubrey that he waz glad Sir John had so far mended his quarrel with the Scholars that he invited them to goe hunting with him. Dr Foxton haz gott a special Hatt for hunting. He putte it on. Then Sir John and the Scholars and all the grooms gott on their horses and rode out of Pipers Hall with Wicked, Worse and Worst-of-all running on before smelling every thinge.

The rain fell all daie. All daie the new servants that Sir John haz hired muddled their work from not having anie good ancient servant set in authoritie over them to instruct them what to doe. The bread did not rise. The butter did not come in the churne. Knives and sickles were blunted from wrong use. Gates were opened that should be shutt. Cowes and horses gott into the wrong fields; broke fences; trampl'd crops. Some wicked boyes I never sawe before climb'd over the orchard wall and ate the apples, then went home with white sicke faces. All through the house I heard the new servants quarrelling with each other.

It is time for the Pharisee to come and bringe me the spun thread. But he does not come.

Grey rabbits bob and looke about them in the summers-twilight, then creepe into the kitchen-garden to eate our sallade-herbes. Owls hoot in the darkening woods and foxes bark. The last of the light is upon Lickerish Hill. It is time for Sir John to come and kille me. But he does not come.

"Miranda!"

"Good evening, deare Scholares. What have you killed?"

"Why, nothing, Miranda," sayz Mr Meldreth in great excitement. "We have had a strange adventure as we must tell you. From the moment that we reached Lickerish Hill, Plato, Socrates and Euclid . . ." [He meanes the dogges that the Pharisee calles Wicked, Worse and Worst-of-all] ". . . ranne as if their dearest Friend waited on Lickerish Hill to embrace them and our horses raced after and we could not halt them. They tooke us to a part of Lickerish Hill which none of us had ever seen before. A great Stagge with droppes of rain upon his speckled flanks stepp't out before us and look't at us as if he waz the Lord of All Creation and not us Men at all. Foxes cross't our path and watch't us pass. Little grey hares look't up from their cradles of stones with fearless faces. But we had no time to be astonished for Plato, Socrates and Euclid ranne on ahead and our horses followed . . ."

"Yes, indeed!" sayz Mr Shepreth. "And one dark sulkie fellow among us cried out that we must have fallen by mistake into some Fairie-kingdome under the ground where Beastes revenge them-selves upon Men for the harms done to them on earth; and Dr Foxton began to speak of wild rides that go on for all Eternity and enchanted riders who cannot jumpe downe for feare of crumbling to duste when they touch the earth. But Mr Aubrey bid us all trust in God and have no feare ..."

"We stopp't suddenlie in a little green meadow in the dark woods. The meadow waz full of flowers and the sulkie man sayd that such flowers had never before been seen anie-where. But Sir John sayd he waz a fool and Sir John sayd he knew the names of the flowers as well as his own—they were Shepherds' Sun-dialls, Milkmaydes' Buttons and Dodmans' Combs. In the middle of the meadow waz a little chalke pit. This old pit waz mostly hidden by tall grasses and the flowers that Sir John had named. And out of the pit came a noyse of humming. The men held back the dogges—to their very Great Distresse—and we went very quiet to the pit and look't down. And what doe you thinke we sawe there?"

"I doe not know, Dr Foxton."

"A Faerie, Miranda! And what doe you thinke it waz doing?"

"I cannot guess, Dr Foxton."

"Well!" sayz Mr Aubrey. "It had a little spinning wheele and it waz spinning wonderfully fast and twirling its long, blacke taile. Quick! cries Mr Shepreth. Say your Spelle, Mr Aubrey! and he leapt into the pit and we all leapt after him."

"I am entirelie astonished," sayz I. "But what did you learne? What did the Pharisee tell you?"

"Nothing," sayz Dr Foxton crossly. "We asked it all our hundred and fortie-seaven questions—which is the reason of our staying so long on Lickerish Hill and coming home so late to dinner—but 'twas the most ignorant Pharisee."

We are all silent a moment.

"But it listened to all your questions," sayz I. "That is strange. It would not so much as come when you summoned it before."

"Quite, Miranda," sayz Mr Aubrey. "And the reason is that we had not gott its name before. The wordes of the Spell and its owne true name held it fast. It waz obliged to hear us out—though it yearn'd to goe on with its worke—it had gott a fearful great pile of flax to spinne. We gott the name by chance. For, as we peep't over the edge of the pit, it waz singing its name over and over againe. We were not at all enchanted by its song. An Ingeniose Spinner, Miranda, but no Poet. Fairies love to sing, but their Inventions are weak. They can get no further than a line or two until some kind Friend teaches them a new one."

We are all silent againe.

"And what did it sing?" sayz I.

"It sang: 'Nimmy, Nimmy Not; My name's Tom Tit Tot,' " sayz Mr Aubrey.

"Well!" sayz I. "I am very glad, deare Scholars, to heare that you have seen a Pharisee, but I am happier still that you have gott safe home againe. Goe to your dinner but I feare it will be a poore one."

Now comes the Pharisee creeping through the evening mist with the skeins of spun flax upon his arme. First I shall guess Solomon then I shall guess Zebedee. But then I must tell him his name and poore Tom Tit Tot must goe howling awaie to his cold and lonelie hole.

Now comes Sir John, all Frowne and Shadowe, on a horse as blacke as a tempest, with Wicked, Worse and Worst-of-all beside him. And when he haz seen the spun flax then he and I shall goe downe together to eate and drinke with the happy Scholars who even now are composing a chearfull song about four gentlemen who once sawe a Pharisee. And all our good Servants shall come home and each shall have sixpence to drinke Sir John's healthe.

"I am writing my historie," sayz I. "Where doe I begin?"

"Oh!" sayz Mr Aubrey, "begin where you chuse, Miranda, but putte it downe very quick while it is fresh and sprightly in your Braine. For remembrances are like butterflies and just as you thinke you have them flie out of the window. If all the thinges I have forgott, Miranda, were putte into His Majesties Navy, 'twould sink the fleet."

Steadfast

NANCY KRESS

Nancy Kress lives in Brockport, New York. She is the author of twelve books: three fantasy novels, six science-fiction novels, two collections of short stories, and two books on writing fiction. Her most recent novel is Beggars Ride, *the third in the trilogy including* Beggars in Spain *and* Beggars and Choosers. *Kress's short fiction appears regularly in* Omni, Asimov's Science Fiction Magazine, *and other major science-fiction publications.*

"Steadfast" is a dark reinterpretion of the Hans Christian Andersen tale of the love of a soldier for a ballerina, "The Steadfast Tin Soldier."

Steadfast

How ow does it feel, Mademoiselle, to be called out of retirement in order to dance at the Opéra gala for the coronation of Louis Napoleon?

That is a silly question, young man. How do you imagine it feels? Are you not in the business of imagining, for your ridiculous newspaper?

But, Mademoiselle, if you will forgive me, at your age it is unusual for even such a great ballerina to be—

You know nothing of great ballerinas. Do not believe that you do.

The first thing he noticed was the blood.

Dried rust-colored stains on the wide stone step: scattered stains, faint in the lantern light. Yet the soldier saw them immediately. He stopped and stared at the step, at the heavy oak door above. The yellow light shone on his uncreased uniform.

"*Allons*, Lefort," his friends called. "The ladies await!"

"He is more fascinated by light-footed charmers."

"Light-skirted, you mean."

"Come along, Lefort, you don't wish to linger here. The dancers have all departed!"

"He likes them limber in the sheets ... Gaspard? *Dis donc*, we will see you later, at Madame Nathalie's."

"The last of our nights, and he studies a doorway ... *au revoir, mon ami!*"

The soldiers moved off, laughing. The lantern, carried by a servant, moved with them. Gaspard Lefort stared at the blood until he could no longer see it in the darkness. Tomorrow he would march to the war in Austria. He was eighteen years old, privately educated, and this was the first time he had ever left his village near the Pyrenees.

The heavy door opened and a woman, backlit from within, stepped onto the wide step. She wore a long dark cape with the hood pulled over her head. "You, there! Tell your master to bring the carriage—I am ready!"

"I am not ... I have not the honor to be ... I mean, I don't know where your carriage is."

She peered at him. "You are not M'sieu Carlaine's man?"

He moved into the light. "I am only a soldier, Madame." He remembered to say, "And General Napoleon's man."

She laughed and threw open her cape, and Gaspard saw his mistake. She was not a Madame. No more than fifteen, dressed in a skirt of filmy white layers that ended startlingly short of her ankles. On the low satin bodice rode a brooch, a silver rose flattened to show tiny scattered pearls like tears. Glossy black hair pulled back and ringed with flowers, mouth painted red, she was the most beautiful girl he had ever seen. The toes of her white slippers were streaked with blood.

"Napoleon's man," she mocked. "Then you are bound for Austria."

"Tomorrow, Mademoiselle."

"Then you must not be late. Those who conquer must be on time." She fingered the rose at her breast and glanced impatiently up the street.

"Yes, Mademoiselle," he said meekly. "Wait, don't . . . don't go inside!"

"Why not? I am cold." But the girl moved closer to him, clear to the front edge of the step, and made no move to close her cape.

"You . . . you are injured. The blood . . ."

"And where do you come from, *mon petit*, that you have never seen a dancer bleed through her slippers? The great Marie Sallé could bloody four pairs of shoes during a single performance!"

"Who is the great Marie Sallé?"

"Ah, you know nothing. But you leave for the war tomorrow, yes? Do you think I'm beautiful?"

The soldier couldn't answer. He nodded.

"I can see that you do. And you have never seen a ballet girl. Ah, *mon pauvre*, watch."

She pulled off her cape and flung it at him. It settled over Gaspard's head. He fought free of it, as blinded by her mocking laughter as by the light wool. On the smooth stone the girl curtsied low, smiling, and rose. She whirled, and danced a few steps, and smiled over her shoulder. She rose on the ends of her toes and balanced there—how could she do that? how was it possible?—and began to dance on the tips of her feet, spinning and swaying and forming such graceful arches with her arms that the soldier turned as hot as if he already heard the Austrian guns.

She danced for several minutes to unheard music, and

ended with one leg high in the air, impossibly high, balanced on the ends of her toes. Nothing moved. The air stilled, and the light from the still-open doorway did not flicker, and the dancer stood on one leg while the world stopped.

A carriage rounded the corner.

"Oh, *vite*, give me my cape! Go away now, he doesn't like to see me with young men . . . go away, I tell you!"

The soldier shrank back into the shadows. The carriage stopped and the girl climbed in, crying, "There you are! I have just this minute come out!" Her voice sounded stretched and sweet. The carriage door closed, and the horses clopped down the cobblestones.

Someone within closed the oak door, but not before Gaspard had studied both the carving above, 'L'École d'Opéra Ballet,' and the fresh blood smeared across the smooth stone of the stoop.

He bent to rub his finger across the stain, and put the finger to his lips.

On the contrary, Mademoiselle, you are mistaken. I know a great deal about your dancing. I have followed your long and astonishing career quite closely.

Tant pis pour toi.

The next day, Gaspard did not leave to join his regiment. By midafternoon he had stationed himself in an alley, from which he could see the oak door. Carters passed by, and peddlers. A laundress, a butcher's boy, a street cleaner. An orange girl, who smiled at him with a provocative dimple. He didn't really see her, nor the dancers as they hurried in at dusk, except to note that none of them was the girl who had danced for him.

At evening he made his way, asking many stumbling directions, through the city's theaters: "Please, Monsieur, is this where the dancers from L'École d'Opéra Ballet rise up on their toes?" At the Opéra, he bought a ticket. In the foyer hundreds of candles glittered in chandeliers. Gentlemen in high-starched collars laughed with women in gowns so flimsy and low that Gaspard blushed. No one in his village wore such gowns. Almost his nerve failed him, but he remembered that he was now a soldier and looked straight ahead, unsmiling, until a contemptuous old woman showed him to his seat and thrust out her hand for a coin. He gave her one and, when her hand stayed out, another, although he was a little frightened that all the old women might then want coins. But they did not.

She was not on the stage. There were other dancers there, skimming along on the ends of their toes, floating like the ghosts old drunken Massine, his father's stableman, used to tell about at home. But not her. This must be the wrong theater. Gaspard was just about to leave, numb with disappointment, when a long line of girls danced out onto the stage and there, at the end, was she.

He sank back into his seat, his legs watery.

She danced for only a few minutes, before the line of girls joined hands and floated off the stage. It seemed to Gaspard during those few minutes that, after all, her leg did not lift as high as the other dancers', nor hold as steady. She wobbled. It didn't matter. He had no heart for anyone on the stage but her, and afterward he waited in the theater alley. But this time a rich man's carriage waited even before she came out the oak door. All he saw was a glimpse of her dark cape, parted for a minute over the flattened silver rose on her breast. One glimpse, and the fresh blood smeared on the stone from her slippers.

The next morning, he left for the war.

Your history, Mademoiselle, your personal history, that is . . . it is most . . . complicated.

You mean I began as a dancer of no particular talent but great beauty, who in the demimonde of that day made her way as a whore, do you not?

You are very frank.

As your magazine is not. A pretty little essay you were planning, n'est-ce pas, about the glory of womanhood under the first Emperor? A marzipan of an essay?

Our feminine readers are refined.

No. They are merely squeamish.

The soldier fought at Ulm. He fought near Vienna. He fought at Austerlitz. In each battle the Emperor was victorious, and Gaspard himself distinguished for courage and loyalty. The shells exploded around him, and men died screaming, and the soldier fought beside his dead comrades with a fury he had not known he possessed. He became someone else, charging across the Austrian battlefield, thrusting his bayonet into the bodies of the enemy. He did not know himself. Afterward, he sat alone beside his campfire and shook his head to clear it, and felt his blood still surging in his veins, exhilarating as drink. His blood, and theirs. The greater the victory, the greater the surging power, as if he had taken into himself the life of those he had slain.

He was only a little surprised to discover how much he loved war.

In April he returned to Paris with the Légion d'Honneur on his uniform. The first night, he looked for the dancer.

She wasn't dancing at the Opéra. He studied the ballet girls as they floated across the stage in tiny delicate steps—*bourées*, he had learned those were called—and as they left by the side door for the carriages of rich merchants or government officials. More than one dancer threw Gaspard an admiring glance, tall and strong in his blue uniform. He ignored them all, until the last.

"Pardon, Mademoiselle, but I am looking for someone
. . . a dancer of this height, with black hair and blue eyes,
very beautiful . . . she was here last summer, dancing in the
chorus, but she did not dance tonight."

The girl wrinkled her pretty nose. "Ah, Amalie Dumont.
You had best forget her, *mon ami*. She is above your reach,
under the protection of Monsieur Endart, the diamond
merchant." She eyed Gaspard's wide shoulders. "But if
you should like some other company . . ."

"Where does this diamond merchant live?"

The girl shrugged. "Discover that for yourself."

He did. He could discover anything, do anything. Walking toward the house rented for her by Monsieur Endart,
it seemed he could *smell* her in the spring air: rose perfume,
and clean sweat, and the chalk rubbed on the stage floor
that rose during the performance to halo the dancers in
ghostly clouds. He went straight to the front door, and the
decoration on his uniform got him admitted by the flus-
tered footman.

She came down the stairs to the trim foyer, with its small
polished table and fashionable rug. Monsieur Endart was
generous. Her glossy hair was piled high on her head; jewels sparkled at her throat. The thin fabric of her dress was
cut low over her breasts, and bulged below. She was heavily pregnant. "Yes, Monsieur?"

He blurted, "We met last year. You danced for me. In
the street, outside the Opéra . . ."

She didn't remember. "In the street? I did? How vulgar
of me."

"I have never seen anything so beautiful in my entire
life."

"I thank you." She dropped him a little joke curtsy. "But
if you would state your business . . ."

"Only to see you again."

She frowned, and glanced up the stairway. "I see no

reason for that. We have never even properly met."

"You are Amalie Dumont. And I am Gaspard—"

"I don't care who you are." A door opening, above. Her eyes darkened. "I am afraid you must leave, M'sieu. You should not have been admitted. But I was told . . ."

She didn't say what she had been told. Gaspard said desperately, "But you danced for me. You stood on the toes of one foot, the other leg raised so high . . . I have fought in so many battles with that picture of you in front of me. I have fought only for you." Even as he said this, he knew it was not true. And yet it was.

She smiled. "How loyal. The constant soldier. But you might better have fought as a means to your own preferment."

"You are my means to preferment," he said, and saw in her eyes how foolish it sounded. "There was blood on the step . . ."

"There will be blood here if you do not leave," she said quickly, as the clumping of a man's boots started down the staircase. Instantly Amalie vanished. But this time the soldier would not shrink into the shadows. He stood his ground.

Monsieur Endart was old. Bent, stooped, white-haired, perhaps blind, or nearly so. He walked slowly past the soldier and never glanced at him at all.

Gaspard smiled at the door through which Amalie had disappeared. Soon the child would be born, in cries and pain and blood. He could wait. Waiting was a necessary tactic of war.

You began dancing during the First Empire, n'est-ce pas? Your first role was in the corps de ballet of Dauberval's La Fille Mal Gardée. *But none of the notices mention you.*

No.

No one knew, then, what you would become.
None of us, young man, can know what we will become.

He was sent to Spain, under Marshal Murat. In Madrid he fought against rioting citizens outraged at the seizure of their homeland, armed with sticks and stones and the tools of their trade. He shot a blacksmith waving a hammer in one hand and a poker in the other, and a stonemason firing a rifle so old it must have belonged to his grandfather, and a baker with flour on his apron. The riot was quelled in less than a day. Later, when Spain was invaded by the English, he went back, serving under the Emperor himself.

He was gazetted a corporal.

At Seville he was wounded: four ribs and a collarbone broken. It healed leaving only a puckered scar and a slight bumpiness where the bones had knit. He caught a disease of the bowels, and then a fever, and survived both.

He was made a lieutenant.

Every night, just before sleep, he pushed aside the face of the stonemason, mouth surprised into a long slit in his rough beard just before the bullet tore into his throat. He pushed aside the baker and the blacksmith and pictured Amalie Dumont, dancing on the stone stoop, one leg raised so high in an *arabesque* that it seemed to disappear into the shadows of the street.

When he returned to Paris, it seethed with soldiers. Danish, Swiss, Dutch, French. Once more he could not find her. Gaspard was older now; he knew people; he had developed an air of command. People answered his questions. He found her not at the Opéra but in a second-rate company just in from the provinces. She danced again at the end of a line of ballet girls: thin, hollow-cheeked, too pale. Her *attitude croisée* wobbled.

In the dressing room she sprawled on a ramshackle chair, bent over the ribbons of her slippers. The other girls, jammed all together in the small room, twittered and stripped.

"Mademoiselle Dumont."

"You!"

"Yes, me. I've come to take you to supper."

She glanced nervously at the door. "I can't."

"Why not?"

"I am otherwise engaged, Lieutenant . . . uh . . ."

"Gaspard Lafort. Break the engagement."

The girls twittered more loudly, exchanging amused glances. She said, "No, no. Please leave."

"Where is your diamond merchant? And the baby?"

"He died," she said, and he didn't know which she meant. It didn't matter. "Please go!"

Gaspard folded his arms across his chest and waited. The man came in, eventually. Not a dancer, nor a soldier. An innkeeper, perhaps, or a small farmer. The innkeeper scowled.

"Mademoiselle Dumont comes with me," Gaspard said. "Good day, Citizen."

"Amalie!"

"I will see you later, Michel." With eyes demure and downcast, her beauty returning with male rivalry.

After the tavern supper, in his room at the inn, Gaspard said, "Dance for me."

She did, briefly, sly *pas de chats* and airy *bourrées*, nothing too difficult. During an *entrechat* she almost lost her balance. She ended with one leg raised high. He saw the bruises on her bare thigh. He pulled her to him—carefully, as if she were glass filigree—and kissed the bruise.

In the morning she was gone, and with her his purse, his kit, his boots, and his sword.

What have been your favorite roles, Mademoiselle?
I have no favorite roles.

He was sent to Russia, the vast, the unknown.

The advancing army, 500,000 strong, met only small skirmishes. The enemy retreated. At night wolves howled, the first Gaspard had ever heard. By October, the cold froze skin and nose hairs. The Emperor wore a peasant woman's shawl over his uniform, for warmth. They took Moscow, but as soon as they had taken it, the Russians themselves burned it to the ground. There was no food, no fuel, no shelter. Only cold. Gaspard fought looters in the burning capital, army soldiers beside frozen rivers, mounted cossacks on steppes so swept with wind that it was hard to stand upright long enough to fire.

Crossing an icy river, the ragged army was attacked. A shell landed beside Gaspard and exploded. His leg was ripped off at the knee.

In the cold, the blood drained more slowly, but not so slowly that he couldn't feel it leave his body, watch it stain the snow red. He lay on his back, frigid wind howling over his face, and stared at the gray sky. In every snowflake he saw Amalie, dancing. In the tavern bedroom, her feet had not bled. They bled now, in memory, and each red drop was the blood of the baker, the blacksmith, the stonemason, the Austrian soldiers, the Moscow looters, the mounted cavalry that Gaspard had shot.

He had not at first chosen to be a soldier. Later, he had loved it. He had given his strength to war, and his will, and his blood, now seeping into ground too frozen to absorb it. Enemy ground. But the enemy must not have his blood power, even though he could not keep it himself. They should not have it. It must go elsewhere.

"Amalie," he whispered. "*Amalie.*"

And fainted.

You have been dancing for over forty years, Mademoiselle. You have seen ballet change, become more refined and exquisite—the phantoms of Robert le Diable, *the disembodied spirits of* La Sylphide, *and of course the ghostly dead brides in* Giselle. *You yourself have refused to dance any of these ballets, refused to dance at all unless the Opéra revived the . . . the earthier works of an earlier time. Why is that?*

No reason.

Come, there must be a reason. Is it loyalty to the . . . Mademoiselle? What have I said to amuse you?

In Paris the chestnut trees were in full flower, and June roses scented the night air. The soldier waited outside the Opéra. He gazed steadily at the door, standing on his left leg, balancing on his crutch. His right leg was a stump, dipped and sealed in hot tar.

She came out alone, as if she knew this was the night he would be there. Flowers ringed her dark hair, and her ballet skirt was pink tulle and blue satin. Gaspard glanced down at her feet. The soft blue slippers were bloody.

"*Bon soir*, Amalie."

"Gaspard. You are—"

"Home. I am home."

She stared at his one leg and he saw the swift recalculations behind her eyes, the shift in reaction. Many people looked at him this way now. She smiled. "I honor your sacrifice for France."

"It was not a sacrifice for France."

She tried to look shocked, failed. "But surely—"

"It was for you. All of it. And when lose it I must, I lost it to you."

Her beautiful face turned wary. "You make no sense, Lieutenant."

"There is no sense to it. Only truth."

"Please excuse me; I am late."

She swept past him, but he grabbed her arm. "Dance for me once more."

"Let go of me!"

"Once more. So I can see what my loyalty has given you."

"Buy a ticket, Monsieur!" She broke free of his grasp and ran lightly down the street. Even in the darkness, even from behind, he could see how much more lightly she moved than she had before.

He bought a ticket the next night, many nights. She was no longer the last ballet girl in the *corps de ballet*. She led the *corps*. She danced in a small *pas de trois* in *Les Amans Surpris*. She danced a brief solo in *Medea et Jason*. Gaspard always stood where she could see him, in a front box or the side aisle or once, when he bribed a stagehand, in the wings. He stood on his one leg and gazed, unmoving, at Amalie.

Did you always plan to be a ballet dancer? Since you were a small child?

I never planned to be a ballet dancer.

But, surely, the discipline, the practice—

I never planned to remain a dancer!

The war had gone wrong. In Paris, they could hear the guns. The tulips stood straight and tall in the gardens of the Tuileries, and the air smelled of hyacinths, decaying meat, drains. People pushed through the streets the Emperor had redesigned, the marketplaces, the quays and wide squares. They carried babies, dragged overladen carts, tugged on frightened donkeys. The enemy was only hours away—the Russians ate roast children for supper— the Prussians used babies for bayonet practice. Get out, leave Paris. *Vite! Vite!*

Gaspard hopped through the crowds, steadying himself with his crutch. Boys in uniforms too big for them, old men from battles nobody remembered—the National Guard prepared to defend the city. Artillery thundered closer.

Crossing a half-built square beside the Seine, where the paving stones were uneven, Gaspard fell.

For a moment, dazed on the ground, he thought he was back in Russia. Then his head cleared and he tried to rise. Some boys, thirteen or fourteen years old, rushed past, knocking him over again. A few yards away they stopped.

"*Dis donc!* A soldier of the Emperor!"

"You mean, of the upstart who stole the throne!"

"My papa says—"

Royalists. Coming now out of their holes. No, not Royalists but children, in another year they would be conscripted to the army, the nonsense knocked out of them. There would not be another year.

"Into the Seine with him, the swine, the traitor—"

They rolled him across the square like a barrel, over and over, the sword clanking at his side each time it struck the cobblestones. At the river three of them, one at each limb, hoisted him to the railing and toppled him over. He splashed into the water and sank.

Amalie. As his lungs grew hot and the current bore him along underwater, he thought, *This is how she feels dancing. Weightless.* Then his lungs burst and he gulped water. A second later his head broke the surface and he sputtered, only to go down again.

This time he saw her, there on the mud and rocks and green-slimed stone wall of the embankment. She was dancing. A slow pirouette while her filmy skirt drifted among the water plants. *Retiré* into *attitude croisée*, the left leg lifted behind, then opening flowerlike into *arabesque*. Gaspard reached a hand toward her, but she *bourréed* away, her smile enchanting. He smiled back. The moment was perfect. They were one.

He was seized from behind and pulled above water. Pain burst his lungs; water streamed out of his mouth and nose.

"Get him aboard, *non, non,* careful—"

"He is dead!"

"He is not."

Amalie—

Two men dumped him onto the deck of the fishing boat. "Lame, poor fellow. There, get him aboard."

"We will take him with us out of Paris. A loyal soldier of the Empire . . . the Prussians shall not have him. Paaaw, but he stinks."

"The river stinks."

"I wonder how he fell?"

Let us talk about the extraordinary reception your dancing received.

Long ago, you mean.

It was said—and I quote from Le Journal de Paris—*that you "dance as if pursued by wolves. Savagely, relentlessly." Was that so?*

Not wolves. Fire. Fire and blood.

I beg your pardon?

You do not have it.

You make no sense, Mademoiselle. Dancing is not war.

It took Gaspard a year to get back to Paris. A fever came on him from breathing the river water; it left him very weak. He recuperated at home, in his village near the Pyrenees. There, nothing had changed. But in Paris the city had fallen, the Emperor been forced into exile. *He will come back*, old soldiers said, *he will return with the violets.*

And he did, escaping Elba, the loyal rallying to his march home. Paris cheered and laughed and danced. In a thousand places the Bourbon lilies were torn down, ripped out, painted over with the Imperial bees.

Gaspard went immediately to the Opéra. Ink on the handbills was still wet:

AMALIE DUMONT *dance* ORPHEUS ET EURIDICE

He caught her leaving her dressing room, dressed for the street in pelisse and bonnet, carrying a silk muff. The dressing room behind her overflowed with flowers and shawls and perfume and fans and small enameled boxes the pink of new skin, the white of exposed bone.

"Amalie. I have come home."

She whirled on him. "What has that to do with me!"

"Everything." He looked at her steadily. She would never dance for him again, he knew. It didn't matter. He would watch her from the stalls, from the pit, from the wings. She could not escape him. He would send her flowers every night. He would wait for her at the alley door, and hobble after her carriage, and wipe the blood from her slippers off stone steps.

"Leave me alone, damn you! Stop haunting me!"

"Never. I will never desert you. I have given you all that I am."

"I didn't want it!"

"That doesn't matter." It was not to be expected that she would comprehend. She was not a soldier.

"Please, please leave me alone."

"Never."

"I can dance now! I never wanted to make my life as a dancer, it was only a means to . . . I wanted to wear silk dresses and drive in carriages and be . . . but now I *am* a dancer. You have done this to me! Now go away!"

He gazed at her, unswerving, without pretending he did not understand. "No."

"Please . . ."

Gaspard said, "One cannot desert blood." She could not be expected to know that either. Blood was not tin. Once blood was shed, it was shed. One could only remain steadfast to the cause of its shedding.

"But I don't want you!" Amalie cried, and hid her face in her long slender hands. She sobbed aloud. Dancers and stagehands stopped in astonishment to look at her. Gaspard looked, too, drinking her in, his fond gaze never wavering until she rushed away into the foyer and then the street, where with his one leg he could not swiftly follow.

Dancing is not war, Mademoiselle. Dancing is . . . art.

Art is no more than whatever animates it, drives it. And what animates us but blood?

Many things. Honor. Courage. Loyalty.

That is what I have just said. Loyalty. It has a terrible life of its own.

Everywhere she went, he was there. He watched her laughing at the Théâtre-Français, strolling on the new Champs-Élysées, shopping for slippers or gloves, stepping down from her carriage for a ball in the rue Chantereine. All of Paris seemed Bonapartist now, the few Royalists gone, or shuttered in their houses, or silent. Gaspard wore his uniform proudly as he watched Amalie. Watched her walk, watched her talk, watched her eat, watched her drive. Watched her dance, one leg kicking high in a *grand battement*. He never tired of watching. He never got enough.

"Go away," she whispered, or shrieked, or whimpered. "Leave me alone. For the love of God . . ."

God had nothing to do with it. He would love her unfailingly, always.

She danced *Les Pommes d'Or*, and the crowds almost tore the theater apart. She danced *La Triomphe de la France*, the music ink still wet, and the Emperor's brother attended, Prince Lucien. She danced *La Vengeance d'une Mère*, and *Le Journal de Paris* called her "a jewel of the Empire. On stage, she is not merely woman, but becomes something infinitely more powerful, infinitely more French. Amalie Dumont becomes the steadfast spirit of France herself."

The only time Gaspard lowered his eyes from her face was when her feet bled, the blood soaking through the soft-toed slippers.

One night in June she danced *Medea et Jason*, the night all the bells of Paris rang for the victory at Ligny. Gaspard stood outside her house in the rue Sainte Marie when the news came, two days later, of the defeat at Waterloo. The coalition marched toward Paris. Many of the rich were evacuating. Gaspard watched the footman fling open the door of her carriage.

"You have waited too long to leave the city, Amalie. The roads are blocked." They were the first words he had spoken aloud in a month.

She stopped, one delicate foot set on the carriage step, and looked at him with hatred so pure it shone, like silver. "Do not try to stop me!"

"You will be back."

She was, by evening. Looters and roving mobs roamed the streets just ahead of the invaders. The mobs plundered houses, fought quick sharp skirmishes, set fires. Smoke rose above the city, and sometimes screams. Gaspard stood stiffly on guard at Amalie's gate, unmoving.

She jumped from the carriage, carrying her valise in one hand and silk muff in the other. Her black hair straggled from its chignon; her pelisse was dirty and torn. The foamy sides of the horses heaved and labored. Blood smeared her left cheek.

"Amalie."

She whirled on him, a move so smooth and quick it

might have been a pirouette. Gaspard smiled to see it. At his smile, something shifted in Amalie's face. She began to breathe in quick sharp pants, and in her eyes leaped something that Gaspard seemed to recognize. He said, "Yes . . . from blood—" and had time for no more before she raised the pistol from her muff and shot him through the heart.

"Mademoiselle!" the coachman gasped. "Mademoiselle—!"

"Inside. Get inside now." She ran into her house just as a burning brand was hurled at the house opposite, landed, and set the wooden structure aflame.

Gaspard never moved as the fire swept toward him. His one good leg stuck out straight, and his hand covered his heart. His eyes looked toward Amalie's house, and never wavered, not even once.

Loyalty has "a terrible life of its own"? I do not understand you, Mademoiselle.

No, probably not. I do not think ghosts are romantic, Monsieur. Not beautiful ethereal maidens floating over graveyards. Not tenderhearted Wilis, bloodless sylphides. Our dead are not beyond loyalty—nor beyond revenge. Their blood imprisons us.

Mademoiselle?

Do you know that I have danced every day since my retirement? Every last day?

Really? Danced every day, for no one?

I did not say that.

I don't understand . . .

You don't need to. But this will be my last performance, thank God. And soon, I think . . .

Yes?

I shall see for myself how much revenge the dead are owed for their loyalty.

Mademoiselle?

We shall see.

Godmother Death

JANE YOLEN

*Jane Yolen lives in Massachusetts. She is closing in
on two hundred books published, and about as many
short stories. Called "America's Hans Christian Andersen" and "America's Aesop," because of her many
children's stories, she is also the author of novels and
poetry for adults that have won the Rhysling Award,
the* Asimov's Readers' Poll Award, *the Mythopoeic
Society's Aslan Award, the World Fantasy Award,
and has been nominated for the Nebula Award.*

*There are many fairy tales that personify death;
they can be found in cultures all around the world.
The Brothers Grimm variant, "Godfather Death,"
was the basis for a terrific story by Roger Zelazny in*
Black Thorn, White Rose. *Now Jane Yolen has her
own unique take on this classic theme.*

Godmother Death

You think you know this story. You do not.

You think it comes from Ireland, from Norway, from Spain. It does not. You have heard it in Hebrew, in Swedish, in German. You have read it in French, in Italian, in Greek.

It is not a story, though many mouths have made it that way.

It is true.

How do I know? Death, herself, told me. She told me in that whispery voice she saves for special tellings. She brushed her thick black hair away from that white forehead, and told me.

I have no reason to disbelieve her. Death does not know how to lie. She has no need to.

It happened this way, only imagine it in Death's own soft breeze of a voice. Imagine she is standing over your right shoulder speaking this true story in your ear. You do not turn to look at her. I would not advise it. But if you do turn, she will smile at you, her smile a child's smile, a woman's smile, the grin of a crone. But she will not tell *her* story anymore. She will tell yours.

It happened this way, as Death told me. She was on the road, between Cellardyke and Crail. Or between Claverham and Clifton. Or between Chagford and anywhere. Does it matter the road? It was small and winding; it was cobbled and potholed; it led from one place of human habitation to another. Horses trotted there. Dogs marked their places. Pig drovers and cattle drovers and sheepherders used those roads. So why not Death?

She was visible that day. Sometimes she plays at being mortal. It amuses her. She has had a long time trying to amuse herself. She wore her long gown kirtled above her knee. She wore her black hair up in a knot. But if you looked carefully, she did not walk like a girl of that time. She moved too freely for that, her arms swinging. She stepped on her full foot, not on the toes, not mincing. She could copy the clothes, but she never remembered how girls really walk.

A man, frantic, saw her and stopped her. He actually put his hand on her arm. It startled her. That did not happen often, that Death is startled. Or that a man puts a hand on her.

"Please," the man said. "My Lady." She was clearly above him, though she had thought she was wearing peasant clothes. It was the way she stood, the way she walked. "My wife is about to give birth to our child and we need someone to stand godmother. You are all who is on the road."

Godmother? It amused her. She had never been asked to be one. "Do you know who I am?" she asked.

"My Lady?" The man suddenly trembled at his temerity. Had he touched a high lord's wife? Would she have him executed? No matter. It was his first child. He was beyond thinking.

Death put a hand up to her black hair and pulled down her other face. "Do you know me now?"

He knew. Peasants are well acquainted with Death in that form. He nodded.

"And want me still?" Death asked.

He nodded and at last found his voice. "You are greater than God or the Devil, Lady. You would honor us indeed."

His answer pleased her, and so she went with him. His wife was couched under a rowan tree, proof against witches. The babe was near to crowning when they arrived.

"I have found a great lady to stand as godmother," the man said. "But do not look up at her face, wife." For suddenly he feared what he had done.

His wife did not look, except out of the corner of her eye. But so seeing Death's pale, beautiful face, she was blinded in that eye forever. Not because Death had blinded the woman. That was not her way. But fear—and perhaps the sugar sickness—did what Death would not.

The child, a boy, was born with a caul. Death ripped it open with her own hand, then dropped the slimed covering onto the morning grass where it shimmered for a moment like dew.

"Name him Haden," Death said. "And when he is a man I shall teach him a trade." Then she was gone, no longer amused. Birth never amused her for long.

Death followed the boy's progress one year closely, another not at all. She sent no gifts. She did not stand for him at the church font. Still, the boy's father and his half-blind mother did well for themselves; certainly better than peasants had any reason to expect. They were able to purchase their own farm, able to send their boy to a school. They assumed it was because of Death's patronage, when in fact she had all but forgotten them and her godson. You cannot expect Death to care so about a single child, who has seen so many.

Yet on the day Haden became a man, on the day of his majority, his father called Death. He drew her sign in the sand, the same that he had seen on the chain around her neck. He said her name and the boy's.

And Death came.

One minute the man was alone and the next he was not. Death was neither winded nor troubled by her travel, though she still wore the khakis of an army nurse. She had not bothered to change from her last posting.

"Is it time?" she asked, who was both in and out of time. "Is he a man, my godson?" She knew he was not dead. *That* she would have known.

"It is time, Lady," the man said, carefully looking down at his feet. *He* was not going to be blinded like his wife.

"Ah." She reached up and took off the nurse's cap and shook down her black hair. The trouble with bargains, she mused, was that they had to be kept.

"He shall be a doctor," she said after a moment.

"A doctor?" The man had thought no farther than a great farm for his boy.

"A doctor," Death said. "For doctors and generals know me best. And I have recently seen too much of generals." She did not tell him of the Crimea, of the Dardanelles, of the riders from beyond the steppes. "A doctor would be nice."

Haden was brought to her. He was a smart lad, but not overly smart. He had strong hands and a quick smile.

Death dismissed the father and took the son by the hand, first warming her own hand. It was an effort she rarely made.

"Haden, you shall be a doctor of power," she said. "Listen carefully and treat this power well."

Haden nodded. He did not look at her, not right at her. His mother had warned him, and though he was not sure he believed, he believed.

"You will become the best-known doctor in the land, my godson," Death said. "For each time you are called to a patient, look for me at the bedside. If I stand at the head of the bed, the patient will live, no matter what you or any other doctor will do. But if I stand at the foot, the patient will die. And there is nought anyone can do—no dose and no diagnoses—to save him."

Haden nodded again. "I understand, godmother."

"I think you do," she said, and was gone.

In a few short years, Haden became known throughout his small village, and a few more years and his reputation had spread through the county. A few more and he was known in the kingdom. If he said a patient would live, that patient would rise up singing. If he said one would die, even though the illness seemed but slight, then that patient would die. It seemed uncanny, but he was *always* right. He was more than a doctor. He was—some said—a seer.

Word came at last to the king himself.

Ah—now you think I have been lying to you, that this is only a story. It has a king in it. And while a story with Death might be true, a story with a king in it is always a fairy tale. But remember, this comes from a time when kings were as common as corn. Plant a field and you got corn. Plant a kingdom and you got a king. It is that simple.

The king had a beautiful daughter. Nothing breeds as well as money, except power. Of course a king's child would be beautiful.

She was also dangerously ill, so ill in fact that the king

promised his kingdom—not half but all—to anyone who could save her. The promise included marriage, for how else could he hand the kingdom off. She was his only child, and he would not beggar her to save her life. That was *worse* than death.

Haden heard of the offer and rode three days and three nights, trading horses at each inn. When he came to the king's palace he was, himself, thin and weary from travel; there was dirt under his fingernails. His hair was ill kempt. But his reputation had preceeded him.

"Can she be cured?" asked the king. He had no time or temper for formalities.

"Take me to her room," Haden said.

So the king and the queen together led him into the room.

The princess's room was dark with grief and damp with crying. The long velvet drapes were pulled close against the light. The place smelled of Death's perfume, that soft, musky odor. The tapers at the door scarcely lent any light.

"I cannot see," Haden said, taking one of the tapers. Bending over the bed, he peered down at the princess and a bit of hot wax fell on her cheek. She opened her eyes and they were the color of late wine, a deep plum. Haden gasped at her beauty.

"Open the drapes," he commanded, and the king himself drew the curtains aside.

Then Haden saw that Death was sitting at the foot of the great four-poster bed, buffing her nails. She was wearing a black shift, cut entirely too low in the front. Her hair fell across her shoulders in black waves. The light from the windows shone through her and she paid no attention to what was happening in the room, intent on her nails.

Haden put his finger to his lips and summoned four servingmen to him. Without a word, instructing them only with his hands, he told them to turn the bed around quickly. And such was his reputation, they did as he bade.

Then he walked to the bed's head, where Death was finishing her final nail. He was so close, he might have touched her. But instead, he lifted the princess's head and helped her sit up. She smiled, not at him but through him, as if he were as transparent as Death.

"She will live, sire," Haden said.

Both Death and the maiden looked at Haden straight on, startled, Death because she had been fooled, and the princess because she had not noticed him before. Only then did the princess smile at Haden, as she would to a footman, a servingman, a cook. She smiled at him, but Death did not.

"A trick will not save her," said Death. "I will have all in the end." She shook her head. "I do not say this as a boast. Nor as a promise. It simply is what it is."

"I know," Haden said.

"What do you know?" asked the king, for he could not see or hear Death.

Haden looked at the king and smiled a bit sadly. "I know she will live and that if you let me, I will take care of her the rest of her life."

The king did not smile. A peasant's son, even though he is a doctor, even though he is famous throughout the kingdom, does not marry a princess. In a story, perhaps. Not in the real world. Unlike Death, kings do not have to keep bargains. He had Haden thrown into the dungeon.

There Haden spent three miserable days. On the fourth he woke to find Godmother Death sitting at his bedfoot. She was dressed as if for a ball, her hair in three braids that were caught up on the top of her head with a jeweled pin. Her dress, of some white silken stuff, was demurely pleated and there were rosettes at each shoulder. She looked sixteen or sixteen hundred. She looked ageless.

"I see you at my bedfoot," Haden said. "I suppose that means that today I die."

She nodded.

"And there is no hope for me?"

"I can be tricked only once," Death said. "The king will hang you at noon."

"And the princess?"

"Oh, I am going to her wedding," Death said, standing and pirouetting gracefully so that Haden could see how pretty the dress was, front and back.

"Then I shall see her in the hereafter," Haden said. "She did not look well at all. Ah—then I am content to die."

Death, who was a kind godmother after all, did not tell him that it was not the princess who was to die that day. Nor was the king to die, either. It was just some old auntie for whom the excitement of the wedding would prove fatal. Death would never lie to her godson, but she did not always tell the entire truth. Like her brother Sleep, she liked to say things on the slant. Even Death can be excused just one weakness.

At least, that is what she told me, and I have no reason to doubt the truth of it. She was sitting at my bedfoot, and—sitting there—what need would she have to lie?

dedicated to the memory of
Charles Mikolaycak

Recommended Reading

Fiction and Poetry

The Robber Bridegroom and Bluebeard's Egg, by Margaret Atwood
  This Canadian writer often uses fairy-tale themes in her excellent contemporary mainstream fiction.
Snow White, by Donald Barthelme
  This is an early postmodern short novel that would be politically incorrect by today's standards.
Katie Crackernuts, by Katherine Briggs
  A charming short novel retelling the Katie Crackernuts tale, by one of the world's foremost folklore authorities.
Beginning with O, by Olga Broumas
  Broumas's poetry makes use of many fairy-tale motifs in this collection.
The Sun, the Moon and the Stars, by Steven Brust

A contemporary novel mixing ruminations on art and creation with a lively Hungarian fairy tale.

Possession, by A. S. Byatt

A Booker Prize–winning novel that makes wonderful use of the Fairy Melusine legend.

Nine Fairy Tales and One More Thrown in for Good Measure, by Karel Capek

Charming stories inspired by the Czech folk tradition.

Sleeping in Flame, by Jonathan Carroll

Excellent, quirky dark fantasy using the Rumplestiltskin tale.

The Bloody Chamber, by Angela Carter

A stunning collection of dark, sensual fairy-tale retellings.

The Sleeping Beauty, by Hayden Carruth

A poetry sequence using the Sleeping Beauty legend.

Pinocchio in Venice, by Robert Coover

Coover often parodies traditional fairy tales in his fiction. His reworking of the Pinocchio tale is particularly recommended.

Beyond the Looking Glass, edited by Jonathan Cott

A collection of Victorian fairy-tale prose and poetry.

The Nightingale, by Kara Dalkey

An evocative Oriental historical novel based on the Hans Christian Andersen story.

The Painted Alphabet, by Diana Darling

This novel is a rich fantasia inspired by Balinese myth and folklore.

The Girl Who Trod on a Loaf, by Kathryn Davis

Uses the fairy tale of the title as the basis for a story of two women, and the opera, at the beginning of the twentieth century. A lovely little book.

Blue Bamboo, by Osamu Dazia

This volume of fantasy stories by a Japanese writer of the early twentieth century contains lovely fairy-tale work.

Provençal Tales, by Michael de Larrabeiti

An absolutely gorgeous collection containing tales drawn from the Provençal region of France.

Jack the Giant-Killer and *Drink Down the Moon,* by Charles de Lint

Wonderful urban fantasy novels bringing "Jack" and magic to the streets of modern Canada.

Tam Lin, by Pamela Dean

A lyrical novel setting the old Scottish fairy story (and folk ballad) Tam Lin among theater majors on a Midwestern college campus.

Like Water for Chocolate, by Laura Esquivel

Esquivel's book (and the wonderful film of the same title) wraps Mexican folklore and tales into a turn-of-the-century story about love and food on the Mexico/Texas border. Complete with recipes.

The King's Indian, by John Gardner

A collection of peculiar and entertaining stories using fairy-tale motifs.

Crucifax Autumn, by Ray Garton

One of the first splatterpunk horror novels; Garton makes use of the Pied Piper theme in very nasty ways. Violent and visceral.

Blood Pressure, by Sandra M. Gilbert

A number of the poems in this powerful collection make use of fairy-tale motifs.

Strange Devices of the Sun and Moon, by Lisa Goldstein

A lyrical little novel mixing English fairy tales with English history in Christopher Marlowe's London.

The Seventh Swan, by Nicholas Stuart Gray

An engaging Scottish novel that starts off where the "Seven Swans" fairy tale ends.

Daughters of the Moon: Witch Tales From Around the World, edited by Shahrukh Husain

A folklorist collects over fifty tales of witches and witchcraft from more than thirty cultures worldwide.

Fire and Hemlock, by Diana Wynne Jones

A beautifully written, haunting novel that brings the Thomas the Rhymer and Tam Lin tales into modern day England.

Seven Fairy Tales and a Fable, by Gwyneth Jones

Eight enchanting, thought-provoking, adult fairy tales by this British writer.

Green Grass Running Water, by Thomas King

This delightful Magical Realist novel uses Native American myths and folk tales to hilarious effect.

Thomas the Rhymer, by Ellen Kushner

A sensuous and musical rendition of this old Scottish story and folk ballad.

The Wandering Unicorn, by Manuel Mujica Lainez

A fairy-tale novel based on the "Fairy Melusine" legend by an award-winning Argentinean writer. Translated from the Spanish.

Red as Blood, Or Tales from the Sisters Grimmer, by Tanith Lee

A striking and versatile collection of adult fairy-tale re-tellings.

The Tricksters, by Margaret Mahy

This beautifully told, contemporary New Zealand story draws upon pancultural Trickster legends.

Beauty, by Robin McKinley

Masterfully written, gentle and magical, this novel re-tells the story of "Beauty and the Beast."

Deerskin, by Robin McKinley

A retelling of Charles Perrault's "Donkeyskin," a dark fairy tale with incest themes.

The Door in the Hedge, by Robin McKinley

"The Twelve Dancing Princesses" and "The Frog Prince" retold in McKinley's gorgeous, clear prose, along with two original tales.

Disenchantments, edited by Wolfgang Mieder

An excellent compilation of adult fairy-tale poetry.

The Book of Laughter and Forgetting, by Milan Kundera

This literate and cosmopolitan work makes use of Moravian folk music, rituals, and stories.

Sleeping Beauty, by Susanna Moore

An eloquent, entertaining contemporary novel that uses the "Sleeping Beauty" legend mixed with native Hawaiian folklore.

The Private Life and *Waving from the Shore*, by Lisel Mueller

Terrific poetry collections with many fairy-tale themes.

Haroun and the Sea of Stories, by Salman Rushdie

A delightful Eastern fantasia by this Booker Prize–winning author.

Kindergarten, by Peter Rushford

A contemporary British story beautifully wrapped around the "Hansel and Gretel" tale, highly recommended.

Transformations, by Anne Sexton

Sexton's brilliant collection of modern fairy-tale poetry.

The Porcelain Dove, by Delia Sherman

This gorgeous fantasy set during the French Revolution makes excellent use of French fairy tales.

The Flight of Michael McBride, by Midori Snyder

A lovely, deftly written fantasy set in the old American West, this magical novel mixes the folklore traditions of immigrant and indigenous American cultures.

Trail of Stones, by Gwenn Strauss

Evocative fairy-tale poems, beautifully illustrated by Anthony Browne.

Swan's Wing, by Ursula Synge.

A lovely, magical fantasy novel using the "Seven Swans" fairy tale.

Beauty, by Sheri S. Tepper

Dark fantasy incorporating several fairy tales from an original and iconoclastic writer.

Kingdoms of Elfin, by Sylvia Townsend Warner

These stories drawn from British folklore are arch, elegant, and enchanting. Many were first published in *The New Yorker*.

The Coachman Rat, by David Henry Wilson

Excellent dark fantasy retelling the story of "Cinderella" from the coachman's point of view.

The Armless Maiden, edited by Terri Windling

Original fairy tales exploring the darker themes of childhood by Patricia McKillip, Tanith Lee, Charles de Lint, Jane Yolen, and many others.

Snow White and Rose Red, by Patricia C. Wrede

A charming Elizabethan historical novel retelling this romantic Grimm's fairy tale.

Briar Rose, by Jane Yolen

An unforgettable short novel setting the Briar Rose/ Sleeping Beauty story against the background of World War II.

Don't Bet on the Prince, edited by Jack Zipes

A collection of contemporary feminist fairy tales compiled by a leading fairy-tale scholar, containing prose and poetry by Angela Carter, Joanna Russ, Jane Yolen, Tanith Lee, Margaret Atwood, Olga Broumas, and others.

The Outspoken Princess and the Gentle Knight: A Treasury of Modern Fairy Tales, edited by Jack Zipes

Presents fifteen modern fairy tales from England and the United States including works by Ernest Hemingway, A. S. Byatt, John Gardner, Jane Yolen, and Tanith Lee.

Modern Day Fairy-tale Creators

The Faber Book of Modern Fairy Tales, edited by Sara and Stephen Corrin

Gudgekin the Thistle Girl and Other Tales, by John Gardner
Mainly by Moonlight, by Nicholas Stuart Gray
Collected Stories, by Richard Kennedy
Dark Hills, Hollow Clocks, by Garry Kilworth
Heart of Wood, by William Kotzwinkle
Five Men and a Swan, by Naomi Mitchison
The White Deer and The Thirteen Clocks, by James Thurber
Fairy Tales, by Alison Uttley
Tales of Wonder, by Jane Yolen

Nonfiction

The Power of Myth, by Joseph Campbell
The Erotic World of Fairy, by Maureen Duffy
"Womenfolk and Fairy Tales," by Susan Cooper
   Essay in the *New York Times Book Review,* April 13, 1975
Tales from Eternity: The World of Fairy Tales and the Spiritual Search, by Rosemary Haughton
Beauty and the Beast: Visions and Revisions of an Old Tale, by Betsy Hearne
The Arabian Nights: A Companion, by Robert Irwin
Woman, Earth and Spirit, by Helen M. Luke
Once Upon a Time, collected essays by Alison Lurie
The Classic Fairy Tales, by Iona and Peter Opie
What the Bee Knows, collected essays by P. L. Travers
Problems of the Feminine in Fairy Tales, by Marie-Louise von Franz
   Collected lectures originally presented at the C. G. Jung Institute
From the Beast to the Blonde: On Fairy Tales and their Tellers, by Marina Warner (highly recommended)
Six Myths of Our Time, by Marina Warner
Touch Magic, collected essays by Jane Yolen

Fantasists on Fantasy, edited by Robert H. Boyer and Kenneth J. Zahorski
  Includes Tolkien's "On Fairy Stories," G. K. Chesterton's "Fairy Tales," and other essays
Fairy Tales as Myths, by Jack Zipes

Fairy-tale Source Collections

Old Wives' Fairy Tale Book, edited by Angela Carter
The Tales of Charles Perrault, translated by Angela Carter
Italian Folktales, translated by Italo Calvino
Daughters of the Moon, edited by Shahrukh Husain
The Complete Hans Christian Andersen, edited by Lily Owens
The Maid of the North: Feminist Folk Tales from Around the World, edited by Ethel Johnston Phelps
Favorite Folk Tales from Around the World, edited by Jane Yolen
The Complete Brothers Grimm, edited by Jack Zipes
Spells of Enchantment: The Wondrous Fairy Tales of Western Culture, edited by Jack Zipes (highly recommended)
  (For volumes of fairy tales from individual countries—Russian fairy tales, French, African, Japanese, etc.—see the excellent Pantheon Books Fairy Tale and Folklore Library.)

Ellen Datlow

Ellen Datlow has been fiction editor of *OMNI* since 1981. She has earned a reputation for encouraging and developing writers such as William Gibson, Pat Cadigan, Dan Simmons, and K. W. Jeter and for publishing Clive Barker, Stephen King, William Burroughs, Ursula K. Le Guin, Jonathan Carroll, Joyce Carol Oates, Peter Straub, and Jack Cady in *OMNI*.

She has edited *Blood is Not Enough*, *A Whisper of Blood*, *Alien Sex*, *Little Deaths* (for which she won the 1995 World Fantasy Award), *Off Limits: Tales of Alien Sex*, *Twists of the Tale: Cat Horror Stories*, *Lethal Kisses*, and with Terri Windling the World Fantasy Award–winning series *The Year's Best Fantasy and Horror*. Datlow has won the World Fantasy Award in the Special Award-professional category for her editing.

Datlow has taught at Clarion West, the Brockport Writers' Forum, and the Suncoast Writers' Conference.

She lives in New York City.

Terri Windling

Terri Windling, a five-time winner of the World Fantasy Award, is the author of *The Wood Wife* and *The Green Children*, as well as works of short fiction and nonfiction. She is also an artist; her paintings (incorporating fairy-tale text and imagery) have been exhibited in museums and galleries across the country. She worked as a fiction editor for New York publishing companies for ten years, introducing many new writers to the fantasy field, including Charles de Lint, Steven Brust, Emma Bull, and Sheri S. Tepper. She created the Adult Fairy Tale series of books, the Borderland "punk urban fantasy" series for teenagers, and has published twenty anthologies prior to this one, including *The Year's Best Fantasy and Horror* annual (coedited with Ellen Datlow) and *The Armless Maiden*. She now lives in Devon, England and Tucson, Arizona but continues to work as an editorial consultant for Tor Books in New York.

11/97   5   11/97
5/98   5.   11/97